LIKE THE SOUND OF A DRUM

D1595713

LIKE THE SOUND OF A DRUM

ABORIGINAL CULTURAL POLITICS IN
DENENDEH AND NUNAVUT

PETER KULCHYSKI

UNIVERSITY OF MANITOBA PRESS

University of Manitoba Press
Winnipeg, Manitoba R3T 2N2 Canada
www.umanitoba.ca/uofmpress
Printed in Canada on acid-free paper by Friesens.

Cover Design: Doowah Design
Cover Photograph: Courtesy Peter Kulchyski
Text Design: Sharon Caseburg
Maps: Weldon Hiebert

Library and Archives Canada Cataloguing in Publication

Kulchyski, Peter Keith, 1959-
    Like the sound of a drum : Aboriginal cultural politics in Denendeh and Nunavut / Peter Kulchyski.

Includes bibliographical references and index.
ISBN 0-88755-178-5 (bound)
ISBN 0-88755-686-8 (pbk.)

    1. Tinne Indians. 2. Inuit. 3. Politics and culture--Northwest Territories. 4. Politics and culture--Nunavut. 5. Tinne Indians—Government relations. 6. Inuit—Canada—Government relations. 7. Nunavut—Politics and government. 8. Northwest Territories—Politics and government. I. Title.

E78.N79K84 2005   971.9'3004972   C2005-905621-5

This book has been published with the help of a grant from the Canadian Federation for the Humanities and Social Sciences, through the Aid to Scholarly Publications Programme, using funds provided by the Social Sciences and Humanities Research Council of Canada.

The University of Manitoba Press gratefully acknowledges the financial support for its publication program provided by the Government of Canada through the Book Publishing Industry Development Program (BPIDP); the Canada Council for the Arts; the Manitoba Arts Council; and the Manitoba Department of Culture, Heritage and Tourism.

CONTENTS

List of Illustrations / vi

Acknowledgements / vii

Introduction / 3

Part One: Names and Places

    Chapter One: The Story Lines / 31

    Chapter Two: The Laws of the Land / 77

Part Two: Concerning the Coming Community

    Chapter Three: The Long Road from Fort Simpson to Liidli Koe / 119

    Chapter Four: On the Ramparts at Fort Good Hope / 151

    Chapter Five: A Certain Kind of Writing in Panniqtuuq / 187

Part Three: Altered States

    Chapter Six: An Essay Concerning Aboriginal Self-Government in Denendeh and Nunavut / 229

Epilogue: Still Hunting Stories / 275

Endnotes / 281

Bibliography / 289

Index / 297

LIST OF ILLUSTRATIONS

Except where otherwise indicated, all photographs courtesy Peter Kulchyski. Maps by Weldon Hiebert.

Map of Nunavut / xii
Map of Denendeh / xiii

Following page 116
The Sahtu region
Flats at Fort Simpson
Treaty day
Yellowknife
Folk on the Rocks festival
Deline on Sahtu
Dene Summer Games (photo: E. Fajber)
Tea boiling (photo: E. Fajber)
Fort Good Hope band office
Fort Good Hope
Drying fish (photo: E. Fajber)
The Ramparts
The Ramparts
Colville Lake
Colville Lake
Graveyard
Airstrip
Panniqtuuq
Pangnirtung Inuit Co-op
Pangnirtung radio station
View from Panniqtuuq
Pangnirtung Fiord
Seal hunt
Near Avataqtu
Pangnirtung Pass

ACKNOWLEDGEMENTS

Thank you. Merci. Nia:wehn. Chi meegwetch. Masi cho. Qoyanamii paa-luk. A hunter and artist of my acquaintance, Jaco Ishulutak, teaches me that what some cultures don't practise can be as revealing about their character as what they do. Traditionally, Inuit rarely said qoyanamii. They didn't have to. The occasional smile of gratitude was enough to acknowledge something that never had to be said. The formal politeness of acknowl-edgement, so insisted upon by Qallunaat/non-Inuit, had no place in Inuit social relations because the bonds between people were too close.

But then, I have also heard those words of gratitude used with great rev-erence in many different languages, including Aboriginal languages. The thanksgiving address is one of the most powerful and beautiful moments of Haudenosaunee peoples. It reminds us that giving thanks itself can be an art form. So I will begin with some words of deep gratitude to those from whom I have learned, my teachers:

My first teachers were my brothers: Tim, my first, best, and closest friend, who taught love of knowledge, reading and ethics, Greg who taught humility and the gentle way, and Wayne who taught rebellion. My mother, Gladys Simard, taught me to fight against all odds to live the good life. My sister L'Annie taught me about courage, my sister Kelly determination. My father John taught me about laughter and dignity, and showed me too clearly the path of self-destruction. All have taught me that material deprivation, however bitter its sting and enduring its scars, does not have to lead to a loss of integrity or the death of spirit.

In San Antonio School in Bissett, Manitoba, my friends Michelle Petznic and Barbara Kirten were gifted classmates. My teacher John Jack, as well as offering as many lessons as he could pack into a one-room school, taught about the value of school to the building of community.

At the government-run residential school Frontier Collegiate in Cranberry Portage, Manitoba, my friends James Kemp, Andrea Long, Rudy Subedar, and Christine Magnussen (now Bennett) were intellectual peers of the first order. I was befriended by many teachers including Sig Ericson, Peter Falk, Gwen Reimer, Jim Davies, and, especially, one of my first great mentors, now an elected politician, Gerard Jennissen.

While at the University of Winnipeg I traded ideas and enthusiasms with Lori Turner, Kim Sawchuk, Fernanda Ferreira, Anne Moore, Janine Tschuncky, K. George Godwin, and especially my extraordinary friend Janet Sarson. I studied geography with Miriam Lo-Lim and Paul Evans, history with Robert Wagner, English with Paul Swayze, sociology with Paul Stevenson, and came to love the study of politics and political theory through the inspiration provided by a second mentor, Arthur Kroker.

At York University I studied social and political theory with Ato Sekyi-Otu, Edgar Dosman, John O'Neill, Neal Wood, Ellen Meiksens Wood; admittedly a mixed bunch, all of whom made important contributions to my world view and in whose shadows I have been grateful to stand. My peers there, and close friends, included Gail Faurschau, Michael Dartnell, Lorraine Gautier, Laurel Whitney, Frances Abele, Michael Kutner, Rich Wellen, Deborah Lee Simmons, Mark Fortier, and that luminous, vivacious, and generous intellect, Shannon Bell. Many of these have gone on to make outstanding intellectual contributions to Canadian academic life. In my years there I engaged in union activism from which I learned many invaluable life lessons. My sisters and brothers in the Canadian Union of Educational Workers included my dear friends Gill Teiman, Leslie Saunders, Pat Rogers, Kevin Moroney, Bruce Curtis, Larry Lyons, Brian Robinson, Charles Doyon, Margaret Little. Julia Emberley had a determinate influence on me in these years and belongs in a category of her own, in more ways than one! So, too, Elizabeth Fajber, whose help and insights impressed themselves on the best parts of my character.

In a place of her own in my heart and mind also belongs a person who transcends the categories of mentor and friend, deserving a paragraph for herself and for whom no words of praise will suffice, Himani Bannerji.

Over years of engagement as a scholar with gainful employment, I have benefited from conversation with a range of friends and brilliant colleagues in and out of Native Studies. Among those out of Native Studies, I will mention Bruce Hodgins, Jonathon Bordo, John Wadland, Julia Harrison, Joan Sangster, Robert Campbell, Deborah Berrill, as well as a courageous group of principled scholars including John Fekete, David Morrison, George Nader, Sean Kane, and the insightful inspirational intellect, Andrew Wernick, whose friendship I prize beyond measure. Michael Berrill and I once tried to prove that friendship could go beyond politics. Our experiment failed. An early draft of this work was carved in 1993-94 out of the currents that swirl around Cornell University: my colleagues in the A.D. White Society for the Humanities that year included Martin Bernal, Richard Burton, Ruth Vanita, Mark Perlman; I am grateful for the encouragement of Susan Buck-Morss, who read portions of an earlier draft of this manuscript, and Jonathon Culler. It was a singular pleasure to befriend and work with Kathryn Shandley. Finally, though he will not detect his influence as strongly in this work, the then Director of the Society, Dominick LaCapra, will find traces of his insights throughout my—admittedly meagre—scholarly productions: this is the best tribute I can offer such a careful and ambitious thinker. Elizabeth Povinelli and George Wenzel provided helpful comments on an earlier draft. I have also been a grateful recipient of the friendship of Gerald Maclean and Donna Landry.

Frank Tough (whom I've studied under and with at Frontier, the University of Winnipeg, York University, and at the University of Saskatchewan!) deserves mention first of those inside of Native Studies, since I have worked with him longest. In my year at the University of Saskatchewan I had the pleasure to teach beside him as well as James Waldram and Winona Stevenson. At Trent University I owe Marlene Brant Castellano innumerable thanks for support and inspiration. There I had the great pleasure of teaching beside Rodney Bobiwash, Don McCaskill, Paul Bourgeois, Shirley Williams, Edna Manitawabi, Tom Jewiss, Colleen Youngs, and, also among the most insightful, honourable and courageous of scholars I know, John Milloy. At the University of Manitoba the motley crew I currently suffer beside includes a great teacher, Fred Shore, a truly great scholar and poet whose name will probably outlast us all, Emma LaRocque, a collection of outstanding junior colleagues including Wanda Wuttunee and Renate Eigenbrod, and that singular character Chris Trott. I affectionately refer to Chris as 'my highly esteemed colleague' because, in fact, I do esteem him highly; if I may be of use to him intellectually in one tenth of the degree to which he has generously assisted me, I will know I have done him great service.

A variety of administrators in Native Studies have shown me that being behind a desk can still involve caring for the human beings who sometimes present themselves. They include Cathy Fife, Chris Welter, Barb Rivett, Anita Speiss, Lois Gray, Gloria Spence, and the amazing Joyce Miller.

I must also thank Anthony Hall and Patricia Monture-Angus, activists and academics who teach that the two need not be exclusive, themselves in and outside of Native Studies.

Among the graduate students who have completed work with me that has had an influence on my own thinking I will mention, from a group too long to list, Peggy Shaughnessy, Alex Levant, Arthur Beaver, Susan Hinds, Aluki Kotierk, Trish Longboat, Daphne Garcia-Taylor, and Kimberley Wilde. Research assistants who have helped me with this project have included Kate Jennings, Aaron Levere, Ramona Neckoway, Wendy Ross, Glenn Tssessaze, and Dawn Sprecher.

From Fort Simpson, although acknowledgements have been made within the text, I will take the pleasure of repeating my expression of gratitude—masi cho—to Herb Norwegian, Bertha Norwegian, Leo Norwegian, Mary-Louise Norwegian, Jim Antoine, Gerry Antoine, and, especially, my friend Eric Menicoche.

From Fort Good Hope I will say masi cho to Isidore Manuel, who has given me many great gifts, Barney Masazumi, Charlie Barnaby, George Barnaby, Lucy Jackson, Everette Kakfwi, and my visionary friends Bella T'Seleie and Frank T'Seleie.

From Pangnirtung I will say qoyanamii paaluk to Sim Akpalialuk, Levi Ishulutak, Ame Papatsie, Margaret Karpik, Hannah Tautuajuk, Pauloosie Angmarlik, Rosie Okpik, Elisapee Ishulutak, Jonasie Karpik, and Jaco Ishulutak. My former student and early guide Kayrene (Nookiguak) Kilabuk also has earned my everlasting respect and gratitude.

From Iqaluit and Yellowknife I gained 'intelligence' regarding northern politics from a variety of friends: Jack Hicks, Lee Selleck, Dorothy
Chocolate, and Marina Devine have been generous hosts, sources, and
friends.

Beyond all of this I must thank my sometimes co-author and close
friend, the woodworking, automobile fixing, sailing, boat building, cabin
building, photograph taking, book writing, world travelling, utterly inde-
fatigable and highly loquacious Frank Tester.

Among mentors and friends the name Gad Horowitz sits in a precious
place in my heart. I thank him and another scholar whose work I admire,
Julie Cruikshank, for giving this work in its manuscript state their careful
attention.

David Carr at the University of Manitoba Press gave me the right
encouragement at the right time to help ensure this manuscript saw daylight and I am in his debt. I am also grateful to Pat Sanders for her outstanding job helping with the nuts and bolts of constructing the final text.
Funding for this study was provided by a strategic grant on Aboriginal Self
Government sponsored by the Social Sciences and Humanities Research
Council of Canada; I am immensely grateful for their help over many years
with my research in the north.

If my many battles with words and institutions now appear to have a
purpose beyond doing what must be done in a world that will not allow
peace, has no time for reason, and despises justice, such a purpose was
given to me by my love for fair Krista Pilz and bears the name Malay. May
your light shine.

Finally, to those of you whose eyes have already travelled this distance,
who are prepared to give these words a small portion of your most precious possession, that measure of duration or temporality we call time
itself—whose transformation into a mere commodity represents the most
insidious sacrilege and enormous debasement embodied in contemporary
social forms—I offer a humble thank you, merci, nia:wehn, chi meegwetch,
masi cho, qoyanamii paaluk.

Nunavut

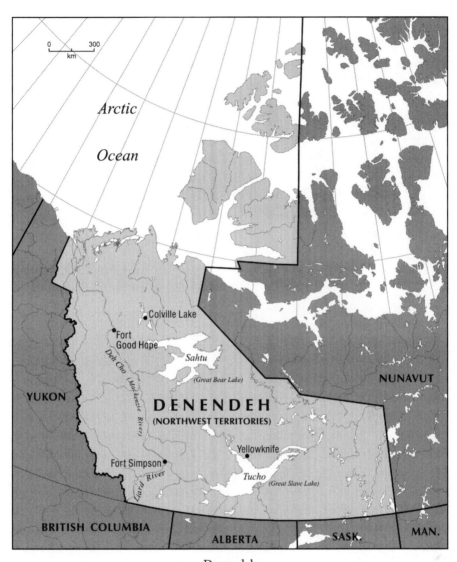

Denendeh

LIKE THE SOUND OF A DRUM

INTRODUCTION

GROUND ZERO

The conquest of the Americas, that vast historical process that dispossesses undetermined numbers of Indigenous peoples to the advantage of European invaders, has not been completed. The liberal consciences of North America today acknowledge wrongdoings of the past, sometimes pausing to note that their own individual ancestors had not yet immigrated to this land (which is to say, they get a free pass on history), sometimes reflecting that past generations did not have the ethical luxury available in our own time, before moving on to other issues. One need not concern oneself so much with past generations and one's own ancestors. In the minutiae of quotidian life, in the presuppositions of service providers, in the structures of State actions and inactions, in the continuing struggles over land use, in a whole trajectory of policies and plans, the work of the conquest is being completed here and now. By our generation. It is our descendants, a hundred years from now, who will protest that they were not there when land claims were being negotiated, when Aboriginal rights were distorted beyond recognition, when the final acts of the great historical drama of conquest were performed. You who remain silent while this injustice continues, you are responsible. Here. And now.

But then again, so am I.

The northern part of Canada is one of the stages for this drama. In the north it is possible to see, to visually apprehend, the imposition of one way of life on another. It is possible to meet and talk over tea with people who were born in another world and saw an epoch of change in a lifetime. In the contemporary modality this struggle is not about the imposition by force of arms of different languages and cultural forms and land ownership patterns, but even today the struggle is about a power that coerces as much as it cajoles. In the north this power is institutionally supported by a trajectory of policies; no single overriding policy or plan says modernization and assimilation are the ultimate destination. Rather, the presuppositions of a whole set of institutional plans and practices in the areas of education, health care, housing, infrastructure, justice, family services, economic development, and all the rest work relentlessly to underwrite the continuing conquest. These policies themselves rest on a fabric of cultural forms that implicitly and with great subtlety help the policy trajectory make sense.

In the northern part of Canada, this policy trajectory is opposed with a creative energy and a spirit of resistance that defy instrumental accountings. Who could have imagined that in the seventies, faced with the might of the world's major oil and gas producers, themselves bankrolled by some of the largest capital centres and State powers, a few scattered Dene communities could successfully halt a major construction project: the Mackenzie Valley Pipeline? Thirty years ago, who would have thought Inuit, most only recently moved to permanent settlements from scattered camps on the land, would today speak in their own voices, in their own legislative assembly, in their own territory? The answer to both questions is not "no one." There were many Inuit and Dene, and others at the time, who rightly believed these were achievable goals. The conquest is not inevitable, inexorable. What our descendants will think of us is as unwritten as the most important of the treaty promises. In what follows, the permutations of this conflict are examined at the micropolitical level of everyday life as much as at the macropolitical level of structure and policy.

The above words were written before the events of September 11, 2001. Since that time "ground zero" has come to have a new connotation. It is not disrespectful to suggest that the term, like the term "genocide," must not be deployed as a singularity, as a reference to one particular historical event. There are other ground zeros, other kinds of ground zeros, including, for Americans of all kinds, the ground upon which we walk.

ONE TIME

One time, while I was engaged in research in the small Dene community of Fort Good Hope, I had an opportunity to travel for two days to the nearby community of Colville Lake. Although Fort Good Hope was small and remote with a population at the time of about 500, located about eighty kilometres to the south of the Arctic Circle on the Mackenzie River (Deh Cho in the Dene language), Colville Lake was even smaller at that time, with a population just over fifty and even more remote, inland to the north and east of Fort Good Hope. Like most students of society and culture who travel in northern Canada, I was interested in traditional Aboriginal lifestyles, without, at the time, having given much thought to the complex issue of what the concept of "traditional" meant. In this vast margin of North America, tradition is still often equated with finding the most northern in the north, the most isolated of the isolated. Colville Lake fit the bill, enjoying a reputation even among the Dene for its traditional economic and cultural life.

It was midsummer in 1985 when I learned that a large airplane had been specially chartered to take a crowd to Colville Lake from Fort Good Hope for Treaty Day ceremonies and celebrations, and that there was room on the plane for me. I eagerly seized the opportunity. I had no idea where I would be staying, what I would eat, what I would do or see, but given that at that time there were no regularly scheduled flights to Colville Lake, it was not a chance to be missed. I joined the small crowd at the airport who quickly filled the Twin Otter for the fifty-minute flight from one small gravel airstrip, over the scrub pines and swamps and giant, rugged hills, to an even smaller gravel strip. Suddenly I was beyond telephone communication, far past the limit of electrical power, in a world of small log houses set in a rough circle on the edge of a huge freshwater lake in bush country. It is somehow fitting that the key cultural event of this first brief visit would involve television.

As our Twin Otter arrived at the airstrip, there was a quick flurry of activity—most of the residents, on hearing our plane in the distance, rushed up to meet it. Supplies and mail were unloaded as we disembarked; letters were loaded that had been finished between the time the plane was first heard and the hour or so later when it left. This, I learned, was the usual routine in Colville Lake: every single one of the sporadic aircraft that arrived afforded a brief opportunity to send out a note or parcel. At the airstrip, relatives and friends greeted each other; the official treaty party—two government officials and a policeman—were escorted by the local missionary to their quarters at the fishing lodge; the whole crowd moved from airstrip to community as the plane left and the normal calm reasserted itself.

It took not much more than twenty minutes for me to walk the entire length of Colville Lake, briefly visit the small Catholic church that was the most prominent structure in town, and then drop in on friends of friends for tea and bannock and dry fish. At that time of year, the rhythm of life in Colville centred on trout fishing: at a leisurely pace, nets were set and checked, fish was cleaned and hung on racks where, in the very dry arctic air, fillets would soon dry into a state that stayed preserved. Orange knuckleberries were just beginning to put in their appearance, so serious picking had not yet begun.

By early evening, the official Treaty Day function was ready to begin. The two government officials, who worked for the federal Department of Indian Affairs, had set up a table in front of a commandeered cabin. They had a list of names and a pile of crisp, new five-dollar bills. Two flags, one of the Northwest Territories and one of Canada, were set up next to the table. Dressed in his formal red tunic, the Royal Canadian Mounted Police officer hovered near the table, overseeing the proceedings. I stood with a small group of young Dene men, who joked around with their newly collected five-dollar bills, letting them wave in the whipping wind. Older men recalled how Treaty Day in the past had been such an important event, the occasion of a feast and a Dene drum dance. Now, even though everyone in town did come to the table, they did so primarily in order to affirm the importance of the treaty. No one seemed sure what kind of social event would be held that evening, but older folks remembered and reminisced about the drum dances that had been held in the past.

The event turned out to be television watching. When the treaty party retired to the fishing lodge, the rest of the community—women, men, children, and one visiting scholar—piled into a tiny cabin where heavy grey flannel blankets had been hung over the windows to block out the midnight sun. A small gas generator was connected to a television and video cassette recorder; four videos rented for one day from the store in Fort Good Hope were watched, one after another, in a six-hour marathon that began at around ten p.m. and ended sometime between five and six the next morning. Every fifty minutes the generator would run out of fuel, the film would be interrupted, and we would creep out of the packed, dark cabin into the bright sunshine (it was summer; we were above the Arctic Circle) for cigarette and bathroom breaks. All the videos had to be taken back with the return flight the next day. No one had work or school to occupy their morning so no one had to worry about sleeping late. My most vivid memory of the night was when, some time after four in the morning, the last film began, a John Wayne feature called *North to Alaska*, and the opening song woke the younger children who had fallen asleep in the front row; their heads bobbed along to the familiar tune.

This story from Colville Lake resonates uneasily with a similar story narrated by Stephen Greenblatt in his *Marvellous Possessions*. He tells of visiting a tiny Balinese village in 1986; recognizing, thanks to the writings of a variety of anthropologists, the communal pavilion; discovering "that the light came from a television set that the villagers, squatting or sitting cross legged, were intent on watching"; climbing nevertheless—"conquering my disappointment"—onto the platform where "on the communal VCR, they were watching a tape of an elaborate temple ceremony. Alerted by the excited comments and whoops of laughter, I recognized in the genial crowd of television watchers on the platform several of the ecstatic celebrants, dancing in trance states, whom I was seeing on the screen."[1] Greenblatt then adds: "We may call what I witnessed that evening the assimilation of the other, a phrase it is well to leave deliberately ambiguous" because "the Balinese adaptation of the latest Western and Japanese modes of representation seemed so culturally idiosyncratic and resilient that it was unclear who was assimilating whom."[2] This anecdote stages, in my view, not so much the "assimilation of the other," a phrase that in the context of Canadian Aboriginal politics is not ambiguous at all, but rather a dynamic of totalization and subversion where, in Greenblatt's words, "to recognize and admire local accommodations is not uncritically to endorse capitalist markets, but it is to acknowledge imaginative adaptations to conditions that lie beyond the immediate control of the poor."[3] Something of this dynamic, where a highly individualizing, serial technology—television—was deployed and recontextualized to affirm a cohesive group identity, was similarly staged for me in Colville Lake.

"One time" is an expression I've heard many of my Dene friends use as the opening to a story: "one time, a few years ago, I went by boat along the

Deh Cho from Simpson to Wrigley." Not "once upon a time" of fairytale fame, nor a mere and efficient "once," but, consistently, "one time." It is a curious expression, denoting as it does the irreducible singularity of the event by reference to the impossible singularity of temporality itself. The narrative form, storytelling practice, is a critical cultural form deployed by Inuit and Dene alike, today as in ancient times. Knowing this, and desiring to write something that might have some appeal especially to northern readers, in my research I left myself open to the possibility of an event. I can be said to have hunted stories: as hunters travel on the land in search of prey, I searched the texts of my journals and memories for narratives. On occasion, this text attempts to follow the rhythm and aspire to the high standard of Dene and Inuit storytelling practice, adopting rhetorical devices commonplace among Aboriginal people in Nunavut and the Northwest Territories but likely unfamiliar to others. Perhaps this written practice will in some way help ensure that this text is of some value to the people it is about. Over the decade that followed my visit to Colville Lake, and especially in the years from 1991 to 1994, when I made a series of visits north specifically for the purposes of this study, there would be many such "one times."

TWO PLACES

The Canadian far north is usually considered that part of the country north of the sixtieth parallel. When this study began in the late eighties, there were two territories in the far north, the Yukon Territory and the Northwest Territories (NWT). The latter was the object of my attention. By the time the study ended, the NWT had divided: a new territory, Nunavut, had been carved out of the northeastern side of the NWT. This event itself speaks to one of the 'facts' of northern politics over the past few decades, the drama of the pace of political change in the north. Every half decade since the sixties has brought with it major structural reconfiguration of one sort or another in the political sphere in the NWT. These include the movement of government from Ottawa to Yellowknife in 1967, the evolution of representative government in the seventies, culminating in an Aboriginal 'takeover' of the territorial government in the late seventies, the proposals and negotiations about dividing the territories and settling land claims in the eighties, and more recently the establishment and creation of Nunavut through the nineties alongside the settlement of the Inuit land claim and the division of Dene/Métis land claim proposals (with the settlement of three of five Dene/Métis claims). To follow territorial politics at a formal level, one must immerse oneself in federal policies respecting Aboriginal rights (especially land claims policy and Aboriginal self-government policy) as well as territorial political structures. As a political observer working with communities in both the NWT and what became Nunavut—the 'two places' the study concerns itself with—through the nineties, I was afforded a unique opportunity to watch some of these changes and to take the development of Nunavut and restructuring of the NWT as part of my inquiry.

Territories in Canada are unusual political entities. They do not have the full status of a province in Canadian federation, but, especially in the last few decades, act with province-like powers in province-like areas of jurisdiction. They do not have a formal vote at the constitutional table, and govern through powers granted by the federal government rather than by the constitutionally determined division of powers that guarantees provinces their autonomy. The NWT is made up of two, broad, ecological areas, the Arctic and the Subarctic, though at times the word "Arctic" is loosely used, like "Far North," to describe the whole area. Nunavut is entirely comprised of ecologically arctic areas. In the NWT three, quite distinct, Aboriginal cultures or peoples occupy this landscape, Dene and Métis in the Subarctic, and Inuit (most of the Inuvialuit or Yupik variety) in the Arctic, while the vast majority of people (about eighty-five per cent) in Nunavut are Inuit.

Technically, the Arctic is the more northern and eastern portion of the territory, defined by being north of the treeline that cuts on an angle roughly from the northwestern corner of the NWT to its southeastern corner. This area, Nunavut, includes all the High Arctic islands and is politically divided into three regions: Kitikmeot, or Central Arctic, among the most isolated of any part of Canada; Kivilliq (until recently called Keewatin), along the northwestern shore of Hudson Bay; and Baffin, which includes Baffin Island and communities in the very High Arctic. All the communities in these regions are occupied by a majority of Inuit people, most still speaking a dialect of Inuktitut, their language. None are connected to the south by road, and all can be characterized as remote communities.

The Subarctic, also sometimes called the western Arctic, is dominated by the Mackenzie River drainage system, which includes two great freshwater lakes, Great Slave Lake to the south and Great Bear Lake to the north. The river is called the Deh Cho, and the lakes Tucho and Sahtu, respectively, by the mostly Dene inhabitants of the area. There are five Dene regions in the western Arctic: that of the Gwi'chin-speaking peoples in the most northwestern corner; a region called Sahtu to the west and north of the lake of the same name; a region called Dehcho to the south of Sahtu, occupied by Slavey-speaking Dene; a 'South Slave' or 'Treaty 8' region occupied by Chipewyan-speaking peoples to the south and east of Tucho; and a 'North Slave' region occupied mostly by Dogrib-speaking peoples. There are also many Cree-speaking peoples scattered about the western Arctic. "Métis," who tend to be concentrated in more southern NWT communities but are scattered throughout, is a term that has a loose application but designates at least three overlapping groups: descendants of the historic Métis settlements in western Canada who may have migrated north in the historic Métis diasporas of 1870 and 1885; descendants of so-called mixed marriages between Dene and non-Dene; and Dene without legal status as Dene. I prefer the term "Denendeh," a Dene term that was used by the Dene Culture Institute and has been deployed recently by June Helm in her book *The People of Denendeh* to describe this area, officially today known as the NWT. Although not all the Aboriginal groups who live there would use the term, it seems to have the broadest relevance and is far better, in my mind, than the "Northwest Territories," which, as a name, has been accepted by default. I will continue to use the term NWT to describe the political reality that existed before the creation of Nunavut.

The 'hinge' in the division between Denendeh and Nunavut is a last region occupied by Inuvialuit and Yupik-speaking peoples to the north and east of the Gwi'chin, near the Beaufort Sea. The Inuvialuit are the only Inuit cultural group to remain in Denendeh, an issue that itself perplexed territorial politics for a considerable period.

In *Home and Native Land*, published in the mid-1980s, Michael Asch distinguished the political approach of Aboriginal peoples in the NWT from that of those in southern Canada and the Yukon:

> The approach to the establishment of aboriginal political rights in the Northwest Territories is based on the following facts: first, unlike the south, the region as a whole is only thinly populated;

second, the sole land-users in the major portion of the territory are the native peoples; third, the native component of the population in each of the two proposed new provinces [Nunavut and Denendeh] has a majority or near-majority status; and fourth, at present, government in the region does not have legislative authority but is, in effect, a colony of the federal government.[4]

Although the division of the Territories has taken longer than Asch may have envisaged, and provincial status seems even further away, his facts remain relevant. They lead him to conclude that, "given these conditions, the issue of political rights for Aboriginal peoples cannot easily be separated from the evolution of sovereign government for the Northwest Territories and, indeed, at the most basic level the two become intimately intertwined."[5]

For any student of politics, Denendeh and Nunavut are very special jurisdictions. They are among the only places in North America where Aboriginal peoples can use their democratic franchise to control a public government at the provincial level. Furthermore, since 1979, Aboriginal peoples have done just that, electing a majority of Aboriginal politicians to the Territorial Assembly in the NWT. Since 1980, all but two of the government leaders of the NWT have been of Aboriginal descent, and the territorial government has described itself as operating on a consensus system that owes as much to the values and traditions of Aboriginal peoples as it does to the Westminster structure of parliamentary democracy. There are seven official languages in Denendeh, five of them Aboriginal; debates in the Territorial Assembly have been simultaneously translated into each, and Inuvialuit, Métis, and Dene politicians make a point of speaking at length in their own language. The evolution of what is called "responsible government" in the north has been seen as in itself the embodiment of Aboriginal self-government aspirations. This pattern has been left intact in Nunavut, where the government leader is Inuk, as are the majority of the members of the Territorial Assembly, and Inuktitut is not merely an official language, but spoken prominently. The creation of Nunavut, though, has led to a rebalancing of power in Denendeh, with something close to a split between Aboriginal and non-Aboriginal voters, where the latter have more influence than they had prior to division.

Substantially complicating politics in Denendeh and Nunavut is the question of land claims. In 1980, all the Aboriginal peoples of the NWT had a legal claim to ownership of the land; that is, they had Aboriginal 'title' to the land, whose status, in Canadian jurisprudence, was and remains largely undefined. In 1984 the Inuvialuit settled the first comprehensive land claim in the NWT, called the Western Arctic Claim. Comprehensive claims are so called by the Canadian government to distinguish them from specific claims, the latter referring to claims that arise as a result of broken or unfulfilled treaty promises. Comprehensive claims are organized on the principle of the extinguishment of Aboriginal title in exchange for monetary compensation, clear (or fee simple) title to specific, much smaller, tracts of land, and other benefits; hence, they can be seen as treaties and have the same constitutional status as the early treaties of Canada. There is a great deal of controversy in the NWT among Aboriginal peoples as to whether extinguishing Aboriginal title was a good thing to do, but by the early nineties, the Inuit of Nunavut had settled a single claim covering the whole of the eastern Arctic, and the Dene political organizations had divided over the issue of claims. The Gwi'chin and Sahtu regions settled claims in the first half of the nineties, while the Dogrib have more recently completed a comprehensive claim negotiation that includes self-government provisions and can be said to "exhaust" their Aboriginal rights rather than extinguish them. Meanwhile Chipweyan are negotiating treaty rights, and the Dehcho region has firmly repudiated the notion of extinguishment of Aboriginal title and is trying to develop an autonomous region, modelled on the Nunavut approach.

Northern Aboriginal politics are as intricate, complex, layered, multidimensional, and dynamic as can be found in any political jurisdiction, anywhere. The situation is rapidly evolving, yet the word "tradition" has enormous resonance. "Culture" is a critical political category, but the concept of "multiculturalism" has little relevance. Gender politics have a very specific trajectory here, especially in the context where negotiation of the public and private space remains a critical political structural issue, yet "feminism" rarely reaches the public stage. For many people, the Canadian north may be seen as the most far-flung sort of backwater, on the furthest colonial margin; yet it is precisely here that the latest theoretical constructs find themselves well tested and it is here that our political language and our ability to think the political have to be stretched to and perhaps beyond their limits. And, in my view, it is here, this kind of place, that has the most to teach us today about the political project of democratic government.

This is a book about two communities in Denendeh and one in Nunavut. I originally wanted to document what Aboriginal self-government meant to the people of these communities, how they thought it might lead to changes for the better, what models they wanted to pursue. I also wanted to test the territorial government's claim that it might act as a vehicle for Aboriginal self-government. And I wanted to document events, provide a snapshot, as it were, of an unfolding politics in the climate of negotiations to settle major, comprehensive land claims in the north. However, as an observer poised to study how macro-level political changes came to bear on local, micro-level, quotidian concerns, I came to see something else, something that escaped the confinements of formal political structures and processes, a politics even more compelling though far less tangible, something like what Fredric Jameson has called a "political unconscious" and that I have come to see as a "cultural politics."

The communities each agreed in advance to allow me to study with them, and in each case I agreed to help the communities in whatever ways they could make use of me. I thought that by working out of band and municipal offices, with the local administrators and politicians, I would get a better feel for the local political dynamics. I also wanted to make whatever contributions I could while I was there so that I would not be engaged in a one-way, appropriative, exchange. I was drawn to these particular communities initially because they embodied distinct models of local government. They came to embody something far more than that: each with its own personality, its own set of difficulties, its own stories, landscapes, laughters, insights, failings, promises.

Fort Simpson is a Dene (south Slavey) and Métis community in the Dehcho region, on the Deh Cho itself where it is met by the Liard River. Political leaders in the community and the region have rejected the logic of extinguishment of their Aboriginal title and, during the period of this study, enshrined that principle in a regional Deh Cho Declaration. Fort Simpson is connected to the south by road. It has a population of about 1000, many of whom are non-Native. It has both a local municipal council and a band council, the latter established in accordance with provisions of the Canadian federal Indian Act legislation, the former through territorial legislation.

Fort Good Hope is also a Dene and Métis community further north along the Deh Cho. It is in the Sahtu region, and, during the period of this study, participated in negotiating and ratifying a land claim that included an extinguishment clause. It has a population of about 800, the majority of whom are Dene and Métis, speakers of the north Slavey dialect, and is not connected to the south save for a winter road. A unique model of local governance, involving a community council that functions both as municipal and band government, has been established in Fort Good Hope.

Pangnirtung, or Panniqtuuq, as local elders would have it, is on Baffin Island in the eastern Arctic, the most remote of the three communities. It has a population of about 1300, most of whom are Inuit. Panniqtuuq is in Nunavut. There is no band council because Inuit are not governed by Canada's Indian Act; a municipal (hamlet) council dominated by local Inuit governs local affairs. In fact, the working language of the hamlet council is Inuktitut and at every meeting I have attended, all the councillors have been Inuit.

In each of the communities, I talked to local politicians, elders, and other community residents, both informally and in tape-recorded formal interview settings. I sat in on local government meetings, on local feasts and celebrations, and on community assemblies or meetings. I read documents in the band/community/municipal council offices. I got out on the land with people in their hunting and fishing camps, and watched and listened and read, letting accidents happen; hunting stories. I also held workshops when asked, wrote funding proposals, drafted legal language for negotiations, acted as recorder at meetings, and tried in various ways to give back whatever I could to the communities. The ethics of such an exchange are constitutive of what is called Native Studies.

The three communities stand in for something broader, though, what could be called the fact of community itself, the fact of community as coming into being, being built or falling apart, as a problem, a construction, a trajectory. In their temporalities and spacings, in their debates and discussions, these communities involve attempts to build a precarious socious; each offers its own example of what such a socious can look like, what kind of social relations can be constructed. That is, each is in some fashion the product of decisions and impositions, negotiations and subversions, actions and reactions at the local level to broader structures and possibilities. Frank T'Seleie, from Fort Good Hope, in a conversation with me, questioned the manner in which communities are often taken for granted:

> The thing that really focusses it away from the traditional system is the focus on the community, the community. I mean that, when you have people [with] the mentality that the world only exists here. To me, I start my learning in a completely different world. I mean that's not my vision of the community, that's a poor mentality. Which, because, we never lived in houses; only now we're beginning to learn how to live in houses.

Communities, as they are now constituted in the north, are relatively recent accommodations and their basic infrastructures are colonial inspirations: the housing designs, the educational systems, the presupposition of concentrated human occupation at a specific site for a lengthy duration, all come with colonialism. Many Inuit and Dene were born to drastically different circumstances on the land or in the bush, and some continue to exist their settlements as base camps rather than as permanent sites of residence. The K'ashogot'ine, the Liidli Koe Dene, the Panniqtuuq Inuit in the three communities did not take the fact of community in its newer appearance for granted; they actively sought to transform the coming together forced upon them by a colonial regime into a new form of social being, something like a community. The fact of community, the daily decisions and practices and languages that go into forging its continual becoming, this too is what these communities represent, and it is exactly the point at which they find themselves frequently in conflict with the colonial State apparatus.

FOUR THESES

Through the course of this study, four theses or considerations emerged as focal points for my inquiries and writings. These deserve summary in a provisional manner here, and elaboration in the discussions of each of the communities.

The first thesis is that in Aboriginal self-government, the politics of form is of considerable importance. Discussion of Aboriginal self-government in the political forum has largely concentrated on the question of the transfer of power from federal, provincial, and territorial governments to Aboriginal communities: how much power will communities have over what juris-dictional areas? However, the form in which power is deployed not only reflects the cultural values of those who deploy it, but it embodies, enacts, and perpetuates those cultural values. Any decision made by an Aborigi-nal community in accordance with the logic of the established order, in accordance with the logic of instrumental rationality and normalization techniques, even if that decision is substantively to do something that will promote traditional values, will be a step in the direction of totalization. The children who watch the deciders will learn that in order to be effec-tive, they must learn the dominant logic. Culture will be separate from everyday life, something to be stored in museum boxes. The debate on Aboriginal self-government must shift to a debate about political forms.

The second thesis is that, if evaluated in meaningful democratic terms, the Aboriginal communities I studied are more than ready for Aboriginal self-government. Much is taking place to 'prepare' communities for self-government on the understanding that, somehow, they are not yet ready for it. This derives from an ethnocentric position that assumes all govern-ment must follow the dominant Western form. However, if we reject that logic, we come to the conclusion that no one is better situated to under-stand and consult the people of Aboriginal communities than Aboriginal peoples themselves and, further, that the mode of consultation must be appropriate to the community and culture, not to the Canadian State. If we argue that 'they' will not be 'ready' for self-government until 'they' can manage committee structures and specific financial accounting techniques, we effectively say 'they' cannot be self-governing until 'they' are like 'us'.

The third thesis is that although the State is itself a relation and a site of struggle, it structurally is positioned to move in the direction of totaliza-tion. The State's objective, aside from the wishes of its individual agents, is to find a mechanism to incorporate Aboriginal peoples into the dominant order. This is a structural exigency and will never cease as long as the dom-inant order depends on the logic of capital accumulation and the expan-sion of the commodity form. It is not this or that individual or even this or that policy that Aboriginal people find themselves opposed to, it is an underlying logic embodied by the State, articulated through a trajectory of policies. Aboriginal peoples in Canada do not experience the State as the protector of their property, the guarantor of peace and order necessary to the individual's search for fulfilment; they experience the State as ruthless, unrelenting, totalizing machinery. The implication is that Aboriginal people's struggle for cultural survival will not end as long as these structural exigencies remain in place: it will always be under pressure from mechanisms of totalization.

The fourth thesis is that, at least in this specific context, the State can be defined as a certain kind of writing. The State will not address Aboriginal people until they learn this writing, this form. Negotiation, indeed discussion, cannot proceed without it. But learning this form of writing means engaging in the logic of the dominant order: a paradox. A precondition for playing the game is surrender. In response to this, the many ancient modalities of writing deployed by Aboriginal peoples, especially modes of writing on the land and writing on the body, are being reconfigured and redeployed in creative ways. To the extent that learning to read these creative inscriptions is a critical aspect of understanding the specific characteristics of this struggle, the study of Aboriginal politics involves many a writing lesson.

Finally, this is not only a discussion of three communities and four theses. It is also a study of a certain public space, what could be called a cultural politics and a political culture. The public governments of Nunavut and the NWT remain a site of investigation here, albeit a decentred site. This study traces the outer reaches of power to determine its effects and map the resistances that take place from that specific structural position or terrain. The establishment of communities that deserve the name may be seen as one such resistance. To another form of those resistances we can give the name or apply the term or enunciate the desire called "democracy." Forcing people to surrender their right to participate in politics by reducing that right to the merest gesture, the written mark, the vote, is deployed as a tool of totalizing power, which everywhere defines itself as democratic and defines democracy by this hollow shell: the vote that establishes 'representative' government. But, in some places and in some times, a different kind of political structure involving the continuance of political responsibility operates. Give up, for a moment, the notion that democracy is defined wholly and exclusively by the exercise of the formal vote for a political representative, to think instead the possibility of continued participation in an ongoing public discussion, beyond the boundaries of the State-sanctioned written word, and through the ethics of mutuality established in performative speech gestures, and constituting something that deserves to be named community, embodied here and now in the contradictory call of Aboriginal self-government.

READING LANDSCAPES AND ARCHITECTURES, GESTURES AND ELDERS

reading. We read for pleasure and for knowledge. Just as our books rub against each other on our shelves, placed together by the accident of category or alphabet, our readings converge with each other; somehow, as the texts are imprinted in our minds, they slip across their covers and merge in strange articulations. Some of us are in large measure the end result of a trail of readings. One can read more than books, though. One can read people, one can read the world. One can read books to gain wisdom and knowledge, power and healing. One can read the bush and the land to gain wisdom and knowledge, power and medicine. One can read the stories inscribed in the landscape with as much care as one reads the narratives of classical history. The differing protocols of these forms of reading need to be respected, and we do well to remind ourselves of the pleasures of the texts.

landscapes. One of the interesting features of northern Aboriginal communities is the way they exist their landscape. It is a commonplace assumption, and one I reject, that Aboriginal peoples are or have been "closer to nature." In my own view, the metaphor of proximity to nature is wholly suspect since nature retains its power within each of our bodies. One cannot be closer or further from that which is within us ("do you need to pee?" is how the Italian novelist Italo Calvino raises the question). However, this is not to suggest that Dene and Inuit communities do not structure different relations to their ecological settings. Furthermore, each of the communities discussed here involves, as a community, a way of making its landscape meaningful, a way of making the very shape of the land become part of the social discussion. The landscape itself as a trace as a story as a setting as an obstacle as a site as a question as an opening as a language surrounded by and representing an embodied inscription.

architectures. The organization of built space within the community, in part a response and reflection and denial of the landscape, is also a critical aspect of community life in northern Canada. Experiments in architectural form—sometimes quite dramatic—have been necessitated by the unique engineering problems posed by arctic conditions. Houses are built on stilts so they will not melt the permafrost underneath, or are anchored down to resist strong winds. Public architecture is always fascinating in these communities, and the construction and use of public and private space are a central concern when these are dealt with across cultural boundaries. The fact of housing itself, so crucial to the fact of community, the ways in which houses are occupied, are telling indicators of colonial political dynamics. Housing has been and continues to be one of the most contested and difficult of local political questions in northern Aboriginal communities.

gestures. Like landscapes, gestures are an embodied writing. The habits of everyday life contain the continuing traces of cultural difference. Attention to the language of the gestural allows us to see how communities are continually in a process of being built and rebuilt. Gestures can be wholly saturated with ideology—as in the salute to authority, the sign of the cross, or most symptomatically the silence that greets the spectacle—though those of interest here are those that move in an emancipatory direction: the habitual gesture that reveals something of the cultural context in which it exists and from which it derives its meaning. Gestures live in the everyday, the quotidian, and invite thought respecting daily difference, modes of being that move along differing trajectories, lines of difference.

elders. Like the concept of tradition, the notion of elders is highly politically charged. Elders have an extraordinary value in contemporary popular culture and hence are made to bear the weight of an enormous desire for 'authenticity'. In Panniqtuuq, in Fort Good Hope, in Fort Simpson, there are elders. Indeed, it is possible to say that the strength of each of these communities in good measure rests on the continuing strength of the elders who remain. Elders can teach with stories and with gestures; they can speak the language of their landscape; they can have an astute understanding of contemporary social issues at the global level or can be largely unconcerned about how their local knowledge relates to broader developments. Different elders have different interests, different kinds of knowledge. In this book, to the extent possible, they have their names: some of the mystification of their status and knowledge disappears when we who write of it accept this form of responsibility, acknowledging the individuality of each elder, whose knowledge is always some reflection of their culture and some reflection of their own idiosyncratic personality. Elders can be respected in their local or regional circumstances and can also be overlooked. Those I have worked with have been humane, humorous, kindly, serious, philosophical, intense, withdrawn, cautious, visionary, grounded, dignified, humble, principled. Contrary to the view implied by their deification, they have not demanded that one agree with everything they say. But one should listen well.

SIX SMALL NOTES ABOUT SIX BIG ISSUES

Note one: culture. The concept of "culture" is under attack. A strain of contemporary social theory would suggest that the concept implies too rigidly bounded, too temporally static a social being to be of value any longer. Since there remains a difference between Dene, Inuit, and Métis lifestyles, values, and views and those of the dominant society, and since other ways of conceptualizing that difference—such as the concept of "race"—seem even more reprehensible than the concept of culture, the latter remains in operation in this work. The challenge is to find a way to represent culture that recognizes the porosity of cultural boundaries and does not presume that culture is fixed in time. This study is not about Aboriginal cultures as they may have been practised and lived in some earlier, more valid, 'pristine' expression. It looks at Aboriginal cultures as they exist today, in contemporary communities, and it puts into play the questions that culture raises about modalities of looking, including how we look at culture.

Note two: history. History gives us some purchase on the present; with Walter Benjamin I would like to think of history not as context and not as a linear sequence that leads to the present, but as rupture and opening, a field of battle in a war over meaning. The purchase on the present becomes more vivid the further back one goes. Classical history, whether of Europe or Asia or the Americas, partly appeals to scholars because it gives something of a longer term perspective, the perspective of vast distance, on our current troubles. If that is so, then the perspective gained from Aboriginal histories, a perspective that must cross the vast chasm of different modes of production, is glacial. No mere accident of reading, then, leads this study down the pathway of classical history: a love of Aboriginal narrative does not have to preclude or negate the value of the Western canon, though one might ask that the attention paid to the oral foundations of *The Odyssey* might also inform the hearing given to certain elders. Perhaps it is only in resonance with some of these most revered of Western texts that an appreciation of the significance of contemporary events and responses to them can be approximated.

Note three: names. Names are withheld in this study as an exception rather than the rule. The words of my Métis, Inuit, and Dene teachers and friends deserve to be attributed, recognized, and acknowledged as surely as the words cited from my scholarly sources. Through this practice, which involves its own ethics, Native Studies unravels the concept of "Native informant," an unravelling that sits closely beside Gayatry Chakravorty Spivak's deconstruction of the concept in *A Critique of Postcolonial Reason*. Colonial nominalism, the rewriting of personal and geographic names, is also at work in the lack of respect accorded to "Native informants." Decolonization involves a righting and a writing of names.

Note four: whites. Inuit call us *Qallunaat*, a word much in use in Nunavut. Dene call us *Mola*. These words are used in their appropriate contexts in this text. The word "non-Native" is also used. The latter has the merit of reversing a five-centuries-old practice of defining Aboriginal people through absences: the Spanish thought of *los indios* as "without God, without kings, without laws." In his influential *The Indians of Canada*, Diamond Jenness structured the work around a catalogue of things that Aboriginal people did not have. Post-colonial reversal positions the colonial inheritors of the Spanish legacy as 'without Aboriginality': I am a non-Native.

Note five: theory. There are those who hate contemporary social theory. No doubt a few can be found practising Northern Studies. There are those who love contemporary social theory. Their lives are sometimes consumed at its sacrificial altars. The three posts of current theory—post structuralism, post modernism, post colonialism—have their place in this study. The concept of totalization, the debates over mode of production, theoretical notions of text and embodiment, these and others allow the refiguring of a political boundary without which politics is impossible. I remain most closely indebted to a dialectical Marxist tradition now largely out of fashion—let the name Jean-Paul Sartre mark this place—but I have allowed whatever current of theory on which a conceptual insight floats to wash over this work. In a small way this work would like to reinvigorate the strong history of theoretical insight in relation to Northern Studies, a line of thought that stretches from Boas to Balicki to Brody, though with terms and concepts of our current moment.

Note six: numbers. The logic of the numerical sequence has been forcefully characterized by Sartre as a serial logic. In northern communities this serial logic, the logic of quantification, of numerical sequence, most frequently serves as a justificatory foundation for imposed State injunctions, while as against it a qualitative logic, defiantly unquantifiable, circulates in stories and gestures. The latter logic, in its unquantifiability, might be called poetic. Methodologically, this study rests on 'qualitative research', though I would designate that concept not so much as another step-by-step sequence of clearly delimited practices as a marker for what can not be defined. The invocation of serial logic in the sequencing of this introduction—here! now!—is a modest attempt to hold a mirror up to the colonial busy-workers statistically projecting economic growth cycles on graveyards.

SEVEN CHAPTERS

This text is organized into seven chapters. The first two chapters may be taken to offer a variety of contexts or frames, though I prefer to think of them as a contribution in their own right. These chapters include stories of the history of public government in the north, description of the different legal status of Inuit and Dene, discussion of land claims negotiations, as well as commentary on a variety of contemporary social and theoretical concepts that illuminate or open up or structure ways of seeing northern politics. The third, fourth, and fifth chapters discuss the local cultural politics and political structures and spaces of Fort Simpson, Fort Good Hope, and Panniqtuuq, respectively. The sixth chapter raises broad questions about the issue of Aboriginal self-government, the four themes and five concerns enunciated above, and the place of the territorial governments. The last, short chapter is a brief epilogue on hunting stories, because the issue of animal rights and hunting is so important to the continued viability of northern Aboriginal economies.

The word "tradition" and the phrase "on the land," which are used extensively in this text, may concern non-northern readers, who these days are keenly aware of how much 'traditions' are constructed and for whom 'on the land' is a signifier without a referent. In the north, these terms are so much a part of everyday discourse that they pass unnoticed. If we remain mindful of the likelihood that where and whenever the concept of "tradition" has been deployed—even in 'traditional' times—it involved a fabrication or invention, perhaps a form of what anthropologist Marshall Sahlins calls "mytho-praxis,"[6] its deployment here need not unduly concern us. It is only when there is a desire to assert the traditional 'authenticity' of this or that cultural practice over others that the term acquires problematic resonances that need to be carefully untangled. To put this in another way, for someone to say "this is the traditional way" could be read as "this is the way we always did things" or "this is the way we did things in the past," which itself is open to interpretation. It is noteworthy that politically, the deployment of the term gives Aboriginal speakers an authority and legitimacy that counter the credentials of their non-Native counterparts. "On the land," a phrase perhaps unfamiliar to southern readers, is used as often for those going out on boats or over ice as it is to describe travel over land. "On the land" designates a reality outside of, but in intimate connection with, community life, a constitutive reality that constantly reflects back on community life, usually related to subsistence food production—fishing, gathering, hunting, trapping—and with as much cultural resonance in the North as the concept of "traditional."

TOTALIZATION AND SUBVERSION

Two concepts that inform this study and have already been partially deployed are best elaborated at the outset. The first of these is totalization. The concept is a well-known Hegelian carry-over into Marx's and Marxist thought; it has been the subject of intense discussion and debate in the last few decades, though the conversation has taken place almost entirely in abstract philosophical terms, thereby reducing its promise as a tool of social analysis. In his *Critique of Dialectical Reason*, philosopher Jean-Paul Sartre argues, "A totalisation has the same statute as the totality, for, through the multiplicities, it continues that synthetic labour which makes each part an expression of the whole and which relates the whole to itself through the mediation of its parts. But it is a developing activity."[7] The homogenization that comes with capitalism, and is increased exponentially in the latest phase of capitalist development, is an expression of the totalizing exigencies at the structural core of the dominant system. Totalization has been experienced by Aboriginal peoples in Canada as a State policy, characterized by many scholars as "assimilation," which has worked to absorb them into the established order. Theodor Adorno, in his *Minima Moralia*, provides an eloquent articulation of how totalization works in the realm of social difference:

> That all men are alike is exactly what society would like to hear. It considers actual or imagined differences as stigmas indicating that not enough has yet been done; that something has still been left outside its machinery, not quite determined by its totality. . . . The racial difference is raised to an absolute so that it can be abolished absolutely, if only in the sense that nothing that is different survives. . . . The spokesmen of unitary tolerance are, accordingly, always ready to turn intolerantly on any group that remains refractory: intransigent enthusiasm for blacks does not exclude outrage at Jewish uncouthness. The melting-pot was introduced by unbridled industrial capitalism. The thought of being cast into it conjures up martyrdom, not democracy.[8]

Fredric Jameson, whose thought in many respects has followed a Sartrean trajectory, has, over the last two decades, established himself as a foremost proponent of the concept of totalization against those, particularly associated with varieties of post-structuralist philosophy, who have attacked it. In his book about Adorno, Jameson suggests that some thinkers in the Marxist tradition have been "stigmatized as 'totalitarian' in their insistence on the urgency and centrality of the notion of totality," arguing that "the misunderstanding lies in drawing the conclusion that philosophical emphasis on the indispensability of this category amounts either to celebration of it or, in a stronger form of the anti-utopian argument, to its implicit perpetuation as a reality or a referent outside the philosophical realm."[9] Jameson is well aware that the concept of totalization is much derided these days as "a properly metaphysical survival, complete with illusions of truth, a baggage of first principles, a scholastic appetite for 'system' in the conceptual sense, a yearning for closure and certainty, a belief in centeredness, a commitment to representation, and any number of other antiquated mindsets."[10] However, on the specific charge that "the concept of totalization means repressing all these group differences and reorganizing their former adherents into some ironclad military or party formation," he argues that "on any meaningful usage—that is to say, one for which totalization is a project rather than the word for an already existent institution—the project necessarily means the complex negotiation of all these individual differences."[11] Jameson's work allows for an understanding of the critical value of the concept of totalization, both in describing the logic and material practice of the dominant order and in constructing forms of resistance to it, counter totalities or, in a Sartrean vein, "detotalizing" totalities: what today we might want to call "viral resistances." A viral resistence acts like a computer virus to reconfigure a total field or, at a minimum, to massively disrupt the project of totalization.

The concept of totalization is indispensable to an understanding of the political project of Aboriginal peoples in northern Canada, a project that can be seen as a form of resistance to the world-as-grid being constructed by the totalizing exigencies of commodity culture. Michael Taussig, among many others and in this instance following George Lukacs, describes commodity culture as "the thingifying quality of commodity-inspired culture manifested in such disparate forms as bureaucratic planning and Warhol's all-alike, endless soup-cans extending over the face of an ever more rationalized capitalist universe," or, in the less abstract terms that Taussig adds, "what hits you as you wriggle out of the congestion of the city to leap westwards in the state-registered steel beast across the George Washington bridge onto Highway 101 starting with Exit 3 and numbered in order all the way to the Pacific coast where the pounding waves stop it short. A Cold War feat."[12] What exit will we take to Nunavut or Denendeh?

Resistance to totalization, for those who do not have the power to directly confront it, frequently takes the form of subversion. Subversion involves a strategy of reading and a practice of redeployment where a sign or structure or object that has been fashioned as a tool of totalization is reconfigured as a mechanism expressing cultural resistance. Jacques Derrida provides an illustrative example in one of his characterizations of Karl Marx: "Marx wants at the same time to extract them from Stirner's witness-text and to use them against him. As always, he grabs the weapons and turns them back against the one who thought he was their sole owner."[13] The following example, offered by Taussig—whose work as a reader of the micropolitics of subversion is perhaps his most significant contribution—is equally illustrative:

> Sometimes the icons of the Church enter into play with the icons
> of the state. Cali, the largest city of the Colombian southwest,
> straddles the angle where the plains cut into the steep slopes of
> the Andes. Overlooking and protecting the city from afar, on
> the mountain's peak, stands an enormous statue of Christ, arms

outstretched, crucified. Down in the city, so I am told by one of its young vagabundos, is a statue commemorating its founder, the great conquistador Sebastian Benalcazar. He stands tensed with his hand to his hip, not to his sword, in anger and disbelief that his wallet has just been stolen. (Cali, it should be noted, is notorious for its pickpockets.) With his other hand he points not to the dream of the sublime and future prospects of the town he has founded, but to another statue, that of the first mayor of Cali (so my young friend tells me), accusing him of the theft. The mayor, in his turn, defends himself by pointing to the statue of another of the city's dignitaries, who in his turn points up the mountain to none less than Christ himself—standing with arms outstretched as for a police search: "I didn't steal anything. Look and see!" The lot of the urban vagabond and that of Christ are thus brought together, both unjustly blamed by the city's founding fathers, conquistadores and good bourgeois alike.[14]

Their "lot" is "brought together" by a subversive rereading of signs—in this case, statues—constructed and placed in order to 'shore up' or glorify the dignity and power of church and State. Subversion is often a micropolitics whose traces are in the sphere of the everyday and pass unnoticed or unregistered, as is appropriate to a gesture against the very process of registration, or official writing, that most often marks State power. While any theory of subversion depends upon a notion of intentionality, subversion is an embodied form of contesting intentionality; the fact that subversion can take place itself illustrates that intentions do not and cannot confer any final truth or guarantee ultimate meaning respecting a text. In western Arctic communities, it is commonplace that Dene, especially older Dene, wear their slippers outdoors with a rubber galosh overtop. The same slippers are sold to tourists. In buying them, the tourists surrender the attempt to achieve ultimate convenience in footwear, slip-ons (Adorno thought slip-ons were "monuments to the hatred of bending down"). The Dene slippers, which require help from the hand to put on, are also are a mainstay of the northern Aboriginal cottage/craft industry. The galoshes worn over them turn them into outdoor wear, but can then be slipped off indoors, turning the slippers back into slippers. Here, a technology developed or intended for wet weather wear is imported and supports the continuance of footwear that is markedly Dene. Subversion and totalization constantly and continually kick each other around.

The relation of totalization to subversion parallels what Jameson describes as a dialectic of ideology and utopia. It is an intricate relation: what is subversive in one moment can quickly pass over into the realm of totalization. The dominating logic can appropriate, usually through commodification, the most subversive gestures. However, the workings of totalization are themselves so complex that even the mechanics of appropriation are open to subversion; this can be learned more from the life practices of the most marginal (and less totalized) people in the world, including Inuit and Dene, than even from the productions of the intellectual classes.

'HERE' AND 'THERE'

> They will fight my fight, with my determination; over there is no more than a here; I am no more in danger 'over there' than they are here; I expect nothing from them (alterity), since everyone gives everything both here and 'over there'. . .
>
> — Jean-Paul Sartre, *Critique of Dialectical Reason*

A final comment with which this introduction can be brought to a close. Clifford Geertz has described anthropology in terms of "being there" and "being here," arguing that "the moral asymmetries across which ethnography works and the discursive complexity within which it works make any attempt to portray it as anything more than the representation of one sort of life in the categories of another impossible to defend. That may be enough. I, myself, think that it is."[15] This text, too, is an attempt to represent one sort of politics in the categories of another. In doing so, the categories themselves come into question, learn to dance in different steps. But this text also represents an attempt to reconstruct the opposition between 'being there' and 'being here' that the newer smallness of the world, created by totalization, allows. In this sense, this text represents part of an attempt to bring into being a new modality of knowledge, which is tentatively given the name Native Studies. Derrida refers to this ethical reconfiguration to some extent in his remarkable dedication at the beginning of *Spectres of Marx:* "at once part, cause, effect, example, what is happening there translates what takes place here, always here, wherever one is and wherever one looks, closest to home. Infinite responsibility, therefore, no rest allowed for any form of good conscience."[16] The situation of an academic discipline called Native Studies equally already implies this. Students who have come from 'there' to 'here'—from around the NWT to Ontario and Manitoba—courses taught 'there'—specifically in Yellowknife and Panniqtuuq—articles written for the northern press, all imply in my mind a different kind of interrelationship and trace a newer modality of responsibility. Eric Menicoche and Robert Tookoome and Kayrene Kilabuk were students in Native Studies at Trent University while I taught there. Bella T'Seleie, James Wahshee, Richard Van Camp, and many others were students in Native Studies courses I conducted for Arctic College in Yellowknife in 1990, near the beginning of this study. Learning and teaching have had to twist around each other in a manner that challenges and enriches both. At least some of the categories and some of the writing strategies deployed 'here' are commonplace 'there'. And this text is directed, aimed, 'addressed', however naïvely or futilely, as much 'there' as 'here'.

PART ONE

NAMES AND PLACES

Growing love of money, and the lust for power which followed it, engendered every kind of evil. Avarice destroyed honour, integrity, and every other virtue, and instead taught men to be proud and cruel, to neglect religion, and to hold nothing too sacred to sell. . . . Avarice . . . means setting your heart on money, a thing no wise man ever did. It is a kind of deadly poison, which ruins a man's health and weakens his moral fibre. It knows no bounds and can never be satisfied: he that has not, wants; he that has, wants more.

—Sallust, *The Conspiracy of Catiline*

The naive supposition of an unambiguous development towards increased production is itself a piece of that bourgeois outlook which permits development in only one direction because, integrated into a totality, dominated by quantification, it is hostile to qualitative difference.

—Theodor Adorno, *Minima Moralia*

CHAPTER ONE

the story lines

SEEING CULTURE

In an interview for this study conducted by Elizabeth Fajber, Mary Louise Norwegian, an amiable, elderly Dene woman who worked as a community health representative in Fort Simpson, told the following story:

> Way back when they used to give glasses, the treaty glasses called. We'd get it once every two years, the free glasses. But when they check up for their eyes, we have interpreter there but they only hire interpreter to look up files, and she cannot be with a patient at the same time as being in the office, so yeah, we have interpreter there, but she's work in the office. So they bring this patient to the room and ask them—because we have so many people in such a short days, just a few days we have to go through all those people—the first thing they ask them: 'do you read?' And those Native people say 'no'. So the kind of glass they give them is for distance, and they never stop to think, these Native women they do embroidery, and sew, and needlework. It's the same distance as reading a book. And then, so I went out of my way and got a dish of beads and a beading needle and thread needle. So I just leave it there with the [unintelligible] sheets, and they take that and if they see a Native woman they give them that plate and they put thread needle around with needle and beads, and so it's working a bit better now. But it's still, you know, they get glasses and they have to wait two more years. They get distance glass, they cannot afford

close range glass, they have to wait for two years. So, you know, that's, that was my biggest concern with eye care, for eye glasses for the Native people, while they have the chance to get it, they should get the right ones.

This story has all the force of a parable, involving as it does questions of seeing, of ways of seeing, and of the visibility of culture itself. Norwegian, the community health representative, notices that women coming for new glasses are being asked by the optometrist if they read and, if they answer negatively, are given glasses for long distance. In a typically Dene fashion, she does not confront the optometrist; instead, she tries to make visible to him what he is not seeing. She does this by leaving beads and needles lying around in this waiting room so he can see that some of the women clearly need glasses appropriate for the intricacies of beadwork.

The story itself is a machine that layers the relation between a non-Native medical specialist and Dene women. The doctor sees the mechanics of eye care enough to offer real help to people. Dene women and men come to him for help. The doctor cannot see exactly what kind of help they need, though of course he thinks he does or he thinks he can find out by asking questions. But an invisible cultural boundary separates him from them, his questions do not account for it, his medical practice is not as helpful as he believes it to be. Norwegian sees the disjuncture in the doctor-patient relation and finds a way of making visible to the doctor his cultural blindness. This whole relation unfolds in the realm of sight, in the realm of what is visible, of what the elderly Dene women want to see and of what the doctor cannot see. This is a story of how to make cultural difference visible and it stages the notion that culture itself is perhaps a way of seeing.

In her *The Dialectics of Seeing*, Susan Buck-Morss argues that the 'trick' in Benjamin's fairy tale is to interpret out of the discarded dream images of mass culture a politically empowering knowledge of the collective's own unconscious past.[1] This is certainly an important and viable program for those caught deeply within the web of late capitalist social relations. But what if the living memory of the collective was politically empowering, not as an unconscious past but as one aspect of the present? What images become politically empowering in such a context? The dialectical images on which Michael Taussig rests so much interpretive power? Or, perhaps, an image of an image, a story of a way of seeing, a story that reveals, makes visible, the limits of a way of seeing, a story that sees seeing itself and, as quietly and insistently as the needle, thread, and beads placed on a plate in the physician's waiting room, implicitly asks us if we need a new pair of glasses.

FOR GINA

Gina Blondin was among the earliest Dene friends I encountered in the Northwest Territories during my first visit, in the summer of 1984. She made it her personal mission to take me a bit under her wing and tried to explain to me some of what the north is all about from a Dene perspective. She was a remarkable person, a strong and vibrant character. She seemed to me to embody something of the spirit of Thanadelthur, the woman who was largely responsible for negotiating peace between the Dene and Cree in the early eighteenth-century fur trade. Like Thanadelthur, Gina could talk. She had an enormous energy and would never sit still, a constant firestorm of movement, meals, papers, picnics, arrangements, thoughts, talk. Talk was her greatest outlet; she spoke rapid-fire, dropping ideas, plans, stories, memories, explanations, justifications in a verbal blizzard, while she whisked her daughter to some practice or other, chopped vegetables, picked up the constantly ringing phone, sorted through mail, dealt with doorbells, and looked over once in a while at her visitor.

She was the daughter of a chief, George Blondin, from the small Dene community of Deline (then Fort Franklin) on Sahtu (Great Bear Lake). Her father, on retirement, became a very well-known storyteller and elder and, thanks in part to her help and encouragement, began to publish traditional Dene stories and histories. Her cousin Ethyl Blondin-Andrew became Member of Parliament for the Western Arctic region for the Liberal party and Secretary of State for Training and Youth in the Liberal government after 1993. Her brother John, until his death in the mid-nineties, was a well-known northern artist, particularly in dance and theatre. She came, in other words, from a very strong family and from a traditional community. During the time I knew her, she was Executive Assistant to the Minister of Education, then Dennis Patterson, and a single mother with a young daughter.

We met through the accident of mutual acquaintances. For no explicable reason we became friends. She offered me meals and paid enough attention to explain something about what was going on, who the key actors were, what their histories were. She helped transform me from another southern researcher stumbling around without a clue into someone who could begin to ask questions. Between 1986, when the study that first brought me to the north was completed, and 1990, when I began the process of starting this study, Gina died of an illness. I found out through friends, from Toronto, a continent away. I never had an opportunity to pay my proper respects. These words, if they are, as Dene might say, "good words," are my only way of returning the gifts she gave me. Two of the stories she told me stayed with me in spite of the fact that I took no notes, and came to inform how I understand the complex dynamic of northern Aboriginal cultural politics.

Like many Dene of her generation, the political leaders in the prime of life through the seventies and eighties, Gina attended a residential school. Dene children were sent to church-run residential schools from primary years up to school completion, returning home for summers and Christmases. The residential school system is famous in Canada as one of the great colonial institutions established by the settler white colony (see John Milloy's *A National Crime*). The legacy of residential schools remains unresolved, and a key component of reconciliation with Aboriginal peoples in Canada will be an accounting of the residential school experience. Because I had attended a government-run residential high school in northern Manitoba (not as harsh an institution as the mission-run schools of the earlier decades, for the accountants of pain to whom this would matter), I was attuned to stories about residential schools and could share experiences. One of those schools in the NWT was a Catholic-run school at Fort Providence, at the south end of the Deh Cho (Mackenzie River), which served many of the Dene communities.

One summer when she was in her teens, Gina was not allowed to return to her family—they were out on the land, or there was an illness—and had to spend the summer at the residential school. She missed her family terribly, and for that reason remembers it as a very sad and lonely period of her life. Gina spent much of her time that summer doing what she was told. The nuns had her working in the dirt, pulling out the plants they didn't like, leaving alone the ones that grew in the mounds, watering, other tasks that seemed very strange to her. Gina had no idea what this was all about. But she was a good, hard worker, she followed instructions closely, she didn't need to know what the reasons were or outcome would be. If the white nuns for their own inexplicable reasons wanted her to wallow around in the mud, that's what she'd have to do. At least she was outside.

The day arrived when something was going to happen to her mounds of dirt. The nuns now had her pulling out little round clumps, brushing mud off them, piling them up. Finally, she recognized them: potatoes! Her reaction, as she explained it to me years later, while leaning across her kitchen counter at the Borealis Co-op in Yellowknife, was something like "yech." She was "grossed out." She had eaten potatoes all her life, they were a staple by then for most Dene families, going along nicely with moose or caribou meat, or fish, or in stews. And now, it turned out, they grew in the dirt! in the mud! they were filthy! For a long time afterwards, Gina had a hard time eating potatoes.

The story remains with me to this day. My intent in telling it here is to dramatize a fact of Gina's life that is typical of many Dene and Inuit. For Hugh Brody, in his recent *The Other Side of Eden*, it is a determinant fact. Dene and Inuit live in some uneasy fashion between two kinds of ways of life; one of those gets its food largely through cultivation, the work of the soil. The other gets its food by gathering or hunting it from the bush.

ON LISTENING

. . . proper listening is the foundation of proper living.

—Plutarch, *Essays*

An astute philosophical analysis on "The Problem of Speaking for Others" by Linda Alcoff concludes with a call that perhaps speaking itself is the problem, that perhaps a willingness to listen would serve better. While the problems of speech and identity politics are much debated these days, much less serious attention is given to the problem of listening, of how to listen. Let Alcoff's end point act as an introduction, then, and one that leads straight to Plutarch, who did address the problem of listening a long time ago in a well-known essay. Plutarch demands that the attitude of the listener not be passive, suggesting that just as in a ball game the catcher must move and change position in a rhythm that responds to that of the thrower, so in the case of speeches there is a certain harmonious rhythm on both the speaker's and the listener's part.[2] One of the main points of Plutarch's essay, which could be read allegorically to deal with the whole problem of listening to 'others', was that a degree of empathy or charity was at least initially demanded, in part because "it is impossible for a speaker to be so thoroughly ineffective and mistaken that he fails to come out with a commendable idea or quotation or overall topic and plan, or at least a commendable use of language and structuring of his speech."[3]

In a society where "power consists in the monopoly of the spoken word,"[4] good listening is hardly a valued attribute. A theme of many of the elders I have talked to—George Blondin, Pauloosie Angmarlik, Paul Wright—has been how people do not listen as well as they did in the past. This is a common assertion of northern Aboriginal elders. For example, Dogrib women told Joan Ryan for her study of Dene traditional justice that in those days people really listened,[5] a lament I too heard repeatedly. This is hardly surprising. Walter Benjamin commented, of course, on the same phenomenon, attributing it to the decline of boredom, "the dream bird that hatches the egg of experience." In Benjamin's view, when the "activities that are intimately associated with boredom disappear . . . the gift for listening is lost and the community of listeners disappears."[6]

Listening to elders, in particular, is a difficult matter. While the contemporary social veneration of elders makes their speech a valuable source of legitimation, to the extent that frequently elders—commonly unnamed—provide the final, 'human' touch to many a politician's speech, listening to their speech demands attention and care of a particular kind. Good listening here means disentangling the web of anthropological practice, exploding the concept of 'Native informant' and the concept of fieldwork, attending to both the immediate power of the individual and the cultural knowledge that the individual bears. And putting oneself in that state of grace, a self-forgetful, distracted boredom, that will allow the story to take root in memory.

Certainly Michael Taussig's concept of "implicit social knowledge" is relevant. Implicit social knowledge involves "what moves people without their knowing why or quite how, with what makes the real real and the normal normal, and above all what makes ethical distinctions politically powerful."[7] Taussig also takes implicit social knowledge to be an essentially inarticulable and imageric non-discursive knowing of social relationality.[8] There must be a way of both respecting the specific, individual views of elders and traditional teachers, and of attuning oneself to their implicit social knowledge. One aspect of the disentangling involves giving one's 'informants' their name: too many texts so carefully cite each textual authority, while conveniently being able to take the utterances of their 'informants' as culturally emblematic, that the names that appear in a text about some 'other' or 'other' are all from the dominant culture. The form in which the images that make up implicit social knowledge are exchanged is itself one critical feature of that knowledge. The narrative form, the practice of storytelling, retains a particular charge among Inuit and Dene alike. The storytelling form as a way of conveying information was and is a refined art among gathering and hunting peoples. This too is a work of stories: stories of communities, of people, of theories, of histories, of ideas, of stories. In the moment of relating these, my only consolation is the hope, like a breath of prayer, that I have listened well.

MODES OF PRODUCTION

Dene and Inuit live on a fault line between two very distinct ways of life: that of the (post)modern, industrial, capitalist world and that of their traditional, subsistence, hunting world. That is, their way of life comes from or is related to an underlying structure that social scientists in the Marxist tradition have called a "mode of production." Fredric Jameson, in proposing a Marxist strategy of interpreting cultural texts, argued that three distinct "horizons of interpretation" could be deployed and that

> such semantic enrichment and enlargement of inert givens and materials of a particular text must take place within three concentric frameworks, which mark a widening out of the sense of the social ground of a text through the notions, first, of political history, in the narrow sense of punctual event and a chronicle-like sequence of happenings in time; then of a society, in the now already less diachronic and time-bound sense of a constitutive tension and struggle between social classes; and, ultimately, of history now conceived in the vastest sense of the sequence of modes of production and the succession and destiny of the various human social formations, from prehistoric life to whatever far future history has in store for us.[9]

In Jameson's schema, a mode of production is the broadest level of analysis, or third and final horizon of interpretation, that can be deployed to understand social phenomena such as cultural texts. Jameson suggests that "the 'problematic' of modes of production is the most vital new area of Marxist theory in all the disciplines today."[10]

The concept of mode of production comes from Marx, who used it to classify differing types of societies. In his notebooks of 1857–58, Marx discussed the different elements of economic analysis in order to frame his argument for the priority of 'production'.

> Production creates the objects which correspond to given needs; distribution divides them up according to social laws; exchange further parcels out the already divided shares in accord with individual needs; and finally, in consumption, the product steps outside this social movement and becomes a direct object and servant of individual need, and satisfies it in being consumed. Thus production appears as the point of departure, consumption as the conclusion, distribution and exchange as the middle, which is however itself twofold, since distribution is determined by society and exchange by individuals.[11]

This "shallow coherence," in Marx's words, of these elements situated production as the generative and determinative point of departure for a social system. Hence, different societies can be classified by the characteristic way or modality that they produce the goods and services they need to survive and reproduce. However, it is important to stress that production, the moment of creation, stands in for the whole social process; a mode of production is not simply a way of making things, but equally implies a way of organizing human relations, ways of ensuring social stability, ways of determining social reproduction, ways of understanding and seeing. A mode of production refers to an intricately interconnected social totality where the moment of economic production, narrowly understood, is itself in part conditioned by the relations it conditions, and where even the notions of what constitutes the "economic," like production itself, are themselves defined and acquire different status within the whole. Broadly speaking, a mode of production implies a way of life, though the former term points in specific characteristic directions that have value for analytic and classificatory purposes, whether we are economic determinists of the older Marxist sort, or assert notions of "expressive causality" or "expressive correspondence" of the structuralist or post-structuralist variety. In the context of northern Canada, for example, it is the concept of mode of production that allows for recognition of a basic structural similarity between Inuit and Dene, despite the extraordinary differences in their languages, ecological strategies, and expressive cultural life. Hence, for Hugh Brody, who has worked with both Dene and Inuit, the rupture between hunting cultures and farming cultures is the critical, defining feature of the cultural difference between 'Western' and Aboriginal peoples.

The anthropologist Eric Wolfe characterizes a mode of production as "a specific, historically occurring set of social relations through which labour is deployed to wrest energy from nature by means of tools, skills, organization, and knowledge," and argues that "the concept of social labour thus makes it possible to conceptualize the major ways in which human beings organize their production. Each major way of doing so constitutes a mode of production."[12] The concept of mode of production has been so widely used, discussed, criticized, and adapted that it is difficult not to deploy without specification. For example, Wolfe clearly sees a mode of production as "historically occurring," whereas political scientist Nicos Poulantzas argued that "the mode of production constitutes an abstract-formal object which does not exist in the strong sense in reality." Poulantzas's suggestion here is important to the degree that it allows us to understand that different modes of production can co-exist within the same social structure; that is, "the only thing which really exists is a historically determined social formation." Hence, in his view, "the social formation itself constitutes a complex unity in which a certain mode of production dominates the others which compose it."[13]

Jameson, while rejecting Poulantzas's form of distinction between an 'abstract' mode of production and a 'real' social formation, because it "encourages the very empirical thinking which it was concerned to denounce," nevertheless accepts and deploys the concept of "social formation."

> Yet one feature of Poulantzas' discussion of the 'social formation' may be retained: his suggestion that every social formation or historically existing society has in fact consisted in the overlay and structural co-existence of several modes of production all at once, including vestiges and survivals of older modes of production, now relegated to structurally dependent positions within the new, as

well as anticipatory tendencies which are potentially inconsistent with the existing system but have not generated an autonomous space of their own.[14]

This is a critical point, because it allows us to think of conflict within specific social fields as conflict between, following Raymond Williams's language,[15] dominant and residual or emergent modes of production. It accords with Marx's argument in the *Grundrisse* that bourgeois forms of production are dominant but not exclusive.[16]

Both Jameson and Wolfe, for different reasons, denounce the common tendency to view modes of production in a sequence of evolutionary stages of the primitive to archaic to feudal to capitalist sort. Wolfe, who proposed to discuss three modes of production, wrote that he had no "intention, in the present context, to argue that these three modes represent any evolutionary sequence."[17] Jameson simply notes that the stage schematic has "generally been felt to be unsatisfactory."[18] Interestingly, Marx, who, with Engels in *The Communist Manifesto*, provided a powerful source for the stage theory argument, showed a much more nuanced understanding in his 1857–58 notebooks, writing, for example, that "it may be said on the other hand that there are very developed but nevertheless historically less mature forms of society, in which the highest forms of economy, e.g. cooperation, a developed division of labour, etc., are found."[19]

One of the merits and contributions of Wolfe's analysis is his definition of three modes of production, "a capitalist mode, a tributary mode, and a kin ordered mode." Although he writes that "no argument is presented here to the effect that this trinity exhausts all the possibilities," his discussion of the tributary mode takes in a wide variety of modes usually given distinct status, including the asiatic, archaic, and feudal. Modes of production are frequently distinguished by the way in which surplus value is 'extracted' from the broad mass of people. In capitalism, workers sell their labour as labour power and surplus value is what remains to the capitalist after they have paid the worker enough to allow the latter to subsist. The capitalist mode, in my own view, is also characterized by three critical features: the generalized expansion of the commodity form, the structural demand for capital accumulation, and the specific separation of the political and economic hegemonic institutions. In the tithe mode, economic surplus is extracted through the bonds of vassalage usually supported by the deployment of repressive force. The tributary or tithe mode, in Wolfe's view, is a mode in which the "primary producer, whether cultivator or herdman, is allowed access to the means of production, while tribute is exacted from him by political or military means."[20] What Wolfe called a kin ordered mode I would prefer to designate as a gathering and hunting mode of production, characterized by nomadic and semi-nomadic bands where the primary producer has both access to the means of production and 'ownership' of the products of her or his labour. Notably, there is no extraction of economic surplus, but rather systems of generalized reciprocity among gatherers and hunters; hence, even this category needs rethinking if it is to be deployed to understand gatherers and hunters.

This tripartite division is particularly useful because it allows us to displace the concept of "pre-capitalist social formations," a concept developed by Marx in his 1857–58 notebooks and used widely to characterize conflict between capitalist and earlier modes of production. The problem with the concept of pre-capitalist social formations, like the concept of "tribal peoples," is that it elides the critical difference between the tributary mode of production and the gathering and hunting mode, between village agriculturalists and nomadic foragers. This difference is critical precisely because there are many features of the tributary mode that are similar to the capitalist mode but do not exist in the gatherer-hunter mode, a point of considerable importance to Brody. For example, both the tributary and capitalist modes are accumulative. The tributary mode involved settlements that allowed for the accumulation of material wealth. Even tributary pastoralists could accumulate, by ensuring that their flocks grew. In capitalism, accumulation reached a qualitatively new dimension with the dominance of abstract wealth in the form of capital. Among gatherers and hunters, particularly nomadic bands, accumulation of goods was not a material possibility. One could only accumulate what one could carry and there was a fairly clear limit to this. Similarly, both tributary and capitalist modes of production are socially structured around class conflict; the gathering and hunting mode was effectively classless. One implication of this is that the word "traditional," used by agriculturalists and by hunters, takes on quite a different resonance in these distinct contexts. Both involve traditional cultures in conflict and collusion with the dominant structures, but one set of traditional values, that of agriculturalists, involves social hierarchy and values directly related to those now in the ascendancy. When hunters from egalitarian cultures use the word "tradition," it retains a critical charge.

Hence, the dynamic of conflict between gathering and hunting peoples and the capitalist mode of production is specific and remains largely under-theorized, to a great extent because of the elision that the concept of pre-capitalist social formations involves. Even Hugh Brody's recent work casts the conflict in terms of a struggle between hunters and farmers, thereby missing the dimensions of struggle that owe their features to the nature of capitalism, specifically. This particular dynamic of conflict has not been helped by many of those who have studied gatherers and hunters with a concern for the search for 'pure' exemplifications of primitiveness, since for the most part they have ignored the conflict altogether. The capitalist mode clearly grew out of the tributary mode and, as a result, even when it imposed itself on the tributary mode, it found social and other material structures that could accommodate its exigencies. The radicality of the difference between capitalism and gatherers and hunters made for an entirely different dynamic, one that continues to this day.

To each mode of production corresponds a mode of social being. This latter phrase may stand in as a working definition for the concept of culture. Reading the traces, in everyday community life in northern Canada, of a gathering and hunting mode of production involves attempting to interpret gestures, structures, stories, talk, objects, for what these may say or how they may point towards a radical alterity, an alterity that operates at the liminal margin of contemporary culture. The most profound differences, which challenge the fundamental structures of being that organize dominant society and which demand operation of concepts suited to the widest horizon of interpretation, are etched in commonplace figures of speech and everyday habits. The work of decoding and interpreting these does not take place for its own sake but has a dual direction: to point towards existing alternative modes of being that may be adaptable to quite different social circumstances, including our own (who and where ever this 'our' can be found), and to better understand and advance the specific struggles of particular Aboriginal peoples in the interest of furthering the project of social justice.

ON MONUMENTS

"One cannot love a monument, a work of architecture, an institution as such," writes Jacques Derrida, "except in an experience itself precarious in its fragility: it hasn't always been there, it will not always be there, it is finite. And for this very reason I love it as mortal, through its birth and its death, through the ghost or the silhouette of its ruin."[21] The monument is the highest expression of the principle of civilization: it reflects this or that particular civilization's mode of public remembrance. And it reflects the notion of civilization itself. It is wise to remember that in ancient times, 'putting up a trophy' was what the victors did on the field of battle to establish and consolidate their victory. All monuments continue to bear traces of the power that can determine what will be remembered.

We are not used to thinking of gatherers and hunters in terms of empires. Gatherers and hunters left no striking monuments of the order of the pyramids. Their histories do not, by and large, tell us the life stories of 'great' conquerors and momentous, nation-building or -shattering events. They left none of the world religions to which millions today bow their heads. What sacred texts they left behind are usually inscribed in, and as an intimate part of, the landscape, as in the story of the giant beaver hides that Dene lawgiver Yamoria left pegged on the south face of Bear Rock Mountain, where "you can see the impression they make to this day."[22] Rather than leaving a substantial material contribution in the form of monuments to what we today might recognize as culture, gatherers and hunters left the most ephemeral but arguably most important of monuments: a set of values socially embedded in a way and a quality of life.

Yet there remains an assumption that the culture of gatherers and hunters is in some way deficient because it is not inscribed in massive architectural structures. And with the enormous self-satisfaction that is one of the society's constitutive features, the assumption that Western society represents the most 'highly developed' way of life still reigns. Critical theory involves a questioning of Western culture from within its own terms, and therefore challenges this assumption. Hence, for example, of the fortunate, privileged, minority, living in increasingly banal suburbs, Theodor Adorno could once write:

> Only when sated with false pleasure, disgusted with the goods offered, dimly aware of the inadequacy of happiness even when it is that—to say nothing of cases where it is bought by abandoning allegedly morbid resistance to its positive surrogate—can men gain an idea of what experience might be. The admonition to be happy, voiced in concert by the scientifically epicurean

sanatorium-director and the highly-strung propaganda chiefs of the entertainment-industry, have about them the fury of the father berating his children for not rushing joyously downstairs when he comes home irritable from his office. It is part of the mechanism of domination to forbid recognition of the suffering it produces, and there is a straight line of development between the gospel of happiness and the construction of camps of extermination so far off in Poland that each of our own countrymen can convince himself that he cannot hear the screams of pain. [23]

A "highly developed" culture indeed, when we systematically destroy the world only marginally faster than we destroy every remaining capacity within ourselves that allows us to appreciate what is being destroyed. While respect for the other does not necessarily depend upon lack of regard for the self—quite the contrary—in the state of officially sanctioned self-satisfaction that the post-communist Western world has stumbled into, a position of criticism grounded upon the values and material strategies of other cultures becomes an almost necessary facet of their appreciation.

In his conclusion to *The Political Unconscious*, Jameson suggests "a reversal of Walter Benjamin's great dictum that 'there is no document of civilization which is not at one and the same time a document of barbarism,' proposing that the effectively ideological is also, at the same time, necessarily Utopian."[24] While we might be inspired to stage an alternative reversal, proposing that "no document of barbarism" exists that is not, at the same time, "a document of civilization," since it is in part the nature and existence of such documents, of the documentary itself, that is in question, we must resist this formulation. Instead of great monuments or documents, instead of "highly developed" self-congratulation, of the gatherers and hunters we have a few scattered inscriptions, a few marginalized communities, a few fragmentary and usually highly distorted observations, passing as they do through the crucible of language before they can be received.

ON LOOKING AT OTHERS

The following passage, by a by-no-means-sympathetic observer, Diamond Jenness, can stand in as an observation and a virtual allegory of the process of observing others. The date was Sunday, August 2, 1914. The place was on the north coast of Alaska. The lengthy excerpt is from Jenness's recently published diary:

> I watched the Eskimo camp ashore through the binoculars. There are 15 people living there, five tents, all of calico, three rectangular gable tents and two oval, like the old Eskimo skin tents, stretched over curving willow sticks. On the beach a man was sitting watching a fish-net stretched in the water on the edge. Presently a boy went down to him and they gathered the fish—salmon trout they looked like—eight in all I think, and flung them up on the beach; then they sat down side by side to chat for a time. Higher up on the bank in front of one of the tents four girls or women were sitting. A young fellow approached, apparently said something to them, then began to run. One of the girls or women sprang up and chased him for a short distance then picked up a clod of earth and threw it after him. Some distance away a man was approaching with a gun—clearly he had been out hunting—probably for ducks. A little while afterwards a little girl in bright red calico dress wandered down to the beach. The same girl ran after her and picked her up and threw her up the bank then scrambled up herself and stretched out on the grass beside the others. Outside another tent a man was gazing placidly out to sea, very likely watching our schooner. The sky was mirrored in the placid water and a little way out from the beach a line of small grounded ice floes stretched along for miles in each direction. Now and again an eider duck or a regiment of oldsquaws flew by. Faint and blurred in the far distance, hardly perceptible to the naked eye, were the Endicott Mountains. Blue smoke curled up from one of the tents and made a dark line across the sky. The whole scene was pervaded with the peace and charm of home, with the melancholy comfort of a sunset.[25]

Watching through his binoculars, from a comfortable distance, observing and recording, Jenness puts himself in what he names the "scene." The searching gaze follows the leisurely pace of the people in the distance, the fishers pulling char from their net, the young women keeping a casual eye on the children or chasing their teasers, the hunter returning home, and comes to rest, finally, on "a man . . . gazing placidly out to sea, very likely watching our schooner." It is at this point that the description of the social scene abruptly comes to an end, and Jenness moves on to the setting and the emotions the whole scene invokes, as if he has reached the point where his descriptive apparatus can no longer accommodate what it discovers.

Attention to landscape here marks a refusal to probe the social. Rather than answers to whatever age-old questions we pose, rather than a revelation or a moral or a piece of evidence, or perhaps as well as these—even from the distance of time, space, culture, that separates Jenness and his reader from the scene described—at the very heart of the "scene," positioned as its virtual "social climax," we find the liminal point of the modernist anthropological project inasmuch as we encounter the fact that our gaze may be being returned.

STILL THINKING ABOUT THE ORIGINAL AFFLUENT SOCIETY

> The Fenni are astonishingly savage and disgustingly poor. They have no proper weapons, no horses, no homes. They eat wild herbs, dress in skins, and sleep on the ground. Their only hope of getting better fare lies in their arrows, which, for lack of iron, they tip with bone. The women support themselves by hunting, exactly like the men; they accompany them everywhere and insist on taking their share in bringing down the game. . . . Unafraid of anything that man or god can do to them, they have reached a state that few human beings can attain: for these men are so well content that they do not even need to pray for anything.
>
> —Tacitus, *Germania*

The anthropological work of Marshall Sahlins has contributed greatly to our appreciation of the gatherer and hunter mode of production in recent decades. His influential essay "The Original Affluent Society" in *Stone Age Economics* retains its power as a lever for toppling age-old biases towards so-called primitives, though, interestingly, the widely read piece has not been as subject to careful scholarly analysis as one might think. The by-now-familiar overall thesis in his essay is that the hunting-gathering economy has to be re-evaluated[26] and such a re-evaluation could well characterize this form of economy as affluent rather than marginal, subsistence, or outright miserable, as has frequently been the dominant assumption.

Sahlins provides two broad reasons for his re-evaluation. On the one hand, he argues that gatherers and hunters have greater leisure time than any of the economies that followed, suggesting that "hunters keep banker's hours" (34–35; note the leisurely tone of the Inuit social space in Jenness's description above). On the other hand, Sahlins argues that there exists "a

Zen road to affluence"(2), that gatherers and hunters can take the path of least resistance, in the language of classical Zen philosophy. Simply put, gatherers and hunters have fewer needs and those needs are relatively easily met. Any individual can make with her own hands the things she needs to survive and thrive. Moreover, there is a material limit that conditions the need structure. This material limit is an exigency that derives from the nomadic way of life of most gatherers and hunters. Again, simply put, in a society where you can only own what you can carry, your ownership or ability to accumulate things has an upper limit. Sahlins writes: "of the hunter it is truly said that his wealth is a burden. In his condition of life, goods can become 'grievously oppressive', as Guisinde observes, and the more so the longer they are carried around" (11). In this social context, objects must be viewed not with the desire that we are increasingly provoked to adopt as an attitude towards things, but with suspicion. For these reasons, Sahlins argues persuasively,

> Hunting and gathering has all the strengths of its weaknesses.
> Periodic movement and restraint in wealth and population are at
> once imperatives of the economic practice and creative adapta-
> tions, the kinds of necessities of which virtues are made. Precisely
> in such a framework, affluence becomes possible. (34)

Conversely, it is the modern world that carefully harnesses its resources and creates massive surpluses, the enjoyment of which is restricted to extremely few, where meaningful, systematic, impoverishment becomes equally possible if not probable: "poverty is not a certain small amount of goods, nor is it just a relation between means and ends; above all it is a relation between people. Poverty is a social status. As such it is the invention of civilization" (37). Revisiting Sahlins's arguments some twenty years after they were posited allows us to recognize both the extraordinary opening they afford in appraising the gathering and hunting mode of production, and the weaknesses and biases they reproduce.

Most critical of these latter is Sahlins's systematic underappreciation of women's work and women's social position. The calculations of hours spent at work, for example, rest on very conventional notions of the concept of labour, almost exclusively focussing on food production. Food division and preparation rarely appear to be considered; discussion of child rearing is non-existent in the essay. In a remarkable passage on the issue of leisure time, Sahlins writes:

> Hunter's subsistence labours are characteristically intermittent, a day on and a day off, and modern hunters at least tend to employ their time off in such activities as daytime sleep. In the tropical habitats occupied by many of these existing hunters, plant collecting is more reliable than hunting itself. Therefore the women, who do the collecting, work rather more regularly than the men, and provide the greater part of the food supply. Man's work is often done. (35)

The focus and bias here are on the hunter, as if the hunter's happiness is of sole importance in Sahlins's economic re-evaluation of the gatherer and hunter mode of production, as if the labour and lives of women, which implicitly in this account might not be so "often done," simply did not matter.

Sahlins's gender biases do not invalidate his general theses, and the work of feminist anthropologist Eleanor Leacock can be read correlatively as both a corrective and a critical contribution in its own right. Leacock's feminist ideology-critique began with the proposition that "the continued separation of woman's position from the central core of social analysis, as an 'and', 'but', or 'however', cannot but lead to continued distortions."[27] Leacock and others have demonstrated that among most gatherers and hunters, it is gathering, one of the important roles of women, that substantively produces the greater proportion of food. Leacock also demonstrated that while women remain primarily responsible for what we would call labour in the domestic sphere, the quality of that labour is substantially improved by its cooperative conditions. Leacock's central thesis was:

> The analysis of women's status in egalitarian society is inseparable from the analysis of egalitarian social-economic structure as a whole, and concepts based on the hierarchical structure of our society distort both. I shall argue that the tendency to attribute to band societies the relations of power and property characteristic of our own obscures the qualitatively different relations that obtained when ties of economic dependency linked the individual directly with the group as a whole, when public and private spheres were not dichotomized, and when decisions were made by and large by those who would be carrying them out. I shall attempt to show that a historical approach and an avoidance of ethnocentric phraseology in the study of such societies reveals that their egalitarianism applied as fully to women as to men.[28]

In effect, gathering and hunting societies can be characterized as egalitarian in terms of gender relations; while women and men occupy clearly defined and differentiated social spheres, there is a balanced reciprocity between the two, rather than an order of hierarchy and subordination, as prevails in other modes of production. Following the general direction of Leacock's work, I have preferred the designation "gatherer and hunter" mode of production rather than "hunter/gatherer" or more simply "hunter," both of which continue to unduly privilege men's activities.

NEOLITHIC BIASES

It is critical to recognize that Leacock's and Sahlins's respective reappraisals of the gatherer and hunter mode of production go against the grain of ancient biases. Hugh Brody's *Maps and Dreams*, on the Beaver or Dunne-za Dene of northeastern British Columbia, begins with an eloquent description of these biases:

> The hunting societies of the world have been sentenced to death. They have been condemned, not in any one verdict, but by a process, an accumulation, of judgements. Among simple societies, the hunters' has seemed the simplest; among flexible and nonindustrial economies, theirs has seemed the most flexible, the ultimately nonindustrial. When adventurers, missionaries, traders, or administrators encountered man-the-hunter, they were sure that here were people whose lives were bare of all comfort, without security, and below morality; people whose prospects for truly human achievement and well-being were minimal. Would-be civilizers concluded that hunters never had, or had lost, the means to achieve a decent way of life; should welcome the benefits of trade, wage employment, and proper religion; should allow their lands to be differently used; and must accept whatever changes are brought to them, however the changes are brought. That is the death sentence.[29]

In my view, the "death sentence" is more a result of "a process"—which will be discussed below—than an "accumulation of judgements," but the judgements have played a critical role in supporting the process. These judgements are the heirs of an ancient, neolithic bias; that is, the bias of settled agriculturalists against nomadic gatherers and hunters. Neolithic bias is not simply a matter of this or that particular judgement but, rather, as Brody illustrates, an accumulation of self-consistent and self-supporting evaluations (such as that which assesses a civilization on the basis of the monumental size of its architectural accomplishments); more importantly, a structure of thought, and an ideology. To those who would accuse Sahlins, Leacock, or myself of an overly romanticized view of gatherers and hunters, one partial response points to the necessity of countering a deep structural bias that condemns them.

The hierarchy of civilized/savage or civilized/barbarian that was developed by neolithic peoples to give them moral authority over their neighbours has been inherited and perpetuated in the industrial era, to the extent that it has become virtually impossible to think with gatherers and hunters, to cognitively work within the categories of gatherer and hunter experience. This, on the one hand, implies that it is difficult to find a way of appreciating the gatherer and hunter mode of production within the terms or language of dominant discourse, which is structured around a series of oppositions, such as civilized/savage, that systematically devalue gatherers and hunters; and on the other hand, it implies that attempts to appreciate gatherers and hunters ultimately draw us away from ourselves, into another language. Plutarch once wrote of Sophocles that he tried "to change the actual nature of language, which has the most bearing on morality and virtue";[30] the insight is compelling, and recalls post-structuralist insistence on the manner in which political values are embedded in language. The critique of ethnocentrism involves a reworking of language or a discursive practice that constantly tests the limits of language. The issue of thinking gathering and hunting within dominant discourse can be staged with reference to the development of Sahlins's work.

What is interesting about rereading "The Original Affluent Society" is the degree to which Sahlins's economics take us to the point of leaving economic thought itself. Derrida's comment that "before your eyes a demonstration ruins the distinctions it proposes"[31] is equally relevant here. Indeed, Sahlins writes at one point that "the hunter, one is tempted to say, is 'uneconomic man.'"[32] The category or opposition of work and leisure, so central to his argument, begins to break down when we closely examine the qualitative nature of the work involved: telling stories to children, decorating a basket or spear so it will be more efficacious, waiting on the plains for a herd of buffalo to slowly drift close enough to the point where the hunters can jump up and frighten the buffalo into a stampede. So much of hunting, conceptualized in dominant culture around the climactic moment of the kill, involves waiting and patience that it is very difficult indeed to determine which waiting is leisure and which is work. Read, for example, Jenness's description of the Inuit camp above and try to determine who is working and who is resting. This holds particularly (doubly) true for work in the domestic sphere, which within the dominant paradigm is uncountable even within so-called 'advanced' social formations, never mind social formations where the public/private boundary is as radically reconfigured or displaced as that of gatherers and hunters.

Within a few years Sahlins would come to challenge the very logic that gives explanatory priority to economic categories. In his *Culture and Practical Reason*, he argued that

> the cultural scheme is variously inflected by a dominant site of symbolic production, which supplies the major idiom of other relations and activities. One can thus speak of a privileged institutional locus of the symbolic process, whence emanates a classificatory grid imposed upon the total culture. And speaking still at this high level of abstraction, the peculiarity of Western culture is the institutionalization of the process in and as the production of goods, by comparison with a 'primitive' world where the locus of symbolic differentiation remains social relations, primarily kinship relations, and other spheres of activity are ordered by the operative distinctions of kinship.[33]

From this, it was a small step to his work on 'mytho-praxis' and *le pensee sauvage* in books like *Islands of History* (1984), which attempted to interpret the mode of operation of a gatherer and hunter "locus of symbolic differentiation."

In the present context, it is enough to summarize with the following: the concepts of mode of production and social formation allow us to think about different categories of social being; at least three modes of production—a gathering and hunting mode, a tributary mode, and a capitalist mode—have existed in human history; although the world today is dominated by the capitalist mode, the gathering and hunting mode exists as a vestige if not as a promise; gatherers and hunters have been systematically underestimated and devalued in dominant Western discourse, which has structured itself around a neolithic bias; it is possible to develop radically different assessments of gatherer and hunter economics, which would characterize them in much less ethnocentric terms; each step in thought towards gatherers and hunters moves us away from the structure and form of Western discourse itself.

To this it is necessary to add that Inuit and Dene in northern Canada, as gatherers and hunters, relied and rely far more extensively on hunting and fishing for subsistence than other gatherers and hunters around the world. That is, they relied less on gathering; this has had important consequences for the position of women in these societies, an issue to which I will return. Thus, although I still prefer the designation gatherer and hunter, it would not be inaccurate or necessarily sexist to refer to Dene and Inuit cultures as hunting cultures.

AGAINST HYBRIDITY

The concept of mode of production, particularly as it is deployed in anthropological theory and practice, has been the subject of intense debate in recent years. Edwin Wilmsen and James Denbow have challenged the gatherer and hunter paradigm, provoking a spirited defence from Richard Lee and Jacqueline Solway. Wilmsen and Denbow argue that "by displaying objectified peoples as exemplars of this category . . . ethnography validates the epistemological program required by the ontological quest. Consequently, the intrinsic realities of these objects are in themselves of little or no interest."[34] This argument is a form of refusal that would deny the value of any analytical abstraction, replacing analysis and critique with a narrow particularism whose only interest would be in recording the presumably infinite variety of human experiences. Wilmsen and Denbow also suggest that the concept of mode of production is ahistorical and ignores "the process through which social formations realize their transformations,"[35] but this is precisely where the distinction between mode of production and social formation becomes critical, since the latter allows for a situating of the former in history, with all its contingencies, necessities, and particularities.

Another, related, assault on the gatherer and hunter model has emerged out of a tendency in contemporary social theory that has come in recent years to celebrate what are called 'hybrid' social forms rather than culturally bounded, seemingly closed or enclosing social forms of the gatherer and hunter type. For example, in his far-reaching critique of notions of 'tradition' and 'authenticity', James Clifford has written:

> Intervening in an interconnected world, one is always, to varying degrees, 'inauthentic': caught between cultures, implicated in others. Because discourse in global power systems is elaborated vis-a-vis, a sense of difference or distinctiveness can never be located solely in the continuity of a culture or tradition. Identity is conjunctural, not essential.[36]

This notion of the "conjunctural" implies that identities are better seen as hybrid than bounded, and the theorist of hybridity is Homi Bhabha, who argues that "the theoretical recognition of the split-space of enunciation may open the way to conceptualizing an international culture, based not on the exoticism of multiculturalism or the diversity of cultures, but on the inscription and articulation of culture's hybridity."[37]

While the notion of hybridity is a critical lever that certainly has value in debunking all-too-dangerous claims of cultural purity, the rush to celebrate creolization and metissage leaves many critical questions unanswered. As Clifford suggests, no cultures can be called pure since all are implicated, connected, related. Hence, all cultures can be called hybrid including the most reprehensible: Fascism may be called a hybrid culture. Degrees of hybridity give no critical purchase whatsoever. There is no doubt that global capitalism, precisely in its totalizing manifestation, is the strongest agent of hybridization in the world today. Celebrating insurgent hybrid forms solely or merely for the fact that they are hybrid misses the point: there has to be some substantive aspect of a culture that is to be valued or criticized, and one cannot determine such an aspect without returning to a language of cultural forms and boundaries. Bhabha himself implies an evaluative process that would distinguish hybrid forms when he suggests "the possibility of a cultural hybridity that entertains difference without an assumed or imposed hierarchy,"[38] here valuing egalitarianism—or, at least, critical of hierarchy—much as those who subscribe to the gatherer and hunter model do. Elsewhere, though, he valorizes hybridity in and of itself, for example suggesting that "the margin of hybridity, where cultural differences 'contingently' and conflictually touch, becomes the moment of panic which reveals the borderline experience,"[39] and for Bhabha this moment of panic, of doubt, of ambivalence and uncertainty, is the desired cultural position. While it may serve the critic and philosopher well, though, it seems as insufficient as the notion of 'diversity for its own sake' in discussing cultures. It is particularly insufficient when we come to think a political project that will be of some value to the people involved.

HUNTERS AND FARMERS

Hugh Brody has come closest to applying and popularizing a version of the concept of mode of production to Aboriginal politics in Canada in his *The Other Side of Eden: Hunters, Farmers and the Shaping of the Modern World*. Although he does not use the term "mode of production," the critical basis of the book is a notion of profound difference between hunting peoples and farming peoples. For Brody, colonialism in Canada is a result of the necessity for expansion intrinsic to agricultural-based societies. The argument in many ways parallels the analyses developed here and in particular demonstrates how the concept of mode of production provides a materialist entry into the question of tradition. While "tradition" is a much-debated and -questioned term, rarely is it pointed out that the traditions of farmers are dramatically different from the traditions of hunters. Looked at from the vantage of the twenty-first century, all old habits are traditions that, depending on one's political perspective, need to be swept aside or reinvigorated. Brody's analysis makes clear that the "aggressive, restless agriculture"[40] of farmers involves a dramatically different set of values from those associated with hunters. The single word "tradition" is today deployed to cover both these markedly distinct sets of social organization and values, while for much of history the two have been in conflict.

Although Brody notes that "more than ever before, this order seems to depend on restlessness,"[41] in my own view he fails to appreciate that the distinction between industrial capitalist societies and farmers is as significant as that between hunters and farmers. The specific dynamic of Aboriginal cultural politics in our own era is driven by the specific nature of totalization associated with capitalist social forms. Hence, for example, in Nunavut and Denendeh the land of hunters is not required for agricultural purposes but as a resource base for ultimately industrial purposes. The ruthlessness, insidiousness, reach, and power of totalization have been dramatically exacerbated by the movement from agricultural to industrial production. Nevertheless, Brody's powerful, expressive language and acute sensitivity to Aboriginal communities allow him extraordinary insight into the dynamics of struggle engaged in by Aboriginal people. Perhaps this work can be seen as marking a modest footnote or supplement to Brody's.

HERE COMES DEMOCRACY

We have travelled a long distance from Gina Blondin's potatoes. The second story that Gina Blondin told me of relevance to this study was a political parable of sorts. The year 1967 was an important year in the history of the NWT. In that year, during Canada's centennial, the government of the NWT (GNWT) moved from Ottawa, where its administrative base had been since 1921, to Yellowknife, the new capital of the territory. The year 1967 is usually represented as a major watershed in the development of responsible government in the north, the year when government was brought to the people and the political moment when the movement towards representative government gained a momentum that, in many respects, has not yet stopped. Thus, for those who like to see history as 'every day in every way things get better and better', 1967 represents a key moment in the north's progressive narrative. The government could thereafter serve the people more effectively by being situated close to them.

Stuart Hodgson, then the newly appointed commissioner, said in his inaugural northern address that "the government has moved so much closer to our people," noting that "this cannot help having a tremendous effect on the attitude of northern residents towards our government and indeed the effectiveness with which we operate."[42] Commenting on this, political scientist Mark Dickerson writes: "The theory was obvious: government from Ottawa had been distant, alien, and unresponsive. Now that government was centred in Yellowknife, it would be close and responsive, and, thus, residents would begin to identify with it. All this was not as simple as it sounded."[43] Gina Blondin, as she discussed this history with me, helped me understand why the issue was much more complex.

She saw '1967' from the perspective of her own community, one of many to which the move north was designed to make a positive contribution. From the community perspective, '1967' did not represent progress, it represented interference. Before 1967, Gina said, in Deline (Fort Franklin) you did pretty much what you wanted to do and you were left alone. No one disturbed you or worried if this or that regulation was being

56 LIKE THE SOUND OF A DRUM

strictly adhered to. If you wanted to build a house, you built it. You didn't worry about zones or lots or codes. You just built it. If there were regulations, if there were funds made available provided you followed certain guidelines, well, you might still get the funds. After all, who was going to check the regulations and ensure that guidelines were followed? There was no need to care about what distant administrators thought 'reality' looked like because, in the language of recent sociology, such as that associated with Michel Foucault and suggested by Anthony Giddens, mechanisms of surveillance were weak.

After 1967, all this began to change. Suddenly the 'white hats' arrived. A closer government meant a government more determined to ensure its edicts were followed. More and more external people were hired whose job was to ensure just that. Government people started coming to communities, checking things out; a colonial administrative apparatus was put in place. If a house was built in the wrong location, if building or other codes were flagrantly ignored, it started to matter. A more responsible government also added up to more government; more government meant more outside interference. A dynamic or process was set into play whose outcome continues to be uncertain but one element of which was and is a dramatic loss of power at the community level. And this in the interest of bringing officially sanctioned democracy.

THE OFFICIAL STORY

The State occupies a critical position in northern Canada. One indicator of this is the extent to which public sector expenditures dominate the northern economy to a much greater degree than in the south. The Yukon, the NWT, and Nunavut have an ambiguous status within Canadian confederation; they are 'territories', enjoying something less than the status that their provincial counterparts enjoy. The federal government occupies a much more prominent place in the north, in part because of the territorial status question and in part because, in all three northern political jurisdictions, Aboriginal peoples, a federal responsibility since the British North America Act (1867), make up a significantly larger proportion of the population than in any province. A brief review of the history of the government of the Northwest Territories, out of which Nunavut was established, is necessary to appreciate its position.

The history begins in 1875, when the North-West Territories Act was passed to provide for governance of a vast territory in the Canadian northwest. By 1905, much of that territory had been carved up into provincial jurisdictions: the provinces of Manitoba, Saskatchewan, and Alberta. In that year the NWT Act was amended to provide for a commissioner and a four-member appointed council. Effectively, governance of the NWT was administered from Ottawa; the first commissioner was the comptroller of the Royal Canadian Mounted Police. Subsequent commissioners—after 1919—were drawn from the Department of the Interior. Until 1921, no council members were actually appointed; the positions existed only on paper. After non-Natives became aware of oil at Norman Wells in the summer of 1920—which would also spark the negotiations that led to Treaty 11, to be discussed below—members were appointed to the council. It had its first meeting in the spring of 1921 and recommended expanding its membership to six; by June the expanded council was meeting. Members were drawn from the government agencies that worked in the north: the RCMP and departments of the Interior and Mines were prominent. In 1929 a senior bureaucrat from Indian Affairs was appointed to the council. Mark O. Dickerson, quoting from a government source, notes in *Whose North?*:

> As the Council was composed entirely of the senior officials of the various federal departments involved in northern administration, it acted as something much more than a legislative body. It became, through the years, an interdepartmental committee of consultation and co-ordination, a general advisory body on all northern administration.[44]

Dickerson's *Whose North?* provides a thorough review of the historical development of Northern government. Effectively, the GNWT started as a colonial government. Not only was it not in any way representative of the people of the north, who were primarily of Dene, Métis, or Inuit descent, it did not consist of political representatives at all, but, rather, administrators. These people passed the earliest legislation respecting the NWT. Dickerson notes that "Ottawa administrators ran a third of the landmass of Canada as though it were their own fiefdom" (57).

Things began to change in the 1950s. In 1947 a non-Native mine manager was appointed to the territorial council, setting in motion a process whereby non-Native northerners began to agitate for greater representation. By 1951 the council was expanded to eight members, three of whom were to be elected; in 1954 a fourth elected member was added. However, Dickerson points out, "Indians were barred from voting prior to 1960. In subsequent elections, however, they did become participants in the electoral process. Barriers prohibiting Inuit voting were removed in 1954, but no constituencies existed in the Central or Eastern Arctic, the home of most Inuit." Hence, "it was not a democracy for Aboriginal peoples" (70). Slowly, the balance on the council between elected and appointed members began to shift in favour of the former, though most of these were non-Natives. In 1967, as a result of a protracted debate about dividing the territory that had led the government to establish a commission of inquiry, the Carrothers Commission, the GNWT was moved to the new territorial capital, Yellowknife, and a new political dynamic began to take shape.

HIGH ABOVE, IN THE SKIES: THE STATE

Dennis Patterson, government leader of the GNWT from 1987 to 1991 and a member of the Territorial Assembly from Iqaluit in the eastern Arctic for many years before the creation of Nunavut, came to Trent University frequently in the winter of 1990 as a visiting Northern Chair. In one of his public lectures, he reviewed the history of the GNWT, pausing on 1967 as one of the watersheds in northern political history. The story of "the move" he told has it that the commissioner, Stuart Hodgson, along with administrators and council, got on a single plane in Ottawa, flew to Churchill, where they refuelled, and then flew the rest of the way up to Yellowknife. This is confirmed by Dickerson, who notes that "in 1967, almost the entire staff and their families (seventy-five people) flew on one plane from Ottawa to Yellowknife" (89). The state, in its local incorporation, came to the north by plane, and still, much of the time, travels to the communities by air, all in the name of something called democracy.

This is peculiarly appropriate. The State flies in, from high above, it circles and lands. The legitimacy of Western-style, liberal, democratic states rests on a specific abstraction (here abstraction stands for a form of intellectual flight: the flight from the qualitative, from the body): political commitment is reduced from the multivarious forms and responsibilities it takes in small communities, reduced and pared down and stripped until all that is left is a single gesture, repeated ritually in periodic intervals, the mark, the indicator, the vote. The existence of the vote then becomes the standard by which political systems are assessed: they are democratic if periodic voting for political representatives takes place; if not, they are not. The vote is an abstraction; it represents the whole political speech and activity of individual citizens, from whom other forms of political speech and activity are no longer required and, indeed, discouraged. The vote is then equated with democracy and invoked constantly as a new mantra: where there is a vote, there is democracy; where there is no vote, there is no democracy. In Canada, this mantra was deployed by the State through the late nineteenth century when it began imposing voting through the band electoral system on Aboriginal communities in the interest of "educating Indians about democracy" and, incidentally, undermining, through a veto, traditional leaders even when they were elected under the new rules. That Aboriginal communities often involved intensely participatory forms of community decision making that comparatively make "advanced" Western political forms look like a hollow joke on meaningful democratic standards, was and is never contemplated, especially by those who still wonder whether Aboriginal peoples are 'ready' for self-government.

Jameson, in this closely following Adorno, has noted that "abstraction is first of all collective and not individual; objectivity is present within the subject in the form of collective linguistic or conceptual forms which are themselves produced by society, and thereby presuppose it," adding that "this has very much to do with the division of labour, and in particular with the primal separation of manual from intellectual labour which is the precondition of abstract thought itself."[45] The logical conclusion is that "abstraction in this sense is the precondition of 'civilization' in all its complex development across the whole range of distinct human activities (from production to the law, from culture to political forms, and not excluding the psyche and the more obscure 'equivalents' of unconscious desire)."[46] This must be read ironically by those concerned precisely to—in Stanley Diamond's words—reinvent the 'primitive' in the modern world,[47] by those of us opposed to the 'civilizing' project. Perhaps our mission is a return to the body: embodiment as the reversal of abstraction.

Abstraction then—in this context—is a tool of totalization, by which the qualitative, lived world is reduced to that which can be counted and exchanged. Socially produced objects, in capitalist societies, are constructed through the lens of exchange value and assigned a number. Labour, whose rhythms and intensities constantly ebb and flow, is constructed as a commodity through the measure of a homogenously construed time. One effect of these processes is to make objects, to make labour, to make lived experience, take on the homogenous, serial, abstract, banal form that systemically represents them. Surely, some of this is what Adorno meant when he argued that "above and beyond all specific forms of social differentiation, the abstraction implicit in the market system represents the domination of the general over the particular, of society over its captive membership."[48] Hence, involvement in the community, in defining and carrying forward the project of the public, is reduced to a single gesture, an abstract representation of the multivarious forms of possible political involvement, the vote, which has become enshrined as the sole determining standard of democracy. In the dominant system, citizen involvement in the major public institutions is circumscribed to an extraordinary degree. The election becomes the nexus of political commitment and consumes whatever degree of political energy remains to a politically totalized, and hence apathetic, body of citizens. Even this meagre measure of democracy was extracted as a bitterly fought-for concession from the ruling powers in the Western world.

In small Aboriginal communities across northern Canada, a different political dynamic exists to varying degrees. Face-to-face politics and community commitments involving a much wider range of citizen responsibilities are, to some extent, the order of the day. The politics of speech prevail. This involves both the daily speech that assesses, announces, questions, challenges, proposes, and the formal speech at public meetings or assemblies. Curiously, at many of these meetings or assemblies, decisions can be made without a formal vote: discussion goes on until all who want to speak to an issue get a chance and the assembly knows if there is agreement or not. If there is consensus, a vote may be taken to solidify it; if not, frequently, no vote will be taken. Participants listen for strong words, effective speeches; the intense and intricate micropolitics of face-to-face exchanges among community members whose speech has the power to effect change, unlike the distant, pre-programmed speech of their representatives. Elections of public figures—mayors, chiefs, counsellors—become one aspect of the range of public engagements, reflecting the latest moment in a shifting political dynamic, rather than consuming the whole political energies of those who have a sense of or stake in political commitment.

From somewhere 'above' these communities, another form of politics announces that it has legitimacy and the power to confer legitimacy. Structures are imposed—these include band and municipal councils—and then adapted in different ways by the people. This State demands to be addressed in writing: its laws are inscribed in a language it alone can read. A political dynamic between these two political forms, one on the air and one on the ground, begins to take place.

THE OFFICIAL STORY CONTINUES

If the period from 1905 to 1921 can be characterized as one in which the government was virtually non-existent, and 1921 to 1967 as one in which the government was largely an administrative apparatus, then the next period, roughly 1967 to 1979, was characterized by the transition from administration to government. Slowly, between 1967 and 1975, the balance between appointed and elected members of the territorial council shifted in favour of elected members. By 1975 the council, Territorial Assembly, consisted entirely of elected members (there were fifteen) led by an appointed commissioner. The council began to look and act less like a coordinating committee of federal civil servants and more like a northern government, albeit highly colonial in nature.

The colonial nature of council was evidenced in its early opposition to Aboriginal land claims. Through the early seventies, it acted in a manner that put the interests and ideologies of non-Native northerners first. Ideologically, this was justified, as it still is, by the code words "progress" and "modernization." This became necessary to the colonial powers because it was at precisely this time that modern Aboriginal political organizations began to develop in the NWT: the Indian Brotherhood of the NWT (later Dene Nation) in 1969 to represent Dene; the Committee for Original People's Entitlement (COPE) in 1970 to represent Inuvialuit; the Inuit Tapirisat of Canada in 1971 to represent all Inuit in Canada, including the NWT; and the Metis Association of the NWT (later Metis Nation) in 1972 to represent Métis and some non-status Dene. Pauktutit and NWT Native Women's Association developed later in the decade. Aboriginal people relatively quickly engaged in a massive organizational undertaking and became much more vocal about defending and advocating their interests. These included both land claims, covering the whole land mass of the

NWT and Aboriginal self-government, a direct challenge to the legitimacy of the GNWT.

In the face of these events, the newly evolving territorial council initially retrenched, formally opposing Aboriginal land claims and in general adopting a 'pro-development' stance that contradicted the position of the Aboriginal organizations. The election of Aboriginal members to the council did little initially to change the approach, because the first Aboriginal councillors were isolated and faced with an entrenched, experienced political and bureaucratic non-Native elite. Two early Dene representatives, James Wahshee and George Barnaby, were elected in 1975 and resigned early into their terms. Nick Sibbeston, who would later become leader of the territorial government, called this a bad period when the government "didn't give credence to Native views." However, in the elections of 1979, a concerted effort was made to use the Aboriginal electoral majority to better effect. That year, for the first time, a majority of the members of the Territorial Assembly were of Aboriginal descent. Furthermore, this took place at precisely the point where the GNWT was making a qualitative leap in its ability to act as a responsible government. The new commissioner, John Parker, began to relinquish control, setting in motion a process whereby the appointed commissioner would, within a few years, effectively have his role reduced to the equivalent of a provincial lieutenant-governor, a head of State but not of government.

RESIGNATION

George Barnaby was one of two Dene members of the Territorial Assembly elected in 1975 who resigned because he did not think that the government was working for the people. He has written about his experience in the important book edited by Mel Watkins, *Dene Nation: The Colony Within*, and discussed his resignation with me almost two decades after the event. His frustration with the non-Native system of government remains strong. In Watkins's reader, he wrote: "The first session of Council I went to, we spent two weeks on an ordinance that had no importance to the people I represented. At this time I asked for more control for the communities. This was voted down. I don't know why."[49] Things only got worse:

> At the second session of Council we talked of political development, where the Council would have authority over the whole

north. I spoke against this, as it would make no difference to the people; it still would not give them any rights to decide for themselves. The power would be only to the Council to decide the future of the North, and people would be forced to follow, whether they agreed or not. I think it was a plan to keep the people oppressed. (121)

Barnaby has a clear, consistent, and powerful notion of what was and is wrong with the territorial government: "Sometimes I say, that if the commissioner and the top executives of the territorial government were all trappers and hunters things would be different, but I see it would make no difference. It is the system which is wrong: wherever only a few people decide for the rest of the population, it oppresses people," or, again, "where the Dene law gives freedom for the individual to do what he decides and take responsibility for his action, the system from the south passes an ordinance which forces a person's action and takes away responsibility. Where our system is set up to serve the people, the people from the south serve their system" (122). Barnaby clearly has a much higher standard of democracy than that adopted by most liberal-democratic polities, whose representative system is structured precisely in the interests of oppression of popular will rather than expression of it.

THE OFFICIAL STORY NEVER ENDS

The 1979 territorial elections were another watershed event in the history of the GNWT. The Aboriginal majority that had been elected dramatically changed the government's official policy positions in a number of areas and inaugurated a period where the territorial government offered official support for Aboriginal rights and for land claims, though its specific positions on these issues frequently differed from those of the main Aboriginal organizations. More remarkably, the politicians surveyed the structure of the Territorial Assembly and decided that, with minor modification, it could be characterized as "consensus government," a form of government that in part reflected the values and traditions of Aboriginal northerners. As the powers of the commissioner ebbed and as more responsibility was devolved from the federal government to the GNWT, an executive arm of the assembly was developed to act as the equivalent of Cabinet, with a leader of government performing the function of premier.

In the early 1980s, it began to be possible to imagine that the public government of the NWT might act as a crucial vehicle of Aboriginal self-government, and that, in effect, the GNWT had been 'captured' by Aboriginal northerners—Dene, Inuit, Inuvialuit, and Métis working together—to achieve this goal. However, other forces were in play. One of these was the fact that although Aboriginal peoples had 'captured' the government, they had not taken control of the State. The State includes the government as only one element of its structure, which usually also consists of police and/or army, judiciary, administration, and public sector service agencies delivering health, education, social welfare, and so on. Hence, a strongly colonial bureaucracy remained in place after 1979 and although it had to respond to a changed climate and radically different leadership, it did so grudgingly, waging trench warfare against initiatives it did not like and engaging as a breaking mechanism on government in general. The tension between administrators and politicians was particularly acute in the early 1980s. Although through the exercise of the vote Aboriginal people could control the government, this did not give them control over the State in northern Canada, a situation that, while the dynamic has evolved markedly, persists.

Nevertheless, very interesting developments unfolded in the decade after 1979. Most of the government leaders of the NWT in the last twenty-five years have been of Aboriginal descent. Party politics, which are the core of the oppositional political dynamic that characterizes formal political discourse in most of the Western world, remain absent from the territorial political sphere. In this situation, the official ideology is one of consensus government in which the Territorial Assembly as a whole has much greater power compared to other political structures. And in this context a fourth watershed, of equal magnitude to those of 1921, 1967, and 1979, has taken place. A formal decision to divide the Northwest Territories into two separate political constituencies, effectively in response to long-standing Inuit demands for their own government and territory, was reached in 1991. The territory was divided beginning formally on April 1, 1999, when Nunavut in the eastern Arctic was created.

YEARS LATER

One of the Aboriginal government leaders in the mid-eighties was Nick Sibbeston, the member of the Territorial Assembly from the Nahendeh riding, which includes the community of Fort Simpson. Sibbeston had first been elected in 1970, took a term off between 1975 and 1979 to complete a law degree, and returned to the assembly in 1979, first as an ordinary member, then as a minister responsible for local government, and, between 1986 and 1988, as leader of the government. I interviewed him in the cafe at the Nahanni Inn in Fort Simpson in the late summer of 1994, a few years after he had retired from electoral politics. In 1994 he was working with the territorial ministry of justice on community justice in his old riding. I asked whether he thought, after all this time, that Dene and Métis involvement in the territorial government was a good strategy or whether it only served to legitimate an imposed system. He replied in a soft-spoken, quiet, and thoughtful manner:

> I know there's two approaches, one is just to stay away and say 'look it's not ours' and the other approach is to get in there and take control. I've been always of the view that, and I guess my whole time in government has been that, to try to exert control and change things but it is a difficult task because you have civil service in place and systems and procedures and policies and so forth that were in place. Even in government, even as a minister, it really gets hard to change, so certainly during my time I did my best to change but I can't really say that I was successful throughout. You know I managed to change things and improve things here and there but if I was to look at my time in government I would say 'yeah, Nick, you had an effect on things but you didn't change the system. You improved things'. You try to make the system work for people. . . .

The question of the relation of civil servants to politicians and some of the tension between the two emerged in Sibbeston's comments as he continued:

> So you do that but it's still the government system and the bureaucracy that carries it out. Often there's not very many Native people in the system. So when I look back I do see that I've influenced in small ways certain policies and procedures and decisions of government but the system's still there and it's largely non-Native bureaucracy. I think, on hindsight, it was the right decision to

become involved because invariably in the long run Native people have to get involved in some kind of government system anyway. It's a good experience. Through the years we did get many Native people in government. I remember in the early [to] late seventies when I became involved it wasn't an honourable thing for Natives to get involved, you know. The best Native brains worked for the Dene Nation, the Indian Brotherhood in those days, but through time we slowly changed government so that it was okay for Native people. Then we went through a period here in Simpson where Native people went after government jobs, so in Simpson here as an example we have changed government where Native people are slowly becoming the majority in terms of government positions. I'm of the view that however you look at it Native people want self-government, they eventually will have to have the experience and get involved in government. I see it as having been good training and as a good, as a necessary evolution or development process to become involved.

Sibbeston's comments represent an alternative Dene/Métis approach to that taken by Barnaby. Both see the dominant system as flawed. Barnaby argued that this made it inherently oppressive and abandoned it, while Sibbeston recognized its limitations but nevertheless became involved and made what changes he could.

Sibbeston stressed a final point, one that is interesting because he was describing the period in the mid-eighties when the territorial government was increasingly describing itself as 'Aboriginal' in form: "At one point we had Native majority, but you never did have that control, you know, that absolute majority Native control where you exerted and used that power, it was never a situation. There's always compromising it seems and it's always following rules that are set in place by the system, by establishment, sometimes by the federal government." On this point, Sibbeston and Barnaby seem in perfect accord.

THE STATE AND TOTALIZATION

Nicos Poulantzas, in his last work *State, Power, Socialism*, sketched an outline for a theory of the State as a mechanism of totalization, as an instrument of totalizing power. This theoretical agenda deserves reconsideration, because it offers a variety of formulations that are of particular relevance to the social struggles of Aboriginal peoples in Canada. As opposed to Michel

Foucault's models and strategy, which involve a critical assessment of the dispersal of State power, Poulantzas offers a theory that remains indebted to the Weberian notion of the State's holding a monopoly on legitimate physical violence. His thesis is that "State-monopolized physical violence permanently underlies the technique of power and mechanisms of consent: it is inscribed in the web of disciplinary and ideological devices; and even when not directly exercised, it shapes the materiality of the social body upon which domination is brought to bear."[50] This is, of course, relatively prosaic by now. What Poulantzas suggests, however, is the beginning of a theory of the State as a machinery of totalization. Two areas in which he demonstrates this are worth reviewing here: the processes of individualization and the construction of the nation through spatial and temporal matrices.

Poulantzas's text contains an interesting discussion of the State as foundation of individual identity and familial form, effectively reversing the dominant view of the public as a condensation or accumulation of the private. In this regard, his analysis may be of particular value to feminists; in few places will the slogan "the personal is political" have such resonance. He argues that individualism "constitutes the material expression in capitalist bodies of the existing relations of production and social division of labour; and it is equally the material effect of state practices and techniques forging and subordinating this (political) body" (67). Poulantzas's central thesis is that "there can be no limit based on law or principle to the activity and encroachment of the state in the so-called sphere of the individual/ private" (71) and, further, "the very separation of public and private that is established by the State opens up for it boundless vistas of power. The premises of the modern phenomenon of totalitarianism lie in this separation and affect the countries in the East as well as the western societies" (72–73). His discussion of the constitution of the family is worth following in some detail:

> Strictly speaking, the modern family and State are not two distinct, equidistant and mutually limiting spaces (private and public): contrary to the now-classical analyses of the Frankfurt School (Adorno, Marcuse et al.), the one is not the base of the other. Although the two institutions are neither isomorphous nor tied to each other in a straightforward relation of homology, they are nevertheless part of one and the same configuration. For it is not the 'external' space of the modern family which shuts itself off

from the State, but rather the State which, at the very time that it set itself up as the public space, traces and assigns the site of the family through shifting, mobile partitions. (72)

Poulantzas's analyses of individualization, the constitution of public and private, and the construction of the family all position the State as a totalizing agency of capital. While Poulantzas himself rarely observes or takes note of the degree to which the process he points to is resisted, his analysis allows us to think resistance and agency in new and interesting ways. I will return to this point below.

Likewise, Poulantzas's understanding of the nation positions the State in a key role as totalizing agent. Elsewhere ("Primitive Subversions," 1992) I reviewed his argument about the State's attempts to construct serial spatial and temporal matrices. He argues that "the modern nation appears as a product of the State, since its constitutive elements (economic unity, territory, tradition) are modified through the State's direct activity in the material organization of space and time" (99). The State attempts to organize space and time along the same principles as the Taylorist assembly line: fragmented, serial, homogenous. Frontiers, borders, divisions assume a new fixity; time, a new linearity. Totalization again becomes a key implication: "genocide is the elimination of what become 'foreign bodies' of the national history and territory: it expels them beyond space and time" (114). The State constructs and naturalizes boundaries of space and time, which, in conjunction with each other, define an exclusive social regime:

> In the modern era, demands for a national State are demands for a territory and history of one's own. The premises of modern totalitarianism exist not only in the spatial and temporal matrices incarnated in the modern State, but also, or above all, in the relationship between the two that is concentrated by the State. (114–115)

Space and time become crucial tools in the construction of conditions suitable for the accumulation of capital and the generalized expansion of the commodity form. The State is the agency by which these conditions are, at times against considerable opposition, imposed.

Poulantzas's formulations in *State, Power, Socialism* offer the outlines of a theory of the State as totalizing agent. As such, there is a great deal in them of relevance to Aboriginal politics in Canada. The stress on the degree to which physical violence continues to underwrite processes of normalization will come as no surprise in the aftermath of Kanesatake or

Ipperwash: the latest of a long series of struggles where the State's coercive side has been felt by those most outside its normalizing techniques of power. Understanding the crucial role of the State in the contested construction of modern individuality and modern forms of subjectivity will likewise seem appropriate to those who have studied this process, long incarnated in the history of the status provisions of the Indian Act in Canada, a process that continues to be enacted in Aboriginal communities. Finally, the passages about suspension of "foreign bodies" from the space and time of the nation seem particularly apposite to the structural position of Aboriginal people in Canada. Poulantzas allows us to see that the Western, liberal-democratic State is, precisely, a totalizing mechanism that contains at its heart the same structural exigencies we find in more explicitly totalitarian contexts. This is something that Aboriginal peoples, of course, have long seen or felt in their life experiences. Furthermore, he allows us to continue to recognize the strategic importance of the State in these processes, something that again accords with the situation of Aboriginal Canadians, for whom the State remains an overwhelming presence.

LINES OF DIFFERENCE: GENDER

The spring of 1997 saw an unusual event take place in Nunavut: a public plebiscite over whether the new territory would have a legislative assembly structured around a formal principle of gender parity. This would be surprising to anyone who had read much of the anthropological literature on Inuit women, where they are most frequently treated as servile caricatures. Though in Diamond Jenness's view, "[Inuit] women had a well recognized position, less inferior to men's than among any Indian tribe except perhaps the Iroquoians,"[51] Jean Briggs's later description of the "warmth and luxury of male dominance"[52] seems to have gained greater acceptance. This acceptance was perhaps supported by the popular images of so-called "wife-trading," the popularity of such images bolstered in turn by the degree to which they conform to dominant male fantasy projections. Not least of the attractions of such films as Robert Flaherty's *Nanook of the North* was the fact that the racial line of difference allowed for the public display and reproduction of Inuit women's bodies, the imagined availability of these being constructed and reinforced by the ethnographically sanctioned stories of "wife exchange" (see my article on Jenness, "Anthropology at the

Service of the State," for a rereading of his observations in this regard, and a recoding of the practice as "partner exchange"). All told, ethnographic description of Inuit women remains a field of ideologically supersaturated discourse, rich with the possibility of rereading.

Similarly, descriptions of Dene women in the ethnographic literature do not do great service to their place in traditional times. Chipewyan women, in particular, inherited the description of them passed on by Samuel Hearne (see Rollaston, "Studying under the Influence"), which Jenness reproduces in the following remarkable passage:

> Strong men plundered the weaklings, and forcibly carried off their women. The latter ranked lower than in any other tribe; separated from all boy companions at the age of eight or nine, married at adolescence, often to middle-aged men, and always subject to many restrictions, they were the first to perish in seasons of scarcity. In winter they were mere traction animals; unaided, they dragged the heavy toboggans. In summer they were pack animals, carrying all the household goods, food, and hides on their backs.[53]

Little room here to imagine the emergence of female leaders and diplomats with the stature of Thanadelthur, or even the intellectual brilliance of Angela Sidney, Kitty Smith, and Annie Ned, whose stories and storytelling praxis, as told to Julie Cruikshank in the remarkable *Life Lived Like a Story*, go a long way on their own to explode these fantasy projections.

The dominant images of northern Aboriginal women served to underwrite a particularly male colonial State apparatus in northern Canada. In the eastern Arctic, almost exclusively men carried out the enterprise of colonialism in the mid-sixties with a northern frontier mentality that stressed male self-sufficiency (see Frank Tester's and my *Tammarniit*). The territorial government was run by and for men. Inuit and Dene women—not, it seems, drawing upon their cultural traditions as they were constructed in Western discourse, but finding some other source of strength, perhaps in part from many grandmothers who did not conform to the caricatures—managed to force their way into the northern public space, to the point where a notion of formal gender parity could be considered for Nunavut, to the point where a whole set of issues at the local and territorial level—from family violence to housing allocation to forms of representation—are insistently a part of public discourse. At the local community level, the gender inflection of politics is particularly intense, interesting, 'personal' in a variety of deeply political ways. The cultural differences in constructing the distinction between public and private are no incidental aspect of this politic.

OUTSIDE OF *EMPIRE*

Among the most compelling recent critiques of colonialism produced by contemporary critical theory is the book *Empire*, by Michael Hardt and Antonio Negri. The analysis refers to the "totalizing social processes of Empire"[54] and offers a reading of the contemporary moment in the history of colonialism that sees both massive extension of colonial reach (hence: Empire) and extraordinary possibilities for global resistance. One of the central points that Hardt and Negri want to establish is that "there is no more outside," suggesting that the logic of capital has reached a stage where it is no longer confronted by anything outside its own version of civilization. In regard to gatherers and hunters, they note that "modern anthropology's various discourses on primitive societies function as the outside that defines the bounds of the civil world. The process of modernization . . . is the internalization of the outside, that is, the civilization of nature" (187), before going on to conclude that "the modern dialectic of inside and outside has been replaced by a play of degrees and intensities, of hybridity and artificiality" (187–188). Themselves writing from the position of the imperial centre—in the case of these authors, the United States and Europe—perhaps only adds to the irony with which these easy pronouncements are read as they reach the margins. While many aspects of their analysis, particularly the philosophical position on immanence that underpins it, do offer critical resources, on the whole *Empire* is informed by a weak anthropology and very weak sense of cultural difference. The book, therefore, is a testament to why a materialist analysis based on reinvigorating the concept of mode of production remains a central intellectual task of critical thought as it grapples with the latest phase of totalizing power.

THE ROAD TO YELLOWKNIFE

Over the ten-year period in which this study was conceived, researched, and written, the force of history, or History in the Jamesonian sense as "what hurts, [what] refuses desire and sets inexorably limits to individual as well as collective praxis, which its 'ruses' turn into grisly and ironic reversals of their overt intention,"[55] marched ever onwards. The most visible reminder of this is the road to the territorial capital, Yellowknife. In the summer of 1984 I drove from Calgary to Yellowknife and found that the pavement ended virtually at the border of then oil-prosperous Alberta and the NWT. Yellowknife has its own attractions as a dynamic, culturally and socially rich, complex, engaging and frustrating city.

In the years that followed, the government of the NWT became ever more responsible as more powers were devolved to it; a massive bureaucracy built up in the territorial capital, Yellowknife, and more and more public sector workers were hired to run its machinery. The town, dominated by working-class miners and Aboriginal peoples, suddenly developed a significant third subculture: that of white-collar workers. Yellowknife became a force of its own, a centralizing tendency, and a name for a political position. Yellowknife, created in large part to service widely dispersed Aboriginal communities, developed its own objective interest. A part of its *raison d'etre* came to be servicing itself. Yellowknife, capital of contradictions.

Yellowknife embodies antinomous directions and tensions, physically enacting the overlay of modes of production and evolving cultural dominants. The Dene bands, living in Detah outside the city, marginalized beyond marginality, across the bay, accessible by roundabout gravel road in summer or fairly direct road across the frozen bay in winter. N'Dilo (once called Rainbow Valley), the Dene sub-band, in prime real estate on the furthest reach of Latham Island, poor people on expensive turf: in 1984 it looked like a South African shantytown; in 1989 that got overlaid with a postmodernish transient centre and other housing emblematic of 'economic development'. The other half of Latham Island is a refuge for the rich: lawyerville and doctorville and senior-civil-servantville, as well as a few hangers-on in the older houses, near squatters, and old Yellowknife money. Then, across the bridge from Latham Island, moving towards uptown, Old Town, a paradise for squatters (in summer), with old-style northern mining town construction, modernism in decay, modernism on the cheap and now looking well worn, a modernism we can feel nostalgic for in the context of Yellowknife. Squatters' shacks squeezed together with mansion-sized houses squeezed together with tourist traps. This leads in turn to uptown, the new city core, a reproduction of any southern city except the buildings are prefabricated: mall culture brought north. A downtown that no comparative-sized southern town would have, so a downtown that physically registers Yellowknife's status as a capital and points to its unusual cosmopolitanism. Here reside the bars and drinking establishments and in these resides one truth of Yellowknife. Beyond this, the mines that are Yellowknife's other source of wealth and bring the third major population group: miners to join the Natives and bureaucrats; though now, of course, it is diamonds further north and a more transient miner population that passes through Yellowknife. And, in the space in-between the appropriately named 'Con Mine' and what I've called uptown, the suburbs. The 'frontier' ideology permeates to such a degree that real estate developers can get away with in the north what would likely be criminal most anywhere else in Canada. Hence, suburban structures densely packed together in a spacious landscape, next to monster houses. But it is not simply the real estate agents who create these suburbs. The occupants of the monster houses all busily put time and energy in reproducing neat little square tracts of empty land, lawns: covering over the—to them—unsightly rock and cutting down the scrub pines to replace them with imperialist grass.

Yellowknife, capital of contractions, its own world set like a dirty diamond north of sixty. In 1984 the talk was all about communities and how Yellowknife could service the communities. The post-1979 territorial governments were mandated to service the communities. Decentralization became a rallying cry, and a series of efforts to decentralize were initiated. But something funny happened. All the people employed to carry out decentralization came to Yellowknife. The bureaucracy had a logic of its own and no politician or group of politicians could easily surmount that logic. Northern politics immediately after 1979 were characterized, in my view, by a struggle for power between a colonial old guard of senior bureaucrats who had been hired by the territorial government in its colonial glory days and the new Aboriginal political elite. As government expanded in the post-1979 period, this old guard watched the gates. Spectacular battles unfolded, as Aboriginal politicians pushed back, hired their own people, and tried to take control of the apparatus of government power. And they were initially successful; the rhetoric of government changed, 'aboriginality' and 'decentralization' came in as local buzzwords. Several bureaucrats who could not make the transition were ousted. By the mid-eighties it looked almost like a new regime.

But success led to legitimation, legitimation led to increased funding, and increased funding led to, guess what, more bureaucrats. The new bureaucracy was different from the old. It was more liberal. It sympathized with Dene, Inuit, and Métis. However, every civil servant needed a house, needed a housing subsidy, had a career, had a family, had a set of needs. Yellowknife was there to fill them. So Yellowknife grew. It had a logic all its own: the logic of capital accumulation. While all around the north, small communities remained roughly the same, Kentucky Fried Chicken and MacDonald's came to Yellowknife; shopping malls came to Yellowknife, and so did shopping mall culture. As well, a whole class of people who occupied the machinery of government came to Yellowknife. I met one of these in the summer of 1994, on the ferry crossing the Deh Cho. We struck up a short conversation, waiting for the ferry to return to our side of the river. She was francophone-Canadian, moving to Yellowknife because she had gained an administrative-support position in one of the more 'progressive' government branches, one dedicated to community government. And, it turns out, she was glad to be leaving Vancouver because it had changed in the last few years, become so much more unfriendly, all those Asian 'foreigners' moving in. . . . Someone whose job involved working in a branch of government devoted to the self-government of people from a non-Western culture, benignly proposing outright racist ideas: somehow this short encounter embodied something of the contradictory nature of the territorial government.

In 1994, when I drove from Fort Simpson to Yellowknife, I found that construction of a paved road had reached north of Fort Providence. Only about 200 kilometres were left to be paved on that trip (albeit, the most expensive stretch because it would have to be cut through the Canadian Shield bedrock). And by 2004 this had been completed. The distance between those who govern and those who are governed thus reaches a qualitatively new level, and this will be heralded in the name of progress. Yellowknifers now never need to leave the pavement. In Nunavut, meanwhile, a similar dynamic poses a similar problem for this new government.

One of the most prominent issues aired in the summer of 1999, the first summer of the new era, related to the new territorial capital. The roads there are in a terrible state.

Shouldn't they be paved?

CHAPTER TWO

the laws of the land

We know that our grandchildren will speak a language that is their
heritage, that has been passed on from before time. We know they
will share their wealth and not hoard it or keep it to themselves.
We know they will look after their old people and respect them for
their wisdom. We know they will look after this land and protect
it and that five hundred years from now someone with skin my
colour and moccasins on his feet will climb up the Ramparts and
rest and look over the river and feel that he too has a place in the
universe; and he will thank the same spirits that I thank, that his
ancestors have looked after this land well, and he will be proud to
be a Dene.

—Frank T'Seleie, *Dene Nation*

Kathryn Shandley, a Lakota Sioux scholar at Cornell University when I
met her, and a friend, once remarked that the most radical thing anyone
in North America could do would be to just stay in one place, 'stay put'.
Coming as she does from a highly nomadic people, the Lakota Sioux,
and a highly nomadic profession, academia, the comment seems doubly
ironic. Yet, it has a remarkable resonance and points to one of the structural presuppositions of contemporary Aboriginal community life in much

of North America and certainly in Denendeh and Nunavut: Aboriginal peoples are among the few people who have a secure knowledge that their descendants will remain attached to a particular geographical territory. Paradoxically, the nomads retain the strongest traces of attachment to home-as-place. Here I reverse Brody's reversal: one of his most original arguments in *The Other Side of Eden* is to suggest that farmers, who need ever-increasing lands, are the true human nomads in the broad view. The attachment of Inuit and Dene reaches far back, to time immemorial, to the traces of grandmothers and grandfathers who came before. And it reaches forward to the generations that will come. If there is an Aboriginal environmentalism, one does not have to be a structural determinist to see that at least in part it stems from this kind of social structural fact: in these communities there is a knowledge that great-grandchildren will see the impact on the land of decisions made today. Hence, in part, the agony of the most conscientious leaders over the impacts of their decisions.

There are other, even more far-reaching, implications to this fact. In his critically important essay on the "Force of Law," the last of the three aporias Derrida writes of has to do with the time of justice. While "a just decision is always required immediately, 'right away' . . . it cannot furnish itself with the infinite information and unlimited knowledge of conditions, rules or hypothetical imperatives that could justify it." Furthermore, Derrida argues, "even if time and prudence, the patience of knowledge and the mastery of conditions were hypothetically unlimited, the decision would be structurally finite, however late it came, a decision of urgency and precipitation, acting in the night of non-knowledge and non-rule."[1] Time and prudence are never unlimited, though, at least within the dominant mode of social being.

If this aporia is displaced onto another mode of social being, other possibilities emerge. Antonia Mills's account of Witsuwit'en law (Witsuwit'en are also Dene/Athabascan peoples, of northern British Columbia), *Eagle Down Is Our Law*, provides one illustration of this point. Witsuwit'en culture in Mills's account involves an intricate layering of land rights, crests, songs, potlatch feasts, and names. Chiefs' names are very important and are distributed carefully; Mills writes that "having a chief's name is an honour and a responsibility, requiring the holder to act correctly and with decorum. The head chiefs are expected to serve as models of correct deportment, to which everyone, and particularly the young, can look for direction and guidance."[2] Furthermore, "feast names are legally related to distinct territory. 'When one chief died, whoever took his name would look after the grounds that went along with the name. That is the way it has always been from the beginning of time.' (Chief Samooh [Moses David])" (143). At a funeral or headstone feast, "if the deceased person has a name, it is passed on. As the Witsuwit'en say, 'Like the flag bearer, whenever one dies, another has to come and carry the flag on'" (65). If the deceased had two names, "both are passed on to different people." Finally, "in the case of a high name, the holder has usually already designated an heir, and this person has previously sat in front of the person holding the name to which he or she is heir" (65). In this mode of social being, the temporality of justice is transformed. The demand for justice to take place 'right away' is reduced: there is, in fact, plenty of time, enough time, for justice. Justice can be carried through the generations, deferred indefinitely, with each passing of the name.

In a world of increasingly generalized commodity production, such forms of long-term ties to specific places are everywhere disappearing. Marx already knew that severing ties to the land was a critical lever in the creation of capitalism; he emphasized the point repeatedly in *Capital*. One aspect of the mode of being of Aboriginal peoples in northern Canada is their consciousness of a debt to the future. Frank T'Seleie, from the K'ashogot'ine of Fort Good Hope, discussed in Chapter Four below, emphasized this in his statement in August of 1975 to Justice Thomas Berger during the Mackenzie Valley Pipeline Inquiry. The extraordinary force of his words in part derives from the radical alterity of the notion of justice they imply and embody. The communities discussed in the coming chapters—and the continuing conversation regarding law and justice plays no small part in these discussions—likewise, in their own distinct ways, imply and embody a mode of social being that presupposes its own temporalities of justice. The question of the land, and of doing justice to Inuit and Dene land rights, has yet to acknowledge this other temporality of justice.

BENEATH THE PAVEMENT

The history of the government of the NWT—and of Nunavut—remains a very partial history. Events I observed in the early nineties cannot be understood without some sense of another history as context: the history of the emergence of the question of land ownership. There are two histories in this context, one dealing with Dene, which is somewhat more convoluted because of a first round of treaty negotiation in the early part of the century, and one dealing with Inuit, somewhat more straightforward. I will briefly deal with the latter first.

Inuit legal status in Canada was a question of some uncertainty because in 1867, when the British North America (BNA) Act was passed, there were few if any Inuit in the then geographic boundaries of the new country. That Act, Canada's constitution, specified that "Indians and lands reserved for Indians" were a federal responsibility; as a result the federal government took measures to negotiate treaties across the country and passed the Indian Act, setting up the system of reserves that came to dominate the Indian reality in Canada south of sixty. However, when Canada's borders expanded northward and Inuit (then called Eskimos) were brought within its jurisdiction, no one knew what their legal status was, and they were treated for the most part as ordinary citizens until a Supreme Court of Canada decision in 1939 established that Inuit were Indians within the meaning of the term in the BNA Act. However, Inuit were not dealt with as Indians within the meaning of the Indian Act. By 1939, meanwhile, the government had stopped negotiating treaties and was no longer recognizing Aboriginal title to any part of Canada that had not already been the subject of a treaty negotiation. Ownership of the whole eastern Arctic remained uncertain until a Supreme Court of Canada decision in 1973 involving the Nisga'a First Nation in British Columbia, the Calder case, forced the federal government to re-establish a process of negotiating Aboriginal title where it had not been surrendered by treaty. The new treaties negotiated through this process were eventually called "comprehensive land claims," which distinguishes them from "specific land claims," the latter negotiated where an existing treaty promise has been broken or unfulfilled. Comprehensive land claims, though complex, have not been comprehensive in the sense of holistic: for many years the federal government insisted that only land-related issues would be discussed at the table, excluding, for example, any talk of Aboriginal self-government. Inuit in Canada's north were among the first in line after 1973, beginning a fifteen-year process of negotiating a comprehensive land claim.

The early part of Dene land rights history has been constructed, with particular attention to Dene perspectives, by Father Rene Fumoleau in his *As Long as This Land Shall Last*, dedicated "to the youngest Indian child in the Northwest Territories." The book is subtitled *A History of Treaty 8 and Treaty 11, 1870–1939*. Two treaties were negotiated involving Dene of the NWT, Treaty 8 in 1899 and Treaty 11 in 1921. Treaty 8 was negotiated because of the gold rush in the Yukon; it dealt with Dene living in northern Alberta and northeastern British Columbia as well as the southwestern NWT, because that region saw a flood of newcomers passing through Edmonton, "gateway to the north," on their way to the gold fields of the Yukon. Treaty 11 was negotiated because of fears of an oil rush after non-Natives learned from Dene about oil at Norman Wells on the Deh Cho in 1920.

Both treaties contained what is now known as the "extinguishment" clause." The word "extinguishment" is not used in this clause, which reads "we the Dene of . . . hereby cede, release, surrender and convey all our rights, titles, and interests in and to lands and waters . . . to His Majesty in right of Canada forever," though it is clear that the effect of the clause is to 'extinguish' Aboriginal title. However, there were irregularities in both treaties, including the fact that many of the x marks that signified assent to the treaties looked suspiciously like they had been rendered by the same hand. Some Dene chiefs may have "touched the pen" to signify assent, but in these circumstances fraud could easily have been practised. Furthermore, the testimony of Dene elders, which Fumoleau (and Justice Morrow of the territorial Supreme Court for a 1973 case) gathered, convincingly demonstrates that the Dene did not see the treaty as a land deal, but rather thought of it as a treaty of peace and friendship. The treaty promise they remember most vividly was that they would be allowed to maintain their life ways. Fumoleau notes that "treaty [in four Dene languages] is literally translated by 'money is distributed'; 'Indian Agent' by 'the one distributing money'. July is 'the month when money is given', and the 'first Treaty' is 'the first time money was given'."[3]

Although a reserve was established at Hay River in accordance with Treaty 8 provisions, and even that in the early seventies, no others were established in the NWT. Dene were in the unique position of having a treaty that specified both the extinguishment of Aboriginal title and establishment of reserve lands, but not having reserves. Annuities were paid in accordance with the treaties, and the treaties came to have great significance to many Dene elders. In the late fifties, the government established a commission to determine why reserves had not been set up. The Nelson Commission found, in part, that Dene had very different ideas about what the treaties meant, which did not include extinguishment of Aboriginal title. By the early seventies, the new Indian Brotherhood of the NWT attempted to file a caveat on lands in their traditional territory, arguing that they still had title to it. Justice Morrow, in his 1973 decision *Re: Paulette*, after interviewing elders who could still remember the 1921 treaty negotiations, agreed with the Dene position. His decision was quickly overturned by the Supreme Court of Canada on the technicality that a caveat can not be filed on unpatented Crown lands, but, in conjunction with the Calder case, was enough to persuade the government to negotiate a comprehensive land claim with the Dene even though Dene were already signatories to a treaty that ostensibly extinguished Aboriginal title. In effect, NWT Dene were in the nearly unique position of negotiating a comprehensive land claim while already having been signatories to a treaty.

By the mid-seventies both the Dene and the Inuit were beginning to negotiate comprehensive land claims, on the understanding that both had Aboriginal title to virtually the whole NWT. Hence, even as the government of the territories, which, in the dying days of its colonial phase, officially opposed both claims, grew in stature and importance, a parallel track dominated territorial politics: negotiations between the federal government and Aboriginal organizations over land ownership.

PLACE NAMES: THE NAME

High in the Arctic, to the east of Victoria Island off the Boothia Peninsula, lies a smallish island with the name Royal Geographical Society of Great Britain Island. In the headquarters of this society in London, in portraits and busts that line its walls, the faces behind many of the place names that can be found in Denendeh and Nunavut are visible. The struggle over land ownership is not incidentally related to the struggle for the righting of names, the struggle over name ownership, and the return of the rich legacy of stories embedded in Inuit and Dene place names. The nominalist struggle informs all levels and layers of territorial politics: from the question of what to call the emerging/residual western portion of the divided territory that emerged in late 1998, to the renaming of communities that makes every map of the NWT and Nunavut outdated as soon as it is printed, to the great collective referents such as Inuit, itself a contested replacement of the denominator 'Eskimo' still used in much of the world, to the names of individuals.

The conflict over names has had a signal impact on Inuit history. Inuit names were difficult to grapple with for colonial administrators. For clarity, the government developed a numerical system in the late 1940s, called E-numbers, and issued small disks, like dog tags, with the appropriate number inscribed to all Canadian Inuit it could trace. The church, meanwhile, moved to produce 'proper' Christian names for Inuit. Inuit have their own cultural practices concerning naming, which had and have a resonant power. For example, children are often named after the community member who passed away immediately before they were born. Such a child became tied in some ways to the family of the deceased, who might continue to call her with the appropriate kinship term. These names are not tied to gender, interestingly, and a female child who has been given the name of a recently deceased male elder might be raised as a male until she asserts her female identity, if indeed she does so. Inuit names are also singular, with no patronym to signal patriarchal descent, as in Angmarlik, the historic leader of the Cumberland Sound whaling station at Kekerton Island in the early twentieth century. One elder woman from Panniqtuuq, Martha, related at a workshop how she resented being given her husband's name as a last name by the Anglican Church because she thought his name was "ugly," but, she shrugged philosophically, "it couldn't be helped."

Places have names that are tied to stories; people have names that link them to their past and to each other. Colonialism was in part a process of reinscription: ruthlessly erasing not only the actual names of places and replacing them with appropriate colonial designations, but also establishing new processes of naming. Northern Canada's microhistory is an emblematic example of colonial nominalism at work. Native Studies, concerned with the righting of names, can not exhibit this concern as long as it follows the properly anthropological practice of citing unnamed informants. Aboriginal peoples and places will have their names again.

ANNIE CATHOLIQUE

There were two powerful moments that dominate my memory of the 1992 Dene Assembly in Pehdzeh Ki (Wrigley) on the Deh Cho. One was provided by an elder named Annie Catholique from Fort Resolution. Dene assemblies have been held since the early seventies, and are gatherings of representatives from all the communities who support the Dene Nation. They are week-long events. The delegates gather in a different Dene community each summer to hear speeches from politicians, land claims negotiators, and key bureaucrats, and to make their own speeches in response. Feasting and drumming and dancing and traditional gambling or gaming take place in the evenings and well into the night. For over ten years, the assembly was the single most important event of any summer in Denendeh.

By 1992, the assembly was a shell of its former self. The Dene Nation was divided, three of five regions boycotted, though one community in Dogrib territory and one from the Sahtu had representatives in attendance. There was confusion about whether quorum had been reached and whether any decisions would be binding. There was uncertainty about which direction the Dene Nation should be taking.

In the Fort Resolution delegation, next to the chief was an elderly woman. Through the discussion on the first day of the meeting, July 14, at various points I noticed her wanting to speak. Her chief would whisper to her "not yet, not yet," and she would sit back. She was a striking figure. She walked with a cane, hunched over, but with a kind of intensity or determination.

That evening, there was a session on Dene history. Rene Lamonthe of Fort Simpson provided an overview, reviewing Dene history and the rough narrative that Fumoleau had researched, focussing on the treaties. He spoke in English, and one thing he said was that "Felix Lockhart told me that, at that time, four copies were made of the treaty. Later, when we wanted to look at them, the church said that its copy had been burned. The HBC said its copy went to England. When I gave this workshop in Hay River, an elder came forward to show me a photocopy of the original treaty document."[4] There are missing documents associated with the treaties: Fumoleau notes that the Treaty Commissioner's "official report as Commissioner cannot be located, though files in the Public Archives of

Canada and at the Department of Indian Affairs were thoroughly searched. Also missing from the files are notes and personal diary of RCMP Inspector Wyndhan Valentine Bruce, who accompanied the treaty party as official escort. . . ."[5] At the assembly, Lamonthe did not mention that official treaty speeches often contained a phrase to the effect that treaty promises would last "as long as the sun shines and the water flows," a phrase that would come up in the discussion that followed.

A few speakers followed Lamonthe. Then Annie Catholique stood up, leaning hard on her cane. The chief no longer dissuaded her from speaking. Her speech was in Chipewyan, and I caught it over the simultaneous translation that was provided. She began by saying, "Seems like us elders know what's happening." Somehow, within a few minutes of her beginning a twenty-minute-long speech, she created an extraordinary feeling, she charged the air with an electricity that had been missing at the assembly. The minutes also record her as saying, "First time they said they had treaty was fifteen dollars. Now the sun is shining, it doesn't go back, we don't want anyone to tell us what to do. They said they were never going to tell us not to hunt or trap, as long as the river is running. We don't want our promise to be broken. They have broken their promise and the river is still running. The Creator put it there. That is Nature there, God is our Boss. They say the paper is lost. Nothing has changed for us. The river is still running, the sun is still shining." My own notes record her as saying, then, "If you go to the south, the white man will not give you a single blade of grass from his lawn." And she said, "You will starve in front of the doors of the white man's houses." For the first time at that assembly, and one of the few times through its entire duration, the delegates rose in a spontaneous standing ovation. The next day, when Grand Chief of the Dene Nation Bill Erasmus referred to the "strong words" that had been spoken the night before, everyone knew he meant Annie Catholique. It was her only speech at that summer's assembly. It was enough.

FIFTEEN YEARS OF NEGOTIATIONS

Both the Dene and the Inuit began negotiating comprehensive land claims with considerable optimism. There was reason to think that within a few years, issues that had long been outstanding could be resolved and newer, fairer arrangements arrived at. The treaty negotiations generally lasted a few days, or at most the whole of one summer. The first comprehensive land claim, with the Cree and Inuit of northern Quebec, had been rushed through in about one year in the mid-seventies. Certainly, there was pressure in that case because of the Quebec government's and Hydro Quebec's desire to construct the James Bay Hydro-Electric project. However, there was every reason to think that, even where there was no major resource development pressure, as was (arguably) the case at that point in the NWT, it would be possible to negotiate a claim within a few years. No one would have imagined how long the process would take.

In 1976 the Inuit Tapirisat of Canada (ITC) presented the government with a land claim, called "Nunavut," to about 64,750,000 hectares of land. However, although the federal government was generally supportive of the initiative, many Inuit leaders felt the proposal did not reflect their real needs, particularly since it accepted the concept of extinguishment. The proposal was subsequently withdrawn. One group of Inuit, Inuvialuit living in the Beaufort area of the western Arctic, broke with ITC and formed the Committee for Original People's Entitlement (COPE), negotiating an Agreement in Principle in 1978 and settling their land claim in a final agreement in 1985. Although the Inuvialuit are small in numbers, their territory is of enormous strategic importance since it is near one of the largest oil and gas fields in Canada: the Beaufort reserves. The ITC, meanwhile, evolved as an organization serving all Inuit in Canada, including Labrador and Quebec Inuit. A new organization, the Tungavik Federation of Nunavut (TFN), was developed to negotiate an NWT Inuit claim. An Agreement in Principle was finally reached by TFN with the federal government in 1990.

In July of 1975, at a joint assembly of Dene and Métis, the Dene Declaration was passed. The Declaration was a Statement of Rights and began with the assertion, "We the Dene of the Northwest Territories insist on the right to be regarded by ourselves and the world as a nation." This was a new rallying cry and would help shift the focus of Indian-government relations. Indians all across Canada, in part inspired by Dene, began referring to themselves as First Nations. "Self-government" became a goal of First Nations. In 1975 the language the Dene used was considered extreme and radical; by the early eighties, Aboriginal self-government had evolved into the key term in government's new paradigm for managing Aboriginal peoples, though the meanings given that term have been hotly contested.

In October of 1976 the Dene presented the government with its land claim proposal, which rejected the logic of extinguishment of Aboriginal title and insisted that self-determination be included in the comprehensive land claims deal. Métis in the region also had a claim to at least some of the same land; they initially filed a separate land claim but the two agreed under federal pressure to negotiate together in 1983. The Dene/Métis positions were not acceptable to the federal government, and although negotiations were held, generally, little progress was made. By the mid-eighties, however, northern Dene communities especially were feeling pressured. Their neighbours, the Inuvialuit, seemed to be making economic progress as a result of the money their claim provided. Leadership of the Dene Nation passed from Georges Erasmus to Stephen Kakfwi. Kakfwi explained in an interview with me a decade later how, in the context of a more supportive territorial government, the Dene Nation made a decision to pursue political objectives through the forum of the territorial government and pursue land issues only through the claim. One major obstacle—the Dene insistence that a self-government agreement be a part of the land claims package—was dropped from the table. In April 1990, Dene chiefs who were gathered in Ottawa agreed to initial an Agreement in Principle (AIP) for a comprehensive Dene/Métis land claim that included an extinguishment clause.

JONAS ANTOINE

In late summer of 1991 I travelled to Fort Simpson in order to ask the band for permission to study self-government there. One of the band councillors at that time was Jonas Antoine, a few years older than I am. Jonas and I spent some hours one afternoon sitting on one of the benches on the high banks of the Deh Cho, looking out over the meeting of two mighty rivers. Jonas explained, in that afternoon, something about his own life history and something about the power, the material and the spiritual power and nourishment, that could be drawn from this site, this place. He said that if you had a hand large enough to stretch across the Deh Cho, even then you would not be able to hold the river back; it was that powerful.

At a band council meeting one evening, newly re-elected Chief Jim Antoine (who had been absent for a few years attending university in the South) reported on the result of the 1991 Dene Assembly, at which a motion to reopen land claims negotiations regarding questions of extin-guishment and treaty entitlements had been passed. Jonas Antoine had his reading glasses on, and had the massive, few hundred pages of legal jargon that made up the Agreement in Principle opened in front of him. In a slow but steady voice, he read out one passage, article 3.1.10:

> Subject to 3.1.12, and in consideration of the rights and benefits provided to the Dene/Metis by this agreement, the Dene/Metis cede, release and surrender to Her Majesty in Right of Canada: (a) all their aboriginal claims, rights, titles and interest, if any, in and to lands and waters anywhere within Canada. . . .

Then he said, quietly and calmly, "I will never sign a document that says this."

THE SPATIAL MATRIX

The thematic of space has assumed increasing importance in social the-ory in recent years. Indeed, Jameson argues in his influential essay on postmodernism[6] that a new attention to space as a cultural dominant, as opposed to the modernist concern with temporality, is one of the con-stitutive features of postmodernism. In another book on postmodernism, David Harvey, a geographer, also emphasizes the increasing importance of the spacial dimension of everyday life in recent times.[7] It is possible to argue that precisely what distinguishes anti-colonial struggles from the classic Marxist accounts of the working class is that oppression for the col-onized is registered in the spatial dimension—as dispossession—whereas for workers, oppression is measured as exploitation, as the theft of time. An argument along these lineaments has been produced by Ato Sekyi-Otu in his careful reading of Franz Fanon: "for a pivotal instance of the ways in which Fanon's texts stage their avowedly 'slight' revision of Marxist analysis is their elevation of spatial metaphors to precedence in the rep-resentation of the structure of domination."[8] It would also be possible to connect the new cultural concern in the Western world with space to a phase of the continuing struggle against imperialism. In this view, the shift that inaugurates postmodernism in the post-war period would be linked to the new nationalism and decolonizing struggles that overthrew formal, political colonies. An unease over decreasing, indeed loss of, space in the metropole in some indeterminate fashion finds its aesthetic impulse in a thematics of space.

Poulantzas provided a nuanced account of how both space and time need to be reconstructed to suit the material exigencies or, in Marx's terms, the presuppositions, of capital accumulation and the commodity form. The world as grid, or the world as hexagon, as central place theorists would have it, is the ultimate spacial vision of the capitalist state. In order to fashion the world as grid, the spacial intelligibility of the dominant logic, serial space as the order of the linear-numerical, has to be imposed and accepted by those who 'live' space. Experience of space must be serialized. Marx emphasized, repeatedly, in Volume One of *Capital*, that no single historical event was more important to the development of capitalism than the tearing away of workers from their roots, from their ability to provide subsistence for themselves from the land. The enclosures in England mark a critical beginning of capitalism. In Canada, the extinguishment policy marks the birth of the nation: it is the oldest continuing policy and practice of Canada, dating at least back to the Royal Proclamation of 1763, arguably the first constitutional document of what would become Canada.

Inuit and Dene have long spoken and written of their feeling for their lands. One could compile a book simply of quotes by elders and political leaders and ordinary citizens about the importance of land (in a sense, Thomas Berger's *Northern Frontier, Northern Homeland* is just such a book). Furthermore, to an economy that continues to rely on hunting as a means of subsistence, land remains a base of local economies. And hunters need more land or territory than farmers, though they will use that land, for the most part, in less intrusive ways. Sacred territories and hunting grounds are the two most common characterizations of land with which northern Natives want to ensure a continued connection.

From the Canadian government's point of view, Inuit and Dene can do what they like with 'their' land; only, what is 'their' land must be precisely determined. Outright ownership of some of the land in exchange for surrender of undefined Aboriginal title to all of it seems a fair exchange to the government, so it continued until very recently to insist on an extinguishment policy as the price of any land claim. The government's term for this is "certainty"; their objective in negotiating a claim is to arrive at certainty. Capital accumulation apparently does not take place in a climate of uncertainty.

The dilemma that confronts Aboriginal leaders in this context is enormous. In the face of economic stagnation, increasing family violence, and suicides, leaders feel that something needs to be done. A land claims settlement that provides investment funds and kick-starts the local economy becomes very attractive. Leaders also fear that elders who have lived much of their lives in sometimes apparent and sometimes real poverty will pass on without their communities' having the resources to both study and record the elder's knowledge in the way they would like to and to provide a measure of material well-being for elders so they can spend their last years with dignity. On the other hand, some fear that their children will grow up in a world where the last bargaining chip, Aboriginal title, has been spent. Effectively, the extinguishment policy forces Aboriginal communities to choose between their elders and their children. This was the choice that faced Dene and Inuit and Métis in the NWT at the turn of the last decade. The struggle over the imposition of the spacial matrix was the locus of totalization in the NWT and provided a dimension of historical significance to the politics of the era.

NUNAVUT

"Nunavut" means "our land," and technically designates two, intertwined, political mechanisms to achieve one dream. Nunavut designates a new political reality, the new territory that was carved from the eastern half of the present NWT in 1999. The creation of this territory was the direct result of a comprehensive land claim, known as the Nunavut claim. Two overlapping mechanisms have led to the emergence of a new political landscape, whose ultimate form is still, only a few years later, uncertain. My research visits to Panniqtuuq took place as the Nunavut land claim was being settled and as the Nunavut territory was being established. The sequence of events that led to this situation began with the comprehensive land claim.

In 1990 the Tungavik Federation of Nunavut and the federal government initialled a 370-page Agreement in Principle (Nunavut AIP) for the land claim. The 17,500 Inuit beneficiaries would gain 350,000 square kilometres of the two-million-square kilometre region, within which they would have mineral rights to 36,300 square kilometres. They were offered 580 million dollars over fourteen years. They would have representation on boards established to manage wildlife and other resources. The deal included support "in principle" for creation of a Nunavut territory by dividing the NWT. And it included a clause that read: "Inuit hereby (a) cede, release and surrender to Her Majesty in Right of Canada, all their aboriginal claims, rights, title and interests, if any, in and to lands and waters anywhere within Canada and adjacent offshore areas within the sovereignty or jurisdiction of Canada. . . ."

In its initial attempt to promote the package, Inuit negotiators, I am told, ran into a difficult time. They had lived in Ottawa for many of the years it had taken to negotiate the Inuit AIP. When they were back in the communities, many people saw them as strangers, as having lost touch with community realities. The apocryphal story is told that, in order to sell the deal, the word "extinguishments" was translated in community meetings as "douse with water."

Finding that the Dene claim was falling apart and the Inuit claim also in danger, the government moved to consolidate its position. Division of the NWT, long the ultimate goal of many northern Inuit, was moved up on the priority list. In the public's mind, Nunavut the land claim and Nunavut the new territory became confused; but suddenly, both were moving ahead. In the context of a new territory, Inuit extinguishment of Aboriginal title seemed somehow less threatening; Inuit would control the public government of the new territory and thereby eventually control public lands. Inuit would also have control over their seventeen per cent of the region. When a plebiscite to divide the NWT passed (narrowly), it became virtually a done deal. On November 12, 1992, sixty-nine per cent of the eligible Inuit voted in favour of the Inuit AIP. On May 25, 1993, the Nunavut Final Agreement was signed. Nunavut became a reality.

Rick Riewe and Jill Oakes, two well-known Arctic researchers, during their tenure as visiting Northern Chairs at Trent University in 1994, told the (also probably apocryphal) story of how Inuit made the best of their "land quantum." Since Inuit are largely coastal people, and since in the High Arctic most of the land of any value is along the coast, the Inuit land quantum theoretically could have been used to select almost all the coastal lands. To prevent this, the federal government limited the total amount of coastal land that Inuit communities could select. However, Inuit know their land very well. They assured Rick Riewe as he was producing the Inuit *Atlas* that much of the coastal land left for the State consisted of sheer cliff fronting the ocean. The value of the story is in what it says about the view of the Inuit land claim: that these negotiators had managed to 'pull off' a much better deal.

The Nunavut claim is widely viewed as a successful example of a comprehensive land claim, in large measure because Inuit were able to do what few other groups could succeed in, somehow tying the issue of self-government and land claims together. Only the Inuit were in a position to use the creation of a public government, the Nunavut territory, as a vehicle for their self-government aspirations, so the model can not be generalized. But it was and is a brilliant strategy and a brilliant way around the impasses created by the federal government's comprehensive land claims policy. That said, it is worth remembering that the Alaska Land Claim was also touted in its time as a new and daring model that would work for the benefit of Aboriginal peoples, including Inuit, there. Every new land claim comes with heralds trumpeting its superiority over past deals.

IQALUIT: NIC AND NTI

In Iqaluit, once called Frobisher Bay after Martin Frobisher, now ironically named as a place "where the fish are" (ironic since "the fish" no longer "are" in Iqaluit), the structural bones of what would become Nunavut were in place by the mid-nineties and embodied in the Nunavut Implementation Commission (NIC) and the Nunavut Tungavik Incorporated (NTI). The former was the advisory body set up to make recommendations on the new public government, the latter the umbrella Inuit-owned corporation established to implement the land claim. Government and corporation, locus of power in the public space and deployer of capital in civil society. Is this an Inuit mirror and inflection of the world constructed by the exigencies of capital, or some strange kind of critical regionalism that enlists the categories of postmodern political and economic life in the name of a cultural form that in some uneasy way directly contradicts the social realities inscribed by capitalism? The actions of both bodies provide some insight.

The Nunavut Implementation Commission offices in Iqaluit seemed in a permanent state of construction, reconstruction, adaptation, renovation, as if reflecting the continuing attempts of the commission to develop something that would become a constitution for the new territory. The commission, appointed by the federal government, itself consisted of six commissioners, representing the different regions and communities of Nunavut, and was led by John Amagoalik, once president of the Inuit Tapirisat of Canada and the Inuit Committee on Constitutional Issues, originally from the community of Resolute Bay as one of the Arctic 'exiles', relocated by a distant State authority from Inukjuak in northern Quebec to the High Arctic in the early fifties.

The first major discussion paper released by NIC was called "Two-Member Constituencies and Gender Equality: A 'Made in Nunavut' Solution for an Effective and Representative Legislature." The paper noted the contribution of the "Mothers of Confederation"—Rosemarie Kuptana, Mary Simon, and Nellie Cournoyea—who were prominent Inuit contributors to the debate concerning Canada's failed Charlottetown Accord constitutional proposals, but argued that at the territorial level women remain severely under-represented. An explicit acknowledgement of the problem of 'formal' and 'informal' politics was made:

> It is also important to distinguish between participation in 'formal' (ie electoral) politics and participation in 'informal' politics (women and men volunteering their time and talents to co-operatively make the communities better places to live), because it is the people who participate in 'formal' politics of legislatures who determine the level of resources that people who participate in 'informal' politics have available to work with.[9]

The discussion paper proposed that all voters in electoral districts be given two lists of candidates, an all-male and all-female list, and that each voter casts two votes, one for an individual on each list. As well as serving the interest of gender equality, the discussion paper noted that the procedure would ensure a sufficient number of legislative members to render it representationally effective. The discussion paper concluded: "The Nunavut Legislative Assembly could be a model for democratic peoples everywhere. Nunavut could have the first legislature in the world to have balanced representation of men and women designed right into its make-up."[10] This last phrase, a disingenuous "right into its make-up," structures into the syntax of a formal proposal a colloquialism, informal language, reflecting perhaps a movement that, if adopted, the gender-balanced representational model would itself structure into the syntax of the political system.

Meanwhile, the Nunavut Tungavik Incorporated, after the election of its first board members and president, had moved into its newer and somewhat more luxurious Iqaluit headquarters nearby. The office boasts the original of the painting that graces the covers of the comprehensive land claim, and a variety of other *objects d'art* (or, *objects d'art* Inuit). The NTI's first president was Jose Kusugak, elected in a hotly contested campaign that ran through the winter of 1993–94.

Two areas of activity seemed to dominate the early, proactive agenda of NTI; its reactive agenda consumed a great deal of time and involved setting up the joint management boards, financial tools, and other structural elements of the claim. Training people to take on new responsibilities was one prominent area of activity; the other was a cash payment or dividend for elders. Young people, who represent the future, and older people, who hold the cultural knowledge that forms the basis of the Inuit project, were thereby given early priority by NTI.

Taken as a whole, these early proposals of NIC and NTI focussed on the elders, youth, and women in a concerted attempt to rebalance the structure of power that favours middle-aged males, through a distribution of political power and economic resources. The possibility remains that this Inuit mirror of dominant structure, the separation of the political and economic as embodied in the State and private capital that is a foundation of capitalist modernism, will be enlisted to support social relations markedly different from those that predominate. It is a dangerous game, though, and the degree to which it depends upon capital accumulation will determine the degree of possessive individualism that can come to predominate, leading in turn to political and economic forms that may wholly undermine Inuit traditions, values, and culture. Early indications were therefore mixed, and, in the spring of 1997 in a plebescite, Inuit voters rejected the proposal for a gender-balanced legislature.

'BREAKUP OF DENE NATION'?

Two meetings have assumed mythical status in Dene politics in recent years. One was the April 1990 meeting of chiefs that ratified the AIP. The other was the Dene Assembly of July 1990 that effectively rejected it. The Dene had consolidated themselves into five different regions: the Gwi'chin to the northwest; North Slavey speakers in the Sahtu region in the central west; Dogrib speakers in the North Slave region in the central east; Chipewyan speakers in the South Slave region in the southeast; and South Slavey speakers in the Dehcho region in the southwest. The Gwi'chin, under some pressure because they occupied lands near Inuvialuit, who had had a settled claim for five years and were looking comparatively prosperous, wanted a settlement. For example, Inuvialuit purchased, among other things, a regional airline company. Inuvialuit beneficiaries could fly on the company for a cheaper fare than non-beneficiaries. Hence, a Gwi'chin on the same flight as an Inuvialuk was paying more. This must have irritated. Others also pushed for an end to the long process. In their view, it was time to move ahead and sign a land claims deal.

I've heard many stories about the April meeting, primarily from those who opposed its result. One was that, after an anxious night of waiting, close to a deal but with the major issue of extinguishment still outstanding, the chief negotiator came back to the room where the chiefs were and said, "We've got a deal." A Gwi'chin chief stood and applauded, and the rest followed. The Dene/Métis AIP was then initialled, and only later did many of the chiefs come to realize they had gone against the principles of the Dene Declaration. An Agreement in Principle with an extinguishment clause, whose provisions included nearly a half billion dollars, was brought back to the north for discussion.

Not long before that, the leadership of the Dene Nation had changed. Stephen Kakfwi, seeing that the land claim was close to settlement, entered territorial politics in order to help steer the self-government platform of the Dene. He would become a cabinet minister and eventual leader of the government of the NWT in the post-division phase. He was replaced at the Dene Nation by Bill Erasmus, younger brother of Georges. There was soon no love lost between the two.

At the Dene Assembly the next summer, the Dene/Métis AIP was the most important agenda item. Again, stories now circulate. A motion sponsored by the Dehcho Tribal Council to reopen negotiations about the issues of extinguishment and treaty rights was presented as something that would not destroy the claim, but, rather, delay it for more discussion. The Gwi'chin hotly opposed the motion. The Sahtu, who also leaned towards a claim, supported the motion on the understanding that it would not be the end of the claim. The motion passed. The Gwi'chin walked out of the assembly, and cherished Dene unity was broken.

The federal government refused to reopen the AIP. And, it broke with its own policy of not negotiating with fragments of a larger body, settling a land claim with the Gwi'chin within two years of the fateful assembly. The Sahtu soon followed suit, left the Dene Nation, and by 1992 had their own AIP. Both were modelled, with slight changes, on the earlier global Dene/Métis agreement and both included an extinguishment clause. Diamonds were discovered on Dogrib land in early 1992 and a diamond rush followed. Without the protection of a federal injunction—which had been in place in the years immediately before the Dene/Métis AIP—diamond prospectors ('stakers') swarmed over Dogrib lands and within months the Dogrib were opening land claim negotiations. However, the evolving federal policy on comprehensive claims had shifted by the time the Dogrib entered into negotiations: by 2002 they had an Agreement in Principle for both a comprehensive claim and a self-government agreement, with the signing of the final agreement in late summer of 2003.

Some called it the breakup of the Dene Nation, and there was much criticism of Bill Erasmus's leadership. Kakfwi, in particular, was relentless in his public criticisms of Bill Erasmus, having watched the strategy he had so carefully crafted over a decade collapse. However, in my own view something was missing from these criticisms: an understanding of the differing situations of the differing regions. As is made clear in the following chapters on Fort Simpson in the Dehcho and Fort Good Hope in the Sahtu, the objective circumstances of these communities are different. In the Sahtu, Dene remain and will remain for a long while a substantial majority of the population. They can, therefore, control municipal and regional governments and through them public lands in the area. In a sense, they are close structurally to the situation of Inuit in Nunavut. In the Dehcho, the presence of a road has meant a substantial influx of non-Natives. There is no certainty that Dene there will control public government and public lands in the future, hence a much greater concern with the impact of extinguishment.

The "breakup of the Dene Nation," I would argue, was the outcome of the very processes of community development and empowerment it was mandated to accomplish. In the late sixties and early seventies, a generation of Dene leaders established the Indian Brotherhood of the NWT; orchestrated the Dene presentation to the Berger inquiry; established the Dene Declaration; with Inuit and Métis seized control of the territorial government; and negotiated and negotiated around land claims, filing the caveat that led to the Morrow inquiry and eventually filing a comprehensive land claim. In the early part of this period, there was a very strong leadership with a relatively small part of it Western-educated. They crafted a vision of Dene unity out of necessity because they needed each other. In fact, the unity was always fragile and required frequent renegotiation between regions with different splits in different periods. Over the years that followed, more leaders emerged at the community level, leaders who could speak more in the interests of their specific community; at that point, the vision of the Dene Nation became the vision of whatever community was behind its leader. The process of stronger communities, in conjunction with a Dene Nation leader who was and is genuinely committed to reflecting the wishes of his constituents, eventually led to a crisis and a new reality emerged: regional tribal councils rather than a central organization would represent the political interests of Dene. The so-called breakup of the Dene Nation in that sense is not a development to be mourned: it is an outgrowth of a deeper political success at community empowerment.

A MEDICINE WAR

In 1991 I paid a visit to George Blondin in his cubbyhole office in the Dene Cultural Institute, then in Yellowknife (it has since moved into a new building at Hay River). George is a well-known Dene elder statesman, a retired chief of his home community, Deline (once Fort Franklin), and the author of two remarkable books of Dene stories and life histories, *When the World Was New* and *Yamoria: The Lawmaker*. I wanted to talk to him about attending the elders' gathering at Trent University, and have some broad discussion about self-government, my own research topic. I followed the custom practised by many Aboriginal peoples in southern Canada and brought him tobacco. Conversations with George tend to follow a certain, meandering pattern. There is talk, most of it from me at the beginning as George, more than trying to understand my particular need or desire, tries to get some grip on who I am. I circle around my objective, explaining the elders' gathering, filling in spaces, making small talk, asking questions, and waiting in some futility for a direct response. Then, from out of nowhere apparent, George fixes his gaze on me and tells a story. I've since seen him do the same thing to others, and he's repeated it with me.

That time, he told me a story about two people who had strong medicine power, one from the north and one from the south. I can not remember most of the story but I remember one thing vividly; a duel was fought between the two, using magic arrows. In the end, the man from the south pierced the heart of the man from the north, ending the duel.

It was a full year before a meaning or a reason for this particular story at this particular time came to me. Many of George's stories, I should say, are about medicine power battles, which is a dominant trope or genre of Dene narrative practice. There is a thread through his narratives about the importance of unity, working together, using medicine power for good ends rather than divisive ones. A clear political subtext underlies many of the stories of medicine power conflict. And yet, in this particular story, the duel was a specific one, on a north-south axis. I now am convinced for no definable reason that it was a story of the division among the Dene; that one line, George's eyes, he repeated it: "the arrow pierced his heart."

IF/ANY

Read the text of the extinguishment clause carefully. In the Nunavut Agreement, for example, it reads, "Inuit hereby (a) cede, release and surrender to Her Majesty in Right of Canada, all their aboriginal claims, rights, title and interests, if any, in and to lands and waters anywhere within Canada and adjacent offshore areas within the sovereignty or jurisdiction of Canada. . . . " All their aboriginal claims, if any. The same language pertains to the Sahtu Treaty and to the Gwi'chin claim. After the 1975 James Bay Agreement with Cree and Inuit who live in the territory to the east of Hudson Bay, the government of the day realized that by extinguishing title, it was implicitly recognizing that Aboriginal title existed. Other First Nations could use such recognition as a lever in pressing their own demands. Undoubtedly, some of the highly paid staff of the ironically named Justice Department in the federal government came up with a two-word solution to that problem and the solution then found its way into all the claims that followed. All their Aboriginal claims, if any. Even in the moment of surrender of Aboriginal title, the very instant of extinguishment that so much energy is spent achieving, the government has not entirely recognized that such title ever existed or had legal force. Hence, the seventy-five million dollars it pays out to Sahtu Treaty beneficiaries, or the half-billion dollars it pays out to Nunavut beneficiaries, are seen by Justice as a payment offered to cover the possibility that something like Aboriginal title exists in law, has legal force, and remains as a possibility to be exercised by Dene and Inuit. This is a Justice that colludes with total-izing power.

There are other clever little legal devices scattered around the text of modern land claims. Since for so many years the government formally refused to negotiate self-government agreements as part of land claims packages, while First Nations insistently pressed for what they saw as 'holistic' deals that would include binding self-government agreements, eventually a compromise was reached: most comprehensive claims began to include a section on self-government. These are not particularly sub-stantive, but they do bind the parties to further negotiation (pursuant to the acceptance of the land claim) on self-government and list the range of subjects to be covered by such negotiations. While comprehensive land claims are constitutionally defined as treaties, and hence have constitu-tional status and protection, a clause in the self-government section of the claim ensures that the whole section does not have such protection, nor does any agreement negotiated as a result of the section.

The astonishing degree of legalism here betrays an unwarranted faith in legal progress. As if, since nineteenth-century lawyers could not craft legal language in treaties that would adequately stand the stresses imposed by time, twentieth-century lawyers are keen to prove they now have the language, the skills. And this betrays a very narrow vision of what modern treaties are about. As in the case of the treaties negotiated a century ago, there is still faith that legal practitioners can produce a text "once and for all" that will stand the test of time, that will work as a document structur-ing relations between Inuit and Qallunaat, between Dene and Mola, into an indefinite future. A curious historical repetition: Aboriginal leaders in the nineteenth century were mostly non-English-language speakers who did not read the documents they were signing. They had their own orders of literacy. The documents had to be read out to them, explained. It is unlikely that, at the community level, Dene or Inuit knew about the clause excluding the self-government section from constitutional protection, for example. Once again, a document is produced that requires outside expertise to understand. Worse, the nature of the document is such that it embodies the most technocratic position on a process that demands broad historical vision. The legal practitioners have added layers of detail, covering over the basic fact of extinguishment (or the exhaustion of land rights, to be discussed below) that continues to underwrite the process. Layers of detail to precisely articulate a narrow vision, if any.

THE EXHAUSTION MODEL

By the mid-nineties, under the weight of decades of criticism, the State began to seriously look at alternatives to the extinguishment clause. Minister of Indian Affairs Ron Irwin famously banned the word from use by his staff (though the word itself is not used even in the clause that achieves its goal). The search for an alternative approach that would still achieve 'certainty' was on. Finally, the Nisga'a agreement of 1999 unveiled a treaty that did not include an extinguishment clause. What it did include was arguably worse. A section of the agreement said that the agreement itself specified all the Aboriginal rights of the Nisga'a ("exhausted" their rights, though that word is also not used). They had nothing other than what is specifically mentioned in the agreement. Although there are many interesting and creative features of that treaty, and as a whole the Nisga'a seemed enthusiastic about a deal they had been struggling for over 100 years to achieve, a key concern centres on the exhaustion model. Extinguishment at least allows a treaty signatory the possibility of rights not foreseen and not specified in the treaty, particularly concerning self-government. The Nisga'a deal includes a substantive and creative self-government package, based on the system that is a part of Nisga'a tradition. The 2003 Dogrib treaty became the first in the north to adopt the exhaustion model and also includes a self-government agreement. The rights provisions of the Dogrib treaty, called the Tlicho Treaty, are complex, but under scrutiny the basic logic of the exhaustion model is clearly recognizable: "2.6.1 Except as provided by 2.10, the Tlicho will not exercise or assert any Aboriginal or treaty right, other than (a) any right set out in the agreement, or (b) the Treaty 11 rights respecting annual payments to the Indians and payment of the salaries of the teachers to instruct the children of the Indians." The treaty fully and exhaustively describes any rights they can exercise. Leave it to the State to find a way to replace one its oldest, most outdated, ineffective, and unjust policies—the extinguishment clause—with something worse.

NUNAVUT AND DENENDEH

Denendeh, in the mid-eighties, was often thought of as a possible name for the Western Arctic, should the territories be divided. Nunavut and Denendeh are dream places, landscapes and territories and homes for Aboriginal First Nations, where there is a possibility that their needs and wishes will be accommodated in a more meaningful way than most of the rest of the continent has been able to achieve.

I come from such a dream place. Manitoba. Land of Manitou, the Cree, the Anishinabwe Creator, established through a Métis rebellion, home of Treaty 1, Treaty 2, and Treaty 5, with territories associated with Treaty 3, Treaty 4, Treaty 6, and Treaty 10. Cree and Métis and Anishinabwe and Sioux and Assiniboine and Dene country. For a short period, a very short period after 1870, there was a promise of something new in the land of Manitou. But it was a short-lived promise. A Métis diaspora, pushed by immigrants from the east, was the first sign that business as usual would prevail. Massive immigration from northern and eastern Europe swamped the Native peoples there. Manitoba became "the keystone province"; a failed project where even the French fact was sacrificed on the grinding wheel of totalization.

Denendeh and Nunavut. New promises. New possibilities. This time. . . .

AN OLD IDEAL

Nunavut and the NWT are among the most interesting political jurisdictions in Canada and perhaps the world. From the perspective of political science, they virtually single-handedly save the country from being accurately described as a long, increasingly esoteric, and sterile debate about the constitutional division of powers. The French fact (whether to establish yet another bourgeois republic devoted to the exigencies of capital accumulation) seems tiresome in comparison. In the NWT and Nunavut, contemporary cultural politics in all its dimensions is being played out with a vengeance. Leaders rise and fall mercurially. Small, minuscule populations rest on enormous land masses.

Government has consciously attempted to adopt Aboriginal values into its mechanisms. Assembly discussion is organized in both territories around vaguely defined principles of consensus. There is simultaneous translation of government discussion in the NWT into seven official languages, five of them Aboriginal. In Nunavut, Inuktitut dominates discussion in the assembly, though not among the administrators.

At the community level, there is room for anyone with an interest and desire to be involved in politics. A typical western Arctic community might include a local band council, Métis local, Native women's association local, hunters' and trappers' association, and a municipal council, and participate in a tribal council, election of a member to the Territorial Assembly, and election of a member of parliament. In communities of 100 to 500 people, this is opportunity enough. But there are also community and regional meetings or assemblies, where one can have an opportunity to speak to whatever issues move one, and the strength of one's spoken words is the only factor that will determine whether they will have any effect.

Out of this 'hothouse' political environment, an impressive Aboriginal leadership has emerged. People like Rosemarie Kuptana, former president of the Inuit Tapirisat of Canada, or Georges Erasmus, past Grand Chief of the Assembly of First Nations and co-commissioner of the Royal Commission on Aboriginal Peoples, or Ethyl Blondin-Andrew, Member of Parliament for the Western Arctic and Minister of State for Youth in the former federal Liberal government, or Nellie Cournoyea, former leader of the territorial government, or John Amagoalic, past president of the Inuit Tapirisat of Canada and of the Nunavut Implementation Commission, have national profiles and reputations. Others, like Bill Erasmus, past president of the Dene Nation, or Stephen Kakfwi, former leader of the NWT government, or Paul Okalik, premier of Nunavut, or Joanne Barnaby, executive director of the Dene Cultural Institute, are highly respected in the territories and have also had an impact on the nation. At the community level, leaders and elders like George Barnaby, or Herb Norwegian, or Frank T'Seleie, or Jonasie Karpik, or Elizabeth Ishulutak are also very highly regarded. Although Aboriginal leadership has been criticized and self-critical in the North for not providing strong enough moral examples in social areas such as substance abuse or family violence— and these comments have not been directed at the people named above—it is, on the whole, an impressive, dedicated, articulate, and dynamic group who have contributed a great deal outside their own sphere. And, again, three Inuit women—Rosemarie Kuptana, Nellie Cournoyea, and then

Inuit Circumpolar Conference president Mary Simon (from northern Quebec)—were called the "Mothers of Confederation" in the Charlottetown round of constitutional talks.

Politics in the NWT and Nunavut is a matter of everyday discussion. There is, in these territories as almost nowhere else in North America, a meaningful sense of 'public' as a sphere of engagement and debate. This is reflected in voter turnouts, which tend to be among the highest of any political constituency in the Western world. In coffee shops in Yellowknife, you can rub elbows with cabinet ministers and tell them what's wrong with their policies. There is a rough egalitarianism of the everyday, which corresponds to but does not equal the traditional egalitarianism of Inuit and Dene. One time, in the Miner's Mess, when it still existed, I sat down for tea with a Dene friend. A member of the Territorial Assembly sat down to talk to him. A chief joined us. Soon another member of the assembly, a cabinet minister, joined the group. Before long I was sitting among a who's-who of the Aboriginal leadership of the NWT. It was a lively though short conversation, and one of my better coffee breaks.

Aboriginal politics, these days organized around land claims and self-government, dominate the north. The political environment evolves rapidly; there is no doubt that by the time these words are read, much will have changed in Nunavut and the NWT. Politics are as complex, Byzantine, as any other jurisdiction in the world. They are reminiscent most strikingly of Middle Eastern politics, often celebrated for the complexities, where ancient divisions, cultures, religions, land disputes, are overlaid with recent geopolitics. Race, class, and gender provide focal concepts for understanding dimensions of NWT politics, but each provides only a partial picture and together they are not sufficient to understand or interpret events. Culture, along the boundary of mode of production, is a more useful and relevant theoretical tool.

The concept of mode of production offers three critical insights that relate to northern Aboriginal politics. First, the concept allows recognition of the fundamental similarities in social structure among Inuit and Dene, while accommodating the extraordinary differences at the level of cultural expression. Through the lens of the concept of mode of production, their politics are jointly conceptualized as those of gatherers and hunters in a late capitalist world order. This does not presume that their similarity of interest has led to the articulation of an automatic solidarity, but, rather, that the fundamental ground of their mutual political struggles is identical. Second, the concept points towards specific aspects of society as critical determinants of change: the forces and relations of production. Little needs to be added to the voluminous literature on the former, but the latter deserves consideration. Social relations in Inuit and Dene communities are the single most important element in the northern body politic. Understanding these turns our attention towards social forms and, in a colonial context, the politics of form itself. Finally, the concept of mode of production allows for a situating of northern Aboriginal politics within a broader horizon, to specify its place in the struggle for social change for social justice.

POLITICAL STRUCTURES

Aboriginal politics in the NWT and Nunavut supports and feeds off an unusual formal political structure: that of the Territorial Assembly. Although Dennis Patterson, one of the leaders of the NWT in the late eighties, characterized the form of government as a creative extension of the Westminster model of parliamentary government, it is possible to argue instead that the NWT has had, for some time, one of the only stable forms of assembly government in existence in modern times. A brief review of four features of the government should be enough to clarify this point.

First, there are no party politics at the territorial level in either territory. This means that members are elected to represent their constituencies, implying relatively little structural bias towards thinking of the 'good of the whole', but stronger regional representation, appropriate perhaps to territories so large. Second, leadership—both government leader and cabinet—is therefore comparatively weak. Unlike provincial or federal legislatures, the leader cannot automatically command the support of her party members and must, therefore, govern much less autocratically, depending on the support of different alliances for the passage of any piece of legislation. Third, committees and the assembly are relatively strong. Meaningful discussion can take place in committees and in the assembly as a whole, because the logic of party control over both—which ensures that the committee and assembly will decide what the leader tells them to decide and makes a mockery of discussion—does not govern. Fourth, discussion in assembly is therefore not structured around a strictly oppositional model.

Members are not trying to 'score' political 'points' for their party, so although this does not necessarily structurally imply a consensus model, as territorial politicians have argued, it does mean an absence of formal or structured opposition. This is not the same as suggesting there is no debate, or that backroom manoeuvring and personal rivalries do not exist. It does suggest a different context within which debate and rivalry operate.

For these reasons, it is arguable that the government of the NWT and the government of Nunavut are, in form, a version of assembly government (rather than either the parliamentary or presidential models). The importance of this is that it signals and represents the markedly different political culture of the two territories and raises the possibility of democratic models different from predominating ones. The form's weakness is that there is no strong structural logic that directs an assembly member to forsake the interest of her region in favour of the interest of the territory as a whole; the government leader's job is to do so, but even she must be mindful of her own constituency's demands and has a relatively weak mandate for the broader job. Its strength, conversely, is that in territories as large and diverse as these, it allows for strong articulations of regional differences. The form also structures in a necessity for shifting alliance politics: on any specific issue, different alliances may form. The most successful politicians may be those who do not completely alienate any of their colleagues, whose support may be needed on another day: soon!

Added to this, it is worth reiterating that proceedings may be conducted in, as well as French and English, one of five Aboriginal official languages: Inuktitut, Slavey, Dogrib, Chipewyan, Gwi'chin. Simultaneous translation or interpretation of all assembly proceedings provides a livelihood for many Aboriginal people and is one of the few ways in which the territorial governments concretely recognize and validate Aboriginal knowledge.

Calling this model "assembly government" has one significant implication. Rather than presuming that the form is an undeveloped version of the models used in southern jurisdictions and that, therefore, 'political development' or progress will come as the system moves towards similarity with those jurisdictions, by suggesting that a whole different logic and structure is at work we have the advantage of assuming this is a fully functioning, fully developed political model. And perhaps one that southern jurisdictions can learn from, rather than dictate to.

IMAGINING

> Utopia is inseparable from death in that its serenity gazes calmly
> and implacably away from the accidents of individual existence
> and the inevitability of its giving way: in this sense it might even be
> said that Utopia solves the problem of death, by inventing a new
> way of looking at individual death, as a matter of limited concern,
> beyond all stoicism.
>
> —Fredric Jameson, *The Seeds of Time*

Fredric Jameson has insistently called attention to the importance of the utopian gesture in contemporary cultural politics, recently in his *The Seeds of Time*, arguing that "there is . . . no more pressing task for progressive people in the First World than tirelessly to analyze and diagnose the fear and anxiety before Utopia itself."[11] In earlier work, Jameson has suggested that culture itself can be seen as "the expression of a properly Utopian or collective impulse."[12] This line of thinking distinguishes Jameson from many of his contemporaries and is one of his signal contributions to critical theory: he cites and attempts to reinvigorate a Marxist version of a positive hermeneutic, situating himself in a tradition that includes Bloch, Bakhtin, the Frankfurt School, Rousseau, Durkheim, and Sartre.[13]

Jameson exhibits a curious uncertainty, however, about the position of gatherers and hunters as an embodied exemplification of this visionary politics. He resists the notion of "a nostalgic-Utopian triad . . . which is handily identified as the Marxist 'vision of history': a golden age before the fall, that is to say, before capitalist dissociation, which can optionally be positioned where you like, in primitive communism or tribal society."[14] Instead, he is concerned to read utopian impulses that seem more future-oriented, in science fiction, for example, or other aspects of postmodern culture. Hence, in this instance, he does not engage the working-through that his own conceptual analysis demands: the concept of mode of production demands no "optional positioning" of the so-called "golden age," but, rather, rigorous critique and argument. There is nothing nostalgic in the recognition of a tradition that embodies egalitarian values and seeks to retain emancipatory social forms, even when it does so at times by deploying the mechanisms invented by totalization itself. In spite of this, though, Jameson's evocative and suggestive work also has the merit of pointing towards a variety of sociologists of 'small group politics' such as the work of Jean-Paul Sartre.[15]

The conceptual apparatus offered by Sartre's *Critique of Dialectical Reason*, particularly the notions of serial collectives and fused groups, are relevant here. Seriality as a concept implies a process of numbering. The logic of the series is founded on numerical sequence: $1 - 2 - 3 - 4 - N$. Sartre argues in his *Critique* that this logic, the logic of the lineup, is the dominant underlying logic of social collectivity in the Western world. Sartre is particularly interested in illustrating how the common interest of individuals randomly brought together as a serial collective, for example in a lineup for a bus,[16] is defined not by themselves but from the outside. An impersonal, extrinsic, and abstract logic substitutes itself for their own responsibility and agency, and this serial logic "excludes the relation of reciprocity" (263), constituting and presupposing the isolated individual as a fundamental social unit. Seriality becomes a part of every individual's way of life and way of thinking; it is simultaneously interiorized and objectified: "there are serial behaviour, serial feelings and serial thoughts; in other words a series is a mode of being for individuals both in relation to one another and in relation to their common being and this mode of being transforms all their structures" (264). The serial collective is a totalizing social form, spreading with and through, at the same time as it helps construct, the conditions receptive to the advance of capital accumulation and the commodity form.

In contrast to this, Sartre suggests a different kind of social reality, that of the fused group. The example he deploys is the storming of the Bastille in revolutionary France, and in general he links the concept to active, though temporary, social movements. Sartre argues that "the essential characteristic of the fused group is the sudden resurrection of freedom" (401), not the freedom that allows "alienated man to live his servitude in perpetuity," but, rather: "against the common danger, freedom frees itself from alienation and affirms itself as common efficacity," thereby producing "in each third party the perception of the Other (the former Other) as the same: freedom is both my individuality and my ubiquity" (401). In the fused group, the group itself determines its project and is united through this determination: "My praxis is in itself the praxis of the group totalised here by me in so far as every other myself totalises it in another here, which is the same, in the course of the development of its free ubiquity. Here there appears the first 'us'" (394). In order for Sartre's concept of the fused group to adequately stand in as a description of gathering and hunting social forms, it would be necessary to do away with the concept of external danger, the 'enemy', or scarcity, that forms critical aspects of it; nevertheless, the concept opens a trajectory of language that points towards utopian longing.

Serial collectivity has been structured into the architectural forms of northern settlements by 'planners' who presume that communities must all look, as they do in the south, suburban. For decades, well-intentioned engineers and architects have applied their best skills to constructing row houses in—to their eyes—highly inhospitable environments. Every northern settlement is in effect torn down the middle by values of people that lead them to insist on meaningful social bonds, and by structures that presuppose the irrelevance of these bonds. Every community is a contested colonial space, a battleground where the value of community wrestles with the totalizing logic of serial collectivity and the possessive individualism it presupposes.

Imagine a sustainable form of social organization founded on the principles of the fused group. The gathering and hunting mode of production may itself be an allegory, a language through which critical theory imagines the utopian dimension in human experience, a metaphor for describing certain kinds of social relations and pointing to their viability. While it may be true that this mode of imagining is in its own fashion difficult to resist, that does not vitiate the continuing strategic necessity of utopian thought.

> Foolhardy as it is to speculate what it might be about the absence of chiefs and property, capital and the State, that would enhance the mimetic faculty—the terms are overly generous—I cannot resist speculation that what enhances the mimetic faculty is a protean self with multiple images (read "souls") of itself set in a natural environment whose animals, plants, and elements are spiritualized to the point that nature "speaks back" to humans, every material entity paired with an occasionally visible spirit double—a mimetic double!—of itself.
>
> —Michael Taussig, *Mimesis and Alterity*

ON THE MARGINS OF THE MARGINS

There are all manner of social arrangements scattered, coexisting, concentrated, and dispersed across the two territories. Interestingly, Hugh Brody's important *The People's Land* begins with an introductory story about the experience of a gay teacher in a small, eastern Arctic community. The story he relates deals with the Qallunaat hostility to the teacher, the Qallunaat perception of an equal or greater hostility among local Inuit— which leads the Qallunaat to forcibly remove the man from town on a charge that he was paying young Inuit boys for sexual services—and finally Brody's discovery that many Inuit felt that "this was not a serious matter, not a cause for real anger against such a likeable man."[17] The accidents of social interaction have made me long aware that Yellowknife has a small but thriving lesbian community or socious, which is largely but not exclusively non-Native, and an even smaller—or, perhaps, more carefully closeted, or, again, simply not prey to the accidents of friendship that allowed me to encounter different subcultures—gay community. Male gayness may pose something of a greater challenge to the patriarchally constructed notion of 'frontier' that continues to circulate among the colonizers, though homophobia undoubtedly exacts a fierce price on lesbians and perhaps those with bisexual orientations. The size and vitality of the lesbian community are both evidenced in the gleeful delight one of my friends takes on hearing of the arrival to the community of an additional sister spirit, calling her "new meat." Among the Aboriginal communities, there is not a great deal of same-sex advocacy; though I have encountered a few Aboriginal people with same-sex partners in prominent public positions, neither closeted nor openly 'out', their sexual identity existing in the ambiguous space of what Michael Taussig has called the "public secret."

In the everyday sphere of community life, sexual borders may be crossed more frequently than we generally credit. In one Aboriginal community, I billeted with a middle-aged, recently single Aboriginal woman, the head of her household and a prominent community member. It is mid-evening, I am half napping, half reading Rosalind Krauss's *The Optical Unconscious*. A female friend of my host comes to visit and the two sit in the kitchen, play cards, and chat, sometimes in low tones, sometimes at a normal conversational level; always in Inuktitut. I fade in and out, assuming that the low tones are an attempt to be polite. The two go off into one of the two rooms—a laundry room and a porch—that separate the living room from outside. They close the laundry room door behind them. I, half awake, assume that the friend is leaving. Suddenly, there is laughter. Heavy laughter. Gusts of laughter, muffled thumps, heavy breathing. A quiet pause. Then more laughter, thumps, breathing. I can hear this all clearly through the thin door. The two come back in after a while, flushed and smiling and breathing heavily, and take their places at the kitchen table, where the card game and hushed conversation continue. I concentrate on my reading, making as little noise as possible so as not to disturb the new sense of intimacy, and after a short while go on upstairs to make the ubiquitous journal notes and sleep.

It's well enough, appropriate somehow, that this exchange between women should exclude men; my own lesbian- and gay-positive attitude, not entirely relevant to this context in any event, will not cross this particular cultural border: the labels themselves do not serve well across the cultural boundary. But a laughter and a pleasure take place within the sphere of, though ultimately inaccessible to, my recording gaze or, more precisely in this event, recording earshot. And that is enough to remind me of the margin on the margin.

Not that the sexual is somehow a hidden truth of this social reality; equally not that the sexual in its multivarient forms is not an intimate aspect of this social reality; rather, the Aboriginal projects of Inuit and Dene women and men, 'straight' or not, are the primary moments of political resistance in northern Canada, over-determining other important identifications on the political level, but not necessarily demanding an erasure of those identifications. This is, in part, the sense in which alterity can remain within the fused group.

LOST HIS CANOE

I own a painting, which I purchased during one of my earliest trips to the NWT, by Dene (Dogrib) artist Archie Beaulieu called *Lost His Canoe*. In his typical, neo-Algonkian style, the painting centres on the head of a man, eyes wide open in horror or pain or anguish or confusion. The body is fragmented, split and distorted into lines that are being swept away with the current of some river. This one figure comprises the whole painting: an image of a moment, of a central character in the process of being decentred. It is a powerful image, enough to induce me in my graduate student days (during which I had moved from the real poverty of my childhood to the new and relatively interesting poverty of graduate school) to buy, for the first time, a piece of original art.

At the time, and still, the painting evoked first anguish and confusion: lost his canoe equalling lost his bearings, adrift and floundering in a river of alcoholism on an individual register and, on a cultural register, lost his culture, his background, his meaning. It is a painting of a certain kind of pain. The central figure's eyes convey some sense of realization just at the moment of loss that loss has come. The eyes are alive, burning with the intensity of that loss. This is not a painting of the monotony of despair, the day-to-day repetition and soul-destroying boredom of the dispossessed. It is, rather, the dramatic realization of loss in its moment, the moment that the self is almost washed away, but some core of self is left to the awareness that it is about to disappear. Lost his canoe.

If any portion of the argument that I have constructed in this part can be accepted, it will be possible to comprehend at least the dimensions of the social trauma that Aboriginal peoples like Dene and Inuit have experienced. The trade for a few simple things that made good lives even better somehow unleashed an underlying dynamic that began to unravel an ancient social order. The aimlessness, family violence, alcoholism, the monotony of despair that comes with colonialism and dispossession, this has its own logic and, it is worth remembering, this logic is fed on by the comfortable: in Adorno's words, "the soullessness of those in the margins of civilization, forbidden self-determination by daily need, at once appealing and tormenting, becomes a phantasm of soul to the well-provided for, whom civilization has taught to be ashamed of the soul."[18] Hence, we have a whole genre of 'social science' literature in Canada that exploits trauma and pain, feeding on images of the most disempowered, and the names of Grassy Narrows, Good Hope, Shamattawa, Davis Inlet are inscribed in the living room conscience as places whose existence offers self-consolation and comfort: "Thank god I don't live there!" Other messages that might be deciphered, especially messages that threaten the stability of the established order, are conveniently elided: somewhere, another way of social being exists that remains at least residually and that is engaged at this moment in a life and death struggle to continue against a totalizing power and logic. In its existence it challenges the fundamental structures of the dominant way of being. The moment of that struggle, 'over there', calls 'here' in two ways: raising the question of our responsibility there while simultaneously throwing into question our way of social being here. Let the name of Grassy Narrows stand in for this dual message: portrayed in Anastasia Shkilnyk's well-known account *A Poison Stronger Than Love* as a place of deep despair, yet, in the last few years showing inspired courage in a struggle to regain control over its forests. Beaulieu's painting, at least, never once evokes what so many of the journalists and academics seem to take for granted: surrender. Lost his canoe.

The concept of individual genius is one of which historical materialists do well to be suspicious. It has always had problematic ramifications and, in the nineteenth century, in particular, served to underpin a series of patriarchal and elitist romanticisms within the logic of the dominant culture. To the extent that the concept has been institutionalized in the academy— much more than people suspect—it continues to perform these functions. Hence, one would like to place the concept 'in brackets' or, better, in the stockade of critical theory. However, the concept of genius may escape its prison if it works away from the individualist premises that have so long rendered it banal. One can think through the socially produced, unsigned texts of a culture and find material worked over through centuries, bearing the richest forms of knowledge and insight. The traces of the genius of culture may inspire as much as the best of the 'great' works of individual genius to which so many in Western culture find it necessary to genuflect, but since these traces are found in the sphere of everyday life, the quotidian, they are often ignored. Yet, the protocols of interpretation one brings to a canonical text would equally serve those who wish to listen to the languages of Aboriginal peoples. The genius of the north, then, though it circles around artists like Archie Beaulieu or filmmaker Zacharias Kunuk, sits on a stoop outside a rundown shack in some remote community, puffing placidly on a pipe; or mischievously yaps like a dog in the Northern store, causing quite a commotion among Qallunaat clerks.

Perhaps it is appropriate that those who have lost their canoe are among the few who are talking about *pimaatisiwin*. I first encountered the word or concept of pimaatisiwin in the Department of Native Studies at

University, which, at the time of this study, was my academic home. Every year at Trent, the Native Studies Department sponsored an annual elders' and traditional persons' gathering, a major event on our social, cultural, and academic calendars. In 1992 the theme of the gathering was "pimaa-tisiwin," a word or concept in the Anishinabe language that means something like "the good life" or "life to the fullest" or perhaps even "the way or path of the good life."

Now, the concepts of "life" and "good" have fallen into disrepute among particularly Marxist scholars, who have rightly argued that both have been deployed for a long time in Western philosophy as links in a chain of essentialist philosophical ideas whose ultimate implication is that everyone should remain satisfied with their 'place' in the socially established order. Curiously, though, no less rigorous a thinker than Gayatri Chakravorty Spivak poses the question "what is the good life?," "cooked on the hot plate in the hotel room" among a few others, as questions "not to produce knowledge about others, but to open yourself to an other's ethic."[19] Perhaps in that spirit, though in this other register or context, and especially among those who have lost their canoe, the concept of pimaatisiwin calls. In any event, the use of an Anishinabe concept to discuss Inuit and Dene social reality is likely more appropriate than the many terms I have already deployed from non-Native social theory.

As it turns out, the concept has a venerable lineage in scholarship and, of course, an even more venerable lineage for Anishinabe. J. Irving Hallowell, one of most important ethnographers of Anishinabe, gave prominence to the concept in his writings: "the central goal of life for the Ojibwa is expressed by the term pimadaziwin, life in the fullest sense, life in the sense of longevity, health and freedom from misfortune."[20] Pimaa-tisiwin does not simply imply an accumulation of 'good' things for the self, but also an ethic of goodness: "there were moral responsibilities which had to be assumed by an individual if [she or] he strove for pimadaziwin" and, Hallowell goes on to note, "it was as essential to maintain approved standards of personal and social conduct as it was to obtain power from the 'grandfathers' because, in the nature of things, one's own conduct, as well as that of other 'persons', was always a potential threat to the achievement of pimadaziwin."[21] In a more recent analysis of Aboriginal environmental-ism, Winona LaDuke has reminded us of—and confirmed—the impor-tance of pimaatisiwin, writing: "Minobimaatisiiwin or the 'good life' is the basic objective of the Anishinabeg and Cree people who have historically, and to this day, occupied a great portion of the north-central region of the North American continent. An alternative interpretation of the word is 'continuous birth'.[22] LaDuke argues that "cyclical thinking" and "reciprocal relations" are "essential to this concept" and "implicit in the concept of Minobimaatisiiwin is a continuous inhabitation of place, an intimate understanding of the relationship between humans and the ecosystem, and the need to maintain that balance."[23] This echoes Frank T'Seleie's words and the discussion of justice with which we opened this chapter. A recent book by Naomi Adelson, called *Being Alive Well*, examines the concept in relation to Cree and issues of community and individual healing.

Clearly, this is a word/concept ripe for commodification. The T-shirt I wear from the 1992 elders' gathering evoked a lot of admiration and commentary when I wore it in one of the major Indian art and culture centres in Albuquerque. New Agers will undoubtedly get excited about the idea. And yet.

Michael Taussig has written, following Henry Munn, "that the sick man, despondent, unsure of himself, decaying in sadness, and almost willfully entering into the realm of death has only one option if he has but the courage to seize it: to become a healer himself." In this sense, there is a direct line from 'lost his canoe' to pimaatisiwin, the line of the logic of pain.

> The cure is to become a curer. In being healed he is also becoming a healer. In becoming one the option is whether he will succumb to the encroachment of death subsequent to soul loss, or whether he will allow the sickness-causing trauma and the healer's ministrations to reweave the creative forces in his personality and life experience into a force that bestows life upon himself and upon others through that bestowal.[24]

Pimaatisiwin resonates with this: both moral force and pleasure principle, an overturning of the injunction that moral goodness involves repression or that pleasure need necessarily be sought in transgression or in the abandonment of an ethical project.

In times of radical injustice, such as the present, it is impossible to live the good life. Those who retire to their comforts, leaving the world in its distress, perhaps guarding themselves with an armour of cynicism to make their choice, if not palatable, at least fashionable, can barely be distinguished from the most self-involved hedonists. Those who devote themselves in the struggle for social justice find their labours reaching towards an ever-extending horizon, their ability to achieve meaningful or lasting success ever waning, their opportunities for self-nourishment increasingly rare. Against these impossibilities a demand: social being must find a way through this labyrinth.

For a politics of pimaatisiwin.

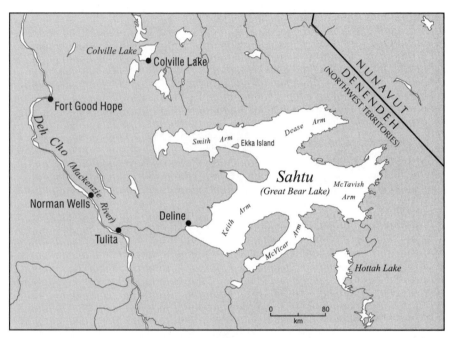

The Sahtu region.

The flats at Fort Simpson, site of the Papal visit, overlooking the juncture of the Laird and the Deh Cho (Mackenzie) rivers.

Treaty Day in Fort Simpson.

View of downtown Yellowknife from Pilot's Mound.

Folk on the Rocks festival, Yellowknife, 1985.

Deline on Sahtu (Fort Franklin on Great Bear Lake).

Dene Summer Games in the field/commons at Fort Good Hope (photo: E. Fajber).

Tea boiling at the Dene Summer Games in Fort Good Hope (photo: E. Fajber).

The Fort Good Hope band office and community hall.

Fort Good Hope.

Drying fish on the Deh Cho near Fort Good Hope (photo: E. Fajber).

The Ramparts at Fort Good Hope from the Deh Cho.

The Ramparts at Fort Good Hope.

Colville Lake from the airstrip, 1985.

View of Colville Lake showing the church and fishing lodge.

The graveyard at Iqaluit, Nunavut.

The airstrip that divides "downtown" from "uptown" in Panniqtuuq.

Panniqtuuq.

The Pangnirtung Inuit Co-op.

The Pangnirtung radio station.

View from Panniqtuuq across the Pangnirtung Fiord to the Kulik River.

Looking south from the north end of the Pangnirtung Fiord at the entrance to
Auyuittuq National Park.

A successful seal hunt near Pangnirtung.

A small rest break from fishing and seal hunting near Avataqtu on Cumberland Sound.

View of Pangnirtung Pass in Auyuittuq National Park near the Mount Thor emergency shelter.

PART TWO

CONCERNING THE
COMING COMMUNITY

Each country thinks that the universal vices and evils of men and society are peculiar to itself. I hear the same complaints wherever I go: the women here are vain and fickle, they read little and are poorly educated; the people here are gossipy and backbiting, always nosing into other people's business; here money, favours, and cowardice count; here envy reigns and friendships are hardly sincere, and so forth. As if things were any different elsewhere. Men are miserable by necessity, yet determined to think themselves miserable by accident.

—Giacomo Leopardi, *Pensieri*

CHAPTER THREE

the long road from fort simpson to liidli koe

In his *Shamanism, Colonialism, and the Wild Man*, Michael Taussig includes a chapter called "On the Indian's Back: The Moral Topography of the Andes and Its Conquest." In that chapter, Taussig is interested in "the way men interpret history and recruit landscape to that task" (287). The landscape he is interested in, of Andean mountains and jungles, was suited to an imperialist moral vision of salvation and descent, good and evil. At the end of the chapter, Taussig writes:

> To imbue a landscape with moral and even redemptive significance is for most of us nothing more than romantic fantasy. But there are occasions when to travel through a landscape is to become empowered by raising its meaning. Carried along a line in space, the traveller travels a story, the line gathering the momentum of the power of fiction as the arrow of time moves across a motionless mosaic of space out of time, here primeval and divine. (335)

At the risk of decaying into "romantic fantasy," it is nevertheless impossible not to say something about the landscape that situates each of the three communities of this study. The concept of "moral topography" at least has the benefit of constantly reminding us that these descriptions have nothing natural about them, are imbued with the powers of narrative. The concept invites reflection on the manner in which a community marks its relation to the landscape in which it is situated. The specific landscape of Fort Simpson allows thinking about it or, rather, thinking it in terms of its particular moral topography.

Fort Simpson is situated at the juncture of two rivers, the Naechag'ah (Liard) and Deh Cho (Mackenzie). Rivers are powerful metaphors, the coming together of rivers perhaps doubly powerful. The Deh Cho is itself the lifeblood, the heartbeat, of many Dene. In the Slavey language, "deh" means "river," "cho" means "mighty" or "great" or "large"; this, at least, is the most common interpretation of Deh Cho. "Dene" itself means "people"—children, women, men, and elders—or "us people," or perhaps even "people of the land." Denendeh brings all these together, focussed on the repeated 'de' vocable: land of the people of the river, people of the land of the river, river of the people of the land: the meanings circle each other, surround each other, repeat each other, reflect each other. Like the sound of a drum. Like the dance it inspires.

The river, in Dene history, ties people together. Materially, it provides a transportation link even today for the communities situated along its banks or the banks of rivers and lakes that run into it. The Deh Cho carries everything away—silt and water, life and dreams—into a distant arctic ocean. The river remains unbridged, a reminder of a force beyond human force, a reminder that human reality has not overcome all obstacles. Once a year, every spring, the river comes to life in dramatic fashion, called "breakup," where enormous chunks of ice crash and thunder and split in the frenetic, explosive tearing apart that leads to renewal.

This specific part of the Deh Cho is one of its most important junctions. Other mighty rivers, the Begade (Keele), the Sahtu De (Bear), the Teetl'it Gwinjik (Peel), flow into the Deh Cho. And the Nahedeh (Nahanni) flows into the Naechag'ah, and, at the present site of Fort Simpson, the Naechag'ah flows into the Deh Cho. "Nahe," meaning "powerful" in both a material and spiritual sense. Nahendeh is another name for the region, used by the territorial government as a voting district. A spiritually powerful land of rivers. Naechag'ah is one of the strongest rivers to be swept up in the path of the Deh Cho.

Traditionally, even the tourists are told, this site was a gathering place for Dene. A coming together place: rivers and people. A sacred place.

The site does not have the drama of cliffs and mountains; for that drama you have to go far upriver, up Naechag'ah, up Nahedeh, to one of the mightiest waterfalls in the world: Virginia Falls, a suitable place to contemplate the mysterious power of the Kantian sublime. At Fort Simpson, the Deh Cho does not inspire an instant sense of drama. When I first saw it, I was not impressed and therefore disappointed: two big, sluggish, rivers coming together: each so wide that the power is dispersed, too big to grasp. On Nahedeh, a much smaller river, you can feel the pulse that is its power, you can not forget it. Deh Cho's pulse is so huge that it's muffled, like thunder in the distance.

I have my own stories of the Deh Cho. Dene spiritual beliefs are intimately tied to, and are an enactment of, their close relationship to their land. Among the spiritual activities that I have seen Dene practise are separate ceremonies involving 'feeding' or 'paying' the land, the river, and the fire. The land needs to be fed or paid, particularly by strangers, who can make small bundles of twigs tied together with string or yarn or other small offerings to express their gratitude and ensure that they will not offer offense. Sacred fires will be lit during assemblies or other special occasions and these will be fed with portions of feast food and tobacco. Feeding or paying the water is important for those who will undertake a journey by boat, where an offering of some tobacco or twigs or branches to the water, with prayers, helps to ensure safety and good travel.

I have my own stories of the Deh Cho. Stories of travel, of camping, of fishing, of hunting moose, caribou, beaver, of picking mushrooms and berries, of sitting with friends beneath the high banks, telling stories. I have travelled on the Deh Cho in small boats with outboard motors, on ferries, in jet boats, by canoe, and along its high banks on foot. The Deh Cho has nourished me, brought me food and friendship, given me passage through great lands and strong, vibrant Dene communities. I have my own stories of the Deh Cho.

The Deh Cho appears in many of the stories people in the area tell. One elder, Leo Norwegian, told us a tall tale as we chatted outside the band office on a hot, dry, summer day. We were talking about the last winter, which had been cold. He reminisced about the coldest winter he had experienced, in the late forties, when it reached seventy-eight below zero. He told several stories that stretched imagination, of crows that froze to death and moose with frozen ears. Then he said, that time, you could hear someone all the way across the river as if they were right next to you, "just like that," he said, gesturing a few feet away, his eyes twinkling. The image resonates, a peculiarly Dene image, of speech and of a river: to be able to talk across the mighty Deh Cho.

After some time, after experiences and stories, after sitting on the banks and talking to Jonas Antoine and many others, after being drawn again and again to the point that overlooks the coming together of these rivers, after walking and running along the high banks, some of the power of the place, of its magnificence, pulsed in me. With friends or alone I have walked along Deh Cho in the early hours and watched the sunset blend into the dawn at this place where people and rivers come together. The moral topography here speaks simultaneously to coming together and being swept along; it speaks to underlying forces and currents of unimaginable strength and to the surface that belies those currents; it speaks to cycles and repetitions; it speaks to the everyday banality and to the moment of extraordinary explosive, irruptive power.

Dene and Métis in Fort Simpson emphasized to me that non-Natives (called Mola by Dene) and Dene/Métis would have to work together. Like two rivers. A moral topography. The question is which river would be swept up and which would carry the other along.

LOCAL HISTORIES

Fort Simpson embodies the history of its region and is an historical site of a particular sort; the lines of history also come together at this juncture. Not least, there is the history of the books and the history of the people, two other rivers. The history of the books, the 'official story', compiled by officials, tells part of the story; the history of the people, circulated in stories constructed from memories, tells quite another. They are different histories, antinomies rather than contradictions; they tell different stories. What matters to the official historians—origin dates, narratives of progress and its occasional interruptions—matters remarkably little to the people. The official story presents itself as 'truth': a narrative that leaves nothing important out, self-contained, fixed around objective points, dates, and numbers; a total history appropriate to a totalizing historical project. The people's history presents itself as this or that story, not linked to each other, with no concern for finding a way of putting them all together, as if that would somehow tell the 'whole' story. When you ask the history books the origin of Fort Simpson, you get the beginning of a narrative that reaches back to the eighteenth century. In the minds of the people, the community as it exists now has a much more recent origin.

In the official story, where colonialism is presented as progress, Fort Simpson was established in the early 1800s as the first fur trading post on the Mackenzie River. It was named Fort Simpson after Sir George Simpson, the first governor of the newly merged (1821) North West and Hudson's Bay fur trading companies, and a dominant figure in the fur trade history for the first half of the nineteenth century. Fort Simpson was thus built in that extraordinary period of fur trade competition that took place between about 1763 (at the end of the Seven Years War) and 1821, when the two companies leapfrogged each other in bids to establish the furthest hinterland post, closest to the direct producers of beaver fur and the richest fur trade grounds, pushing the fur trade far into the Canadian northwest. Fort Simpson was a North West Company post, built after North West Company trader Alexander Mackenzie made his 'historic' 1789 trip up the river to which non-Natives (and their maps) have given his name.

The unofficial story tells us that the people used to live on 'the flats', the part of the community right at the juncture of the rivers, below the high banks that run along the Deh Cho. This is where they gathered in ancient times, meeting every spring to share stories and gifts, to celebrate, find marriage partners, argue, feast, make music, gamble at hand games, and dance. The flats are perfect campgrounds, easy to get to from the river, still on the banks of the clearer Naechag'ah. When people began to settle permanently in the community, they built their homes there. The fur trading post stood on the high ground, befitting a non-Native cultural logic organized around the domination of nature, in spite of the relative impracticality of this location (water having had to be brought uphill). In the early sixties the Deh Cho overflowed, there was a flood; the flats had to be evacuated, people's homes were destroyed. The flats, which had been a perfect campground for nomadic hunters, proved not nearly so suitable for a permanent settlement. The community was rebuilt higher up, on the banks of the Deh Cho. By then, the non-Natives had occupied most of the prime, riverfront property. And the community would not be reconstructed in material terms that corresponded to Dene views of community: for example, cabins circling a commons, or in a semicircle facing the river.

A different kind of place came into being just above the flats, leaving the latter space empty, a constant reminder of what had been. This community of straight streets at right angles to each other, where access to the river was impeded by Mola ownership of the strip of land along the riverbank, was designed in a manner that turned away from its own landscape in a peculiar fashion.

TAKING THE TREATY

The difference between the official story and the people's story is most dramatically staged, and has its most important implications, in the story of the treaty. The difference between literal readings of treaty, involving interpretations of the treaties based on documents associated with treaty, and readings of treaty based on the 'spirit of the treaty' adduced from the oral accounts of elders, remains a key theme in Canadian Aboriginal politics generally. The treaty signing in Fort Simpson was a very specific event that did not follow the pattern even of many of the other signings of the same treaty, Treaty 11, along the Deh Cho that summer of 1921.

Rene Fumoleau's *As Long as This Land Shall Last* reproduces both versions. Fumoleau quotes Treaty Commissioner Henry A. Conroy on the treaty negotiations. It should be noted that Conroy had been given a treaty prepared in Ottawa prior to meeting any of the Dene; it was his job to get the Dene to sign this treaty. Calling the meetings "negotiations" in this context could be something of a misnomer, except for the fact that the Dene viewed the process as one of negotiation, and attempted to secure conditions that were not dealt with in the written treaty. In Dene views, the treaty consists of these oral promises as much as the written documents. Conroy and his treaty party, which included the Catholic Bishop Breynat, Royal Canadian Mounted Police Inspector Bruce, and translators, had already 'taken treaty' at Fort Providence, and reached Fort Simpson on July 8, 1921.

Conroy's account glosses over treaty negotiations. As quoted by Fumoleau, Conroy wrote of Fort Simpson in a letter to the Superintendent General of Indian Affairs that

> we found nearly all the Indians awaiting our arrival. At first the Indians at this point were nearly unanimous in their decision to let 'well enough' alone and remain in the condition in which they had

been heretofore, but after several talks and explanations, they all entered into Treaty, and elected their chief and headmen entirely to the satisfaction of myself, the Agent and all the white inhabitants, whose opinions count for anything.[1]

Treaty negotiations lasted three days. Fumoleau writes: "There was a problem little discussed on Sunday, July 10. The chief who had been chosen for Treaty negotiations was Joseph Norwegian, but he 'wouldn't agree because he wasn't too sure what would be the outcome of the treaty.' When Joseph went away for lunch, Old Antoine was designated as chief, signed the Treaty and received his Treaty money" (174). Bishop Breynat noted many years later that "I may say that I am responsible for the treaty having been signed at several places, especially at Fort Simpson" (173).

In 1973 the Indian Brotherhood of the Northwest Territories filed a caveat with the land registrar of the territory, arguing that their title had not been extinguished by treaties 8 and 11, and therefore they still had a claim to ownership. The land registrar turned their application over to the courts and Justice Morrow held a judicial inquiry into the legitimacy of the caveat, ultimately ruling in favour of the Dene. Part of the inquiry involved soliciting testimony from elders who had been present as adults or teenagers at treaty negotiations and could still remember the events. One of these was Louis Norwegian from Jean Marie River, for many years a sub-band of Fort Simpson. Norwegian's testimony is worth quoting at length.

> My grandfather, the old Norwegian, is the one who tried—the Fort Simpson band tried to make a leader out of him or a chief out of him, and he was the one who was speaking for all the Indians at Fort Simpson. Every time they wanted to give money, the grandfather who was supposed to be chief, he did not want to take the money for no reason at all.
>
> [. . .]
>
> I remember that they have meetings to try to pay the treaty, and the Commissioner who paid the treaty tried to make the Indian leader take the treaty first, and they had a meeting for three days, so my grandfather did not want to take the money until he wants to be sure what it is all about, and my grandfather told me, 'I am not going to give any money for nothing, and five dollars means a lot, and we want to find out, and why do we take the treaty, so we

did not want to take the treaty right away'. And they mentioned this to my grandfather, that he knows the sun rises in the east and sets in the west, and the Mackenzie River flows, and what I will have to promise have been said by the treaty date, and as long as the words exist, whatever the Commissioner told the Indians, the word would never be broken. My grandfather wants to know why they have to take that money from the people, and the Commissioner told him that the treaty is going to be developed in future years, that there would be lots of white people and if the Indians took the money they may be registered, and if there is enough white people in the country, the government will know wherever the individual Indian is going to be, and that is all the treaty amounts to.... [...] What happened is that they had a 3-day meeting and they have something to eat and when they went home and got supper there was one Indian Antoine was left behind, and they said there was no harm in taking the treaty, so the old man took the treaty. He was not elected, and that is what happened.[2]

Conroy's account stresses that the Dene in Fort Simpson "elected their chief and headmen entirely to the satisfaction of myself, the Agent and all the white inhabitants, whose opinions count for anything," significantly leaving out whether the election was 'entirely to the satisfaction' of the Dene who were to be represented.

Although the Dene accounts of treaty signing in Fort Simpson point to a certain illegitimacy of the treaty—specifically the fact that it was signed by an individual who was not the genuine representative of the people—nevertheless the sanctity of the treaty and its status as a symbolic representation of solemn promises not to interfere with Dene life ways, guaranteeing the continuance of those ways for as long as the "sun rises in the east and sets in the west, and the Mackenzie River flows," remains a crucial basis of Dene politics in the Dehcho region. That is, Dene in Fort Simpson do not want to argue that the treaty was a fraud and should be torn up. Rather, they want their understanding of the treaty, a treaty of peace and coexistence, respected. A concern to maintain the sanctity and integrity of the treaty was one of the reasons that many Fort Simpson Dene challenged the comprehensive land claim Agreement in Principle that had been negotiated in 1990. To understand this, we need to understand the particular circumstances of the community today.

THE ROAD TO FORT SIMPSON

Fort Simpson's geopolitical status in the northwestern fur trade made it one of the early centres of the north. That means it has had a long history of comparatively long occupation by non-Natives. This occupation was given an enormous boost in the late sixties, when construction of the Mackenzie Highway connected Fort Simpson to southern Canada. Among the impacts traced to the highway were increased social problems associated with increased access to drugs and alcohol. The community had also had a large experimental garden and served as a food supplier to many communities along the river. The road made southern produce available more cheaply and ended the life of the garden.

The road has had an extraordinary political importance to Fort Simpson and has led to a defining structure of the band's position: the population of Fort Simpson, about 1200 people, is mixed. Most of the community is Dene or Métis (mostly Dene, at about a five to one ratio) but about forty per cent of the people are non-Native. Fort Simpson has to cope with 'the fact' of non-Native presence in a way few other small northern communities have had to. This distinguishes it from Fort Good Hope and Panniqtuuq, as well, neither of which is connected to southern Canada by an all-season road. The physical structure of Fort Simpson reflects this fact.

The highway sweeps down a hill, crosses a bridge that connects the island Fort Simpson is on to the mainland, and promptly turns into the main street, on which are the main grocery stores, two hotels, gas station, other stores and offices, and off which run neat streets of suburban-style row housing. Fort Simpson looks more like a suburb than any of the more isolated Dene communities, which have an architectural logic all their own. There is even something of a suburban grid, with '102nd Street' and so on. The highway that turns into a main street is a given in most prairie towns in Canada. You cannot see the river from the main street in Fort Simpson; at least, not until the road passes through town and meanders along the last few houses, merging with the street that runs along the banks of the Deh Cho. Along that street are a few government buildings and a row of decidedly suburban homes, most of which are owned or lived in by prominent non-Natives in or from the community, and many government employees.

The two streets merge and trickle along into the bush until they come to an abrupt halt, near the north end of the island.

In order to 'escape' the community, which was seen as rife with social problems, and to accommodate growth, two satellite communities emerged. One, called Four Mile, is on the Naechag'ah, and looks something more like a more northerly community: less organized on a row-housing model, opening up on to the river, constantly 'speaking' the river in its physical structure, only partly connected by service infrastructure. The other, Three Mile or Wild Rose Estates, is well off the river in a fairly densely wooded area, but better serviced in terms of the amenities available.

At the south end of the island, off to the right of the road just after the bridge that leads in to town, are the flats: a large field that now bears a huge wooden teepee, a concrete sculpture, a large cross, a partially enclosed meeting place, and a baseball diamond. This is the area where Treaty Days and other important events marked by feasts or drum dances might be held in summer, and where Pope John Paul II delivered a papal address and blessing to the Aboriginal people of Canada in the summer of 1988.

HIS HOLINESS

Fort Simpson was chosen as a site for the papal visit, during the papal tour of 1985, where His Holiness could make a statement to Aboriginal Canadians. Fort Simpson was appropriate for many reasons. It was a traditional gathering place and a sacred site, where two mighty rivers flowed together. There was the factor that the community had some infrastructure, open ground, organizational abilities, and northern 'hospitality'. It was in the north, and therefore relatively accessible to the northern Aboriginal peoples who might otherwise feel excluded, given that the pope was speaking in a number of southern Canadian centres. And it was accessible to southern Aboriginal peoples, because of the road.

The 1985 visit never happened; a fog appeared and made it impossible for the pope's airplane to land, hence the need for a return visit duly held a few years later. Thousands of people were expected for the visit, but no one knew exactly how many would actually come. To meet the need, among other things, a long chain of outdoor toilets was set up on the flats. Many of these remained during my visits in the early nineties, and were another part of the material text or legacy of the visit, which led to the construction of the teepee, the concrete sculpture with four Dene drums circling the earth, and the large wooden cross. People refer to the remaining outdoor toilets affectionately as the "vati-cans."

GESTURES I: THE OPEN DOOR

In spite of the road to Fort Simpson and the degree of suburban-style design in its physical structure, it is possible to find daily practices that are not the norm in southern Canada. One of these could be called "the open door," an attitude that exists in each of the communities discussed, including the Dene/Métis part of Fort Simpson. Briefly put, the protocol when visiting is not to knock at the door and wait for someone to come and answer, but rather to walk right in and call out to see if anyone is home. If no one is home, or answers, one can leave, or settle down in a chair to watch television or rest and wait. There is no doubt that the exigencies of winter make such an approach to visiting more practicable: why leave your guests waiting outside in the cold as you rush to turn down the stove, put the baby in a safe place, turn down the radio, and finally get to the door and your near frozen prospective guest? And, if one is not home, one's prospective guests—friends and relatives—will likely need warming before they venture the return journey. As a guest, why tax your host with the demand that they interrupt their card games or cooking or conversation or television watching to come and open the door for you, something you are perfectly capable of doing yourself? In fact, the open door attitude is so prevalent that knocking and waiting outside instantly mark the visitor as a non-Native, likely an agent of State surveillance: social worker or police.

These gestures, these habits of everyday life, are worth far more careful reading than the monuments and canonical texts of dead cultures. They inscribe traces of the genius of a culture that continues to thrive in radically new material circumstances. Of particular concern here are those traces, such as the open door, that point in the direction of community, that work towards the establishment and the continuance of forms of social being that stress the community over the individual. The open door as a feature of everyday community life—practised unconsciously as a norm of social existence—represents, evokes, and embodies a value that has been almost entirely erased from the dominant culture, a value exiled with such a totalizing ruthlessness from metropolitan life that its continued existence in this distant context comes as something of a shock that paralyzes many who reach its threshold. This value, foundational to any project of community that deserves the name, is sometimes called "trust."

The gesture of the open door, as in the case of other gestures to be discussed in other chapters, can be read to mark an aspect of Aboriginal community life largely absent from non-Native social centres: a certain kind of socially generated trust. This trust has material preconditions and survives because of these. In the first instance, the distribution of wealth is not so great at the community level that there are enormous disparities. Hence, although petty theft can be a problem, it has not been a problem to such an extent that it has caused most people to lock up. More importantly, the singular fact of Aboriginal community life is that the inhabitants know— on the level of implicit social knowledge—that they will live together for the rest of their lives, and that their descendants will likewise very likely live together. Although living close together in permanent communities is a practice that developed with colonialism, the precondition of extensive contact with particular people over long periods of time likely structured earlier social relations. The structural precondition of most Mola communities is that the likelihood of living one's whole life in one place is slim, the likelihood of one's descendants living in the same place even more remote. While in a community like Fort Simpson the Mola might be fair game, stealing something significant or valuable from another Dene or Métis involves a social rupture that will remain, possibly for generations. It is easier not to worry about locks, not to tax your guest with waiting, not to tax your host with answering, but rather to leave the door open.

THE ELECTORAL BAND COUNCIL SYSTEM

The particular historical circumstances of Fort Simpson have given rise to the political structures that govern the band at the local level. Although Treaty 11 promised that "His Majesty the King hereby agrees and undertakes to lay aside reserves for each band, the same not to exceed in all one square mile for each family of five, or in that proportion for larger or smaller families," a reserve was not established for Fort Simpson Dene, or for most of the Dene in the NWT. In large measure, this had to do with the fact that Dene did not believe they were extinguishing their title to land when they signed the treaties and the Indian Agents knew quite well they would resist being confined to reserves. Historian Kerry Abel quotes Catholic Bishop Breynat as stating, in the late 1940s, that the Dene "conception of a Reserve was to be placed in a kind of Fort with walls around it!"[3] The non-establishment of reserves became one of the reasons why the federal government agreed to negotiate comprehensive land claims with Dene in the seventies.

However, as a direct result of the treaties, other provisions of the Indian Act were implemented, including the band council electoral system. The Indian Act itself had been modelled on pre-Confederation legislation developed for the specific circumstances that prevailed in Upper and Lower Canada in the mid-nineteenth century. A Civilisation Act of 1858 had become, with Confederation, an Enfranchisement Act in 1869, evolving into the Indian Act of 1876. This had been revised numerous times, including the addition in 1884 of the band council electoral system. Although this latter aspect of the Act had been justified as a measure to introduce Indians to 'democracy', as the provisions evolved it became clear that they were being adapted and deployed by Indian Agents to undercut the influence of traditional leaders, particularly the well-established matriarchal governing structure of Iroquoian nations. By the 1920s, the band council electoral system was well established, though important modifications took place in 1951.

Effectively, the system allows for the election of chiefs and councillors, though the Indian Act to this day reads that the process is initiated by the federal government: "whenever he deems it advisable to the good government of a band, the Minister may declare by order that . . . a chief and councillors, shall be selected by elections to be held in accordance with this Act."[4] Hence, the band electoral system imposed a single political structure on the diverse cultures of Canadian Indians. Only Indians recognized as such, that is, having 'status' as defined by the Indian Act, can participate in the band council electoral system as voters or politicians. Until 1951 Indian women could not vote or run for office. The Indian Act specifies that "the council of a band . . . shall consist of one chief, and one councillor for every one hundred members of the band, but the number of councillors shall not be less than two nor more than twelve and no band shall have more than one chief."[5] Powers of band councils, which "may make by-laws not inconsistent with this Act or with any regulation made by the Governor in Council or the Minister," are specified in section 81 and range from "(c) the observance of law and order" to "(j) the destruction and control of noxious weeds," though in general the powers are municipal-like. Band council resolutions are known colloquially as "BCRs." Section 82 states that bylaws have to be forwarded to the minister within four days of being passed, and come into effect forty days after that, "unless it is disallowed by the Minister within that period."

This structure shows clear limitations as a model for local governance. The most striking limitations are in the form of governance—a model based on representational democracy that determines the size and scope of councils—and in the overarching authority of the federal government. The project of Aboriginal self-government in many southern jurisdictions involves, as a crucial component, rewriting these sections of the Indian Act to give band councils more powers and to allow them to adopt forms more appropriate to the specific cultures and traditions of each First Nation. Fort Simpson is in the unusual position of having a band council elected on the model of the Indian Act, but having no reserve. Management of reserve lands is a preoccupation with many band councils. Interestingly, the electoral band system allowed communities like Fort Simpson to simply elect 'traditional' leaders, who formally functioned in a very minimal way, usually present at Treaty Day and sometimes intervening in an informal way in the administration of justice. These individuals were recognized as community leaders, though, and often exerted a strong moral influence locally. Through the sixties and seventies across the western Arctic, and in Fort Simpson, band councils became much more formal, establishing offices and taking responsibility in a whole series of areas—housing being one of the most crucial—as a new generation of younger, more activist leaders took over. The band council in Fort Simpson, in form, follows the guidelines of the Indian Act—no one I talked to, for example, seemed to question the fact that there would be a specified number of councillors or thought of increasing the number as a step towards a more representative structure—but in action rarely limits itself to the areas specified. It acts, broadly speaking, as a political voice of the Dene of Fort Simpson and is engaged in and concerned with a whole range of activities that likely fall outside its official scope.

POLITICS ACROSS THE PRIVATE AND PUBLIC

The rigid distinction between public and private that informs so much of political life in liberal democracies, or rather, is a critical and often shifting terrain of struggle in the dominant order as 'left' and 'right' attempt to articulate very different visions of what properly belongs to each sphere—has a markedly different inflection in small northern communities. This was made clear to me in two interviews with Bertha Norwegian, one in Fort Simpson in 1993 and the other in the nearby community of Kakisa in 1994. Bertha was born and raised in Simpson, and had worked in the early nineties as a staff person for the band before moving on to a new job in the territorial government as an advisor to the minister responsible for the Status of Women. Bertha emphasized that "basically I think that the women are stronger, when you look at the overall population" in Fort Simpson. She insisted there was a powerful core of women leaders in the community.

> I think that the women seem to have a better sense of what self-government is all about. I think that, well, women have, basically a lot of women run or take care of their household, whether they are single parents or are married. They're the homemakers, financial breadwinners, they're the ones that hold the good jobs, basically they're the ones that have more control than the husbands.

Women occupy many of the office jobs in a community where other wage-labour opportunities are quite restricted, while, in Bertha's view, "the men are, they love to go out on the land. I mean the women do too, [but] the aspect of going out on the land is better for the men than for the women." For whatever reason, it seems clear that there was a strong group of women who were not involved at that time in the band council structure, though "a lot of them are keeping their own families together. A lot of them are involved in different community organizations: the Friendship Centre, the Housing Authority, or whatever." These community organizations form a critical aspect of the local political dynamic and provide alternative structures particularly for women to make their views heard.

Rather than calling these an "informal" political sector, in opposition to the band and municipal councils, designated as the "formal" political sector, in my view these bodies are an integral aspect of the overall political dynamic, and many influential women in the community gravitate towards this aspect of the dynamic rather than to the band council. This may be because, in Bertha's view, the women have their own agenda of concerns. In our conversation in 1994, she said, "Well, I think that a lot of the issues [of concern to women] have to do with social issues, such as family violence or that women and children have to leave that environment and go into a safe home rather than the men going into some kind of program." The community organizations tend to be more directly concerned with dealing with social problems and issues of concern to women.

Certainly, there was some criticism of the band council in this regard: "Anytime women have concerns and bring it to the council they're just kind of brushed off. The council isn't addressing women's issues." However, in our conversation in 1993, Bertha had noted with approval the more recent participation of women on the council:

> It's really good to see [more women on the band council now] because ... like there's an elder woman who's a band councillor ... who you wouldn't expect to say a whole lot at the meetings and yet when there's something really crucial that comes up that needs a good decision, you know, she just does it, you know, she doesn't agree with it, she gives her reason why she doesn't agree, and why it's the way it is, and it's too bad it's that way if they don't like the response.

One of the more telling examples Bertha used was her own application for a house. It is worth noting that the housing issue is particularly crucial across the country; it was over this issue that women like Yvonne Bedard struggled in the early seventies against the sex-discrimination provisions of the Indian Act. The written discriminatory provisions in the Act concerning the issue of Indian status themselves marked or outlined much broader discriminatory attitudes that developed, in part as a result of the legislated patriarchy. These are frequently displayed when it comes to the vexing local problem of housing:

> Like, for example, I applied for band land and I was flatly, absolutely refused without being given a reason. And the reason was that I was a woman—single!—why should I be entitled to band land. I'm a band member. And I said, at the time I was thirty-six years old, 'I'm thirty-six years old. I worked all my life. Why can't I have band land so I can build my own house or buy my own mobile home, whatever?' But I was refused and it took four months to get the band land and it was the men that refused me. They told me—[it was] last May, you know—there was no reason.

[I got it] just through persistence, you know, it's my treaty right to get the band land. And yet they gave the land to single men who hadn't even worked. I can only assume they didn't give me the land because I was a woman. The women on the council thought I should get it . . . .

In Fort Simpson, although women were in a minority on the band council, they still had a great deal of influence and any political leader would be unwise to do something that would anger the prominent female band members. Bertha's own story illustrates both the discriminatory attitudes of some of the male leaders, and her own ability to, with persistence, achieve her—in this case personal—goals. In each of the communities I studied, I found a collective of very strong, articulate women, most often not as a group running the local council, though in each case at least one member had a seat on council and could liaise with the rest, bringing the message back to council when "a good decision" is needed. This dynamic was certainly operative in Fort Simpson, where Lorayne Menicoche became band manager in 1994, Mary-Louise Norwegian remained on the council, and women like Ethyl Lamonthe, Bonnie Cli, Jean Lafferty, and many others have a great deal of influence. In Bertha's words, "there's a lot of really strong women that are not in the limelight." But, in effect, Bertha was predicting something that would become a reality a few years later, in 1997, when Rita Cli was elected chief in Fort Simpson.

MEETINGS, MEETINGS, MEETINGS

I attended four different kinds of meetings in the communities I visited. Small, informal meetings with individual staff members to work on specific programs or proposals were the most frequent and also the most similar to meetings I might attend in southern Canada. Band council meetings were more structured, formal affairs, whose logic was governed in part by the Indian Act and in part by Dene ways. Community assemblies were open community meetings that ran in what appeared to be a less structured manner. Regional (or the Dene) assemblies were highly structured, though discussions frequently went beyond structural parameters. The assemblies were occasions for formal speech, for highly nuanced rhetorical style.

Fort Simpson is a very politicized community. As well as a band council, there is a municipal council; the latter presents itself as the government of the whole community, though, in practice, it tends to represent the Mola (non-Dene) interests. The band council likewise sees itself as the legitimate government of the community. It is certainly the case that the band council will operate without consulting the municipal council, while the latter would only at great peril make a major decision without consulting the band council. Politics at the community level, nevertheless, have a great deal to do with the interaction between the two communities, Dene/Métis and Mola, as embodied in the two local governments, band and municipal. Local politics are more complex because of the presence of a Métis Nation local, a Native Women's Association branch, and other organizations, like the Friendship Centre. The community participates in electing a member of the Territorial Assembly for the Nahendeh riding and a member of parliament for the Western Arctic riding. The Nahendeh representatives have included Nick Sibbeston, a Métis who became a leader of government, and Jim Antoine, for many years chief of the local band. All this points to the high degree of politicization in the community. It is relatively easy for anyone who wants to be politically engaged to find an organizational outlet or to have friends or family involved in one or another of the organizations, and this, of course, is not withstanding the whole dimension of politics that takes place outside these structures.

The relations between Mola and Dene were staged for me during a band council meeting I sat in on in the summer of 1990. Other guests at the meeting were a local Mola businessman and a regional government official in charge of tourism. Interestingly, the government official did all the talking, speaking for the businessman, who was silent the whole time. In this context, it was clear whom government was serving. In his very first comments, to the effect that it was unnecessary for him to be asking the band for support, the official had probably unknowingly antagonized everyone in the room, tantamount to saying "you're not important, but I'll generously talk to you anyway!" He then explained that the businessman was applying for a licence to run boat tours on the river. This would enhance the tourist potential of the area, create jobs, and generally boost the local exchange value economy. The reason for coming to the meeting was to get band council support for the licence application, even though, the official hastened to stress, such support was technically not necessary. The official thought he was going out of his way to 'consult' with the band council, that he was presenting a proposal that was eminently desirable and uncontroversial, and perhaps even that he was building bridges to the Dene community. His discourse was liberal, friendly, helpful, sincere. The chief at the time was still Jim Antoine. Chief Antoine asked the official why Dene, who had lived on the land all their lives, could not get licences as tour guides. The official explained that territorial standards included ensuring that guides take a course or program in guiding. Chief Antoine pressed the issue, saying that people did not want to leave the community to take courses, and, after all, already knew the land better than anyone else; it was Dene who should be holding these jobs and taking advantage of tourist opportunities. As far as the official was concerned, this was "off topic," but he was willing to discuss the issue, explain the government's policy, and work to get more local community members into the proper courses. The band decided it would discuss the issue further and let the official know its decision. He shook hands all around and left with the businessman in tow. The latter never spoke. The discussion had taken about a half-hour. He left cheerily, with no sense that from his opening comments onwards, he had shown enormous disrespect. After he left, a councillor turned to me and said, "You see the kind of assholes we have to deal with." Bridges had not been built. The irony is that the federal government of Canada uses or deploys the image of Dene tour guides to promote itself and the north: an advertisement promoting Canadian tourism in *The New Yorker* magazine in the mid-eighties featured a two-page colour photograph of Sunblood Mountain in Nahanni National Park, with a smaller photograph in the upper left of "your friendly Dene guide."

In this context, the Dene community strategy is to seriously think through being together with the Mola. This may involve, in the words of the chief who followed Jim Antoine, Gerry Antoine (which he said to me when he was no longer chief, but vice-chief of the Dehcho Tribal Council, in an interview in May of 1993), "minding your own business." He argued that "that's probably an element of how people saw what the Treaty 11 is, is that, okay, there's gonna be non-Dene people here and we're gonna be minding our own business, and because of that there's a treaty, and we'll live the way we want to live and they'll live the way they want. That's how I'm beginning to understand what self-government is." Gerry Antoine described both the crucial element in the way many Dene see the spirit of the treaty—a promise to allow Dene to live as they had always lived—and the local strategy for self-government. Extinguishing Aboriginal title in a community like Fort Simpson would mean giving up any future leverage it might have on what would happen on public lands. Replacing certain parts of the treaty, which was also an aspect of the 1990 AIP, meant violating the integrity of the treaty and agreeing to see the treaty as this written, literally interpreted, document. Small wonder Fort Simpson was a vigorous opponent of the 1990 AIP.

BAND POLITICS

The Dene band in Fort Simpson is by no means a homogenous entity; it involves a complex of interests and perspectives. These tend to be organized around family lines. The families—Deneyoua, Menicoche, Antoine, Norwegian, Tetso, and so on—are roughly divided into 'upriver' and 'downriver' people, the Deh Cho again providing an organizing principle that reaches into the heart of the social. Through the years I worked and studied in Fort Simpson, there were three different chiefs, Jim Antoine, Gerry Antoine, and Herb Norwegian. Discussion of the leadership styles of each of these, whom I interviewed and worked with to a greater or lesser extent, will give a sense of the dynamic of community politics.

In 1985 I attended a drum dance held for Chief Jim Antoine, who was leaving the community to attend university in the south. From Marie Lafferty's house, I could hear the pulsing of the Dene hand drums across the school field and, drawn by that sound, joined others from the community and wandered towards the school gymnasium. There I found a packed hall and much of the community out to celebrate and honour their chief, who, still very much a young man, had made a great contribution to building the band council infrastructure. By then, Jim Antoine had a reputation as an articulate spokesperson and 'radical' Dene chief. He had been quoted in the Toronto *Globe and Mail*, threatening to "blow up" the pipeline that was built between 1983 and 1985 if community demands for jobs and environmental protection were not respected.

Antoine told me in an interview in 1994 that he had had no great desire or sense of mission that led him to become chief. He had been asked by community members immediately before a community meeting in the early seventies to run as chief. This meant standing in opposition to an older generation of chiefs, who had been more traditional but did not seem to be achieving anything for the community. He did not, in his view, so

much run for election as allow his name to stand and says he did not campaign or actively seek office in elections that followed. He let it be known
that he was interested in re-election, and people knew him and voted for
him, and he gained office. During his first tenure as chief, he struggled to
establish a band office and an effective community governance infrastructure for the Dene band. He was one of a very strong generation of new
Dene leaders, but, unlike many others, stayed focussed for many years on
community-level politics.

   He left office in the mid-eighties to pursue a university education
in the south and was followed for a short term as chief by his brother,
Gerry. Gerry Antoine followed his brother as chief twice, once in the
mid-eighties and once in the early nineties. He also followed a non-
campaign style during elections. After his first term as chief, he served
a difficult term as mayor of the community. In contrast to his brother,
who is a forceful speaker with clear agendas, Gerry Antoine is more philosophically inclined, modest, soft-spoken, carefully thinking through problems and issues. Jim Antoine returned from the south, was re-elected as
chief, helping in a few years to reopen the 1990 AIP, and then left local
politics, gaining election to the territorial government. At the 1992 Dene
Assembly, he was still making the transition from Dene to territorial politician; it was clear that he was much more comfortable speaking at Dene
assemblies or community gatherings than in the Territorial Assembly.
Gerry Antoine was elected for a second term, following his brother's resignation, which was interrupted when he, too, resigned after a few years
following a major internal, administrative conflict, which will be discussed
below.

   In the election that followed, Gerry Antoine ran again, using a non-
campaign style, and was opposed by Herb Norwegian, a long-time Dene
activist from the community, who had run in the early eighties for the
presidency of the Dene Nation. Herb Norwegian has more of a populist
orientation; he is a genial, positive, and active man whose conversational
refrain is "good stuff." Norwegian ran something more like a campaign,
going door to door and actually pulling his supporters out on voting day.
He won the election and served several consecutive terms as chief.

   It is important to note that these elections did not lead to deep-seated
resentments or divisions. All three men continued to work together
on issues for the community on a daily basis, and are more often allies

on these issues than opponents. It is equally important to note that in Fort Simpson, where a number of women are very influential politically, no woman had been chief until in the summer of 1997, when Herb Norwegian lost the office to a woman, Rita Cli.

In 1994 when I interviewed Jim Antoine, he was a member of the Territorial Assembly. I was curious about how he felt about the transition from often fighting the territorial government on behalf of his community to being an active participant at its highest decision-making level. He said that the rules of speech in the assembly were difficult for him to adapt to, having to address people as "the honourable this" and "the honourable that," as he put it. As well, keeping speeches within allotted time frames was difficult for someone trained in a social climate where high rhetoric is practised in its most refined forms and it often takes an individual five or ten minutes simply to warm up to a subject—that being often the full time allotted for a question or statement in the assembly. He had had to make an oath to the Queen in order to take his seat. He told me, "read the oath, not the translation, what I was supposed to say, but the Slavey version, what I actually said."

That same summer, I had the opportunity to closely watch Gerry Antoine at the Dehcho assembly in Kakisa, where he was running to be Grand Chief of the Dehcho Tribal Council. His opponent again ran an active campaign, reaching out to people, keeping track of votes, articulating a program. Through all this, Gerry Antoine simply continued to go his own way, as if nothing were happening. The election mattered a great deal to him but he did not show it in any outward manner, rather going about his business, being present, continuing to think and speak about issues when they mattered to him. During the evening of the election, when the candidates gave their speeches, he spoke quietly, outlining his achievements, speaking thoughtfully and at length. Not once through the preceding three days did I see him do anything that could have been called campaigning or actively seeking office. In a vote whose narrowness surprised many people, he won the election.

At the Fort Simpson Treaty Day in 1994, out on the flats in the middle of the afternoon, Herb Norwegian made a speech about the importance of the treaty. It was a hot, dry day. People were there to take treaty, get their treaty money, or the nets and traps and twine that were handed out from the back of a truck as part of the process: still useful items for hunters.

Later that evening there would be drumming and dancing. But the afternoon was an occasion, and words were needed, and it is the chief's job to speak those words. Chief Norwegian spoke at great length in Slavey, then translated himself, giving roughly the same speech in English. It was not a large crowd, and those who attended were relatively inattentive, but the task was still an important one: the treaty promise of non-interference, the treaty philosophy of living side by side in peace, had to be re-explained, rearticulated, and, in spite of kids running around, and whether or not anyone was listening, he gave his speech and it was, as he would have put it, "good stuff."

The talk of these three men, whether forceful or genial or philosophical, whether in a meeting or a conversation, marked them as quite distinct from each other. Their talk was clearly an integral aspect of their leadership abilities but it was not defined by any single, clear style. Yet all are Dehcho Dene, respected leaders in and out of politics.

A CONVERSATION WITH LEO NORWEGIAN

Leo Norwegian, an elderly man, could be found most afternoons around the trailer that serves as a band office in Fort Simpson, having a smoke outside, chatting with the staff, or the chief, or any number of non-Dene. He acts as an advisor to the chief, the band manager, the council, and some of the committees established by council. We talked a number of times and it is always a great pleasure, whether he is telling tall tales about the coldness of winters gone by or talking more seriously about the community. He has lively eyes and a mischievous grin. I could see the child he had been as he told a story about playing a prank on his sisters, getting spanked by his mother to teach him a lesson, which he duly learned, saying of the spanking: "I still feel it!" I learned a great deal from him. Two issues emerged as a strong theme in our conversations, overlapping each other: that of Dene law and that of social assistance.

On the question of law, Leo was firm in his belief that Dene law "would [work today], if they let us." He expressed a great deal of frustration with the dominant legal system, noting that "Dene, even if they don't know the [Dene] law, they don't recognize the European idea, don't want to recognize . . . government says 'well, you don't recognize my law you go to jail.'" This dissatisfaction was not, interestingly, with the local administration of justice, a point he emphasized: "at the present law system the RCMP is doing a good job, I think, they're doing what they're told to do. They're going by the books. They don't bend the law. But I think we the people should be working with those people, meet them halfway." The metaphor of 'bending the law' will reappear in later chapters, as will the theme of law and books. The dissatisfaction was rather on a deeper level, in part, I would argue, with the form of law, the manner or shape of law's structure, the boundaries of law: "some places there shouldn't be a law and there's a law, and some places there should be a law and there's no law there!"

Leo Norwegian provided a lengthy and interesting description of how Dene law worked in the past, in comparison with the dominant legal system:

> When I was a kid, they still used the law a lot, you know. Today if somebody commit a crime or broke the law, [they] bring [him] to the court house and they put him in front and they point a finger at him and the dirtiest thing they can find they throw it on there and work him down. Dene law, I seen a guy that, I wouldn't say what crime it was but he committed a crime, and so it was brought to the group and they put up a feast and he's in the crowd there, they didn't tell him why, he's in the crowd there, and everybody had a feast, everybody ate, and after everybody eat they set the fire, they pray, they set fire and then they start talking about different things but related to that guy. He's in the crowd but they make sure that he gets the message, by the time it's finished, he gets the message. And then, they never mention his name or anything, they just will be already, we don't know who they're talking about, but finally he got up and said 'I promise I'm not going to do that no more'. He said, you know, 'I want to live with you people'. He says 'I don't want to be sent away and I don't want to be put to death or', you know. He just got up and say that. They never mentioned his name, nobody look at him, just talking and he got the message, and from then on he became a really, one of the leaders later on. That's the way they used to work.

Among the many things that could be said about this description, I want to note the repetitions: the style of repetition is itself so important to Dene storytelling, and the particular repetitions here—he's in the crowd, they had a feast, they set the fire, they never mention his name, he gets the message—are all critical. This is a public event, food is shared, a fire is set (perhaps in the manner of the sacred fires used by Dene in 'feeding the fire' ceremonies, which are an important aspect of their tradition) to signal the importance of the words spoken, the individual is never signalled out but recognizes himself in the talk that takes place, until finally he acknowledges receipt of this address. The focus is on rehabilitation, on achieving a voluntary acknowledgement by the lawbreaker of his misdeed.

Norwegian's view (and Angmarlik's, discussed in Chapter Five) contrasts dramatically with the view Joan Ryan attributes to Dogrib elders in her *Doing Things the Right Way*, where, once placed in a 'justice' circle, "the offender was kept there until he or she admitted guilt, at which point the senior people and leadership would give the person 'harsh words'."[6] Norwegian's description, rather, emphasizes how the individual is not singled out. Instead, a deliberate strategy of misdirection seems to be deployed so that whatever critical words need to be spoken will be enunciated in such a manner that they are not spoken directly at the individual (the approach is not unfamiliar to the European imagination: the same strategy is used by Beatrice, her early words to Dante regarding his failings are addressed to nearby angels but in his earshot, in the *Purgatorio*). The individual can therefore come to realize her or his misdeeds at their own pace, in their own way, and voluntarily acknowledge them, at which point there is no longer a need for harsh words.

Norwegian also had a great deal to say about social services and was convinced that "social service, that's something that should be handled by band." He talked about how people drift into town from elsewhere and end up being supported, in an apartment, drinking away welfare money. It is the waste of human life that concerned him greatly, and he used the example of two elders who wanted money to help them get back on the land but were refused, as a contrast, saying "that's deadly wrong." The system encourages people to stay in the community and do nothing, rather than supporting people who want to try to be independent and live more on the land. Yet he also had great respect for the basic idea of social support: "like the social service, it could be, it's a good program—it's a good—if you do [it] the right way, you know."

In effect, both of Leo's critiques are directed at the problem of form, although in the case of justice he clearly has more respect for the local administrators than for those responsible for social services. That is, in both instances it is not the existence of a program that is of concern, but the manner of its operation. In this context, his respect for Dene forms is noteworthy: "Dene way, a lot of ways it's good you know. We survived for thousands of years. It's not written down but just passed down from generation to generation." This leads to the question of self-government, self-government as a mechanism to re-enact or reinscribe Dene ways, not least in the areas of justice and social assistance. Leo Norwegian gave one of the strongest or clearest statements about what the project of Aboriginal self-government means, interestingly also illustrating a strong identification with the political project of self-government in his deployment of the 'we' form here: "self government, we're not trying to say we want to kick everybody out of office and take over. What we're saying is, what we did before, for thousands [of] years, if we did do it, we could do it again. But it's not in a big way, you know, slowly take over."

CHAOS AND COMMUNITY DEVELOPMENT

The year before I arrived in Fort Simpson to begin this study, a serious conflict had developed in the band's administration, focussed on a controversial band manager. The conflict was still on people's minds, and people would often mention to me that they were 'supporters' or 'opponents' of that manager, so I gathered together at least some of the threads of the story, which had a lasting impact on the band office and community politics. Since that band manager was long gone, I did not interview him and therefore will not use his name in this study. The manager was from the south, and both his supporters and his detractors insist he was an excellent program developer. He was successful at getting things started and at bringing in money. Many saw him as just what the band office needed, a force that would turn things around in the community and give it direction, organization, and development. However, the women who worked in the band office, according to one source, or the financial officer, according to another, found themselves in a power struggle with him because they noticed he was siphoning off funds for his own personal gain. Some viewed this benignly: he was bringing in so much, if he wanted to reward himself with little extras, so be it, he deserved it. Others were outraged, saw it as out-and-out corruption, misuse of band funds. The incidents the people later related ranged from the trivial to the quite extraordinary. He charged the ice-cube trays in his home to a band account. One evening, the band council signed over $9000 in personal expenses to him.

At some point, the struggle escalated. The band manager fired the financial officer. The chief returned to the community to find the band office in uproar, a minor uprising of the staff on his hands. He sided with them and asked for the manager's resignation, which he got. Four members of the band council, who strongly supported the manager, then resigned en mass. A community meeting was held, quite well attended, where both sides vented their feelings. The chief, Gerry Antoine, felt forced to resign as well, and elections were held for both chief and council. A whole new slate was elected, Herb Norwegian as chief, and the office management changed. The interim band manager, Deborah Dupont, came into a situation of near chaos, without the benefit of a predecessor who would tell where basic files could be found.

Fort Simpson has something of a reputation in Yellowknife for disorganization, and this incident certainly did nothing to dispel that reputation. But disorganization at the band office administrative level never translated into confusion or disorganization at the level of political position, something that many people in Yellowknife never understood. It was often said that the Fort Simpson Dene did not understand the AIP or the treaty, or the relation between the two, and that was why they rejected it. In my view, they rejected it because they understood it all too well, and the model it implied did not suit their specific circumstances.

The chief and council were aware of the administrative problems and made serious attempts to find a financial officer and develop a general administrative apparatus up to the tasks. By the summer of 1994, a very competent local woman, Lorayne Menicoche, had been hired as band manager and a southern financial expert hired as financial officer. But staff turnover and administrative problems continued to plague the band office and were the priorities of the new band manager, who was faced with the task of putting the band on a solid administrative foundation while at the same time overseeing and expanding the programs and projects run by the band.

It should also be noted, in an epoch when 'band corruption' is a staple topic for news media and federal politicians, that in the northern communities I studied, the standards of integrity were very high. Leaders were weighed down with responsibility. Here and there, as in the story of this band manager, a scandal usually involving very small dollar values erupted and became important precisely because questions of individual integrity were in play. In the context of, for example, the infamous, over $100 million, federal 'sponsorship' scandal, one wonders where the real problems of accountability lie.

A DECLARATION

While these events were going on, and seeming to confirm the negative judgements often cast in Fort Simpson's direction from Yellowknife, another series of events was taking place. One of the most important lessons I learned from my study of northern communities emerged as a result. The community of Fort Simpson had stood front and centre in its opposition to two aspects of the 1990 AIP: the extinguishment clause that effectively would have removed any Dene claim that they had Aboriginal title to their traditional territory, and the notion that the AIP would replace certain sections of treaties 8 and 11, thereby violating the integrity of the treaties and implicitly acknowledging that the treaties only amount to the written pieces of paper recorded and disseminated by Mola.

In the summer of 1993, at the Dehcho Assembly, a "Declaration" was passed that read as follows:

> Declaration of Rights
> Deh Cho First Nation
>
> We the Dene of the Deh Cho have lived on our homeland according to our own laws and system of government since time immemorial. Our home is comprised of the Ancestral territories and waters of the Deh Cho Dene. We were put here by the Creator as keepers of our Waters and Lands. The peace treaties of 1879 and 1921 with the Non-dene recognize the Inherent Political Rights and Powers of the Deh Cho First Nation. Only sovereign peoples can make Treaties with each other. Therefore our Aboriginal Rights and Titles and Oral Treaties can not be extinguished by any Euro-Canadian Government. Our Laws from the Creator do not allow us to Cede, Release, Surrender or Extinguish our Inherent Rights. The Leadership of the Deh Cho upholds the teachings of the Elders and the Guiding Principles of the Dene Government now and in the future. Today we Reaffirm, Assert and Exercise our Inherent Rights and Powers to Govern Ourselves as a Nation. We the Dene of Deh Cho stand firm behind our First Nation Government.

The Declaration re-establishes the authority of the treaties and of elders and rejects the principle of extinguishment. These words were as sharply criticized by Mola in government as the Dene Declaration of 1976 had been. They were called "unrealistic" and "nothing new."

However, what is good for a community, for its sense of itself, for its ability to have a political project that ties people together, gives them direction, offers a sense of pride, may often be quite different from this or that program or policy that offers supposed immediate alleviation of social or organizational problems. A community can have the strongest administrative structure imaginable, and thereby only sever the band office from the community it serves, feeding a sense of elitism and alienation and perpetuating the cycle of hopelessness and poverty that is too common in Aboriginal communities. On the other hand, as is the case, I think, in Fort Simpson, it can have nearly the worst administrative structure or make decisions that, on the surface at least, seem unpractical and yet begin to instil a sense of pride, or belonging, or community, that serves as a meaningful ground for re-establishment of self-sufficiency, by taking on a political project that resonates in the affective life of the people.

What is often called "community development" is ordinarily understood as having something to do with building a human and physical and structural infrastructure that will efficiently and effectively administer resources and oversee programs and services. Communities are "developed" when they can run this infrastructure on their own. Such a set of infrastructures is entirely compatible with, and may even be an aspect of, serial collectivity, alienated forms of social being: community development in this sense fits comfortably into community dysfunction and social pathology. This is the development most often promoted in northern communities by both federal and territorial governments. But administrative capacity should never be confused with community. What deserves to be called "community development" takes place when a sense of project and a sense of pride circulate among people.

Chief Norwegian, here reflecting an attitude shared by most Dene in his region, was enormously proud of the Declaration and believed it to have historical significance. At the Dehcho Assembly in the summer of 1994, framed copies of the Declaration were presented to the community chiefs and to visiting dignitaries. In an interview with me, Chief Norwegian mentioned that in a talk with government officials, they stressed to him that their authority comes from specific pieces of legislation passed by the federal government, and asked him about his authority. He said, laughing, "I pointed to the Declaration. I said 'my authority comes from there'. They didn't like that." The Dehcho now has its own written words to set against the policies, the laws, the forms, the documents, with which government confronts it. They have a written code with which to oppose the State.

FROM FORT SIMPSON TO LIIDLI KOE

> descriptions . . . may not indeed be held tributary to ontological universals, but neither are they discrete events, sovereign acts of naming isolate particulars. Rather, descriptions are implicates of what I would call semantic formations, achieved essences elicited from historical existents, optimal properties which critical usage has salvaged and distilled from time. Something like this strategy of naming—one that is distinguishable from both ontological essentialism and a corrosive nominalism—informs Fanon's account of class relations. . . .
>
> —Ato Sekyi-Otu, *Fanon's Dialectic of Experience*

Through the cold winter of 1993–94 another change was taking place in Fort Simpson: the band searched for a new name, no longer wanting to be known as the Fort Simpson Dene Band. By the spring it had arrived at or reclaimed a name that had been circulating and in use in other ways for a number of years. Fort Simpson Dene are now known as the Liidli Koe First Nation. "Liidli Koe" means "people of the forks." One part of the process of community development for the community—claiming its right to name itself, to give itself a 'proper' name—had taken place. Although the substantive name change is important, even more important is the process of reversing colonialism's deep-rooted nominalist power, the process of establishing that the Dene community can name itself, a critical decolonizing aspect of its right to determine its own mode of social being.

The distance between Fort Simpson Dene Band and Liidli Koe First Nation may seem trivial to some, but it cannot be reached by road and it speaks at least to the possibility of something vast. Liidli Koe is based on the principles of the Deh Cho Declaration, a place where the people, having proclaimed and asserted their rights, do not allow outsiders to determine and control the community's agenda. Liidli Koe is a place with a project, internally focussed at the moment on healing the scars left by two centuries of colonialism and on establishing the community itself as a foundation from which other values and ways of being can be re-established, towards the "situational transcendence of existing relations," to borrow Dominick LaCapra's fortuitous phrase.[7]

Liidli Koe is a place where the sound of strong drums is still heard, reaching over the waters of the Deh Cho and Naechag'ah. As on Treaty Day, 1994, when, after feasting and dancing and dancing and dancing in the circle that says and repeats the bonds of friendship that establish community, on the flats where two mighty rivers come together and where the dancing had taken place year after year, we could walk up the hill, watch the rising moon over our shoulders, the sun still well up after midnight, its light reflected in the water of the Deh Cho, the pulse of the drum in the rhythm of our steps and, following us home, reminding us that somewhere, the dance continues.

CHAPTER FOUR

*on the ramparts
at fort good hope*

THE RAMPARTS

W.J.T. Mitchell has argued for understanding landscape "as something like the 'dreamwork' of imperialism, unfolding its own movement in time and space from a central point of origin and folding back on itself to disclose both utopian fantasies of the perfected imperial prospect and fractured images of unresolved ambivalence and unsuppressed resistance."[1] The intricate connection between landscape painting and colonialism has been studied in the Canadian context by Jonathan Bordo, who, in his analysis of the canonical work of the Group of Seven, has extended the chain of connections to include contemporary modes of relating to landscape as wilderness, noting that "it is in the correlation between wilderness piety and correct conduct that the question of aboriginal presence and its erasure unexpectedly emerges."[2] It is impossible to write about landscape without participating in a language historically shaped by colonial nominalisms. It is equally impossible to write about a community like Fort Good Hope without out evoking the surrounding context of local meaning-production. The landscape that situates Fort Good Hope remains in tension with the community: metaphors generated from the landscape reach into the interiority of the socious, symbolic representations are inscribed on the landscape in an attempt to bring together disparate discourses of the sacred, the physical structure of the community opens itself to the river that many of its inhabitants depend upon for subsistence. And, of course, my own narratives of landscape always fall perilously close to repeating those marked by colonial desires for mastery, twisting around a history of representations that are never easily shed, even when self-reflectively acknowledged.

The only way of driving to Fort Good Hope is along a treacherous winter road, open only when the cold weather allows the swamp, lakes, and rivers to freeze solid enough that a road can be ploughed over them. Even then, the road is for the stout-hearted, with plenty of emergency supplies and hope of good weather. It's not an everyday sort of trip, although travel to Norman Wells is a bit more frequent. I've rarely gotten to Fort Good Hope by way of the winter road. Flying, or, in summer, by boat along the river are the more common ways of reaching the community, located about 100 kilometres south of the Arctic Circle on the Deh Cho and relatively isolated by most people's reckoning.

Fort Good Hope (the Dene language name *Radeli Ko* is not used in everyday talk) is a small but important Dene community of about 800 people, the majority (about eighty per cent) of whom are Slavey speakers. The remaining ten per cent are nearly equally divided between Métis and non-Dene, making the latter group relatively small indeed. The importance of Fort Good Hope is both intangible and incalculable; it's known for the strong Dene leaders who have come out of the community, the leadership provided by the community in opposing the construction of the pipeline, the establishment of a unique model of governance for the community based on the consolidation of the municipal and band councils into a community council, and many other contributions to Dene political life. It is also known as one of the most beautiful Dene communities in a gorgeous setting.

The town stretches northwards from a boat-landing site near a small river, Jackfish Creek, which winds into the Deh Cho, which also flows north. From this point, the bank slopes up a bit more gradually than elsewhere, allowing a road to connect the river to the town. Both this point, the end of the peninsula, and another space, which I designate as "the commons," open the community up to the river that runs along it. It is hard to be anywhere in Fort Good Hope and not be aware of the presence of the Deh Cho, and all paths and roads seem to lead down, to invite, to pull towards it. At the top of the hill, the first building is one of the most prominent in the community, its Catholic church. Constructed in the middle of the nineteenth century and partially finished by the missionary and amateur ethnographer Emile Petitot, one of the most important early European recorders of Dene ways, the church is now an historic site. From the church, on the left of the main road, are prominent government buildings—a nursing station and RCMP office—leading to a drop-in centre and community fire hall, and, finally, one of two centres of town, the Northern Store. Out front of the Northern Store, across the main road, is a bench from which the comings and goings of pretty much everyone in town can be watched and commented on by those who have the time and inclination to do so. Along the right side of the road are private homes, looking over the pines that slope down to the creek. Behind the government buildings are also a few houses, some overlooking the Deh Cho. They lead to the lone hotel in the community, owned and operated by the community council's development corporation. The Northern Store and the Ramparts Hotel are two corners of a baseball field or 'commons', a large field in the centre of town, half circled by two groups of houses.

The houses, according to another friend, Barney Masazumi, can each be identified in connection with the housing program that provided the funds to build them, which are in turn associated with the various Indian Affairs ministers who were in office at the time. There are the 'Hugh Faulkner' houses, and the 'John Munro' houses, and the 'Jean Chretien' houses, and so on. Each type of house, prefabricated, or log cabin-type construction, is one of a series. Many of the houses have teepees outside them, made of the plywood used to package the housing construction materials sent up by barge every summer. The teepee smokehouses usually consist of bits of bright blue or red plastic tarpaulins, which augment the plywood. The teepees are often as tall as the houses, and are used to smoke or dry meat or fish, and sometimes as storage areas.

The far end of the commons, opposite the Northern Store, is a hill, with houses built about halfway up. On the east side of the hill, away from the river, is the T'Seleie School; on the west side, overlooking the commons and the river, is the second centre of town and gathering place, the community office. This is a large, log-construction building with a hall and a few offices including that of the community radio station on the first floor, meeting rooms and offices on the second, and a large, flat, wooden platform at the entrance. The main community council meeting room is a beautiful room on the second floor featuring a painting of a wolf by Dene artist John T'etso and a balcony that offers a view of the river and the main part of the community.

Further north, houses stretch along the river and in small subdivisions in among the spruce trees, with a gravel strip airport about a kilometre east. The gravel road that connects all this leads up past the biggest hill that overlooks the whole of town, past the refuse dump just over a kilometre, and continues north until it ends, just a few kilometres later, at "Rabbitskin" River, on the maps called Hare Indian River. This is a popular place to swim or to fish or to picnic on the hot, dry summer days that are common to Fort Good Hope.

Fort Good Hope is situated about 800 kilometres north of Liidli Koe on the Deh Cho, just south of the Arctic Circle and at the north entrance to the Ramparts, one of the most prominent features of the Deh Cho. A rampart is defined by *The Oxford Paperback Dictionary* as "a broad bank of earth built as a fortification, usually topped with a parapet and wide enough for troops etc. to walk on." Ramparts are defensive barricades. The Ramparts that stretch for a few kilometres south of Fort Good Hope are steep cliffs, of a rusty orange, brown, and yellow colour. The Deh Cho is itself almost two kilometres across, so the cliffs form a broad canyon: they are one of the few landscape features not completely dwarfed by the Deh Cho.

One time, in 1985, during a visit to Fort Good Hope, my research assistant and friend Rita Kakfwi toured me through the Ramparts. She showed me the island that was the giant's overturned canoe, and the places—breaks in the cliff—where the giant's head and hands and feet had rested when he stretched out across the river. I saw the thousands of bird nests that cluster along the cliffs. I saw hunting cabins placed at different points along the Deh Cho by different families from Fort Good Hope. I saw the falls or rapids at the south entrance of the Ramparts. Two huge, heron-like birds, frightened into the air by our small boat, wafted away. Fish were to be found in nets set along the bottom of the cliffs. Later, on other trips, I also saw the campground where community assemblies are frequently held.

This is a landscape suited to a culture in a defensive posture, buttressed against and actively resisting the ruses of totalizing power. The Ramparts and the river that runs through them: both gateway and obstacle, invitation and last-ditch stand. The moral topography of a barrier—one cannot easily climb the Ramparts to get at the land beyond it—and of a majestic entrance—one passes through this magnificent canyon to reach Fort Good Hope from the south by boat—where the culture and economy of a people focussed on the land and river still breathe, somehow in struggle reproduce themselves, dance their dialectic of totalization and resistance, still standing strong and proud of their place on this powerful part of this powerful river against the world-historical forces ranged against them.

THE COMMUNITY COUNCIL

The political structure of Fort Good Hope is markedly different from that of Fort Simpson/Liidli Koe, reflecting the differing circumstances of the two communities. Fort Good Hope is governed at the local level by a community council, which functions both as a band council and as a municipal council. This is one of the ways in which Fort Good Hope has shown creativity and initiative in local governance, effectively subverting the imposed political structure and creating something genuinely new and unique out of its material. The community now wants to use the movement towards self-government to push this process even further, though whether it will be successful remains to be seen.

In the late sixties, as with many Dene communities, there was a local band council that had minimal official responsibilities: its role was largely confined to Treaty Day celebrations. One of the old-timers in the community, who preferred "not to have his name in any books," told me that in the old days, after the treaty, the chief was not elected but "instead people just raised their hands," pointing to an interesting distinction between the individualism presupposed by the more recent secret ballot system and the collective/public implications of the older show-of-hands system. As government began to get more involved in the community, particularly concerning housing programs, both the band council and the Métis local responded by themselves becoming more active, agitating on behalf of their members in the community. Meanwhile, the newly energetic post-1967 territorial government established a settlement council to act as municipal government, in a similar fashion as it had done in many other northern communities.

Frank T'Seleie, who comes from a prominent family of community leaders and was himself elected chief several times, told me about how in 1974 he became "the youngest chief at that time." Although, he said, "most of the old-timers, they provided me with really good advice," he also inherited very little in the way of administrative structure: "when I became chief I was handed a shopping bag! That was the office. No resources to work with. Up until just before that the territorial government established with the Dene chiefs up here core funding for administration, so that was in place, but I had very little to work with." But the biggest obstacle to community governance was the establishment of a separate political structure:

> We lost a lot of control when the territorial government moved in in 1967 and began establishing their own administrations in the communities, and completely bypassing the authority of the bands. One of the first things that we done was we started a process of regaining our control by doing away with the administration that they set up and the way that was accomplished was by the people refusing to vote and reinstating the chief and council.

T'Seleie also noted that there were "mainly non-Natives [on the municipal council], people like the priest and contractors."

George Barnaby, another prominent political activist in the community, told me that "we don't like that municipal style government, so we develop[ed] our *own* and we put all the people as the authority on [it] and the council as the representative and their leadership under." In Barnaby's view, the replacement of the municipal council by the community council helped the community achieve control over its governing institutions, particularly in allowing the mechanism of community-wide meetings or assemblies to play a prominent role:

> The assembly came out of the, all the, what happened with the settlement council. That time, the way that the constitution, the local government ordinance, settlement council act, it said, you know, there'd be six councillors and a chairman, they'll have all the responsibility and the right, have everything. The public has no say in it. And if they persist in saying something, like, you have to leave, you know, throw them out. The people didn't like that. They wanted guarantee that the people in the community are going to have a say. So they put it right in their constitution, right there. The assembly is the main authority with anything new, strategy for band, or something, have to be approved by the assembly, so.

The settlement council became a competitor with the band council as local governing authority. When it began to make decisions without consulting the people of the community or their representative bodies, it lost legitimacy. People boycotted settlement council elections, and it became defunct. Its functions were taken over by the band council, which then became a community council, in charge both of federal Indian Act functions and of municipal government functions established by territorial legislation.

Barney Masazumi, with whom I worked closely in the summer of 1992, told me a story that graphically demonstrated the need for local government. We were standing at the airstrip, looking up towards the high hill, which Barney said was where trails leading inland to Colville Lake, the nearest community, ran from, leading along a ridge of land going eastward and inland for miles. One day in the early seventies, people heard a loud sound and found out that a bulldozer was on the hill, clearing land to build something, perhaps a fire tower. Some of the people immediately ran up the hill to put a stop to this; in their view it was sacred ground, not to be flattened. That someone had thought they could just go ahead and build where they wanted to build and bulldoze where they wanted to bulldoze brought home to the community the need for an effective local government; more importantly, that they were able to stop the bulldozer brought home the fact that they could have an influence on events, that they had power.

The community council is run by local Dene on a band council structure—that is, with a chief and council, the number of councillors being determined by the relevant Indian Act provisions. The community has no official settlement status with the territorial government, so the band assumes municipal responsibilities. A major community assembly is held once a year to determine general direction and policy; open community meetings are held with some regularity to discuss particular issues of importance. The council meets frequently, about once a week, usually in the morning, with most business discussed in English.

There are three broad kinship or family or 'clan' groups in Fort Good Hope. These are inland or Colville Lake people, river people, and mountain people. Anthropologists call them Hare or Hareskin, though the people I met called themselves North Slavey speakers. The families— Kakfwi and Barnaby, T'Seleie and Tobac, Granjam and Pierrot, Bucan and

Kochon, Masazumi and Manuel—have all participated in the community council structure, though the chief has tended to come from among one of the larger family groups, the Barnaby/Kakfwi family network, which the chief at the time of my research, Isidore Manuel, was connected to by marriage.

In Fort Good Hope, at the local level the 'ethnic' government is also the 'public' government. The Dene and Métis have direct control over all local affairs, but the federal and territorial governments still define what constitutes local affairs and handle many programs and policies in which the community feels a need for some input or control. This is a unique model and one that the local residents want to extend.

TUSI KO

Fort Good Hope, like Fort Simpson/Liidli Koe, has its own sense of history. One important part of it circles around Tusi Ko. A version of the Tusi Ko story is printed in *"Mom, we've been discovered,"* a Dene Cultural Institute publication, as "A Dene Discovers the White Man," told by Suzanne Gully. In Fort Good Hope I was directed by my friend and sometimes research assistant Bella T'Seleie to an older man who knew the story. When I visited his house one afternoon, he did not like the idea of being interviewed and told me that a photographer had once taken his picture without his permission, later running it in a newspaper. This incident had disturbed him greatly. However, during the course of an afternoon-long conversation over tea, he said I could certainly pass on his words and refer to him as "an elderly gentleman," since he preferred not to have his name in any books. He has since passed away, but I must respect his wishes. In outline, as he told the story, Tusi Ko (Dry Loon) may have been from the Colville Lake area, but had a fish camp on the Deh Cho. One time, he found some wood chips floating in the river that had not been made by a beaver. Tusi Ko had a dream and must have had medicine power because he decided to follow his dream. He decided to try to find the source of these chips.

He travelled far up the Deh Cho, carrying four marten skins, hiding from other people, until he found the cabin of a man with yellow hair. At first, he hid and watched from afar. But, after three days of this, he revealed himself. He told the white man something about the river and people on it, and received from the white man an axe and some clothes (or, in other versions, a gun and a pot, these latter being the two most important goods brought by fur trading companies as staples of the trade), which he took back to the people. The next year Alexander Mackenzie, guided by old Beaulieu and three other men, travelled down the Deh Cho. This initiated important changes in the life of Dene.

There are slightly differing versions of the story, but also some remarkable consistencies. Most interesting from my perspective is the way in which the story claims agency for the Dene in making their history. The Dene take responsibility for bringing the fur trade, rather than being its passive recipients. Furthermore, the story inverts the logic of discovery: a Dene explorer 'finds' the white man just as Dene and Métis guides would show Alexander Mackenzie the river that inappropriately bears his name.

So too, today, Fort Good Hope Dene are taking on, reconfiguring, subverting, restructuring, absorbing, marking, the wood chips, documents, proposals, forms, guidelines, policies, laws, floating along and through the mail, couriers, fax machines, e-mails, meetings held to disseminate them. Following against the current, Dene have for more than a century been tracking these to the source, trying to decide what to bring back. Stephen Kakfwi from Fort Good Hope, living in Yellowknife as premier of the territorial government. Ethyl Blondin-Andrew, also from the Sahtu region, in Ottawa as a junior minister in the federal government. What will they return with after the arduous journey homeward?

SAHTU

Fort Good Hope is in a region called Sahtu, a Dene name for Great Bear Lake. There are four Dene communities in Sahtu: Deline (formerly Fort Franklin) on Sahtu; Tulita (formerly Fort Norman) at the juncture of the Sahtu De (Great Bear River) and the Deh Cho; Fort Good Hope further north on the Deh Cho; and Colville Lake (inland north and east of Fort Good Hope). Another community, Norman Wells, situated between Fort Norman and Fort Good Hope on the Deh Cho, is a largely non-Native oil town, though many Dene and Métis make it their home. The Sahtu region was the second Dene region to opt for a regional comprehensive land claim after the failure of the 1990 AIP. The general feeling was that Sahtu delegates had voted in favour of renegotiating the AIP during the summer of 1990 because they were persuaded that this would not 'kill' the claim; when the Dene position did lead to an impasse and the Gwi'chin just north of them negotiated their own regional claim, the Sahtu Dene followed suit.

For much of the eighties, the Dene Nation president was Stephen Kakfwi, an articulate Dene leader from Fort Good Hope. Kakfwi had crafted and overseen a Dene Nation policy that separated the issues of self-government and land claims. The former would be pursued through the vehicle of the territorial government, the latter through the federal comprehensive land claim process. By the late eighties, with the land claim nearly settled, Kakfwi felt it was time to leave the Dene Nation in order to make progress on the self-government issue. He ran for the territorial government as a representative of Sahtu, was elected, and remains one of the key territorial politicians. But in his absence, the Dene Nation first rejected the land claim and then split into regional tribal councils with quite different positions on the crucial issues of land claims and self-government.

Kakfwi advocated a regional land claim for the Sahtu, based on the 1990 AIP model. This is what the Gwi'chin had negotiated. Sahtu negotiators hoped to achieve something more, and this was structured symbolically through a reconceptualization of the approach to comprehensive land claims: the Sahtu claim would be called a Sahtu Treaty. The region was slower to negotiate a claim, and somewhat less well prepared and organized than the Gwi'chin, but nevertheless soon established an Agreement in Principle. The Sahtu Tribal Council, centred in Fort Norman, was led by George Cleary; the chief negotiator of the Sahtu Treaty was Norman Yakelia.

The Sahtu Treaty contains an extinguishment clause, number 3.1.9, which reads, "in consideration of the rights and benefits provided to the Dene/Métis by this agreement, the Dene/Métis cede, release and surrender to Her Majesty in Right of Canada all their aboriginal claims, rights, titles and interest, if any, in and to lands and waters anywhere within Canada."[3] It also contains a provision that replaced specific aspects of Treaty 11. For much of the three years spent in my study of Fort Good Hope, political discussion focussed on the question of whether to accept the claim, which was to be voted on in the summer of 1993. Some communities wanted to be able to opt out of the claim by voting on a community-by-community basis. This was rejected by the federal government: it was an all-or-nothing deal, to be established on a regional basis.

A KIND OF COUP

In the summer of 1992, a kind of *coup d'état* took place in local governance of Fort Good Hope. The story of this coup stages many of the issues and dynamics of local politics, and involves in one way or other many of the local politicians. It began with a now near-mythical event, the attempt by some band councillors to go out and stake land, using money provided to the community as part of the land claim negotiations process for land selection.

What the councillors were attempting, what their intentions were, remains open to question. What they actually did is clearer. They chartered a private float plane using land claims funds, which, significantly, landed on the Deh Cho at the north end of town, away from the more public dock and loading area at Jackfish Creek. Some saw this as evidence of their guilt—they wanted to hide their activity by having the plane load and unload in a less public location. In any event, they certainly were not successful in hiding their activity, if that was the intent. One of the councillors was seen with a pile of wooden stakes, walking down to the plane. In the intense, hothouse, political climate of Fort Good Hope, where discussion of land claims was the main issue on people's minds, the incident provoked comment. The comment spread. Curiosity—what were they up to?—quickly turned to concern—they are band councillors, supposed to be working for the people, why doesn't anyone know what they're up to?

Staking land implies establishing private ownership; this is something that band councillors should not have been using band funds to do. Two theories circulated. On the one hand, some people thought the councillors were guilty of fraud: they were staking or trying to stake land for their personal gain. Perhaps they hoped to select lands that would then be selected by the community, in which event the government might have to compensate them. Perhaps they were simply using the privilege of access to an aircraft to claim land for their families. Either way, it was seen as dishonest, from this view. One the other hand, a second theory went, perhaps they were staking land so that the community could eventually control more than the land it would be allotted ownership over through the

Sahtu Treaty. In this view, they were attempting a misguided strategy to benefit the community: by staking land they would add to the land quantum the community would control. The strategy was misguided because in order to maintain ownership of staked land it has to be 'worked' or 'improved' enough over the years to satisfy government that there is an active interest in the land; if individuals were to stake out enough land to be of significant benefit to the community, they would then have to spend all their time 'improving' that land, and even then might not make a significant dent in the community land quantum. The "stakers," as they became known—a few members of the band council, not including Chief Everette Kakfwi—were called on to account for their actions.

The forum of this accounting was a public meeting at which, in the words of one of the four people who told me this story, they were "caught with their hands in the cookie jar." They were directly confronted and publicly lost face, both rare events in Dene community dynamics, in my experience. A formal land selection committee was set up to accomplish the task of choosing the lands that would make up the community's land quantum. The committee was led by three women: an older woman who was a justice of the peace, a younger woman who was a 'youth' representative, and an energetic, middle-aged woman who was clearly the driving spirit of the whole group. The group also consisted of an ex-chief, a young man who had returned north from university, an older but quite active local 'diplomat', and another man who was on the band council but not a staker.

This group took over the process of selecting the community's land quantum, but also played a role as an informal check on the community council, a kind of alternative political structure that was seen by many as a more legitimate representative body. It had been appointed at a very well-attended public meeting, rather than by the less immediate voting process for chief and councillors. And it acted with an assertive moral authority in the context of a band council that had lost some of its legitimacy and moral authority. That it was dominated by women, as opposed to the community council, which was dominated by men, meant it also gave a structure or vehicle for the politically strong women of the community to intervene in more active ways than they had previously in the formal public sphere.

Two events in its functioning are worth comment here. At one of its early meetings, which I attended, the subject of funding was brought up.

There was a lengthy discussion of what had happened to the money allocated for land selection, whether it had all been spent by the band councillors in their "high-flying" way, and whether it had been adequately accounted for. There was concern expressed that the committee would have no money with which to function. At that point, the president of the Métis local, who was in attendance and whose local had also been allocated funds for land selection, simply volunteered their funds to the committee, whose work would help both groups. These funds would help the committee initiate its work while it determined what happened to the monies provided to the band. The offer and its acceptance demonstrated the close working and trust relations between Dene and Métis in the community.

A few days later, a community council meeting was held. The land selection committee attended the meeting in force. Ostensibly, it was there to report to the community council and gain formal approval and support for its proposals on how to proceed. However, the political dynamic in the room was clearly highly charged and largely reversed the reporting relationship. At the meeting, the council was performing under the watchful eye of the committee. Not only did the council not dare to challenge any of the committee's ideas, but on other agenda items—for example, hiring an employee—it was clear that the council was minding its p's and q's; a relative of one of the council members was passed over for the job.

This event was an exercise in governance that reveals and stages, in my view, the very interesting and healthy political situation where an alternative power structure was developed to challenge the formal structure, because the latter had lost its legitimacy in the eyes of the people. That there was structural room for such an event to take place testifies both to the level of political involvement, creativity, and engagement of community members, and to the flexibility of local governing structures in a situation where "face-to-face" politics still has relevance. Among the eventual outcomes were a more systematic, community consultation process in the actual selection of the land quantum and a transition in the membership of the community council. The stakers eventually resigned, and the next election saw a dramatic change in council membership.

A PAINTING AND A STORY: TWO CHIEFS

The main office area of the community centre features a painting of a man, a portrait in realist style, the man dressed in camouflage greens, against the background of the Ramparts. The man is Charlie Barnaby, for many years the chief of Fort Good Hope. Charlie's style was a joking, populist approach. Two consistent themes of his conversations with me were street encounters—the notion of face-to-face meetings that he regularly deployed as a metaphor to explain the issue he was discussing—and talk, conversation. Both these came together in one statement he made to me, to the effect that "you know what kind of guy I am, I never faced away from people. But I don't talk you know for a few minutes, I go crazy. I gotta talk. I see someone going there, it's good to say hello. Some people, they don't want to see you, you know. They go the other way." Talking is emphasized in the work of Pierre Clastres, among others, as a critical function of the chief: "talent as a speaker is both a condition and instrument of political power."[4]

Although he formally retired as chief, Charlie Barnaby remains active in community politics. He was on the land selection committee in 1992 and back on the band council as a councillor in 1994. He has an outpost camp upriver, past the Ramparts, near where the Hume joins the Deh Cho; a beautiful spot. These days, he plays a teasing, tricksterish-like role, poking fun where it won't cause offence, being serious when the occasion demands. In conversation with me and Charlie Tobac, a local counsellor, he emphasized the theme of sharing:

> To be honest, you know, it's good to talk in front of one another, eh? Because people are, Native people you know, when it comes to think about it and really look at it, we always been sharing, eh. If somebody shot a moose down here, me and him we could run down there. We get a chunk of meat. But if you go down Edmonton you never see that! And that's what I mean, the past history, we always been well known for sharing. Now somebody packing fish up here. Like yesterday, I ask a guy about fish. He would give me some. Won't say 'gimme dollar' or something. Next time I seen with fish, give him some too. But a lot of this next generation, they don't know that. . . .

Charlie Barnaby often alternated as chief with Frank T'Seleie, who, in that sense, might have been seen as his political rival, yet I never heard any expression of bad feeling between the two. They worked on the band council together for many years, one as chief, the other as councillor. And they worked together, in whatever capacity they found themselves, for the good of the community. In a conversation with me, T'Seleie emphasized responsibility to the land: "The way we were brought up like each clan or family unit was responsible for certain places or geography on our land. . . . Philosophically our people understood their resources of their land. They were really strong. I was brought [up] on those principles, taking into consideration all of creation or the whole. . . ." He told me about how he had found an ancient campsite and could 'see' how land had been used in the past. He referred me, in that context, to stories that inscribe the relation between the landscape and the social:

> You could see it, visualize how the land was governed. Some of it was stories and legends associated with certain landmarks, Pelican, Anderson River areas is really interesting, one of the landmarks there is associated with the creation story. A lot of knowledge is for teaching. We were coming around the river, these boys and I, just above Sansu. There's a long straight stretch, cliffs on one side, you've seen it, one place there's a figure of an animal sitting way out on a rocky ledge, way out by itself. That's supposed to be a wolverine that turned into a rock, and it's used for teaching, for like here the wolverine jumped out to the rock where someone had stored, had a cache and he's trying to steal it, turned into a rock, you know. That's spiritual voice I guess, teaching about stealing, about taking what's not yours, that kind of stuff: legends of, ideas of, good and bad, right and wrong. That kind of stuff is all in our language but in order to understand it, it's got to be, like to sense in our own language. It loses a lot of its meaning when you translate it. There's another one that's, it ends somewhere around here, the story, there's landmarks. It ends in Cambridge Bay.

Teaching stories, stories inscribed in landmarks and landscape: 'how the land was governed'. Stories that reach far into the distance, one end in Fort Good Hope and another end in the Inuit community on Victoria Island about a thousand kilometres northeast; and reach deep into the social, "about stealing . . . ideas of good and bad, right and wrong."

ON THE RAMPARTS

Near a bend in the Deh Cho as it passes though the Ramparts, about half-way up the cliff and dwarfed by it, is a statue of Mary in blue robes, arms outstretched. Rita Kakfwi called my attention to it on my first trip through the Ramparts, and I've noticed it on every subsequent trip. In the Fort Good Hope Catholic church, among the many very bright paintings of biblical scenes—including one that shows very white angels condemning a dark-skinned Satan to hell and damnation—is a painting by Father Bern Will Brown from the fifties that shows a Dene woman having a vision of a figure on the Ramparts. The painted vision and the statue, apart from size, look remarkably alike. Stories circulate about the figure on the Ramparts. I've heard differing accounts of who put it there, and why.

It recalls the story, told by Eduardo Galeano, of the Caribbean Island-ers who were given by the Christians a number of statues and Christian iconographic figures. When the good Christian Spaniards returned a year later, they found that the Caribbean people had buried the figures in the ground. In punishment for such disrespect, they slaughtered the islanders. They never realized, or wanted to realize, that the Caribbean people had buried the figures because they believed the Spanish, they believed that the Spanish gods had power(s), and put them in the soil hoping the power would improve fertility and guarantee successful crops. They had done the most respectful thing they could with those figures and been ruthlessly punished for it.

Michael Taussig, too, tells of symbolically laden objects whose mean-ings twist around and subvert both official church narratives and older spiritual beliefs, in the chapter called "The Wild Woman of the Forest Becomes Our Lady of Remedies," in his book *Shamanism, Colonialism and the Wild Man*. There, he suggests that the everyday stories of 'popular ico-nography' do not merely involve "the strumming of the string of defeat and salvation that creates multiplicity of versions concerning the Virgin, the juggling with the semiotic of the miracle" but also "the way the heavy tone and mystical authority of the official voice of the past is brought down to earth and familiarized with gentle and sometimes saucy wit."[5] Interest-ingly, Taussig frequently deploys landscape metaphors to textually moti-vate this discussion of semantic richness, as in: "we can describe a 'sacred' contouring of land made from interconnected chips and fragments of place meanings," though only, in his view, if "we endorse a notion of sanctity that endorses the strength of human weakness";[6] here the repetition of "endorse" in the sentence seems to grammatically act out the "human weakness" being invoked.

The figure on the Ramparts evokes a Dene version of this story, told and retold in the New World, the world that Dene storytellers like George Blondin would implicitly call an old world, a tired world, no longer new, a world where magic has been disenchanted and healing power weakened, where the spiritually powerful must gain and give strength to the same land that gains and gives strength to and from the people who live with it, where the power of the sacred places, the powerful places, must be brought into contact with the power of the bible, of Jesus, to ensure that both work for each other, with each other, in the same way that the people must work for each other, with each other. In a good way.

GESTURES II: THE GIFT OF FOOD

Sometimes the sacred enters into the everyday unannounced, not bounded by ritual or prayer, as if it were a comet that one grew accustomed to after the first week of nightly viewings so that it became merely another part of the night sky, so much so that one forgets it will not reappear in a lifetime, or two, or a thousand. It is this way with the gift of food, the differing but related food-sharing practices of Dene and Inuit. This gift is hidden in the protocols of everyday life. When one visits for a chat, the protocol is to 'help yourself' to the tea or coffee and bannock that are usually ready on stove and counter. One does not tax one's hosts with the demand that they serve such daily necessities, and one would not want to tax one's guests with the obligation of patiently waiting until food and drink are offered. Food sharing among Aboriginal peoples, which has been written about extensively in the social science literature and goes under the imposing term "generalized reciprocity," continues to be practised extensively in northern communities like Fort Good Hope, particularly with regard to so-called country food, wild meat or fish. But the practices are also inscribed in everyday politenesses, in everyday gestures or forms of conduct that assume and enact a commonality necessary to community. Communities, whether the term is used to encompass nomadic but stable social arrangements or peoples settled in close proximity to each other, deserving the name "community" are built and inscribed in gestures of this sort.

FROM COLVILLE LAKE

as Colville Lake is to Fort Good Hope, as Fort Good Hope is to Yellow-knife, as Yellowknife is to Ottawa, as Ottawa is to Washington, as Washington is . . . The periphery. The site of wildness. Of a 'healing' calmness. Of a mythical reality. Since my first visit to Colville Lake, its image has remained forcefully lodged in my memory: a 'traditional' community. In Fort Simpson, when I mention Colville Lake to Leo Norwegian, his eyes light up, he smiles—"fish!"—and so much more. For a while, it seems as if everyone I talk to in Fort Good Hope traces their family back to Colville Lake, wants to be connected with it in some way, associated with its ephemeral, ambiguous power.

In the late eighties, Colville Lake decolonized itself, established itself as a separate band, rather than a sub-band of Fort Good Hope. It got electricity. And a new band office, a building that could finally compete in the architectural landscape of Colville Lake with the church and privately owned fishing lodge, owned by Bern Will Brown, transformed by marriage from 'Father' to 'Mister'. Colville Lake, the community, is situated on the lake of the same name, called in Dene *K'ahbamitue*. It is inland, accessible by air or skidoo or foot.

The small houses in Colville circle a commons and open up onto the lake itself. There are still about 100 people living there. Most of the houses are small log cabins, built some time ago by the people who live in them. Newer houses are going up as the community grows, usually prefabricated houses, organized around the fact of electricity that Colville Lake now has, along with other amenities.

Yet, something of the place called to me, calls me still. The absence of amenities couldn't hide the presence of something else, a rhythm of life, which remains even with the newer amenities. After two summers in the early nineties in Fort Good Hope, by 1994 it was time to go back to Colville. By then there were 'scheds': regularly scheduled flights, one direct from Fort Good Hope. When we got to Colville and settled in, we (my then partner Elizabeth and I) got directions to Rita Kakfwi's place and knocked and opened the door—"YOU!" she exclaimed, "I never thought I'd see YOU again!"—and there was much laughter. For the first time, with her young family and friends all piled into a boat, I got a chance to go out on the lake and catch a few of the delicious trout waiting to be caught.

We learned some painful things about Fort Good Hope. Talking with some of the older women, Elizabeth confronted the difficult issues being grappled with by the community: sexual assault, violence. These are as much a part of Colville Lake's reality as the rhythm of its life. They won't easily go away. And there is not much support for the women who want to work through them. The painful things linger. And still, Colville Lake calls to me. It is, to Fort Good Hope, as . . .

THE SAHTU TREATY

On June 29, 1993, as the day approaches when a decision must be made about the Sahtu Treaty, a public meeting is held to discuss the matter. George Cleary flies in to explain the terms of the claim and to answer questions. The meeting is well attended. By this point, there is a feeling that a vote in Fort Good Hope could go either way. Chief Kakfwi has been interviewed on the radio, sounding quite critical of the claim, many people have serious doubts, opinions seem to hang in the air, ready to be blown by whatever strong wind comes.

Cleary explains the Sahtu Treaty well, emphasizing its strengths. There is no one to speak against the claim. He stresses that only minor parts of Treaty 11 will be modified: they will no longer be entitled to reserve lands specified in that treaty; the chief's treaty right to a new suit is surrendered; and hunting and fishing rights under the treaty are exchanged for more clearly specified rights under the new claim. The trivial and the profound are thrown together. There is concern about what would happen if the Sahtu Treaty is rejected. Cleary notes that there is no guarantee a new federal government would provide more generous terms (a federal election was due and in fact took place, in which the Conservative government was replaced by a majority Liberal government, which had promised to replace the extinguishment policy) and that the freeze or moratorium on land development will be lifted. The spectre of the diamond rush then taking place on Dogrib territory is mentioned.

Earlier that day, Isidore had said to me that "we need to get united. I think we should go for it [the claim]. I think we have to stop bickering.

I'm going to go for it. At least it'll give us something to work with, to carry on with, and we can go from there." He had made up his mind: the unity of the community was the critical factor informing his judgement. By late in the meeting, Chief Kakfwi spoke also in favour of the claim, saying that "it's up to the people to make up their minds," but also indicating his own—albeit cautious—support for it. George Barnaby, who had written in *Dene Nation: The Colony Within* that "the land claim of the Dene is a claim not only for land but also for political rights,"[7] was of the opinion, which he had expressed to me earlier that week, that the land claim "was just a real estate deal" and that the real action would be in self-government negotiations.

After the meeting, people, especially the older men in the room, huddle around the large map of the area that has been put up, indicating what lands have been selected. Fingers touching the differently coloured areas of the map. Questions. Comments. Concern. Somehow, it is clear to me that the vote will go in favour of the Sahtu Treaty.

Isidore Manuel, trying to express his frustration at the difficulty of explaining the treaty terms to people, once showed me the definition of a tree in the treaty:

> 'trees' means a single stemmed, perennial woody plant growing to a height of more than eight feet, and which is found in a wild state in the Northwest Territories, including *Pinus* species including Jack Pine and Lodge Pole Pine, *Larix* species including Tamarack, *Picea* species including White Spruce and Black Spruce, *Abies* species including Alpine Fir, *Salix* species including Beaked Willow and Pussy Willow, *Populus* species including Trembling Aspen and Balsam Poplar, *Betula* species including White Birch, Alaska Birch and Water Birch, *Alnus* species including Speckled Alder and Mountain Alder, and *Prunusn* species including Choke Cherry and Pin Cherry.[8]

Who can read this? he implicitly asked. How do you even know where to start? Whereas the earlier treaty had been written in English (although written in legal English in its day, the treaty is relatively short, a few pages, and today is relatively easy to read; in 1921, it is the fact that it was written in a foreign language that took the official version of the treaty out of the hands of Dene), a language not widely spoken and even less widely read by Dene in 1921, so that Dene would have to rely on their own version of what the treaty said, this later treaty was written in the language of lawyers, equally foreign to the people who were supposed to decide whether they were 'for' or 'against' it. Not much more than a week later, in a vote held in the Sahtu according to the procedures established by the comprehensive claims negotiation process, the Sahtu Treaty was ratified by the people.

JIM PIERROT'S MORAL MAP

That summer I was treated to another version of what a written treaty looked like. I was staying in Henry Tobac's house while Henry, then on the band council, was away with his family in Edmonton. He had given me the use of his truck, and I tried to repay his generosity by giving rides to anyone who needed one, especially older people. One afternoon, I found myself giving a ride to one of the older community councillors, a man named Jim Pierrot. He said he had been on the council, off and on, since 1967. I had seen him at council meetings, where he tended to be one of the quieter members, though he gave off an air of thoughtfulness. We talked for a long time, sitting in the cab of the truck, outside the log house where he wanted to be dropped off. He had many concerns about the land claim and said he thought many of the older people felt as he did. He said they were especially concerned about the land selection part of it, drawing lines on the map, dividing up the land.

At some point in our conversation he pulled a piece of well-weathered, lined writing paper out of the side pocket of his nylon jacket. He carefully unfolded it and showed it to me. It was a map of sorts, though it took me a few minutes to make it out. It showed the Deh Cho, I realized, and the community, as well as a mountain south along the river and an inland lake; it had the words "f.g." (for federal government) and "band" written across the top. Along the side, it read "treaty." With this as his basis, he launched into a lengthy discussion of treaty relations, of peaceful coexistence. This is what treaty means to him, and he sees its presence in the landscape. The treaty as a 'writing' on the land, about the land and the people. The treaty as a kind of moral topography, an inscription of social relations embodied in a landscape of rivers, lakes, mountains: a community of river people, mountain people, lake people.

One can read into that piece of paper, or read out of it, the network of social relations and the degree to which they are over-inscribed by newer lines of power. The river, lake, mountain, and community: a moral topography of Fort Good Hope itself, seen in terms of the most important family groups. 'Above' this social/landscape setting rest the power relations: band and federal government. No landscape representation for these abstract forms of power, which must relate to each other and to the landscape and to the community through something called treaty, which runs along the side, in some way encompassing this whole, both of it and out of it, along it and inside of it. This way of seeing, of seeing the people, the land, the writing, as integral, layering each other, circling around and through each other, is one reason why the Comprehensive Land Claim of the Dene in the Sahtu region of the NWT is called the Sahtu Treaty.

'SO THAT THINGS WILL WORK BETTER ALL THE TIME': A PLAN FOR SELF-GOVERNMENT

A territorial government official and friend once mentioned to me that George Barnaby is thought of in some circles as the 'philosopher king' of the western Arctic, and this has always seemed to me entirely apposite. He is certainly a diplomat of the highest order; along with Isidore Manuel, he was one of the very few people who moved back and forth between the community council and the land selection committee in the highly charged political climate of the summer of 1992. This was not an easy feat to negotiate, but he managed it ably. There were two things that convinced me the official's assessment was accurate, apart from that observation. George Barnaby had a lengthy experience in territorial government, being one of the first Dene to be elected to the Territorial Assembly in the early seventies and staying active, in one way or another, in politics ever since. He also had a consistent vision, a coherent philosophy, of politics, which he has spent most of his life struggling to enact.

As noted earlier, though the story bears repeating, Barnaby had written about his mid-seventies political experience in the first part of "The Political System and the Dene" in *Dene Nation: The Colony Within*. Reading this, one can still sense the frustration he must have felt as one of the only Dene on the territorial council: "the first session of Council I went to, we spent two weeks on an ordinance that had no importance to the people I represented. At this time I asked for more control for the communities. This was voted down. I don't know why."[9] In an interview with him in 1994, he said he resigned from the council because he became convinced it was not serving the people: "So I told [Justice Thomas] Berger that I can't stay in a government like that, doesn't serve the communities, doesn't recognize community rights—I forget the exact words I had. So I said I'm resigning, making an official announcement that I'm resigning as the representative for the Great Bear Region and going to work with the Dene Nation to develop a Dene government." He held a press conference to express his concerns, publicly rebuking the territorial government system. For a few years, he worked as a vice-president of the Dene Nation, but the pressures and feeling of not accomplishing his goals led him to resign from that position, which he did in a particularly Dene fashion: he went off into the bush for the spring hunt. After a while, his absence was noted and no one could find him in order to determine what his plans were. He returned to his home community in the eighties and concentrated his energies on politics at the local level, trying to find a way of achieving his goals there and putting his talents at the service of the community. He has served on the band council for two terms, but has never been chief. He has always been active, attending band council meetings and in the nineties assisting with the self-government 'portfolio' at both the regional and community levels, characterizing his role "as a consultant to the band, mostly on political and other community issues . . . I negotiated . . . for the community. I guess that's the kind of work I'm doing for the community, political stuff, developing new ways of, you know, of dealing with issues that concern the community so, you know, [we] get our own government, our own constitution, our own way of doing things."

His political philosophy is also enunciated in the article on "The Political System and the Dene." It involves enacting Dene ways, at the political levels, Dene ways of making decisions: "The way decisions are made is another law. No one can decide for another person, everyone is involved in a discussion, and the decision is made by everyone. Our way is to try and give freedom to a person, as he knows what he wants" (120). Barnaby argued that the system of territorial governance "is wrong: wherever only a few people decide for the rest of the population, it oppresses people" (122). George Barnaby's philosophy is democratic through and through; not the formal democracy of Western political systems, but a participatory democracy that questions the nature of representation as a vehicle for expressing and enacting the wishes of the people. I asked him about his model for community self-government, and he replied:

> Well, basically I guess it's community control, then under that it's, you know, there's the Aboriginal Rights, so that could be the band council and then there's the public. Then we're creating a charter community so that could fall under that hat. Same council but not all councillors deal with all subjects. The Aboriginal deal with everything but non-Aboriginal wouldn't deal with, none of the band stuff. So basically it's community control.

The model here is not to have a separate Dene government, or even a Dene 'house' or Senate with veto powers over specific areas. Rather, it is to have a public government with Dene representatives having exclusive jurisdiction over specific areas, those related to band matters, and non-Dene participation through normal representation mechanisms. However, the model also features community assemblies as the foundation and final authority.

In the eighties, as the Dene Nation moved to separate out the logic of negotiation of land claims and self-government, Barnaby crafted a self-government strategy for the community of Fort Good Hope. By 1992, a version of this strategy was embodied in two documents, one called "A Model for Self-Government," authored by The Fort Good Hope Dene Community Council and dated March 21, 1991, and the other called "Government of Fort Good Hope: Self-Government and Program and Service Responsibilities," dated May 14, 1992, with no author listed. The development of this model was encouraged as a pilot project funded by the territorial government. There are three basic principles enunciated in these documents: 1. community government would be open to all members of the community, band government would only be open to Dene band members, and the two would form a concentric circle; 2. community and band assemblies, open to all members, would be the highest decision-making bodies and would meet regularly; and 3. the community would be recognized to have authority over all programs and services delivered at the local level, but responsibility would be transferred only at the community's request.

The model comes out of a clear sense of the specific history of the community and its current situation. Among the issues George mentioned in our conversation, here related to the colonial history, was a certain 'de-skilling' of the people: "if . . . we look at capability and deal with administrative skill or self-government skill, but the other one is the capability to work together. I mean after living under the territorial government for twenty-five years, you know, a lot of problems been created in the community." Interestingly, the skills being emphasized have to do with cooperation at the community level, rather than administrative: the 'skills' that people need for the project of democratic government to succeed. He added that "people used to really work good together, live, and they cooperate, have respect and good feelings. Now there's lot of bad feelings, lot of jealousies, back-stabbing and all that stuff. In order to manage and run our things you have to deal with that as well."

In 1992, as the last pieces of the Sahtu Treaty were being negotiated, I worked with Barney Masazumi and George Barnaby to draft legal language that could be used in the Sahtu Treaty to incorporate this model. George would spend the morning talking with Barney and me, and we would sit in front of the computer through the afternoon, writing and revising. Ironically, the model was a few years ahead of the proposed self-government provisions of the Charlottetown Accord, a set of proposals for revision of the Canadian constitution that was rejected by the Canadian public in the fall of the same year. The language we worked on, a "Draft Agreement for Sahtu Regional Self-Government," "Draft Proposed Amendments to the Sahtu Treaty," and "Sahtu Dene and Métis Self-Government Framework Agreement," were not incorporated into the Sahtu Treaty or negotiated in a separate package with the territorial and federal governments.

A critical question in this political vocabulary relates to the politics of form, in this instance evidenced at the level of political structure. George Barnaby noted, in response to a question I asked about the turnover of political leaders at the local level, that it was "the same as Canadian politics. You don't like conservatives, you elect the liberals, or, but really, it's the system, the structure, everything's got to change. So as we keep trying to elect better leaders we provide training and workshops. . . ." He put it nicely in the context of some broad statements about self-government, saying that "if it's the same guys working on it, then nothing will change, it's the same. Same guys, only thing is, elect them this way, don't use an x, use an o. Really nothing changes. Same structure." The structural change that needs to be made, in his view, involves extending democracy:

Make some structural changes. It's like building a new car I guess, you keep identifying problems, keep changing, it gets better all the time. So we're not going to live with something we know doesn't work very well. And that's what Good Hope did with settlement council, it wasn't what they wanted so they, they couldn't change it so the only answer was to get rid of it. Then they went with the band, but they didn't really write a constitution to change it. After getting rid of settlement council, then they went with the band, but they brought the bad habits and procedures from settlement council. They're starting to end up the same structure, only with more people in it. With the change in council . . . after a couple of years they wrote up this new one to put the people on top, the assembly, so that's what we have now but there's still something missing. It's that human, community, development. Healing, getting rid of the bad things, putting good things, working together, then, the training completed are needed, so that things will work better all the time.

Here, the political vocabulary leads almost inevitably outside the realm of the political narrowly conceived, circling around notions of community healing, community well-being, community development, in the search for a political structure that will embody and address these issues.

In 1993, George worked on a plan for restructuring the council's electoral system. The plan would have involved representation by family group, to ensure that each of the major family networks had a representative on council. At a public meeting on June 28, he raised the issue for discussion. Everette Kakfwi, then chief, noted that there were both large and small family groups and the proposal would be difficult to implement. Isidore Manuel spoke in favour of it, saying it would ensure smaller families were represented on the council. A woman on the band council spoke against the proposal, arguing it might lead to pitting the families against each other and suggesting instead that voting by areas within the communities would be a better system. Others spoke in favour of this. George then spoke about the need to ensure that more women were on the council, another problem. A few people mentioned that it would be a good idea to consult the elders on this, and the meeting turned to the next agenda item. The idea was dropped; no consensus or agreement had been developed.

In the summer of 1994 the community was working on a self-government plan to negotiate transfer of programs and services to the community. The core idea of the plan was that the community would determine its priorities and readiness to take over each specific area—social work, health care, education, justice, and so on. At that point, they would notify the federal and territorial governments of their readiness to take complete or partial control, and it would be transferred.

Many people have suggested that Aboriginal self-government is an undefined concept for which Aboriginal people are not ready. In the case of Fort Good Hope, there is a clearly defined vision that is coherent and consistent, workable yet working towards the achievement of ideals that correspond with prominent critical notions of social justice. Much energy has gone into developing proposals, models, legislative language for this vision. That it remains a vision and not an actuality is a testament to the failure of the dominant political system, not to the lack of definition or the unpreparedness of the people of Fort Good Hope.

A POSSIBILITY WORKING AT THE HEART OF FORM

The Fort Good Hope self-government model is interesting precisely because it is less concerned with what powers the community should have than with establishing a way of transferring powers based on a recognition of community authority (that power derives from the people) and with establishing a system of community governance that ensures active and meaningful participation of community members (that power derives from the people). This touches on the question of the politics of form, of establishing a form—in this instance, community control through enhancing participatory democracy—that would work within and challenge the dominant form.

In another, vastly different, context, Rosalind Krauss has named this process or challenge "informe," writing:

> let us think of informe as what form itself creates, as logic acting logically to act against itself within itself, form producing a heterologic. Let us think of it not as the opposite of form but as a possibility working at the heart of form, to erode it from within . . . a structure destabilizing the game in the very act of following the rules. To create a kind of 'mis-play', but one that, inside the system, is legal. The spring winding backward. Like clockwork.[10]

Here, the form structure or logic of the dominant system, a logic of abstraction in the name of an ever more illusory, banal, eroded, and alienated democracy, is turned towards itself; its own claims are used against it. The challenge is from within. A "logic acting logically to act against itself within itself . . ."

A PUBLIC MEETING

The public meeting on June 28, 1993, at which George Barnaby proposed his restructuring of the community council, had three items on the agenda: elections, band membership, and community concerns. A short discussion of the council structure took place under "elections." Also under that item, dates for nominations and elections for chief and councillors were announced. The band membership discussion also involved a quick report. The "community concerns" item, on the other hand, led to a long, emotional, and intense discussion of the community's alcohol policy. The meeting had been scheduled to start at 7:00, but actually got underway at about 7:45. It was held in the downstairs hall of the community centre. About fifty adults attended, and about one-third were women. Lucy Jackson, a local justice of the peace, provided translation services during the meeting for the elders, since most of the meeting was conducted in English.

Fort Good Hope, like Fort Simpson, has an alcohol rationing system that sets daily limits on how much alcohol any individual can bring into the community. Since the community is not easily accessible by road and does not have a liquor store, the ration system works to keep the community somewhat 'drier' than Fort Simpson, where there is a liquor store. The rationing policy had been determined by the community in a referendum and was long established, in spite of occasional challenges.

A group of young people proposed that a local beer dance be held in the community on the same weekend when nearby Norman Wells holds its annual summer Black Bear Jamboree. This would help to prevent boating accidents and the funds raised could be used to build a community basketball court. A series of young people spoke in favour of the proposal, adding details, and then an older man and the chief spoke against it.

A series of people then started to try to talk; voices were raised. George Barnaby called for order, asking that other people who wanted to speak be allowed their turn. Voices for and against the proposal were heard, more of the latter emerging as the meeting progressed. By this time more people had crowded into the meeting. The community centre can be seen from most of the town. When a lot of trucks are parked outside in the evening, residents know that something is up and they start to gather. Clearly, the rumour that a big discussion was going on had spread, and the intensity of the discussion brought the smokers in from outside as everyone waited their turn to speak, or watched and listened and assessed.

After the first hour, a series of strong speeches by a middle-aged woman, who chastised the band council for allowing the idea to come to a public meeting, a young woman who spoke passionately against the proposal, the local drug and alcohol counsellor at the drop-in centre, and a female and a male elder, all strongly opposed, silenced the proposal's supporters. Chief Everette Kakfwi then suggested drawing the discussion to a close, admonishing the recreation committee that they were "not in place to come up with this sort of activity that half the people don't agree with," to which a younger woman from the committee responded with the comment that it had come forward "as a suggestion to raise ten thousand dollars for a scoreboard" and not meant to cause harm. The first elder who had spoken then summed up that there was "no agreement on it. We can't talk about it all night. Let's throw it back on the council." No vote was taken, and it was clear from the tone of the meeting that the council would reject the proposal. The young man who had first raised the idea, and his friends, were upset and dejected.

The meeting, though, continued. A young man suggested limiting gambling in the community to weekend nights. There was no comment on this. Another man suggested establishing a neighbourhood watch system. Then an elderly man, who hadn't spoken all evening, responded to the gambling suggestion: "There's too much complaining here," he said. "You don't want us to have any fun. What kind of fun can we have without gambling? People will start drinking again. There's nothing to do around here, it's just dead!" A shorter discussion ensued, following a similar trajectory to the earlier one. The chief then closed the meeting by noting that "these are the two most troubling issues" in the community, which was "always going to be dealing with them." By then, it was late in the evening. The meeting had slowly emptied, and the last twenty to thirty people stretched, chatted, drifted outside into the long late evening light, lit cigarettes, unwound, went home.

The issues had been difficult and there were no final resolutions. But there was active participation of a good proportion of the community. And a demonstration of the passion and emotion with which people held different concerns and ideas in the community. And, for me, a practical demonstration of the effectiveness of George Barnaby's ideas, that community assemblies could work as the basic decision-making bodies in a context such as that of Fort Good Hope. Consensus is often thought of colloquially as "full agreement," a much harder to reach goal than that of "general agreement." This meeting demonstrated consensus on two distinct but important levels. One was that of the ethics of speech, the guiding rules of discussion that allowed everyone who wanted to speak to be heard, every voice to be treated with respect. The respect of community members for each other, even across the boundary of heated opinion, was constantly being demonstrated, enacted. Secondly, the eventual outcome—more so in the instance of the electoral system discussion but arguably also in the beer dance discussion—involved a consensus of the negative sort. Because there was no general agreement, action would not be taken and this was understood without a vote. Action could only be taken, not necessarily only with full agreement, but if there was strong enough support that the dissenters, after having been heard and themselves noted the tone of discussion, voluntarily ceased their dissent and allowed a momentum of supportive opinions to carry the day. The intricacies of face-to-face politics, a multiplicity of subtle nuances, tones, momentums, shifts, continue to structure the basic political life of Fort Good Hope.

AN ELECTION

The same meeting had its share of on-the-side dramas. One of these had to do with the upcoming election of chief and council. Isidore Manuel, my close friend, was running against Everette Kakfwi, the chief who was also brother to Stephen Kakfwi, one of the most prominent Dene politicians in the NWT. Everette himself had won the position as chief on a platform of spending more time in the community; past chiefs, during the years of federal constitutional negotiations, had been called on to spend much of their time out of the community. Everette was committed to addressing local concerns and to being present to deal with individuals who had problems. That summer, when I interviewed him, he was officially on holiday, and not only met with me, but, during the hour I spent, was called on by several people for small favours or help that he as chief could dispense, and was finally called away because a cheque needed urgent signing.

He was, and is, a dedicated man and lived up to his promise of spending more time in the community. In my first encounters with him, I found him difficult to get to know, but professional and well organized. Later, I would find that, perhaps because of not having the worries and responsibilities of the office of chief, he was much friendlier and kinder, and I grew more impressed with his leadership abilities. However, one thing did impress me from the outset, and that was his dedication; he took the job seriously and was constantly on the run.

His sole opponent was Isidore Manuel. I never saw Isidore actively do anything to seek office, though he may have campaigned more when I left. His sole tactic seemed to be that when people came up to ask him if he was running for chief, he would nod, smile shyly, and finally say "yes." The people who came up and asked would then say, as a few did during the community meeting, "well, you've got my support." There was a quiet strength in these exchanges, a calmness and determination. Isidore never said anything negative about Everette, though there was much talk about how things needed to change, the band office needed to be more responsive to the community. Isidore's strengths were his seriousness, his dedication, his experience with the band council, his having gained some education outside the community, and his close connection with people from many different families. On the basis of this fairly random evidence, I was not surprised to hear, weeks later, from Yellowknife, that he had won the election. On the phone to me soon after, he said he was going hunting to get some moose for the community assembly. He had begun his career as chief.

POLITICS AND FRIENDSHIP

Two delicate matters. The next summer, when I came to Fort Good Hope, Chief Manuel was out of town at a meeting of the Sahtu region leadership to discuss issues pertaining to the land claim. I discovered that the election margin had been very narrow—a bare handful of votes separated the two candidates. The outgoing chief was very upset, especially because the turnout had been quite low and there was some concern that proxy votes had not been used. The whole council had changed dramatically; more young people had been elected as councillors. However, on the council, Everette had slowly come around, apparently, and impressed me as an able and concerned council member; it was almost a year later and he had taken his defeat in stride, now doing what he could to contribute positively. Meanwhile, Isidore now had a furrowed brow and was worrying more than ever about the community, about whether the land claim was going to work out properly. Isidore and Everette had reached, with some difficulty, the position where they could continue to work together to achieve the goals of the community. I wondered if, in part, a new generation of leaders was following the practice, or rather, political dynamic, established by their predecessors: as Frank T'Seleie and Charlie Barnaby had worked together over the years, each serving terms as chief, would Isidore Manuel and Everette Kakfwi do the same? It turned out not to be the case.

In my discussions with Leo Norwegian from Liidli Koe, he had described in some detail what he thought it took to be a good chief. He had said in part that "you got to be really strong to be chief. I don't think I could ever be chief, my temper is just too bad [laughing]. . . . If the people like you, they support you. You have to work together." The stress was on bringing people together, being the pacifier, and this meant that there was no room to be self-centred or temperamental. In speaking about an 'old-time' chief he admired, Old Man Cli, Leo had said, "He's very, very level-headed man. Some people call him names and it don't bother him. . . ." Isidore, by temperament, struck me as in this way a 'traditional' chief, someone primarily concerned with ensuring that people are getting along, keeping his eye on the main long-term objective of community well-being.

It became clear to me that in his term of office as a new chief, Isidore was slowly feeling his way, hesitant to assert the authority of office, wanting to use the office in something like a traditional manner, to help people. But he was not having an easy time of it. He spoke to me of the frustration of going to regional meetings "where all they want to talk about is setting up this or that board of this or that development corporation." He could not find a way of getting real community problems, or the issue of healing that was then being widely talked about in Fort Good Hope, on the agenda. Frustrations, worries, hesitations, doubts: the job of a chief. But even those who criticize him commend him for his dedication, and the most they would say in criticism is that he needs more time.

Nevertheless, in the next election, Isidore lost the position to John T'Seleie, who had recently returned to Fort Good Hope from Yellowknife.

T'Seleie himself lost the subsequent election to none other than Everette Kakfwi. It was almost as if Fort Good Hope represented a mirror image of Liidli Koe. In Liidli Koe an administration in turmoil was counterbalanced by a fairly stable political leadership; in Fort Good Hope the administration, which did change over the years, was remarkably stable while the political leadership went through dramatic change. In each of the following three elections a different chief was elected: Fort Good Hope had become a political hotbed in which leadership experience was being circulated through a select group of women and men.

A DAY ON THE DEH CHO

One time, Isidore and Millie Manuel took me along on the river from Fort Good Hope to Norman Wells and back. We left early in the morning for the five- or six-hour, depending on stops, trip. The first forty minutes take us through the Ramparts; for the next few hours the landscape is dominated by the river itself, until we begin to see mountains as we get closer to Norman Wells. On the way down we discover that the Dene camps along the river this summer—including Bella and Frank's—are much preoccupied with picking mushrooms for the Japanese market: a new short-term cash source has been discovered that supports the subsistence economy. Each of the camps we stop in at has fish or moose or caribou meat ready to offer guests, along with tea and bannock. We offer news, make sure everyone is doing well, visit for a half hour or so, and continue on our way.

That time, on our return trip, we found about three other boats of travellers, also returning home to Fort Good Hope. After about an hour, we find the other boats drifting together: the lead boat, the fastest one, is out of gas. They've been sitting for a while, sharing smokes, chatting. Isidore passes over some gas, as does someone in another boat, tanks are refilled, and we're off again. About an hour later, the same thing: a second boat is out of gas. Difficult calculations are made, gas is redivided, the party starts off, but Isidore confides that, now, none of the boats has enough gas to make it back! Nevertheless, it goes without saying that the problem is shared among each of the boats. We travel on, what else is there to do? At worst, after we all run out of gas, we'll drift in to town, carried along by the powerful current. Isidore tells a story about the last time he drifted with a boatful overnight, through the Ramparts, into town. The fastest boat skims on ahead, the others slowly spread out, trailing along behind. Then, as the boats are gathered together a third time, as if by some miracle, a boat with two young men, partying, dangerously charges up. They have nothing but gas and laughingly pass it out, enough for all. By some serendipity they just happened to be out on the river, cruising around. They tease Isidore, saying, "You're chief, you'll have to make sure we get paid," and, also, "I guess we're just like 9-1-1," and he gracefully accepts the teasing; it never disturbs his dignity or upsets his equanimity. The boats all start off again. We start off first, but are slowest. One by one, each of the other boats passes us. As the last ones go by, Isidore takes out a paddle, pretending to 'speed up' by paddling alongside the boat, enjoying the joke: the chief has the slowest boat.

That time, we came through the Ramparts just after midnight, as the sun was starting to set. The cliffs on the west side were dark, in shadows, but along the east shore, where our boat travelled, the setting sun splashed across the Ramparts, bringing out a vibrant, stunning gallery of colour, dominated by orange and yellow, lit up as if by an internal light, and we watched as, through the twenty-odd minutes it took us to get through the Ramparts, the shadow cast by the earth itself as it turned away from the sun painstakingly crawled up the cliff.

In an interview some days later, I ask George Barnaby, "What's the goal of self-government—is it a mechanism to achieve something else, or an end in itself? What do you ultimately want to achieve?" He pauses, thoughtfully. His answer: "I'm not really sure. Part of a, like I said, part of a big picture. Because really the goal is to have a good life in the community." The good life. Somewhere, it can be found. Perhaps echoed in the midnight sun on the Ramparts on the Deh Cho.

EPILOGUE: BREACHING THE RAMPARTS

In recent years the proposal for a Mackenzie Valley Pipeline has resurfaced. This time, the plan appears to be, according to my friend Petr Cizek, to bring natural gas down from the Beaufort Sea and the Sahtu region to the tar sands of northern Alberta for use in processing the crude oil there: natural gas is needed in massive amounts in the production of this oil, and do not ask questions about the logic of using 'clean' energy to produce 'dirty' energy. This time Aboriginal people are to be partners, or, at least, the development corporations established by land claims agreements are contemplating buying equity positions in the megaproject. There can be no doubt that the current land claims (modern treaty) model, which turns First Nations into capital holders who must make wise investment decisions, sets in motion the events that lead to these kinds of 'buy-ins'. A map produced by the Canadian Arctic Resources Committee shows a spiderweb of pipelines around Colville Lake that will be a likely result, or worst-case scenario, depending on your view, of the project. Fort Simpson and the Dehcho region continue to oppose the project, which will have to cross their unsurrendered territory. Some of the people I know in Tulita and Fort Good Hope are now working for the pipeline company. Others oppose the pipeline but the best they can do is try to drive a hard bargain, ensure they get ongoing taxation, rent, or resource-sharing revenues for the life of the pipeline. If the companies and State think this is too much and decide not to build, they'll cry crocodile tears. Perhaps the time I have spent in Fort Good Hope and Colville Lake will have to be filed under the category: witness. Perhaps twenty years from now someone reading these words may say, "That is what it was like then," as they survey the wreckage of one, ten, a thousand Norman Wells-style oil towns in the NWT. But it is still my preference to think of the political dream embodied in Fort Good Hope not as a nostalgic throwback to a distant past or a fading present, but rather as the promise of a possible future.

In a recent visit, Frank T'Seleie takes me hiking up the Ramparts and teaches me something new about them: they were perfect summer fish-camp sites. Instead of a mere backdrop, as I have tended to discuss them in this chapter, they were actually the foundation of the summer gathering of peoples, a safe, resource-rich, place on the river. Runners carried messages along the trails at the top of the Ramparts from camp to camp. In the still evening air I can almost see the smoke from many fires, hear the laughter of children, smell and taste the dry-fish. For the energy companies, breaching the Ramparts means building along their banks. For myself, breaching the Ramparts means recognizing them not as backdrop but as ground, as a foundation, for a community that reaches into the heart of the land as much as a land that reaches into the heart of a community.

CHAPTER FIVE

a certain kind of writing in panniqtuuq

COMMUNITY INSCRIPTIONS

Panniqtuuq announces itself. Consistently, insistently, it tells you, reminds you, of its presence. And it's not as if it has to. To reach Panniqtuuq, you travel by air or sea. There is no road, no winter road, no proposals for a road, no dream of a road. Panniqtuuq is located near the Arctic Circle on the east side of Baffin Island, on a fiord, the Pangnirtung Fiord, that runs northward off another large body of water, Cumberland Sound, which runs westward. It is hard to imagine reaching Panniqtuuq—having taken the trouble to get there—or being in Panniqtuuq and thinking that you might be someplace else or wondering where you are.

However, if for some strange reason you forget, there it is, written in small white stones that make up large white letters, a short way up the smaller of the two mountains that overlook the community: "Pangnirtung, NWT," the anglicized version of the name written in English and Inuit syllabic print (more recently it has been amended to read "Pangnirtung, NU"). And further along, on the same hill, a little higher up, the words "Welcome to Pangnirtung," in the same white stones, in the same English and Inuit syllabic forms, translations, though which is a translation and which the original, and for whom, are open questions. A strange (double) repetition: "Pangnirtung, NU" and "Welcome to Pangnirtung," the only words inscribed in the hills that overlook the community, in two languages, a kind of doubling, a repetition and a difference. One welcomes, one announces: both in two languages and two forms of writing, inscriptions in stone on the land, both specify: Pangnirtung.

Should your gaze not wander so far out of the community, you would still not be at a loss for location markers. The fire station, in small white wooden letters, says "Pangnirtung Fire Station." The Co-operative grocery store says "Pangnirtung Inuit Co-op." The post office says "Pangnirtung Post Office" not once, but twice. The community radio station is marked as the "Pangnirtung Radio Station." It is as if Panniqtuuq cannot resist the opportunity to inscribe itself, remind itself of itself.

On a rock between the 'downtown' and 'uptown' parts of the community, divided by the airstrip, can be found what was for many years the only graffiti in town. Here, presumably some of the younger folk, in a fit of daring, flaunting convention and authority, leave traces of their generational energies and "weak messianic powers." On this rock, they scrawl in black spray paint: "Pang." Their youthful exuberance doubles over with their 'proper' citizenship, as if a crew of rebels had taken great risks to establish control of the governor's palace because they wanted to decorate it in a manner better suited to the dignity of the office. Some years later, an expletive so well known to speakers of English that one need not violate the sanctity of the academic text by repeating it here, gets added in a different colour (reminding us of how the supplement can overturn the meaning of that to which it is added), and more graffiti proliferates around the community including, among the more typical and expected scrawls, an unexpected "have a nice day."

Much of this could be said to be both normal and benign. After all, many communities—perhaps all—mark themselves. But the double inscription on the land, on the hill overlooking the community, is peculiarly insistent, certainly unusual, and over-determines a reading of the other inscriptions. Something here relates to Fredric Jameson's reflection on landscape in *The Seeds of Time*, where he suggests that "this kind of analysis effectively neutralizes the old opposition between the rational and the irrational . . . by locating the dynamics of meaning in texts that precede conceptual abstraction,"[1] texts like the inscriptions on landscape, or the landscape itself. Jameson goes on to suggest that in these texts "a multiplicity of levels is thereby at once opened up that can no longer be assimilated to Weberian rationalization, instrumental thought, the reifications and repressions of the narrowly rational or conceptual" (23). In a community where, as I will illustrate, elders have stressed the colonial relation by deploying the metaphor of over-inscription—"they wrote their laws over ours"—this gesture, this inscription on the landscape, marks perhaps on one level a written response, the construction of a different sort of text. Panniqtuuq's improbable insistence on itself reflects, not least, the politics of being that is a key feature of Aboriginal politics in Canada. It equally reflects something about writing, about the being of writing, about kinds of writing: a certain kind of writing and, perhaps, a certain kind of writing lesson.

AUYUITTUQ

Jameson writes of landscape potentially as "a space that is somehow meaningfully organized and on the very point of speech, a kind of articulated thinking that fails to reach its ultimate translation in proposition or concepts, in messages,"[2] and, in reference to a text from the Pacific Northwest called in English the *Epic of Asdiwal*, argues that "the various landscapes, from frozen inland wastes to the river and the coast itself, speak multiple languages (including those of the economic mode of production itself and of the kinship structure) and emit a remarkable range of articulated messages."[3] What message is evoked by Auyuittuq, "the land that never melts"? Auyuittuq is a valley that stretches northward from the end of the Pangnirtung Fiord, along the Weasel River and across the Arctic Circle through a stretch of mountains named by the Qallunaat after Norse gods, up to Summit Lake, then down along the Owl River to the fiord at the north end, on which is an island that holds the community of Qiqiqtarjuak. Auyuittuq is glacier country: glacial moraines, glacial streams, tundra, landslides. Here, the world is new, still being carved, still being formed. Now a national park, Auyuittuq provided Inuit with a way of passing across this peninsula of Baffin Island: it was and is well-travelled-upon country. Though nowadays, physically fit tourists with expensive hiking gear do most of the walking.

Panniqtuuq is perched near the entrance of the fiord that leads to Auyuittuq, the fiord slowly widening as it winds southward from Auyuittuq to Panniqtuuq. By the time you reach Panniqtuuq, the world is no longer new, the landscape well formed, presenting a more established aspect. This is ocean and mountain country, far north of the treeline, with a moral topography all its own. And it is a spectacular setting for a remarkable community, a community in conversation with its landscape like few others.

Panniqtuuq is a kind of coastal community. Not quite coastal in the way the term usually designates, because for much of the year the ocean is frozen and travelled on by snowmobiles. Even in summer, the boats have to navigate around the floating debris of ice packs that can on occasion squeeze together tight enough to make themselves unpassable. Hunting, here, involves most frequently going out on the water or ice. The community itself is perched on a tidal flat, so the rhythm of tides dominates life in summer, and, in winter, creates a zone of broken ice that must be navigated over in order to get to the smoother ocean ice.

But there are also trails that lead overland, and hunting parties that follow those trails, as in the one that goes through Auyuittuq. Inland, following those trails that wind along creeks and rivers, surrounded by mountains and rolling hills, meadows and valleys, moss and boulders, a different kind of reality prevails. It's somehow more pastoral, serene, nurturing: no longer the harsh exposure of the open ocean. Walking overland here invites poetic reflection of the sort John Moss so eloquently practises in his writings on arctic landscape.

In the Pangnirtung Fiord the dramatic highs and lows of the kind of moral topography Taussig talks about have relevance. So do other oppositions: inland and coastal, or winter and summer, though going high up the mountains seems to be a comparatively rare venture, much less frequent than going out on the ocean (whether frozen or not). Certainly, this is a landscape that invokes the sublime: Auyuittuq, especially, provides the kind of contrast, starkness, and impressive, awe-inspiring quality that might be associated with the sublime. While camped across from Crater Lake, near sleep, I hear an enormous roar that sounds as if it comes from just above the tent. It continues, not thunder, a landslide, growing louder. We sit up and look out. Across the valley, kilometres away, we watch for almost twenty minutes as the roar continues, marking tons and tons of rock, ice, and snow, falling down sheer cliff and mountain, making a vast pile at the bottom, soon to become just another part of the moraine, one I am glad not to be under.

An earthly place, marked by stunning, unearthly beauty. The clearest air I've ever seen: ocean air. Wild, wild winds. Mosses and other small plants, covering all the ground: a giant feeding field for caribou and other wildlife. The best time of year to see this terrain is May, when you can travel by snowmobile across the frozen ocean or along and over the land ridges, across valleys and valleys, high up to see ridges fading into the distance, or low along valley floors, wandering along frozen rivers and streams, the dry air working to lessen the feel of coldness, which has dissipated enough to have lost its sting. And no trees to block the view: better to be a hunter than prey here.

My Inuit students in southern Canada can not quite get comfortable with the presence of trees: trees are always 'in the way' of the view. One northern Inuk I talk to, when asked what he remembered most about a recent visit to Toronto, gave the distinctly Inuit answer: "all the trees." Who else would associate Toronto with trees?

A WALK THROUGH PANNIQTUUQ

The variety of global changes in political and economic structure currently taking place in Nunavut—involving both the land claim and the new territory—have had little immediate impact on the architecture and social landscape of Panniqtuuq, and in fact appear almost to derive from their community-based embodiments. Which is to say that a community like Panniqtuuq primarily gets built from the ground up, gets built from a variety of everyday and strategic decisions made by local people, albeit sometimes at the behest of opportunities made available from the outside and frequently drawing on outside technical assistance. The site of Panniqtuuq was chosen by Attagoyuk in the early 1920s, who advised the Hudson's Bay Company that it would be a good place for them to set up shop. Perhaps he deliberately chose a location not used as one of the semi-permanent family bases scattered around the Sound. The name "Panniqtuuq" translates as "where the bull caribou are."

A walk from one end of town to the next takes about forty minutes at an easygoing pace, and will serve here as an adequate rhetorical structure around which a description can be fashioned. Walking, like reading, allows thought to travel across inscribed space; small wonder that thinking so frequently converges in the two activities. In this walk, the trace we follow is that of the road that stretches from one end of town to the other; although not connected by road to the south, there are many vehicles—mostly trucks—in Panniqtuuq and a well-established road and trail infrastructure.

The two main parts of this community of about 1500 people are called 'downtown' and 'uptown'. The former is the older part of the community. Here, one can still make out the traces of the old Anglican mission and training school, the freshly painted, bright white and red Old Blubber Station from the Hudson's Bay Company's flirtation with the whale and fox fur market, the remnants of appropriately named 'matchbox' houses from the earliest government-sponsored housing programs next to the more spacious and solidly built houses of recent years, as well as other new additions to the community: three commercial stores, a substantial medical centre, and something resembling a public square or triangle with the Auyuittuq Visitor's Centre, the Angmarlik Cultural Centre, and the Uqqurmiut Artists Co-operative facing each other. Standing on the road amid these buildings, it's possible to look along the coast and see the Hamlet Office building and, further along, the building that supports the local commercial fishery.

This architecture embodies the three major sources of cash income for the community, tangible representations of the community's economy. Tourism, primarily oriented towards wilderness hikes in Auyuittuq National Park, brings a steady midsummer trickle of clients to local businesses, including Inuit outfitters who usually carry tourists by boat to the park entrance, and sometimes take tourists out on fishing or hunting trips, or out to the more distant territorial historic park at Kekerton Island. The tourists also provide some support for a second source of cash income in the area of art production. The Uqqurmiut Artists Co-operative (the name "Uqqurmiut" means "people of the lee side," referring to the situation of the community at the foot of Mount Duval) produces an annual catalogue of prints and tapestries, all made by local Inuit artists, for sale at the outlet in Panniqtuuq as well as in southern markets through a variety of art dealers. Finally, the commercial fishery allows individual Inuk, primarily through hook and line fishing, to sell turbot and Arctic char to southern markets.

What is striking about these three economic activities is the degree to which they conform to and support a fourth activity, one that takes a dramatically different form. That is, of course, what is called the subsistence economy, life on the land. The fishery, the ecotourism, and the arts and crafts all serve to support movement out of the community and into the ecologically rich Cumberland Sound hunting and fishing territory. Each provides the money that allows for the gas, bullets, and other supplies now necessary for getting from the community to the hunting grounds or hunting camps. The brilliance of Panniqtuuq rests in this, more so than in the architecture or even the setting; it has found a way, its own unique way, of making the cash economy and the subsistence economy support each other. This would not be feasible if the cash economy depended upon large, non-renewable resource extraction projects—mines or oil wells—which demand time, skills, work discipline, and social organization antithetic to the demands and rigours of life on the land (of course, the environmental damage that comes with these projects also mitigates against subsistence hunting). Each of Panniqtuuq's main sources of cash involves and supports going out on the land, as going out on the land supports the art production, ecotourism, and fishery.

For this to work, Panniqtuuq has also had to be innovative in the use of technology. Strikingly, at about the time that most people moved out of their hunting camps, which had been widely dispersed along Cumberland Sound, newer forms of mobility allowed them to continue to use virtually the whole of the area. Snowmobiles and motorized boats allowed people to take advantage of settlement life while still having access to wildlife-rich areas quite remote from the community. In his very exhaustive and engaging study of social structures of Inuit in the region, *Inuit, Whalers and Cultural Persistence*, Marc Stevenson suggests that "the advantages of the snowmobile were realized soon after its introduction in 1964; the hunter could now cover more ground in less time, which allowed travel to traditional hunting grounds and back within a day."[4] It is not uncommon to find Inuit hunters or outfitters today equipped with the latest in satellite location devices; they have been quick to take up any technological innovation that is of practical use. For many families, the community acts more like a base camp, a secure place to return to in the worst seasons or when one suffers an injury or begins to find life on the land too demanding. As a result, fewer people spend extended periods of time in their hunting camps. The physical structure of the community is strikingly open to the spectacular landscape that surrounds it, not so much in the interests of beauty as in the interests of access, though the two serve each other well. Comings and goings are more hourly than daily events, organized around the tides.

If we walk further, past the airport that cuts the town in two (the short-cut right across the airstrip was once marked by a light on a pole, which flashed to warn of the impending arrival of an airplane, but eventually Transport Canada realized the dangers inherent in this and blocked the shortcut), to the newer 'uptown' part of the community, we find an equally dense community infrastructure. More of the homes here are larger and newer. This part of town holds the two schools, a new Adult Education Centre, an arena. On its margins: warehouses, electrical generators that produce a constant, somewhat discordant, mechanical hum, and, along the coast, graveyards and massive oil containers.

Further along, our walk ends with trash, refuse, debris: the garbage dump. The garbage dump is situated about a kilometre down a gravel road that stretches along the coast northward. Garbage disposal is a problem in the north, where the dryness and coldness of the air make for very slow decay. In Iqaluit, the garbage dump has been a stain on the landscape, as refuse falls over, slides down, and litters the dark bank on the ocean with whitish smirches in full view of the rest of the community. In Pan-niqtuuq, the dump is closer to town but less obvious, more adequately contained, though smoke from the almost continual burning acts as a con-stant reminder of its presence. The road appropriately enough ends at the stink of the dump, the final resting place of the detritus of civilization, the terminus of things. However, this reflection is cut short by a student, Tara Wittman, who, while working on a project in the dump, notices that the bulldozer-driving staff daily wait to begin their burning until a small group of regulars has picked over the refuse. Local recycling. Northward, the coast stretches invitingly towards a peninsula with a high hill that prom-ises a view, and stretches further towards Overlord Mountain and Auyuit-tuq. Straight inland from the dump is Mount Duval, the taller of the two mountains at whose feet Panniqtuuq rests.

One of the post-1999 Nunavut impacts has been the construction of housing and office units on the far side of the small river (simply bear-ing the name *ku*, river). Slowly this area is evolving into its own suburb: a ghetto for government workers. While creating jobs at the community level is a Nunavut government priority, and decentralization is one of its mantras, there is a worry that the creation of areas of a community with government housing and government offices will bring to Panniqtuuq a newer version of a colonial social structure marked by a colonial architectural structure. A critical mass of Qallunaat who do not need to interact with local Inuit might make an indelible impression on the place: ironic that Nunavut should be the initiator of such a process.

TEA WITH ROSIE

Rosie Okpik's house near the end of her life was in the middle of downtown, one of the older private homes in the community of Panniqtuuq, with the rundown and comfortable feel of an old, southern farmhouse, although it was much smaller. From her dining room window, Rosie could look out along the coast at the small mountain and, in mid-afternoon, find inscribed on the cliff edge a face, perpetually and resolutely turned towards the sun: a gaze forbidden to mere humans.

I first met Rosie in Peterborough, at the elders' gathering, where she had been invited, along with two other Inuit elders, to speak. She came to my home, attending a feast that Inuit students sponsored for their elders, and gave me a small gift, a bookmark made at the tapestry studio, and invited me to visit when I next travelled to Panniqtuuq.

I visited her several times, for conversation, tea, and bannock, as well as a formal interview. We would sit at her table, place a teapot between us, and talk away the time. She would tell me that "a good thing would happen if we would adopt our own culture," and how when she goes out on the land, "it's a good feeling, a good life" where she's "at peace" and "it's good for your mind and body." She "worries about what's going to happen, next twenty years." She emphasized the need for people to "teach their children" Inuit culture because "we will never become Qallunaat" and, significantly, "we should have it written, so we can teach the children our own." She also said, "When you learn, when you're [at an] early age, you don't forget those, what you learn, outside of your parents. And again, when you learn from your parents, and you don't forget them either. Even [when] your parents die, they [are] long gone, you know, their words, it's right there in your mind. When you have to use them it's right there." Although a very devout Christian (an Anglican gone Pentecostal!), Rosie Okpik has great respect for her own and other Aboriginal traditionalists, commenting on how impressed she was by the strong traditional spiritual presence she observed at the elders' gathering she had attended in Peterborough, for example, or taking great interest in braided sweetgrass. The questions of cultural survival interest her, and, in "her little house" where she is "not rich" but "comfortable," she said emphatically, "we can talk all day!" about these issues.

Rosie nearly always had the radio playing in the background, as did many people in the community. Local broadcasts in the daytime hours featured community announcements and Inuktitut-speaking hosts playing music. During one visit, Rosie insisted that I "go over the radio" to say a bit about who I was and thank the community. I gladly agreed, and then found this was as easy as picking up the phone and calling the station; suddenly I was "on air," fumbling my way through a thank you to the community for welcoming me and helping me with my research, which Rosie then translated. And the "thank you" extends, since I must here thank Rosie for showing me the proper form; one more "thank you" in the infinite chain that circles around the many ritual and spontaneous expressions of gratitude offered by Inuit, by Dene, by Anishinabe, by Cree, by Haudenosaunee, to their friends, relations, creators, so often for that good life.

GOVERNANCE

Inuit are not subject to the Indian Act. They have constitutional status in Canada as Aboriginal peoples (s 35) with Aboriginal rights, but, thanks to the outcome of a 1939 Supreme Court of Canada legal decision,[5] were not defined as "Indians" in accordance with the provisions of the Indian Act. Therefore, there is no band council structure in the community and no reserve lands. Instead, formal politics in the community are focussed on a hamlet council, a municipal government nominally open to participation from anyone in the community—Inuit or Qallunaat. However, since the vast majority of the community is Inuit, the council is dominated by Inuit representatives. In the years of my study, there was not a single Qallunaat on council, so meetings were held in Inuktitut. Instead of a chief and council, whose resolutions must be approved by the Minister of Indian Affairs and whose powers are defined by the federal Indian Act, in Panniqtuuq a mayor and council have powers under territorial legislation and, rather than the Department of Indian Affairs, in the nineties worried about MACA, the Department of Municipal and Community Affairs of the territorial government.

In these circumstances, self-government takes on a markedly different inflection. Self-government in Panniqtuuq, as in the rest of Nunavut, involves gaining increased power for local public governments. It is not seen as a distinct, separate, or ethnic government. The democratic franchise takes care of Inuit participation. Hence, there is no need for restructuring the Indian Act or any of the other key elements that will work to establish self-government among other First Nations. The political project here, rather, has been to gain as much power as possible for regional and local public governments. The establishment of Nunavut represents an enormous move in this direction. A Nunavut government now passes legislation of its own respecting municipal councils. The degree to which communities will have control and responsibility for management and delivery of programs and services such as education, health, social welfare, justice, and so on, is being negotiated. However, the negotiations are dramatically different from those most band councils will have, because they take place in the context of an Inuit-controlled territorial government, a context that may imply that communities will not have as great a need to establish ownership over broad program and service areas. The whole discussion of self-government at the community level is moot, to a point, because of this context, while at the same time the general project of Aboriginal self-government remains as relevant to Panniqtuuq as it does elsewhere.

The Panniqtuuq Hamlet Council meets regularly in the boardroom of the community centre. The mayor in the early nineties was a young man named Jaypetee Akpalialuk. Most of the councillors were men, though an active female councillor was on council during the early nineties and it appears that one or more women have been involved since then. The council also included a youth delegate who was female. The council meets regularly, both in regular work hours and in the evenings, as circumstances demand. The agenda is dominated by municipal affairs: determining what will happen on what lots, how municipal buildings will be used, what social events would be held in the centre, appointment of municipal staff including a "bylaw officer," usually referred to as "the bylaw," who acts as a quasi local policeman, and so on. The council, as representative of the community, will also be asked by outside bodies to express its views on broad issues and to name delegates to regional bodies. Two things of ongoing concern in Panniqtuuq are the speed at which municipal vehicles, particularly water and sewage trucks, are driven because in the everyday chaos of children, roads, trails, the potential for serious accident seems of concern; and the constant, lingering, unresolvable problem of dogs roaming freely around town. One of the bylaw officer's main responsibilities is, following council directives, to go around and shoot loose dogs on designated "dog days."

Administration of the council's affairs was managed by an efficient local staff. The senior administrative officer (SAO) in the early years of my study was a Qallunaat man. There had been serious conflict between him and the mayor, which led to the mayor's handing in a resignation and the SAO's feeling uncomfortable, frustrated, and distressed. However, over the course of about a year, the mayor somehow retained his position and the SAO gladly moved on, making way for a local Inuit woman, who held the position for many years. Tension at the office, which always worked relatively efficiently, seems to have been markedly reduced. A typical council meeting in Panniqtuuq will likely begin within fifteen minutes or so of the announced time. The meetings are open to the public, though I never saw other observers. Occasionally, as when discussing the highly charged resignations and counter-resignations of mayor and SAO in the summer of 1993, meetings might be held behind closed doors.

The boardroom in the community centre features a picture window view looking down the Pangnirtung Fiord to Overlord Mountain and Auyuittuq. On the windowsill is a heavy and quite large soapstone maple leaf, about one square foot. An outline is carved into the maple leaf, which roughly corresponds to the landscape outside. The maple leaf, in a land without trees, remains a signifier that still works to mark 'Canada' in spite of the fact that the literal referent—the leaves of maple or any other trees—are not part of this reality. 'Canada' then, embracing and written over by the Pangnirtung Fiord: the fiord marking 'Canada' and 'Canada' marking the fiord: a dialectical image, one that equally inscribes the totalizing power of the dominant nation and a subversive capturing of that power to invest a local landscape with national significance: an imaginary staging of the dramatic tension between ideology and utopia. A fitting image to think through the position of the Panniqtuuq Hamlet Council, which itself sits at the interstices of power, power derived from legislation that comes from the federal government via the territorial government as much as it is derived from the people of Panniqtuuq. Somehow, uneasily, the Panniqtuuq Hamlet Council oscillates between, and is accountable to, both; like the Pangnirtung Fiord, over-inscribed by a maple leaf, written in stone.

LIVING HISTORY IN THE ANGMARLIK CENTRE

Living history: a history that is alive: a life that is historical: a history that "hurts." The Angmarlik Centre in Panniqtuuq, the community's cultural centre, dramatically stages a relationship between history, nature, and culture. The centre consists of four, distinct, interior-architectural components: a reception area, the entrance where shoes are left behind, and a front desk, like any other front desk, occupied by very friendly and helpful staff (all female through the course of this study); a small community library, with a good collection of northern, Panniqtuuq-related and Auyuittuq-related books; a museum that focusses on traditional Inuit culture in the area and the history of the community, special attention being paid to whaling in the early part of the twentieth century; and, finally, an elders' room, where elders can frequently be found, playing cards, drinking coffee or tea, sewing, and chatting about old times and new.

The museum is situated in the centre of the building, surrounded by the reception area, library, and elders' room. The most striking display in the museum is the first one: a frame dwelling, with a wide variety of traditional clothes, tools, toys, that can be worn, handled, played with, set in front of a blown-up photograph of the Pangnirtung Fiord. This leads to a picture window view of the real scene, in front of which is a bench and table with a series of photography books, which contain images of the past organized along themes such as whaling, old days, the land, elders, Qallunaat/friends, and so on. Around this, behind the signature display, a series of small museum pieces focus on life on the land, missions, whaling days, the early history of the community.

The photographs would make for an interesting study in themselves. Many are subtitled, with the names of their subjects in syllabic Inuktitut and English. Other subtitles are commentaries, often with no immediate relation to the image: stories, reminiscences, reflections, comments.

The images and texts represent only one aspect of the centre's living history. The elders, who provide the centre with its pulse, are another.

The elders gather during regular weekly hours. They are available to chat with and will tell stories or ponder over the photographs, centre staff providing interpretation. The school can bring classes who will sit in on storytelling sessions. The elders are organized as in no other community I have visited, to be consulted, interviewed, or simply for conversation. For this study, I set up in a small side room with my interpreter, Kayrene Kilabuk (formerly Nookiguak), and tape recorder. We approached the elders as a group, introduced me, explained the project, and asked for direction. Elders were eager to participate, and during interviews, whenever I asked if they were too tired or wanted a break, they always replied that they enjoyed the chance to talk about the past and would be happy to talk as long as I had questions. Elders who had spent their early years growing up on the land, before the community existed, could relate from their varied perspective a whole history of contact and relations with Qallunaat.

The history itself is organized into roughly four periods: a period before the Qallunaat, when Inuit lived in dispersed hunting groups entirely on the land; a period in the mid- and late nineteenth century, when there was a whale boom in the Cumberland Sound area, leading to a period through the first half of the twentieth century when whaling was replaced by a fur trade and a redispersal along Cumberland Sound; and a more recent period after 1962, when people were brought in from their dispersed camps to the community and Panniqtuuq began to take its present form.

Inuit have great pride that derives from their memory of the first period, when they were self-sufficient and Inuit ways thrived. Elders, especially, remember those days with great pleasure and speak evocatively of bringing back the old ways. At the same time, they stress the difficulty of life in the old days, the hardships, near-starvation experiences, and the dangers. It is not, therefore, an idealistic and nostalgic representation of the past that lingers in these images and stories; rather and arguably, what lingers is an implicit critique of the modern. The memory of the past provides a position or a standpoint from which the modern can be assessed and the weaknesses of the modern, particularly in terms of social relations, are exposed, rendered visible.

The whaling period is a source of dramatic historical events, reflected in the dangerous chase for the whales themselves. The hunt of whales roughly parallels the hunt to near extinction of buffalo in the great plains in the same period. Curiously, both large mammals provided critical raw materials for industrial technologies, lubricating oil from the whales and leather belts from the buffalo, though commercial products were made from both as well. The shallow waters of Cumberland Sound, an area biologically rich in sea mammals, provided a major successor for a depleted Davis Strait whale industry in the mid-nineteenth century. Whaling stations at Kekerton and Blacklead islands attracted hundreds of Inuit and hence led to a period of population concentration. The centre is itself named for the most important male leader of the whale hunt in the last stages of this period, Angmarlik, whose strong persona is still vividly and fondly remembered by elders in Panniqtuuq. One of his adopted sons, Pauloosie Angmarlik, provided my most interesting and complex conversations in the community during the early years of my involvement with it.

A combination of depletion of whales and changing technologies that rendered some of the whale products unnecessary led to a decline of whaling in the early twentieth century. Inuit dispersed again to hunting camps along Cumberland Sound, within a few decades finding that the value of fox furs, the hunting of which was quite compatible with hunting for the main dietary staple, seal, was sufficient to allow for the purchase of store-bought goods that had become increasingly necessary. In effect, a kind of retraditionalization took place as Inuit moved away from the sustained, regular contact with Qallunaat and the subsistence economy enjoyed renewed importance. In the early 1920s Panniqtuuq was established at its present site as a Hudson's Bay trading post.

A sketch from the 1920s that is noticeably absent from the centre refers back to the earlier period. A.Y. Jackson, one of the Group of Seven painters who refigured perception of the Canadian landscape in the twenties and thirties, travelled with the Eastern Arctic Patrol in 1927, and included in a portfolio of printed sketches from that trip are three of Panniqtuuq. I first saw two of these sketches on display at the McMichael Gallery northwest of Toronto in the mid-eighties and was excited simply because of that great Western conceit: "I have been there." Four sketches of Panniqtuuq are reproduced in *The Arctic 1927*. Two show Inuit and their skin tents against the backdrop of a view towards the mouth of the fiord. One looks inland, an overgrown moraine, at the hills of Panniqtuuq. The other depicts Inuit in a small camp on the present site of Panniqtuuq, and a view, the same view, always the same, of the Pangnirtung Fiord, looking northwards, toward Overlord Mountain, towards Auyuittuq. Jackson's gaze, too, could not avoid that direction. The sketch, remarkably, stages virtually exactly the same image as the primary display in the centre, evoking the first historical period, though seen from the perspective of the second.

The summer of 1962 marks a fourth period. At that time, there were buildings at the present site of Panniqtuuq—a nursing and police station, a mission school, the ever-present Bay store—and a small group of Inuit permanent residents, but the site acted more like the centre of an extended group of people who occupied camps all along the shoreline of Cumberland Sound, in places like the shallow bay of Avataqtu, where Arctic char are to be found in great numbers in the late summer. In 1962 an epidemic struck the dogs, killing them off in great numbers. Without the dogs, which meant mobility in winter, life on the land was too dangerous. The 'authorities' gathered up the people—in camp after camp they were swept up in a purge that left few out—and took them to Panniqtuuq, where they were 'settled'. The community, its present social being and the architectural and urban infrastructure that together form the social landscape, began to take its present shape.

These four periods of history circle around each other and are represented in the stories and images focussed in the Angmarlik Centre. The view of the fiord, the artistic representations, the artefacts, the images, the elders, the books: nature, culture, and history folded over each other. The three periods, likewise, playing off against each other: images of traditional life ways remain vivid through the latter two periods. The Angmarlik Centre is a kind of university, a kind of museum, a kind of library, a kind of art gallery: a cultural centre, a repository of knowledge, a site of conversation, dialogue, exchange, discussion, and a fitting stage for the intricate intellectual life of Panniqtuuq. That it is 'open' to the community, that it is 'legitimated' by the tourist traffic in the summer and its 'function' of organizing rides for English-speaking tourists with Inuktitut-speaking 'outfitters' to Auyuittuq, that it is likewise 'open' to a breathtaking view of the Pangnirtung Fiord, the light from which providing enough open air that tourists and researchers can photograph the feature display, the frame dwelling and photographic image of the fiord behind it, 'as if it were the real thing', an image of an image, simulacrum, whose power doubles back to say 'tradition', that it has become all this and more: a certain kind of writing, what could be called a writing against the State.

THE TEMPLE OF NATURE

The Angmarlik Centre is in striking contrast to the nearby Auyuittuq Visitor's Centre. Both exist in part to serve a tourist clientele, though the former is at least equally oriented to local people. The latter, with an oblique entrance, is much more forcefully directed towards outsiders. It contains five distinct areas: an office area like those of recent, fluorescent-light, numbing style; a room dedicated to the park; a room dedicated to 'nature'; a room dedicated to art; and a workshop-like meeting room. The room dedicated to the park is in the centre of the building, the other four areas surround it. It is made up of maps, photographic images, and displays that provide the expected useful information about the geology, flora, and fauna in the park. Most useful is the map that shows recent polar bear sightings. To the side are two temples, one to art, the other to nature. A separate room, artificially lit in the spectral tones of a ritual space, is devoted to art works: large sculptures produced by local artists. Next to it is a room with a display of all the wildlife one will not see on a hike through the park. A huge, stuffed polar bear leans over a stuffed seal, while the dead gazes of lemmings and owls and foxes survey the scene, on a backdrop of ice and cliffs. A dead nature, here, animals treated with the most extraordinary disrespect, offered as spectacle, as a stand-in for what the northern tourist wants but will not likely see. Tape-recorded sounds of animal and other 'natural' noises enhance the simulacrum, strive to create an ever-receding aura. The workshop room stages in its physical structure the dialectic of seeing. The room is brighter than any of the others, one wall being of glass, allowing for the view. The room is filled with chairs, all of which face away from the window, away from the view, to a giant television screen where one can listen to park regulation and safety lectures and, more importantly, watch the video representation of the park; infinitely preferable, it seems, to turning one's head around.

ISLANDS OF HISTORY: KEKERTON

It takes a few hours to travel by the small, distinctive Panniqtuuq boats from the community to Kekerton Island. Now a territorial historic park, the island was for decades a major focus of Qallunaat whaling activity. In a sense, the Inuit of Panniqtuuq can lay claim to having had some of the longest sustained interaction with Qallunaat, compared to other Inuit in Canada, though in the nineteenth century the limited ability of Qallunaat to withstand Arctic conditions—quite inhospitable, to their way of thinking—meant that Inuit were in a better position to control or at least influence the interaction. Kekerton was enough of a hub of activity that when the fledgling Canadian government wanted to do something to assert its sovereignty over the High Arctic, a sovereignty passed on to it by Order-in-Council from Great Britain in 1880, they sent representatives to 'plant the flag' there. William Wakeham, a fisheries patrol commander, wrote in his journal for August 17, 1897:

> Landed and hoisted the Union Jack in presence of the agent, a number of our own officers and crew, and the Esquimaux, formally declaring in their presence that the flag was hoisted as an evidence that Baffin's Land with all the territories, islands and dependencies adjacent to it were now, as they always had been since their first discovery, under the exclusive sovereignty of Great Britain.[6]

The Union Jack remains hoisted on the high lookout hill, once a marker of colonial dominance, now a reminder of colonial history. Kekerton Island is also the place where Franz Boas conducted the research that would lead to, among his many other publications, *The Central Eskimo*. If we accept Boas's place in the canon of anthropological inquiry, it can be argued that the whole practice of fieldwork so central to contemporary professional anthropology, and indeed perhaps even to the concept of cultural relativism, was invented in this place, with the participation of the great-grandparents of Panniqtuuq Inuit.

To visit Kekerton today is to visit a spectral landscape, a landscape of traces from the past, only partly contained by the relatively minimal newer boardwalk and site-explanation devices. No structures remain, though the outlines of buildings and tent frames remain clearly visible. Scattered bits of machinery and other ancient refuse litter a relatively small area where the old station was located. One reconstructed whalebone tent frame is now the most prominent structure, a large pile of rusted barrel rings the most prominent pile of debris. On the climb up the hill, to look out as in older times for whales, or to look at Wakeham's flag in its latest incarnation, or just to look out at the view, one passes usually by accident the most striking feature of the park. Around the outskirts of the old station are Inuit burial sites: old barrels and wooden coffins, covered sometimes with just a few stones, unmarked, scattered in no discernable order except that they have been placed outside what was once the site of settlement. One stumbles across these almost always by accident, finding oneself suddenly haunted, in the presence of death, sometimes surrounded by coffins: once you spot one, others become visible and they are all around. No crosses. No inscriptions. No names, and none are necessary since these are passed on to the next generation. Marked only by themselves.

OUR QALLUNAAT FRIENDS

There are Qallunaat in Panniqtuuq, many of them small-business owners, on the frontier of capital accumulation, making their way through the maze of government tenders and the high-risk business opportunities that exist: store owners or managers, a private fishing company owner, construction company owners, and the like. For the most part, the men are not soft-spoken; they swear as easily as breathe, a colourful language where polite forms stand out like an Inukshuk in a southern city. They know the community well and are happy to share their knowledge. The Qallunaat women tend to come in the stereotypical roles of nurses, teachers, and welfare workers. Hugh Brody's chapters on 'whites' in *The People's Land* remain quite appropriate. Writing in the early seventies, Brody remarked that "the Whites of the far north are class-conscious to a remarkable degree, and the nature and minutiae of their social life are informed by that consciousness."[7] In Panniqtuuq the Qallunaat frequently speak of the 'troubles' in the community: alcohol addiction, drug addiction, violence, family violence, assault, sexual assault. In this world view the community is a kind of rural ghetto where, borrowing their idiom, 'these people'—Inuit—are not succeeding at the painful process of adjusting to modernism. They are at pains to reveal this to me, the naïve southern researcher, to ensure that I 'see' this 'reality', and to save me from the danger of idealizing or sentimentalizing. Although they do have a much deeper understanding of the community than I can hope to, the kind of understanding that only comes from duration, from lived experience, a kind of under-standing I have great respect for, and although they also, each in his own way, have admiration and genuine care for their Inuit employees, co-work-ers, friends, clients, yet, over and over again, their description of the com-munity is exhausted by a litany of horrors, each example, each story, more revealing of inner weakness, more revealing of trauma and failure, than the next. To them, I respond: "All right. I see it. And I see something else, too. Since you are so capable of telling the one story, it is this 'something else' that I've chosen to write about." There are other kinds of Qallunaat as well, who have stayed even longer, established more permanent con-nections, maintained a degree of empathy, interest, excitement; their well-told stories also deserve careful attention.

In the Angmarlik Centre, one book of photographs features "Our Qal-lunaat Friends," photos of whalers, police officers, missionaries, and others who spent sometimes large parts of their lives in Panniqtuuq. There are Qallunaat friends living in Panniqtuuq today, including the businessmen, those in the 'helping' professions, and many Qallunaat visitors, including researchers, including me, taking up time and space. There are many Qal-lunaat who live in or visit Panniqtuuq and want to 'give something back' to the community. But that is not as easy as we would wish it.

DELEGATIONS

Watching and reading through the record of the more open-ended portions of hamlet council meetings in Panniqtuuq is a study in micropolitics. The open-ended portions of the meetings are where non-agenda items can be raised, usually through two mechanisms: a regular agenda item that allows 'delegates'—anyone from the community, as well as guests who come in some official capacity—to make a statement before the council; and a regu-lar agenda item called "council concerns" that allows councillors to raise any issue of their choice. Reading through council minutes from the past few years, more often than not these two agenda items reflect in an unusual context what Anthony Giddens once referred to, in relation to modernism, as "this unique conjunction of the banal and the apocalyptic"[8] and reveal a good deal about the internal political dynamic of Panniqtuuq.

Delegates to Panniqtuuq Hamlet Council meetings frequently include everyday citizens coming to speak their minds on a wide range of issues, from the mundane to the profound. A select sample from the year 1992 is illustrative. At the January 6, 1992, meeting, one of the three delegates is Mosesee Nakashuk, who says, in the language of the minutes,

> this has been on my thought for some time now, we the people of Pangnirtung elect our leaders of this community, there have been job opportunities that I have tried for, I only see that we the locals are put aside when the applicants are selected it seems only out of town people get hired. Cr. Sowdloapik answers why weren't they acknowledge by letter for their interest in the job. Council wishes to conduct interview as a whole, sometimes Finance committee is delegated to conduct interviews and report to council. Mosesee is appreciated for coming to council.

The initial gesture should not go unnoticed: Mosesee begins by berating the leaders with an appeal in classic democratic rhetorical style—"we the people of Pangnirtung elect our leaders"—before going on to lodge a serious complaint. The recorded response is a discussion of a more minor, technical aspect of the problem, but the council deferentially thanks the citizen for coming forward with his comments.

Rumours of complaints circulate as freely as other stories. A representative to the Baffin Regional Health Board, Leah Akpalialuk, in her regular report to council as one of ten different delegates on March 16, 1992, is recorded as saying: "we were told to make people more aware of cigarette cancer. We were also informed from Arctic Bay, when they sended a dead body down south for autopsy, the body was sent back in a garbage bag, when they should not do that. . . ." An unusual combination to report: a following through, perhaps, with the official form of reporting what you are told to report embodied in the cancer warning, followed by what was really interesting that was heard, a story that ends with a moral imperative—"they should not do that"—a story testifying at least to a perception of the everyday brutality of racism, something of a distant, colonial echo to Benjamin's warning that "even the dead will not be safe from the enemy if he wins. And this enemy has not ceased to be victorious."[9] The command, dutifully carried out, is directly followed by criticism, as if somehow one calls forth the other, cannot be left to stand alone; there is something here too of the overturning logic of the supplement.

Very serious issues sometimes are brought forward by delegates, reflecting concern about the deep social problems in the community and perhaps a belief that somehow, by talking about these issues, by raising them in the public forum, in some way this talk—a public version of the 'talking cure' that psychoanalysis posits for private, personal, individual psychic illness—will effect something mysterious but desirable called "healing." At the November 30, 1992, meeting the first delegate lucidly confronts the problem of mental illness:

> Meeka Arnaquq—Mental Health Committee: Meeka has had a concern, for a long time, about the terminally ill patients sent home from the hospitals, and their families. It can get stressful on the families caring for the patient 24 hours a day. The intentions of people who offer help is good but when there are people there all the time, they have to realize the patient and family needs peace and quiet sometimes. Families sometimes end up caring for a patient up to a year and this can take its toll on families. b) Also there's an increase in mental illnesses, not just stress or hard times but actual illnesses. Health isn't doing much for these people.

Once again, as with Mosesee Nakashuk, who said, "This has been on my thought for some time now," and Michael Kilabuk, another delegate who "wanted to come here before, but never did till now," Meeka Arnaquq stresses the gravity of the problem as something that "she has had a concern, for a long time, about." It is tempting to read the last statement, which refers to the Department of Health, in its more general valence: "health isn't doing much for these people," their health alone will not help them from the debilitations brought on by social problems. Or perhaps it can be read allegorically as a reflection of the almost classic working-class attitude that health is not worth guarding when life offers so little: "health isn't doing much for these people." Her concerns, about the support network for terminally ill people and about the increase in mental illness, are not easily addressed:

> Council discusses strategies to improve terminal patient care and to work with other organizations like the Member of Legislative Assembly, Baffin Regional Council and Baffin Regional Health Board and that they will persist with this issue until Health has some solution.

The response reflects a registration process, a registering or acknowledgement that the problem has been noted, that renewed efforts will be made, that "they will persist with this issue until Health has some solution." Through this process a concern is noted, an affirmation is provided; speech and response take place in the political forum. Finding no resolution, the talk, the conversation, will continue and perhaps it itself, mere speech, will remind and cajole, reflect and project, startle and distract, persist, persist, persist, "until Health," perhaps health itself, "until Health has some solution."

COUNCIL CONCERNS

Often, delegates presenting at a meeting are the councillors themselves, who "remove themselves from council" in order to represent some other interest from the community. However, the councillors also have an opportunity for open speech in a "council concerns" agenda item. A reading through the same sample year, 1992, reveals a similar overlay of discussions, reflecting the micropolitics of the community. An eclectic range of local problems gets raised, as in this list from the October 19 meeting: "A. Evic wants the Garbage drivers to pick up garbage more often. A. Dialla thinks it would be a good idea to get a alarm system for the Post Office. I. Kilabuk is concern about the dogs being loose around town, he is wondering if they can be shot on sight." The concern about loose dogs, according to the first Senior Administrative Officer, Bill Bennett, whom I interviewed in 1993, was the most frequent, raised repeatedly by delegates and councillors alike. It is also peculiarly ironic, given that the most common reason for the community's coming into being was an epidemic that killed dogs and forced people off the land. They were relocated as a result of an absence of dogs to a place where the continued existence of dogs would prove one of the most persistent problems of everyday life.

Sometimes, what seem to be simple problems prove intractable, revealing in their very existence the difficulty Inuit have fitting their life ways into the structures determined by outside forces. The following council concern, from the November 30 meeting, is a case in point: "Councillor Ipeelie Kilabuk—Education Representative—Qammaqa [snow houses] are used at the schools as part of education. GNWT Dept. of Safety has put all kinds of regulations on their operation, like they have to have two exits, and this is causing problems. Cr. Qaqasiq doesn't think this is good." Councillor Qaqasiq's wry comment is equally a warning and a reflection of a sense of uneasiness. This issue—not being able to teach children about Inuit cultural ways as embodied in snow houses because 'buildings' have to conform to fire regulations that stipulate the necessity for two exits (just as, in residential schools, children could not be brought wild food from local trappers for use in the cafeterias, because such food would not conform to safety standards)—unfolds the whole tissue of rules, presupposing values, imposed by outsiders, the Qallunaat, on Inuit. This issue, one of extraordinary urgency, is addressed frequently and directly by the council, particularly in its discussions of law and the administration of justice, the arena of rule formation *par excellence.*

THE POLITICS OF POLICING

The embodiment of the repressive State apparatus in Panniqtuuq is the Royal Canadian Mounted Police, with whom the council had an uneasy relationship in 1992. What is interesting about the council's record in this matter is the way in which the council tries to exert its influence in an area where it has no 'official' jurisdiction or power. The RCMP officers frequently appear at council meetings as delegates to 'give reports' about the community. At the March 16, 1992, meeting, a tense, highly charged exchange takes place, beginning with the officer's report:

> B.L., RCMP read his report for the month of February, he said it was the most violent month since his 3 years up here. These were alcohol related, charges have been laid, there was an attack on his house, and someone broke his window. He is concern about the safety of his family, and he is asking council if he can work with them.

A dramatic appeal, but one that does not find a sympathetic response. One of the council's most consistent concerns is that of overly strict law enforcement, leading to a too-high-frequency incarceration rate of Panniqtuuq Inuit. A councillor, Sakiasie Sowdloapik, responds by confronting this latter issue, which other councillors raise in different contexts through the course of the year:

> Cr. Sowdloapik tells him that he is just grabbing too many young people from coming in from out of town. Most of the young

people don't want to go out of town anymore, even to work. Also the one who broke your window, I think he was provoked by you, you just grabbed him, he was coming in from work. You are also hurting the airlines, I talked to your headquarters in Iqaluit, they told me you just can't grab anyone without reasonable grounds to search. I want to work with you B., but you are over doing it.

The appeal here reveals, firstly, that Sowdloapik knows who is responsible for breaking the window—a peculiarly 'ideological crime', directed as it is at the embodiment of State repressive power—but, secondly, will not reveal or divulge that information and, thirdly, has sympathy with the miscreant.

At subsequent meetings in 1992, officers other than B.L. presented the RCMP reports, as in the case of the July 8 meeting when "RCMP D.F. gave the June/92 report noting that it was a quiet month with few offenses reported. Concern was raised about the Centre operation. Council thanked Mr. F. for his report." A much more benign discussion. At the September 28 meeting, a new officer introduces himself:

RCMP Corporal S. has been in the service for 16 years, 6 years in the North. He is looking forward to meeting all. He read the monthly report for September. There has been complaints about pellet guns, when they are suppose to be prohibited. In his report, cpl. S. stated that the Centre is open too late. J. Veevee tells him that Recreation Committee will deal with the Centre's hour at the next meeting.

In this instance, interestingly, the council does seem prepared to work with the officer, operating not on the basis of the structure, but rather of a face-to-face ethic: the 'new man' will be given a fair opportunity.

The politics of policing are intricate in Panniqtuuq; a local ordinance against drinking is deployed by police with great intensity, providing an excuse for them to engage the machinery of disciplinary power that founds them. The heavy-handed administration of justice is a frequently addressed concern of the council, which has limited ability to act but nevertheless uses its influence and apparently with some effect. The council in a state of being against the State, as a State against the State, on this plane of community politics. But the question of law and justice plays itself out on other planes, as well.

A MATTER OF LAW

A special meeting of council was held on August 24, 1992, for the purpose of discussing the issue of justice. Members of the community, including elders and community activists, were invited to the meeting to express their views. Special guests at the meeting were the Baffin Regional Judge, Beverly Brown, and Justice Scott Cooper, a prosecutor with the Department of Justice. The language of the minutes for this meeting is particularly ambiguous, untidy, incomplete, resisting grammatical structure almost as if it were reflecting resistance to the rules and law it addresses. The intent of the meeting seems to have been to consult with community members about the administration of justice and to establish a justice committee in order to promote ongoing consultation.

After the preliminaries, the issue is joined by councillor Sakiasie Sowdloapik:

> Juridical system is not working for the Community and a lot of parents seen that their children are going through the system. Creates a lot of stress for the whole families and that elders present stressed that they were able to solve and counsel the persons problem.
>
> —has lost a lot of traditional knowledge and has not been able to utilize the white Society. Court system does not use the forgive and help life style looking at all the Committee present have a lot of resources a program in the Community.

The stress here, as elsewhere, is on using Inuit mechanisms to deal with problems, rather than the imposed legal system. Other councillors add comments, one noting that he had not even seen a police officer in the first years of his life: in those days none were needed.

Having duly allowed the elected representatives to speak, establishing the tone and direction of the meeting, other guests intervene. An important elder, Aksayuk Etuangat, notes that there was "No alcohol in our days. Alcohol and drugs play a major part in getting into problems in the Community." Another elder, Pauloosie Angmarlik (both these elders were adopted children of the whaler Angmarlik), returns to the issue of traditional justice, which becomes a theme for much of the rest of the meeting:

Traditional knowledge passed on from one generation to the next, we did not have the white mans system and they have created more problems and expect them to be able to correct their problem and parents are expected to pay their children's fines or restitution payments we need to understand what would be the best alternative to solving these problems.

This puts the question rather directly: Qallunaat have created a problem they now want Inuit to resolve. Sakiasie Sowdloapik follows soon after, referring the issue back to policing:

Police have no knowledge of Inuit life style— Laws are so thick and follow these Laws and Inuit must understand these laws and you don't understand these principals. We need to work together in solving problems. We need to understand the nature of crime and researchers dealt with. Studies have been done and it shows that white society do not allow us to make changes to the present Laws.

The "thickness" of the Law, an unusual but appropriate metaphor to explain the difficulty Inuit have in understanding and following Qallunaat law, though Sowdloapik also notes that Qallunaat "don't understand these principals" of Inuit law as well. The elder, Pauloosie Angmarlik, speaks again, soon after: "Laws have been written by the white society and Inuit have verbal laws and these laws would never have been over ridden by the written laws— White society are responsible for the Crimes being committed and we are not saying that have stop in sentencing criminal." Even through these layers of mediation, Angmarlik and Sowdloapik both speaking in Inuktitut, their comments hurriedly translated and roughly recorded in minutes, it is still clear that they are saying something about the difference between Qallunaat law and Inuit law, something about the difficulty Qallunaat and Inuit have in understanding each other's law, something about the difficulties created by the imposition of one law over another.

As a result of the discussion, that which was aimed for in its initiation is achieved, a justice committee is established. The committee, which will come to serve in an advisory capacity assisting in the sentencing process, meets three times by September 28, and provides regular reports to Council thereafter. One of these involves the following exchange at the November 30 meeting:

> Cr. Evic asked if the Judicial Committee could do something about the time frame of incidents and the charge being laid. There are charges getting laid for incidents that happened years ago. Cr. Veevee responded, saying that the time frame is of Federal jurisdiction and that only they have authority to change it. Cr. Kilabuk suggest that an option for the defendant would be to approach the committee before going to the RCMP to lay the charges. Cr. Papatsie ended his report telling Council, the Committee will need all the support it can get.

Once again, the imposed legal order establishes a structure that community members cannot easily circumvent in the name of their own conception of justice.

The discussion is entirely revealing of the conflict between the imposed Qallunaat system of law and that which lives in the memories of elders and in the culture of Inuit. In this instance, Panniqtuuq provides a microcosm for the whole debate about the continued existence of Aboriginal culture in Canada. The nature of the legal structure that underlies social structure is not an incidental aspect of this debate. In Panniqtuuq, most frequently the conflict is embodied in the removal of people from the community to distant discipline centres for distant reasons. The prisons where offenders are sent allow them to make connections with gangs and more often than not become training grounds for criminals: prisons as colleges of crime. Community leaders and elders have a clear, lived sense of the dimensions of the problem, and in this demonstrate a far-sightedness, a nuanced vision of the intricate layers and sedimentations of cultural imposition, an alternative ordering of the temporality of justice.

PAULOOSIE ANGMARLIK

During my reading of the minutes of the special hamlet council meeting of August 24, 1992, one statement stood out, or struck me, as particularly resonant. This was made by the elder Pauloosie Angmarlik, who had said, "Laws have been written by the white society and Inuit have verbal laws and these laws would never have been over ridden by the written laws. . . . White society," he added, "are responsible for the Crimes being committed." This notion of the fact that Qallunaat laws are 'written' and that this allows them to verride Inuit 'verbal laws', creating a responsibility, seemed an allegory for the whole process of colonial imposition.

I decided during my 1993 visit that I would like to speak to Pauloosie Angmarlik. My research assistant, Kayrene Kilabuk, assured me that he was a very respected elder, a "wise old man," and that we would have little difficulty finding him. On the morning of August 4, 1993, I met with him in his small house, one of the older houses in the downtown part of the community. It was the first of many meetings, interviews, and conversations. He was a small man with a full head of white hair, and was wearing a light blue T-shirt with dark blue pants held up with red clip-on suspenders. Kayrene simply asked if he was willing to be interviewed and he said, without hesitation and through welcoming smiles, that we could go ahead. I ask one question, about if he remembers his comments to the special council meeting at about this time last year, and his eyes widen, eyebrows moving up in the expressive Inuit facial gesture that means an emphatic "yes!" He goes to a nylon jacket hanging over a chair near the sink, pulls out a neatly folded piece of paper, on which is written, in Inuktitut syllabics, his speech on justice, which he proceeds to read to me.

In *Tristes Tropiques*, Claude Levi-Strauss used "A Writing Lesson" to unfold a whole theory on the dynamics of State power. He wrote, in part, that "the only phenomenon with which writing has always been concomitant is the creation of cities and empires, that is the integration of large numbers of individuals into a political system, and their grading into castes or classes."[10] Derrida uses a reading of this passage as one of the signature gestures of deconstruction, deconstructing the opposition between speech and writing and challenging the ethnocentric presumption that there are societies without writing: "to say that a people do not know how to write because one can translate the word which they use to designate the act of inscribing as 'drawing lines', is that not as if one should refuse them 'speech' by translating the equivalent word by 'to cry', 'to sing', 'to sigh'? Indeed 'to stammer'."[11] Derrida's comments are usually taken as dismissive of Levi-Strauss's association of writing with the State and power, but if we read closely, we find in Derrida the trace of a more nuanced account. It is possible to construct an argument whose lineaments suggest there are different modalities of inscription, some that are associated with State power, some, like the writing on the body that Pierre Clastres theorizes, may be writings against the State. Clastres suggests that a society against the State "dictates its laws to its members. It inscribes the text of the law on the surface of their bodies"[12] and, it should be added, on that other body, the landscape. For Clastres, "in its severity, the law is at the same time writing. Writing is on the side of law; the law lives in writing and knowing the one means that unfamiliarity with the other is no longer possible. Hence all law is written; all writing is an index of law."[13]

Unlike Clastres, Angmarlik stresses the opposition between speech and writing. But Pauloosie Angmarlik's writings, it seems to me, may also be seen as writings against the State, which is itself nothing other than a certain kind of writing, the kind that overrides or imposes itself. In Angmarlik's view, it seems clear that Inuit law, which existed in speech and memory, occupied a space that appeared empty to the Qallunaat colonizers, a space that could then be overridden by a certain kind of writing, the writing of Qallunaat law. In response, in his small house in Panniqtuuq, Pauloosie Angmarlik prepares or composes another kind of inscription, one reflecting the outlines of something called Inuit law, so that this time, it cannot be written over.

Angmarlik's speech is similarly a complex praxis. My interviews with him were so tentative. At times, by accident, I ask a question that elicits a lengthy treatise; at times I ask questions that elicit a bafflement that seems to say, "of what possible relevance could that be?" Confusion on my part is the main, structuring element of our talk, but talk takes place. When I listen to these tapes now, more than any others, I find myself thinking, why didn't I ask something to pursue that point further! and regretting directions not taken. And yet, in the midst of my confusion, Angmarlik has a great deal to say. One of his themes is the disastrous consequence that derives from delaying trials: on May 12, 1994, he said through Kayrene, who works as a legal interpreter and was familiar with Pauloosie, having frequently interpreted his statements in court,

> he's never agreed with the white man's law before because it does not work for him. For someone that is supposed to go to court and his court date is usually moved to another date, that is usually the case up here and some people tend to commit suicide because they tend to get worried and think that they'll go to jail and all that, and he said that is one of the factors for people committing suicide nowadays because suicide is a problem up here.

The same theme, virtually, is repeated and elaborated by Angmarlik on August 10, 1994:

there's sometimes delays—like that person's scheduled to be in court today and the judge said that the trial date would have to be set to another date—it would be delayed and all that and it's kept in someone's mind that they have done something wrong and he [Angmarlik] feels that they should be dealt with right away and not try and say so many hurtful things to that person because somehow it's destroying his mind and his inner self and sometimes when court dates are delayed there's often suicides done by young people and he [Angmarlik] feels that it's not very good because if it was dealt with right away some people would not commit suicide, he said that's a factor.

The fact that twice, both times at length, he makes this connection between deferral of justice and suicide, the second time using the most vivid kind of language to try to convey the interiority of mental anguish the delay creates—"it's destroying his mind and his inner self"—is a clear indication of the importance Angmarlik gives this particular subject. Here, the face-to-face circumstances of the community demand that justice not be deferred; here, again, another problem with the temporality of justice emerges.

There are other themes that repeat themselves in Pauloosie Angmarlik's speech. This, from the May interview:

he was saying that nowadays people are going through the court system and people who did something wrong are sent to jail. How he would handle it, how it would have been handled in the past, was that those two people, or more than that, they would be brought together and there would be a discussion with those two people or other people and they would try and find out solutions to their problems. The Qallunaat law and the Inuit law are two very different laws and they cannot seem to work together and he's never agreed with the white mans law before because it does not work for him.

Interestingly, the Inuit law is not seen by Angmarlik as more flexible because it involves resolution of conflict through discussion, but rather as more structured: "He's stating that the Inuit way of life seemed more structured in the past because there were discussion groups of where the hunting was going to take place and if there were conflicts in the camp people were brought in together to discuss the problems." The purpose of the law, in Angmarlik's view, is to help the people resolve conflict: Inuit law as a process of conflict resolution through discussion. Hence, the consistent concern that imprisoning people is not achieving anything, not helping anyone, not solving any problem, but, rather, creating new problems. "The Inuit law it was to help out other people that needed help. I'll give an example: if someone was fixing something and that person was not too good at fixing it someone else would teach him how to fix it. These days that's not the case, so it's the person that can fix something better will just watch and not try and help out." Imprisoning does not 'fix' anything because it doesn't teach anything. There is a remarkably consistent and powerful world view embodied in these reflections; strikingly, it moves from the everyday to the abstract, from people being taken out of the community to serve sentences or delays in trials leading to suicides, to the question of the purpose of law, to provide a set of strictures that must constantly be enforced or to continually contribute to the formation of community by centring the process of discussion.

Another consistent theme of Angmarlik's is that of the relation of law to writing.

> The Qallunaat law is written. Some non-Natives make it look as if it's the only law to follow. That is not the case up here. Inuit have always had their own laws which are not written, since paper was not available and used to write in the past. The Inuit law is kept in memory and the Qallunaat law, since it's written it's—I'll give an example of my house, if I was following the Qallunaat law my law books could catch on fire if my house burned down and there would be nothing else. The Inuit law has been passed on from my ancestors and the only way the Inuit law will not be available is when I pass away.

This is an issue I was particularly interested in; what drew me to Angmarlik in the first instance were his comments to the judge about the overlay of Qallunaat law on Inuit law. On August 9 he added:

> The Inuit law was not written because papers and pens were not available that time and the Inuit used to keep things in their mind. They always remembered what was told to them and the Qallunaat law was written and given to the Inuit not thinking about the Inuit law at all, they thought the Qallunaat law would be suitable for the Inuit too.

I asked him about the relation between Inuit law and Qallunaat law several different times and in several different ways. Among his replies,

The Inuit law is stronger and it would have worked if it still existed, well, if it was written. It would make it seem that the Qallunaat law would not step up on the Inuit law and nothing could take over the Inuit law, because it kept going in one direction and the Qallunaat law takes all different turns and curves and all that because that's how I see it, it doesn't seem to work for the people up here.

[. . . .]

The Inuit law and the Qallunaat law are very different and they cannot seem to work together. It seems as if there's always a blockage between those two and if the Inuit law was written the Qallunaat law would not go on top of it.

While he saw the possibility of Inuit and Qallunaat law working side by side, especially if Inuit law were written down, he also said that "the Qallunaat law should be used by the Qallunaat and the Inuit law should be used by the Inuit."

When I pursue this, when I chase down the specifics of Inuit law—give me an example, I ask, or, how did it work? or, what did it say?—I consistently draw a blank, it eludes me. Angmarlik sketches an outline of the law, which consists of insisting that the law—Inuit law—exists, and very little more. The written Inuit law posed against the written Qallunaat law does not consist of an alternative sequence of injunctions, lists of crimes and punishments, intricate mechanisms for specifying how particular problems will be dealt with, but rather of just that: that Inuit law is, just as Inuit are, and now that this much has been written, the space is no longer so clear for Qallunaat law to operate unimpeded. So, too, Inuksuit, literally "resembling people"—rocks piled to mark a trail or look human-like in order to scare animals—marked the land, a writing on the land that may indicate nothing but the fact that the land is occupied, like the word "Panniqtuuq" inscribed on the hillside, the being of Inuit placed in a new writing, one that this time, I hope, the Qallunaat will be able to read. "We are here."

I interviewed Pauloosie Angmarlik three times. The subsequent interviews, referred to above, took place in the spring and late summer of 1994, and were in the Angmarlik Centre. In these interviews, Pauloosie used all the means of expression at his command to stress the seriousness of the issue of law, the problems that sprang from this overriding of Inuit law by the written Qallunaat law. Listening to the tape recordings of these interviews some months later, I can hear something else. My questions,

Kayrene's interpretation, Pauloosie's Inuktitut answers, and, in the latter two interviews, Kayrene's new son, named Imo after her father, his cries on occasion overriding our conversation, inarticulate, seemingly formless, but clearly demanding, in a language only his mother can understand. With me in this small room, an elder, a younger Inuit woman, her new child, thrown together in the enterprise of understanding Inuit law.

PAULOOSIE ANGMARLIK IN CONVERSATION WITH JACQUES DERRIDA

A conversation can be staged in many ways. It is clear that, sometimes, the books one reads have a bearing on the things one sees and hears. The reverse, of course, is equally true. This conversation, between some of the books I read and some of the people I talked to, may perhaps strike sparks. Whose authority legitimates whose here? Readers of Derrida may learn to listen to Angmarlik, just as readers of Angmarlik may learn to listen to Derrida. In any event, it is clear that the conversation has happened.

Pauloosie Angmarlik, August 24, 1992:

> Laws have been written by the white society and Inuit have verbal laws and these laws would never have been over ridden by the written laws— White society are responsible for the Crimes being committed and we are not saying that have stop in sentencing criminal.

Jacques Derrida, *Of Grammatology:*

> If writing is no longer understood in the narrow sense of linear and phonetic notation, it should be possible to say that all societies capable of producing, that is to say obliterating, their proper names, and of bringing classificatory difference into play, practice writing in general. No reality or concept would therefore correspond to the expression 'society without writing'. This expression is dependent on ethnocentric oneirism, upon the vulgar, that is to say ethnocentric, misconception of writing. (109)

Pauloosie Angmarlik, May 3, 1994:

> It seemed as if the Inuit law kept going in one direction, the right direction, the Qallunaat law seems to go in different curves and all that. . . . I never knew if anything else was added on, I knew that it kept going in one direction and there were no curves or whatever. . . . The Inuit law is stronger and it would have worked if it still existed, well if it was written, it would make it seem that

the Qallunaat law would not step up on the Inuit law and nothing could take over the Inuit law, because it kept going in one direction and the Qallunaat law takes all different turns and curves and all that . . . it doesn't seem to work for the people up here. . . . The Inuit law and the Qallunaat law are very different and they cannot seem to work together. It seems as if there's always a blockage between those two and if the Inuit law was written the Qallunaat law would not go on top of it. . . . If the Inuit law was written they could have worked together if their minds were similar if they had similar ideas on certain issues they could work, but in some cases they would not be able to work together because of the differences.

Jacques Derrida, "Force of Law: The 'Mystical Foundation of Authority'":

Tonight I have agreed by contract to address, in English, a problem, that is to go straight toward it and straight toward you, thematically and without detour, in addressing myself to you in your language. Between law or right, the rectitude of address, direction and uprightness, we should be able to find a direct line of communication and to find ourselves on the right track. Why does deconstruction have the reputation, justified or not, of treating things obliquely, indirectly, with 'quotation marks', and of always asking whether things arrive at the indicated address? (15–16)

Pauloosie Angmarlik, August 9, 1994:

Whatever was passed on to me, I remember it as being straightforward. The Inuit law being straightforward and being another point that I just mentioned was that Aksayak, he's older, and we both know how the Inuit law works: it's more straightforward than the Qallunaat law. . . . The Qallunaat law does not work for me because I had known another law before the Qallunaat law was introduced. I work with the court party now and I try to somehow make the two laws work together but at times there is certain laws that do not connect together and its hard on me sometimes in my mind because I know that another law, how to handle a situation. Another thing is that the court party says you have to do it this way and I feel that the Qallunaat law has a lot of curves and the Inuit law is straightforward. . . . I feel that I have an idea why [the Qallunaat law is] crooked. That the laws are, I see them as being so strict and mean towards the Inuit. . . .

Jacques Derrida, *Spectres of Marx:*

> The perversion of that which, out of joint, does not work well, does not walk straight, or goes askew (*de travers*, then, rather than a *l'envers*) can easily be seen to oppose itself as does the oblique, twisted, wrong, and crooked to the good direction of that which goes right, straight, to the spirit of that which orients or founds the law (*le droit*)—and sets off directly, without detour, toward the right address and so forth. (20)

The dialogue continues, indefinitely, without end.

GESTURES III: SMILES

You are walking down a dusty gravel road. It's a grey day, with spitting rain and just enough fog to block the view. Your hands are weighed down with grocery bags, the plastic handles biting into your skin. You trudge along, enumerating worries for the future, regrets from the past, and present miseries to yourself in a feast of mental self-punishment. Ahead, in the periphery of your vision, someone approaches. In the city you ignore them and walk on by. In a small town you wave hello, or nod or smile curtly, or exchange a few words. In Panniqtuuq, you give the biggest and brightest smile you can manage. And you get one in return. Those offered by the elderly people, in particular, never fail to lift your spirits.

The "smiling" Inuit: one of the dominant images that circulates in the south. And one that has a basis in Inuit practice, though it does not mean that everyone is happy all the time! There is, still observable today, a certain smile, a certain presenting of a face that is happy to greet the other, a certain leaving of troubles behind. When you encounter people walking along the road, especially older people, a smile will always be greeted with a broad smile in reply, a smile over the burdens that are being carried. This is, in Inuit communities, a protocol of everyday life, a gesture that builds the community because it says "I am happy to see you" and it says this even if the name, language, or face of the other are unfamiliar. The first step in building familiarity and friendship is to express pleasure at encountering an other. There is a world of wisdom in those smiles that carry those faces above their troubles, that offer to share only happiness, that refuse to pass on their burdens, that greet the meeting in pleasure.

Walking with Kayrene Kilabuk to Meeka Arnaqaq's home for an interview, she tells me that a twelve-year-old boy is missing in her home community of Broughton Island (now Qiqiqtarjuak). He had been adopted by his grandparents but now his grandmother is also dead and his absence was therefore not noticed until yesterday. Earlier that day she had heard about two suicides in another Inuit community, Clyde River. Walking, telling me this story, smiling, "So you see, there are lots of things happening in our communities. . . . " Smiling.

HANNAH TAUTUAJUK

In two of my visits to Panniqtuuq, I boarded with Hannah Tautuajuk. She was born a Nakashuk, and married an older man, a hunter, who had died some years before. She has three children, one in Yellowknife, one who had lived in Ottawa for many years before moving back to Panniqtuuq, and a daughter, Julie, the youth representative on the hamlet council, who, with her young daughter Tina, lives with Hannah. Hannah is the perfect hostess, accommodating, stretching her English to its limits to be able to talk, teaching the odd bit of Inuktitut, baking bannock, cooking char, ensuring I felt at home in her house.

The first time I stayed at her place, she was out on the land when I arrived. I had come on a Saturday, and she returned from her hunting trip early Sunday evening. She had been on her snowmobile, far across the frozen fiord, hunting the small Baffin caribou. She came into the house like any worker returning home, with big, expressive movements, stamping, warming up, sitting on the couch to take her ankle-high boots off, bringing with her the smell of far-off winds and the aura of pride in a well-done job, a successful trip. Her group had gotten five caribou. She herself had gotten one. She thought nothing of it, it was one of many for this hunting woman whose activity would unravel many an anthropological theory.

ROSIE'S LAST LOOK

When one sets out to deliberately engage in a sustained exchange, dialogue, or conversation with a particular elder, one almost inevitably puts oneself in a situation of intense affect. Rosie Okpik had cancer. By the last years of the twentieth century, it had eaten away much of her life. In the summer of 1997, I went to visit her; she had been out of Panniqtuuq, receiving medical treatment, for much of the time when I was in town. When I heard she was back, I made sure to take the time to visit her. The house was bustling with visitors and relatives, but I recognized Rosie's sharp, rasping voice as soon as I entered. We sat at the table with tea and *pulauga*, chatting. I was soon to be leaving town for another year. When it was time for me to leave, she got up and went to the window, leaning on the sill with a cigarette. I slowly put my boots on, leaning against the doorframe, half bent over, tugging on the heels, then the laces; finally ready. We looked across the room at each other. She was lit in sunlight at the window as if a figure from a Vermeer painting, but the look she gave me was something else, filled with sadness, finality, resignation. I have only ever come close to seeing it in Robert Mapplethorpe's final self-portrait, the one where, holding a skull-cane, he gives us and history the look with which he faced his impending death. It was a look that told me all I needed to know. We would not see each other again. Her words to me, thrown under the look as our eyes held each other for a moment—"goodbye, Peter"—were also somehow resonant beyond the words themselves. She knew, I knew, how final that goodbye was, perhaps one of a chain of final goodbyes she was making. But it is the look that stays with me. Goodbye, Rosie.

COUNTRY FOOD

Gathering country food is work unlike any other, with enough rewards to ensure that it is an embodied deconstruction of the binary opposition between work and leisure. Kayrene Kilabuk ensured that, late in the summer of 1993, I had an opportunity to go out with her father-in-law, Ipelee Kilabuk, who would later be on the hamlet council and had already served a term in the NWT government. The day begins early, we are loaded into the boat—Ipelee, his marriage partner Aittaina, their adopted grandson Ben, Kayrene, my good friend Julia, and myself—and on our way by 6:45

in the morning. The boat is one of the typical Panniqtuuq sea boats, just over five metres long, with a small cabin and open back and a 110-horse-power motor driving it. It's a very cold, hour-long boat ride, across the Pangnirtung Fiord and down the coast of Cumberland Sound, threading our way through huge, floating chunks of ice to a small, shallow bay called Avataqtu.

Avataqtu is a place where fish are plentiful. This I discover as soon as my hook reaches the water, about two minutes after stopping, as tea is being heated to warm us up, bang, an Arctic char. Everyone in the boat, every single person, child included, catches char. We fill up a fish box with char. Through the morning, about four other boats arrive, all with the same intent. I can see char swarming for my hook when I cast out, and fishing is a matter of nudging the hook towards the biggest-looking char. A few hours go by deliriously, as we rake in the fish. A second box begins to fill. Suddenly, a shout. What is it? A seal. Someone has spotted a seal. We're all looking up, scanning the bay for the telltale ripples that indicate a seal, but before I can spot it—bang—this time a shot, and the seal goes down. While I was distractedly going, "oh, how nice, a seal, where is it?" the others had business in mind. The boats all converge on the spot; it turns out there was a second seal and we move out of the bay, searching intently, rifles at the ready, waiting for it to come up. No luck, this time. After a bit more fishing, we go back to the bay, now our gaze turned down into the shallow water, searching the bottom for the seal that was hit. All the boats are engaged in this; we circle around, trolling for fish, watching for the seal on the bottom.

This takes a long time, but eventually the seal is found. It's hauled up with grappling hooks, and the boats are tied to a large, floating chunk of ice where the seal is laid out. Everyone gets out of their boats, stretches, and the seal is methodically butchered, the meat and innards distributed; each of the families receives a share. Virtually all of the seal is put to use; even the intestine is cleared and wound up, the liver is prized. By now it's mid-afternoon, both fish boxes are full, the boats leave in a convoy that slowly spreads out, and, against fairly heavy winds in the open stretch of Cumberland Sound, we make the cold ride back.

The boat is unloaded and the char placed near it. Aittaina begins to clean, working fast with her ulu, the traditional woman's 'moon knife'. Kayrene starts to help, so I join in as well, fumbling and much slower with my Qallunaat knife, as does Julia. Here, it seems, the cleaning is woman's work—Ipelee casts a bemused look in my direction—but nothing is said and we feel that we must do our share for the ten char that Julia and I will keep. Later, a few of those ten char will go towards encouraging a new intake of Inuit students at Trent University to visit my home, where we plan and set up an Inuit Students Group. But then, walking up to the house we were staying in, sinking exhausted after the fresh air, cold, and work, I had that same feeling, a job well done, and pimaatisiwin.

PART THREE

ALTERED STATES

Never will my name appear on filthy government paper.
—Charles Baudelaire, *Lettres à sa mére*

. . . bureaucracy was the result of a responsibility that no man can bear for his fellow-man and no people for another people.
—Hannah Arendt, *The Origins of Totalitarianism*

CHAPTER SIX

an essay concerning aboriginal self-government in denendeh and nunavut

Decolonization in the Canadian context means engaging in the perpetual work of maintaining relationship, not so that it can be circumscribed and terminated, but so that it can carry us all into the future.

—Joyce Green, "Towards a Détente with History"

A DRUM WORKSHOP

Among the cultural events that take place in the NWT capital of Yellow-knife is an annual summer folk music festival, called Folk on the Rocks, in part because of the setting. Long Lake, just across from the airport at Yellowknife, is surrounded by the igneous rock and boreal forest typical of the Canadian Shield, providing a glorious background, midnight sun included, for the event. This is the landscape of my own northern Manitoban childhood, and one that therefore has extraordinary personal resonance. The festival places some emphasis on northern musical talent, including Aboriginal performers. Traditionally oriented Inuit throat singers and Dene drum groups join the usual folk-circuit blues, country, folk, bluegrass, jazz, and rock performers. Many of the latter are northern non-Natives or Natives as well.

On July 23, 1994, I attended a drum workshop by Dogrib elder Gabe Doctor at that summer's Folk on the Rocks. It was a mid-afternoon workshop, on a hot summer day. His niece was along and provided translation and commentary as Gabe Doctor worked a caribou hide, stretching the skin and fixing it to a wooden frame outside, near a stage, and then going inside a teepee where the hot coals of a fire allowed him to heat the drum, contracting the skin so that it fit tightly on the frame. The heat from the coals drove most of the sparse, scattered onlookers, including us, outside for that part of the workshop. Drum making takes skill and patience, we learned; when we returned inside, the niece beat a short song on the newly made, partially complete drum. Gabe had meanwhile gone outside, back to the stage, with a pre-made drum, to sing a song. A woman, likely his marriage partner, kneeled in the shade of a nearby tree the whole time.

On stage, he asks his marriage partner to join him; they stand together for a prayer, then they both sing as he beats the hand drum. At first, their voices sound thin and weak from the distance, but when a microphone is moved close so that the wind no longer drowns their song, the rich, full sound surrounds us. The song moves me through layers and ranges of moods. At first, I hear a kind of stark sadness, the nearness of death, a lament. Later, I hear the sound of still proudly beating hearts, voices weaker than when young, yet remaining strong enough to sing, to celebrate life. Two voices and a drum, distinct but blended: the song is long, and I can finally hear both of these moods—the sadness and the celebration—merged or walking the tightrope of ambiguity, reminding me of the Rembrandt self-portrait at sixty, where both the twinkle in his eye and an endless void of sadness can be found in one look.

A SHORT HISTORY OF ABORIGINAL SELF-GOVERNMENT

The notion of Aboriginal self-government itself walks a tightrope. The name "self-government" has been given to State-sponsored institutional changes among Aboriginal governments, changes that work largely in the interests of totalizing power. At the same time, the concept of self-government has reached the national agenda as the result of agitation and persistence from Aboriginal activists because it bears the promise of representing a site of resistance. A few words on the historical dimensions of the appearance of the concept lay the groundwork for understanding this curious situation.

Within the broad sweep of the conquest-history of the northern part of North America, the status of self-government emerges from the status of the political moment itself. For much of the history of what would become Canada, affairs between Aboriginal and non-Native peoples were governed primarily by an economic logic, the exigencies of the fur trade. If an Aboriginal and non-Native person were talking, say in the period between 1600 and 1870, the chances were that the latter was a trader and the talk was about the terms of trade. In the last half of the nineteenth century, the fur trade declined in importance for Canada, though it remained critical to northern Aboriginal community economies. The economic logic was replaced by a political logic and the State replaced the fur trading companies as the most important hegemonic institution in the lives of Aboriginal peoples. In the twentieth century, if an Aboriginal and non-Native person were talking, chances were the latter worked for the State as Indian Agent or as social service provider of one sort or another.

The Indian Act became a critical tool in the State's arsenal, though it was not applied to Inuit and Métis peoples. From the 1880s, the Indian Act included provision for local-level, municipal-style, band governance. The provisions were controversial from the beginning and were amended many times in the first few decades of their existence. Although they were justified as a mechanism that would teach the Indians about democracy, in fact they were deployed in an attempt to establish more pliable, comprador governments on reserves across Canada. The last major changes made to the band governance provisions took place in 1951, when the worst repressive elements of the Indian Act were dropped and Indian women were given the right to vote for band councils. Much of the language in the Indian Act, including the governance provisions, has been in place since the late nineteenth century. It is a one-size-fits-all model that leaves the minister ultimately with overseeing authority in most areas and a narrow range of delegated powers for band-level governments. With the historic struggle and victory to prevent implementation of the Statement of the Government of Canada on Indian Policy, 1969 (the so-called White Paper), Aboriginal people were in a position for the first time in over 100 years to seize the political initiative.

What policy makers and legislators in Ottawa desired was never exactly what took place in the communities. In Akwesasne, for example, the electoral band system was not operative until it was imposed, by force, in 1899.[1] In northern Dene communities, leaders were elected by show of hand until the sixties and even later. Frank T'Seleie is fond of telling me (as I reported in Chapter Four) how when he was elected chief in the early seventies, he was handed a plastic grocery bag full of all the band office files and documentation. That was it, no office, no phone: a small pile of papers in a plastic bag. The call for self-government came to national attention partly as a result of the patient, continuing assertions of Haudenosaunee peoples that they had never surrendered their sovereignty. It also came from the Dene, whose mid-seventies' well-publicized declaration asserted, "We the Dene of the Northwest Territories insist on the right to be regarded by ourselves and the world as a nation."[2] Although officials at the time were skeptical, within a decade the language of self-government as a partial acknowledgement of the sovereignty concerns of Aboriginal peoples had become a part of the status quo. And increasingly Indian bands began calling themselves First Nations: the language of nationhood and governance was forced on to the agenda by Aboriginal leaders.

As might be expected, the State moved to co-opt the discourse. A major parliamentary report in the early eighties, *Indian Self-Government in Canada: Report of the Special Committee* (or the Penner Report, as it is commonly known, after committee chair Keith Penner), endorsed the idea of self-government and recommended constitutional entrenchment. Although its major recommendations were ignored, the report helped pave the way for broad public acceptance of the idea. By 1985 two pieces of community-based self-government were in place: the Sechelt Act based on delegated municipal-like powers for that BC First Nation, and the Cree-Naskapi Act that flowed from the James Bay and Northern Quebec Agreement, a comprehensive land claim (or first of the recent treaties). Since the Cree-Naskapi Act was passed pursuant to the land claim, itself since 1982 constitutionally protected, there is an argument that the Act itself is the first constitutionally protected self-government legislation in Canada. Subsequent land claims, where they included sections pertaining to self-government, contained a clause specifically exempting self-government provisions from constitutional protection.

Progress on self-government was slow, partly because of the issue of whether deals would have constitutional protection. In a sense, the issue strikes at the core of the self-government debate. Without such protection, legislated self-government can be changed at the will of the federal government. Any time a First Nation engages in an activity that seriously challenges the logic of the established order, it could have its authority revoked. Such 'self-government' is barely self-government at all, but, rather, delegated authority. By the mid-nineties several things had changed. Amendments to the Indian Act in the mid-eighties to secure equality rights in marriage for Indian women had also included provisions allowing band councils to develop their own citizenship codes, as many moved quickly to do. The settlement of several major northern land claims in the early nineties led to agreements to negotiate self-government in the Yukon, the agreement to establish Nunavut (a public government in one of the Inuit homelands), and the federal government's agreeing to recognize the 'inherent right' of First Nations to govern themselves.

Two recent events have sharpened the focus of debates. In the land claims or modern treaty era, settlements by the Nisga'a in British Columbia and the Dogrib (Tli'chon) in Denendeh have included self-government agreements. These have not been agreements to proceed with negotiations as in previous cases, but actual models of self-government included in the treaty and constitutionally protected. Both First Nations agreed to apply or adopt the constitutional Charter of Rights and Freedoms, which implies that at this historical point the trade-off for constitutional protection is adoption of the charter. Since the charter is premised on individual equality rights, there is reason for concern from a cultural perspective: effectively, these deals mean that the federal government will not have immediate authority but that the values it represents will be accepted by the First Nations governments themselves. It should be noted that some of those values might be intrinsic to traditional cultures: for example, among the Dogrib, traditional respect for individual autonomy might sit comfortably next to provisions of the charter. But the general stress on collectivity and community associated with Aboriginal culture will not benefit from such a deal. The language in the Tlicho Treaty is "7.1.2. In addition to anything else necessary in relation to the Tlicho government, the Tlicho Constitution shall provide for . . . (b) protection for Tlicho Citizens and for other persons to whom Tlicho laws apply, by way of rights and freedoms no less than those set out in the Canadian Charter of Rights and Freedoms." In my travels around northern communities, I have been consistently struck by the many idiosyncratic Aboriginal individuals I have encountered. This leads me to the observation that the dominant society, which stresses the value of individualism as a social foundation, is nevertheless profoundly based on conformity in practice and produces cookie-cutter suburban subjects, while so-called collectively oriented Aboriginal communities appear to do a much better job of nurturing significant social differences and producing strikingly unique individuals.

The second recent event was the draft Governance Act, a legislative initiative late in the Chretien regime. The draft Governance Act technically was in response to the Corbiere case at the Supreme Court of Canada, 1999, which determined that status Indians living off-reserve had the right to vote for and participate in their band councils. Instead of merely changing or striking down the relevant section, as the Corbiere decision warranted, the Governance Act proposed replacing the whole of the electoral band system with a new model, determining three sets of codes that bands would have to develop and establishing the broad criteria for the codes. Specific elements of the Royal Commission on Aboriginal Peoples' (RCAP) report were also incorporated into the Governance Act, particularly those pertaining to accountability (for example, recommendation 2.3.40 deals with codes of conduct for public officials and other accountability mechanisms that broadly resemble the approach used by the draft Act).[3] Although the initiative was fought off by an Aboriginal leadership concerned about the one-size-fits-all aspects of the model, and its reassertion of a colonial 'we know what's best for you' approach to dealing with community governance, it raises a concern that the State sees local Aboriginal government as a way of downloading responsibility while maintaining Western institutional forms of decision making.

THE ROYAL COMMISSION ON ABORIGINAL PEOPLES: SMALL NOTES ON A BIG REPORT

Two large sections of the Royal Commission on Aboriginal People's (RCAP) voluminous report are particularly relevant to this discussion. Volume Two, itself composed of two parts, is called *Restructuring the Relationship* and deals with treaty relations, economic relations, lands and resources, and governance itself. Volume Four, *Perspectives and Realities*, which separates out particular Aboriginal interests, including those regarding women and youth, includes a section on "The North." Taken together, the section on governance and the section on the north provide a strong analysis with detailed recommendations regarding Aboriginal self-government in Denendeh and Nunavut. The RCAP report was sometimes criticized for being too large to absorb (five volumes, with one of those divided into two parts), though given the likelihood that the federal government would not be responding favourably to it, a longer report with carefully thought-out positions on a whole range of areas made sense: the report will continue to inform debate into the next decade and its impacts are more than likely to be felt over the longer term. In general, here one can join with Alan Cairns in calling for the State to give more serious consideration to the recommendations. Furthermore, giving piecemeal attention can lead to undesired consequences, as the example of the Governance Act demonstrates. Rather, one must look at the whole trajectory of policies suggested by the RCAP and, while not being bound to implement each one, should look to them for guidance on a set of policies or a policy trajectory that would lead to meaningful change, to the betterment of Aboriginal communities. It should be noted that co-commissioner Georges Erasmus is from Denendeh and in general it is clear that northern models and experiences are certainly taken into account, if not central to the paradigms deployed. For example, the hunting economy gets serious attention, as in the manner in which the discussion of leadership in the RCAP borrows from the description of a good hunter and leader developed by the James Bay Cree Cultural Education Centre in Chisasibi.[4]

In terms of governance, although the commission recognizes that "many Aboriginal people see revitalization of their traditional forms of governance as playing an important role in reform of current governmental systems" (137), there is no specific recommendation dealing with "revitalization of . . . traditional forms" and the concluding paragraph in the discussion of this matter ends up somewhat weaker on this issue than might be hoped:

> many Aboriginal people are in the process of revitalizing their traditional approaches to government as part of a larger process of institutional innovation and reform. While some nations propose to establish institutions based on traditional forms, others favour

approaches that use contemporary Canadian models, while drawing inspiration from traditional Aboriginal governance. Written
constitutions do not tell the whole story, however. Whatever form
Aboriginal governments take, they will likely be influenced by
less tangible features of Aboriginal cultures. The fact that some
Aboriginal governments may resemble Canadian governments in
their overt structure does not preclude their being animated by
Aboriginal outlooks, values and practices. (139, emphasis added)

This is the exact point where, in spite of much excellent work, the RCAP
takes a serious misstep. As I will argue below, the issue of forms is not
one aspect of the struggle for self-government—"whatever form Aboriginal governments take"—but is the central issue. "Whatever" form indeed
is the critical factor in determining whether this or that self-government
model is in collusion with processes of totalizing power or whether they
mark a moment of disjuncture and resistance. The notion that "written
constitutions do not tell the whole story" is critical here: arguably, the
"less tangible features" that will influence Aboriginal governments are
themselves forms of writing. Totalization does its work by deploying one
form of writing; Aboriginal resistance deploys another form, contradict-
ing it in the very modality of its existence as embodied inscription. The
commission entirely sidesteps the issue and makes a weak endorsement of
Aboriginal forms of governance—in spite of an extensive discussion of the
issue and much research about it—that ultimately amounts to no endorsement at all.

As noted, the recommendations do not include a specific endorsement
of Aboriginal traditional forms as a basis for Aboriginal governments,
though, to be fair, they do create a structure that would be much better
than what currently exists at allowing those forms to flourish. The recommendations are strong in detailing the value and nature of the inherent right to self-determination and -government, and are sensitive to the
varied circumstances of Aboriginal communities across Canada. The latter is one of the clear strengths of the commission's report and the value
of that should not be underestimated: very few commentators resist the
temptation of using their own geographic area of experience as a basis
for recommending national models (and this study itself clearly is based
on northern circumstances). The most controversial position taken by
the RCAP is to endorse national-level government rather than community

self-government, largely as a capacity-building issue. But if democratic rather than administrative capacity were the central issue, community government would clearly be the best repository for any new models; this is one area of clear disagreement between RCAP and my own approach.

The section on "The North" in the RCAP report, while again useful in providing a relatively recent map of the northern context, is disappointing on several scores. Not least, the report, in my reading, tends to de-emphasize the extraordinary human strengths at the community level in Denendeh and Nunavut and, although it notes that "the North is the part of Canada in which Aboriginal peoples have achieved the most in terms of political influence and institutions appropriate to their cultures and needs" (Vol. 4, 386), it never seems to gain inspiration from that fact. While Thomas Berger's *Northern Frontier, Northern Homeland* remains worth reading for the richness and variety of voices that inform the discussion, the RCAP report is more bureaucratic in inflection: though quotation is extensive, the majority of voices quoted are from the elected leadership level. Community voices are muted. Substantively, although the report emphasizes the value of the traditional hunting economy (389), few of the recommendations deal with it. There are recommendations suggesting that social assistance and income supplement programs be examined "to make them effective instruments in promoting a mixed economy and sustain viable, largely self-reliant communities."[5] Hunter-support programs are discussed, but there is no general recommendation that supports the hunting economy; the only recommendation specific to the traditional economy is 4.6.18: "Government employment policies accommodate the demands of traditional economic activities by increasing opportunities for job sharing, periodic leave and shift work" (493). The substantive discussion of what the RCAP calls the "traditional mixed economy" is very good, but it does not lead to any strong overall endorsement of its value and centrality to northern communities. There are additional recommendations in the "Lands and Resources" chapter of Volume Two regarding wildlife harvesting that would no doubt be better than the current systemic undervaluing of the hunting economy, as well as some in the chapter on "Treaties," but even these do not place the issue anywhere near the centre and it remains surprising that so little is said of this issue in the chapter on "The North."

238 LIKE THE SOUND OF A DRUM

By now, an Aboriginal self-government machinery exists in Canada. A branch of the federal department of Indian and Inuit Affairs is devoted to the issue. The federal government, with the support of many provincial governments, officially endorses the idea. Something, which will be given the name "Aboriginal self-government," is unfolding. With this unfolding, a discourse is being produced. Specialization in Aboriginal self-government is now a possibility. Courses, seminars, and workshops are offered, papers and articles are written. Administrators are involved, can become specialists, and write reports. Politicians are certainly involved, can become specialists, and have written reports. Lawyers, not wanting to pass on such an important opportunity, have gotten involved, can become specialists, and have written articles and drafts of legislation and opinions. Academics, neither last nor least on this list, are involved, have become specialists, and have written academic papers and books. In these ranks this book may now be included, another cog in the Aboriginal self-government machinery.

Among the academic texts that precede this one, and which this one must necessarily respond to, is Menno Boldt's *Surviving as Indians: The Challenge of Self Government* (1993). Although Boldt makes a series of complexly related arguments, the general thrust of his work points in a different direction from that I have suggested in the foregoing pages. To be fair, this is undoubtedly in part because Boldt's work comes from the context of his situation at the University of Lethbridge, where the concerns of prairie First Nations, and their specific politics and history, must have had some influence. For example, Boldt suggests using the treaties as a key concept with which to orient Aboriginal relations to non-Natives, but this has only partial relevance in the north, since Inuit did not negotiate treaties and do not think of the comprehensive claim as a 'modern treaty' the way many other First Nations do. Similarly, Boldt's text deserves respect and acknowledgement for its treatment of the problems of leadership in some Aboriginal communities. The Indian Act band electoral system was developed in part to ensure a class of leaders who would collude with government; there are many people involved in Aboriginal politics largely for the personal economic benefit they can derive from it, particularly in circumstances where opportunities are severely limited. Boldt does bring to bear extensive experience working with communities and offers insight into a range of problems they face.

The crucial difference between Boldt and the approach taken here is in our assessment of Aboriginal communities and what might be called a community-based approach. As an aside, in an argument that criticizes government, Boldt refers to "the horrendous conditions that prevail in all Indian communities,"[6] a remarkably sweeping statement that could just as easily, or in my view more easily, be applied to most urban centres and the dominant society. Boldt dismisses the subsistence economy, noting that "while a few remote northern bands/tribes still derive part of their subsistence from traditional means, even these derive the largest part of their income from government social assistance" (229). Finally, these evaluations lead to Boldt's dismissal of the democratic impulses at the community level. In one context, writing about elite and poor classes on reserves, he suggests that "perhaps the long habituation of both classes to colonial rule has functionally and psychologically incapacitated them to such an extent that revival of the traditional systems and norms of government is no longer a realistic goal" (144). Hence, self-government, in Boldt's view, must be achieved from the top down:

> During a century of colonial rule, Indian people have acquired a deep sense of alienation, and resignation and apathy about their future. To overcome this mind set, *the people will need to be tutored* in effective political attitudes, skills, and experience. This can come only from ongoing participation and influence in the decision making process in their communities. It will also require complete self-resocialization by Indian politicians and bureaucrats to traditional attitudes of service and accountability to their people. Only such a process can achieve the decolonization and emancipation of the Indian lower class. (160, emphasis added)

The re-education of Indian people, teaching them democracy: this was a project of the Canadian State in the late nineteenth century and led to the development of the band electoral system that self-government projects now seek to displace. If "the people will need to be tutored," and a political project of consciousness raising is to be the foundation of the effort to achieve Aboriginal self-government, then the battle is already lost.

Hence, several of Boldt's pronouncements about Aboriginal communities, which he does not sustain even with data, are dangerous and misguided. They imply a set of ethnocentric judgements about people's capabilities and about what people think. How does Boldt know that Aboriginal people "have a deep sense of alienation, and resignation and apathy"? Certainly these feelings exist in Aboriginal communities, as they do among the poor in Canada generally, but they are not specific to Aboriginal people. Boldt repeatedly and consistently assumes he knows something about what Aboriginal tradition is, and what Aboriginal people think, that extends beyond what Aboriginal people themselves may know or think; hence, he offers statements like: "Indian leaders impose meanings on their concept of land title that are derived from the Euro-Western lexicon, not from traditional *Indian* philosophies and principles" (27, original emphasis). Interestingly, and to stress his point, throughout his book, Boldt deploys a certain kind of doubling method, writing Indian as Indian and *Indian* as *Indian:* "nor is such a definition required for the survival of Indians as *Indians*" (27, original emphasis). How Indian does an Indian have to be in order to be an *Indian?* By *Indian*ing Indians, Boldt allows himself the authority to determine what is or is not traditional, and how viable traditional culture is in the world today. Boldt can charge Indian leaders with "proceeding from an acculturated perspective" (43) and, when he is not telling us what *Indians* think, can tell Indian leaders what they should think: "Indian leaders must always keep this in the forefront of their minds" (47). Absent the conceptual tools provided by the idea of modes of production, absent an anthropology; even a lucid, experienced, and careful thinker of Menno Boldt's calibre can wander into a minefield of unguarded prescriptions.

At least in the communities I studied, those discussed in this text, it is precisely a sense that "the people need to be tutored" that limits and circumscribes a meaningful project of Aboriginal self-government. This is the basic, ethnocentric assumption that government officials bring with them when they visit these communities. It is the approach that continues to underwrite policy: the recent Governance Act proposals entirely reflected the same set of assumptions. In contrast, both something called "tradition" and something called a "subsistence economy" have relevance, indeed are, in my view, best seen as a foundation, of the project of Aboriginal self-government in the northern context.

INDIAN GOVERNMENT: ITS MEANING IN PRACTICE

Among the crucial texts produced by the Aboriginal self-government machinery is a book by Frank Cassidy and Robert Bish called *Indian Government: Its Meaning in Practice*. Cassidy and Bish make a serious effort to put the concept of Aboriginal self-government into practice. Their work is largely based on a survey of a variety of band and tribal councils in southern Canada. It directly reflects the political position of many southern status Indian political organizations. For example, on the very difficult and politically fraught question of legal Indian status in the post-Bill C-31 context, they review band council criticisms of that legislation. However, they do not touch on the criticisms made of band councils by Aboriginal women's organizations.[7] The book focusses on four elements of governance—citizenship, policy development, service delivery, and financing—and tries to illustrate how these elements are now being dealt with and what implications Aboriginal self-government may have in each of the areas. As was the case with Boldt, their work largely ignores the differences between northern and southern approaches to Aboriginal self-government, and, also like Boldt, their work is concerned with 'Indians', not with Métis or Inuit.

Although Cassidy and Bish have a somewhat narrower vision of Aboriginal self-government than Boldt, their view more closely resembles that of southern Aboriginal political leaders. They argue that

> Indian peoples and their governments have been quite clear about what they want from Canada. They want constitutional recognition of the inherent jurisdiction of their governments. They want to deal with Canada as First Nations on a government to government basis. They want an understanding of their diversity as well as their unique cultural and linguistic identities. They want a just settlement of their grievances concerning their traditional lands was well as compensation for past wrongs and due attention to the special status in law that arises from their aboriginal rights. They want to govern themselves. Their wishes have not been recognized.[8]

They start from the premise that Aboriginal governments already exist, even if in a form that remains highly circumscribed. This gives their analysis some force, as they orient themselves towards improving and strengthening what already operates, rather than attempting to project something completely new.

Cassidy and Bish do not recognize the objective interest of the Canadian State in vitiating a meaningful project of Aboriginal self-government. They situate the problem with achieving Aboriginal self-government as a problem of 'inadequate' federalism, of the tension between a federalist model of governance that predominates in Canada and the centralist biases that remain inherent in the Westminster model. For example, they suggest that

> Federalism can accommodate different governments. It allows for a recognized basis for independent powers. It enables citizens to be citizens of two or more governments simultaneously. It uses judicial institutions as mediating mechanisms for disputes between citizens and governments as well as those between one government and another. Federalism, in fact, is characterized by all of these conventions; yet Canadian federalism, as practised, particularly in light of the Westminster model, has not accommodated fully recognized Indian government on the part of Indian peoples. (163)

There is a good deal of force to this argument, which implicitly suggests that ethnocentric or racist logic underlies the refusal to provide Aboriginal governments with the same powers that provincial governments have, and also suggests a structural reason in the centralizing tendencies of parliamentary democracy, presumably, for example, in the doctrine of parliamentary supremacy, on the Westminster model.

In another context, Cassidy and Bish note that "comprehensive [self-government] arrangements, at the present time, must be regarded as experiments aimed at more fully integrating Indian governments within the federal system" (155). But the Indian governments they discuss were created by the existing system, and integrating the governments as they stand has been a long-term policy objective of the federal government, embodied in the Indian Advancement Act of 1884, which sought to turn band councils into municipal councils, in the White Paper of 1969, which sought to turn responsibility for delivery of Indian social services over to provincial governments, and more recently in the Governance Act, which sought to strengthen "accountability" mechanisms in band governance. This is a policy objective that Aboriginal peoples have continually struggled—in practice—against.

There are, then, two critical problems with Cassidy's and Bish's approach. First, they do not recognize the politics of form. That is, Indian governments will be recognized within a federal system when they become governments that reflect the dominant view of what a government is or should look like. They understand that decision-making "procedures would likely show considerable variance across Canada because of widely differing traditions in First Nations communities. They would, however, reflect a strong emphasis on active citizen involvement and the use of consensus" (166), but they do not see the degree to which these kinds of "procedures" contradict the basic logic of the established order. Second, Cassidy and Bish do not see the State's function as a totalizing mechanism in late capitalist society. Although it is true that "federalism can accommodate different governments," it can only accommodate governments whose basic form meets certain requirements, it can only accommodate governments that resemble it, that speak to it in its own language, that write back and that work within the same logic, a logic conducive to the accumulation of capital and the expansion of the commodity form. Any governments or political groups that attempt to do something different will feel the relentless force of the State's ideological or repressive apparatuses.

CITIZENS PLUS

In a brief, intellectual autobiography in the introduction to *Citizens Plus*, Alan C. Cairns lets his readers know that early in his career he worked as a senior staff in the team that crafted the *Hawthorn Report*, which is credited with giving impetus to the idea that Aboriginal peoples should be considered "citizens plus" in the Canadian polity. For the next thirty years his research focussed on "federalism, the Constitution, constitutional reform, and the role of the courts in constitutional change."[9] He has now returned full circle, deploying his depth of knowledge as a senior scholar in politics in an attempt to revive the abandoned concept, to respond seriously to the Royal Commission on Aboriginal Peoples report, and, in effect, to bring a voice from the discipline of political studies into the debates about self-government. This is an ambitious undertaking, and one fraught with dangers. Revival of older concepts poses the possibility of being charged with "a failure of imagination" and the possibility of seeing the whole approach as "the last gasp of an imperial mentality"; to his credit, Cairns acknowledges these dangers.

That, indeed, is one of the strengths of this book. There is an honesty in this engagement, a tone of soul searching, that breathes life into what might otherwise be another dull-as-warm-summer-concrete Canadian constitutional analysis. Other strengths that a scholar of Cairns's or Boldt's experience brings to the table is breadth of knowledge—in Cairns's case a range of references that spans from studies of Old Order Amish in the United States, theoretical material about cultural hybridity, demographic studies of ethnic minority marriage patterns—and depth of knowledge—particularly regarding the whole panoply of legal, political, and philosophical studies of Aboriginal rights and citizenship—that lend considerable gravity to their judgements and that, without fail, provide readers with valuable resources for pursuit of these issues.

What follows is a serious attempt to come to grips with my own considerable distance from many of Cairns's positions: to take up the glove he has thrown down for a reasoned debate. If, then, I do not pull many punches, I do so out of respect for an enterprise of thought I presume would want to be read with a rigour and determination equal to that which informed the manner in which it was written. Let me state my differences with Cairns through six propositions, which counter some of the more deep-rooted positions he stakes and emphasize the issues from a northern community-based perspective.

First Proposition: at this historical juncture, the ground of relations between Aboriginal peoples and newcomers must philosophically be an acknowledgement of alterity. The most basic premise of Cairns's approach is that "one of our essential tasks is to foster a sense of common belonging to a single political community, as well as the recognition of difference. If we achieve only the latter, our triumph will be pyrrhic" (180). A good deal of the book is devoted to a critique of Aboriginal separatism in the sphere of self-government discourse, but Cairns is not by any means an assimilationist. Rather, he wants the 'plus' of "citizens plus" to take cognizance of the 'citizens', he wants to promote the development of an Aboriginality firmly within the rhetoric of Canadian commonality. He advocates what he calls a "modernizing Aboriginality" in which "individuals and communities remake themselves by choosing from the options at hand" (105). This implies that those trajectories of policy that aim to promote autonomous, self-governing, Aboriginal political entities are misguided, for Cairns, because they rest on a notion of Aboriginality "defined in terms of an authenticity with roots in the distant past" (105).

The position is not without considerable philosophical power. Dominick LaCapra once argued that "the comprehensive problem in inquiry is how to understand and negotiate varying degrees of proximity and distance in the relation to the 'other' that is both outside and inside ourselves,"[10] which could well encapsulate a moment of agreement between Cairns and my own position. However, given the history of colonial power relations that have created the current inequities, and given the continued extraordinary degree to which the culture of newcomers to Canada has simply not understood or respected Aboriginal cultural difference, it is disingenuous to the point of naïveté to suggest that commonality rather than difference should be the ultimate objective of policy.

I share with Cairns a Western legacy: a respect for the tradition of civic humanism that shifts like an ineffable current through the last two millennia of north African and European thought and practice. But the cultural and historical perspective of Aboriginal peoples gives lie to the principles that the Canadian State enunciates as its own ground for being and pretends to inherit. For Aboriginal peoples, the State has not been a benign liberal-democratic arena where the nature of their insertion into the body politic as a whole may be freely debated. The State has been a totalizing agent, a structure of power relentlessly imposing its forms and logics on Aboriginal communities, bodies, lands. Cairns appropriates two Aboriginal analyses, that of John Borrows and of the Federation of Saskatchewan Indian Nations, to suggest that (in this instance referring to a position paper by the latter) "only by becoming fully involved in the Saskatchewan community will Aboriginal peoples become part of the province wide 'we' community and thus have the moral levers to engage the majority as fellow citizens in tackling poverty and social malaise" (208). But their position, as I read it, is more that the dominant society must begin to learn from Aboriginal peoples and cultures for the betterment of both: this can happen only if Aboriginal cultures are not taken for granted, if there is an acknowledgement that there is much about those cultures not yet understood. That is, we must begin from the humility implied by a premise of alterity, the otherness in the sense of unknown or difference of the other, rather than from the arrogance of presuming a universal understanding, if there is to be any hope of a meaningful accommodation.

Second Proposition: the trend toward urbanization of Aboriginal peoples must not become a 'fact' deployed to diminish the particular claims of those in rural communities. Cairns argues that the tendency of the RCAP to focus on land-based models of self-government ignores "the choice of half the Aboriginal population" to live in cities, which may put it "on the wrong side of history" (185). The numbers argument is frequently deployed these days, by Cairns and others, to suggest that Aboriginal leaders who do not represent the views of urban Aboriginal peoples are out of touch with a growing reality. Here is another fact: in the twentieth century, numbers have rarely served a small group of people living for the most part in isolated parts of the country. The claim of Aboriginal peoples for justice was never based on their proportion in the population, but rather on qualitative claims of cultural difference and historical claims for legally enshrined rights. There are as many people now living in northern Aboriginal communities—more, actually—than there were at the turn of the century. They have been a minority for a long time. Now they may be, or soon become, a minority within that group of people who are descendants of the original occupants of this land. Their call, their claim for justice, remains as strong as it always was. The many and compelling issues regarding urbanization of Aboriginal peoples do demand a response, perhaps even a response along the lines delineated by Cairns, but that response must not be applied to those for whom the statement "ours is an urban civilization" continues to have no relevance.

Third Proposition: the notion of cultural hybridity is a dead letter that cannot provide a basis for any form of critical cultural politics. The time was sure to come when a liberal line of discourse would find the value in that stream of post-colonial thought, *pace* Homi Bhabha, that valourizes hybridity, the mixing of cultures. Hence, it comes as no surprise to see Edward Said's statement that "all cultures are involved in one another; none is single and pure, all are hybrid, heterogenous, extraordinarily differentiated, and unmonolithic" (quoted in Cairns, 103). The point that hybridity theorists have been trying to make is that, when in power, a cultural purist discourse can have reprehensible results; when deployed towards minority cultures, a cultural purist discourse can become a cage. The theoretical point that all cultures are, and have always been, marked by interaction with other cultures has a place. However, when raised to an uncritical celebration of the hybrid, the discourse implodes: I suggested in earlier chapters that

Fascism was as hybrid a form, even in the manner it deployed a discourse of its own purity, as any postmodern cultural transgression. Hybridity on its own merits does not tell us anything—all cultures are and always were hybrid, it insistently repeats—about whether a particular cultural form is worth attention, respect, admiration. Only the substantive way a particular people have responded to their particular problems, and to the problems that appear to face most of us in our existential being, can give us a basis for engaging in cultural politics. For Cairns, the fact of cultural hybridity underwrites the modernizing Aboriginality he sees as an alternative vision: "now, with the new story line, going for a Big Mac, or becoming a lawyer, are simply contemporary ways of being Aboriginal" (104).

In the end, surprisingly, this view, coupled with the notion of urbanization, actually makes Aboriginality a matter of so-called 'blood' rather than cultural choice. An Indian working for a multinational corporation is as much an Indian as the Cree trapper he is dispossessing. There is a truth to this statement, of course, a truth for which Duncan Campbell Scott would cheer. Cairns wants to develop a politics for Aboriginal peoples that does not exclude the urban, hybrid individuals emerging. He ends with a politics solely for their benefit. And once again, the isolated and marginalized, too culturally pure to be in fashion, since, after all, many of them speak their own language, are comfortably silenced.

Fourth Proposition: Aboriginal nationalism and political agency, in its many diverse forms, is not imported. This is a point about history, and here we find Cairns repeating a discursive trope that seems particularly endemic to discussions of recent Aboriginal history. In his discussion of 'how did we get to where we are?' Cairns offers two explanatory points. The first he treats briefly: the notion that Aboriginal people were a vanishing race "lost credibility." The second is that "domestic developments could not have brought us to where we now are without the support offered by the international environment" (40–41). He then reviews in a page or so the global history of decolonization as a context for Canadian decolonization. There can be no doubt that there is some truth to this. But how we got to where we are becomes a more compelling story if two other truths are foregrounded: material conditions of life, including poverty, and the emblems of oppression have always been the basis of social movements; and secondly, indigenous leaders, local women and men, are the primary makers of local history. They did not need someone from elsewhere—one thinks of Reagan's mythic Cuban infiltrators in El Salvador—to tell them they were oppressed. This notion pervades Cairns's historical account. Although, for example, he shows an awareness of the importance of the Dene Declaration in giving impetus to the language of nationhood that became common in Aboriginal politics (106), he still states that the "1976 Parti Quebecois victory gave Aboriginal peoples the opportunity and incentive to couch their demands in constitutional terms" and "reinforced a nation-to-nation definition of the situation" (171). Aboriginal peoples did not need incentive from Quebec (not to follow Cairns's path and presume that both Quebec nationalist separatism and Aboriginal nationalist separatism are the same, does not likewise presume that the former is inherently problematic and the latter will lose its sheen if the two can be connected). And the nation-to-nation definition of the situation owes at least something—never mentioned by Cairns—to the fact that for centuries European powers in the Americas treated the Aboriginal peoples they encountered as nations.

Fifth Proposition: ecological and environmental grounds of Aboriginal self-government must inform the political dialogue. One thing absent, entirely absent, from Cairns's account is a sense of the ecological field within which humans operate. This is convenient, since it allows him to ignore the fact that the small proportion of Aboriginal people who live in rural Canada are the effective occupants of a majority of Canada's land mass. And what is the best way for them to live? Might it not be too presumptive to suggest that some use of local ecological resources may have the best chance of providing a sustainable economy in those places? Might not one of the issues that Aboriginal self-government is really about be the question of how that land is to be used: as a giant storehouse for the urban civilization that Cairns treasures, or as a homeland for distinct cultures, to frame the question in a manner that approximates Thomas Berger's model? Perhaps the issue is not so much that the RCAP and others put too much weight on land-based models of self-government, but rather that the question of land base is one of the most fundamental questions in the discourse of self-government.

Sixth Proposition: Aboriginal peoples are peoples. A small point of linguistic moment: the term "Aboriginals" has steadily come creeping into everyday language. Cairns uses it interchangeably with "Aboriginal peoples." I wish he wouldn't. "Aboriginal" is an adjective. It qualifies another word.

That word is "people." With "Aboriginals" we are a bare step to a word that became offensive in the Australian context and could become equally offensive here.

I have a variety of other concerns regarding Cairns's book: why does he not challenge the work of Menno Boldt and Taiaiake (Gerald) Alfred, political scientists like himself who might have a stronger argument about the relevance of a nationalist discourse in Aboriginal matters? Why is he so unconcerned with Nunavut as a public government that in many respects might be said to meet his own standards of citizenship-inclusion, treating it rather as another exercise in separatist self-government? Why are some authors, Emma LaRocque, John Borrows, whom Cairns agrees with, identified as Aboriginal scholars while others, those he disagrees with, James (Sakej) Henderson, Mary Ellen Turpel, are never given the same acknowledgement? But these are of smaller moment.

In the midst of such radical disagreement, let me add some additional words that point to the considerable strengths of *Citizens Plus*. For newcomers to the field, the book does provide, for the most part, a sound overview of the issues, histories, and positions that have emerged in the debate regarding Aboriginal self-government. The chapter on the RCAP, in particular, does convey the main impulses of the voluminous report and is one of the better summaries and engagements with that work. I would echo Cairns's view that "the federal government's response to the Erasmus-Dussault commission is an embarrassment" (122). Cairns is very strong on the legal advocacy literature that deals with Aboriginal rights and the reader comes away from his text better informed on the many positions that derive from that arena.

What Cairns offers is a particular liberal perspective on a debate that passed him by. His view is that the notion of "citizens plus" was lost in the 1969 controversy over the White Paper, and was replaced in the next decade by a notion of Aboriginal rights, which focussed exclusively on the 'plus' part of the equation, and by Aboriginal nationalism. He does not seem to notice that, by the seventies, Aboriginal peoples were not interested in their Canadian citizenship for good reason: the State had spent a century trying to enforce citizenship on them at the expense of their rights. By winning the battle over the White Paper, they blew the lid off the whole range of discursive logics that confined their political aspirations and so a whole new terrain emerged. Finally, they were allowed to talk substantively about what Aboriginal rights meant. The notion that a reinvigorated concept of "citizens plus" offers a new or better path out of the current conflict is not compelling and raises more questions than it resolves: what is there in this polity that is supposed to attract the attention and loyalty of those whose values and ideals as embodied in culture it ruthlessly, relentlessly attacks?

WHITHER INUIT SELF-GOVERNMENT

In July of 1993 I had the opportunity to assist with a set of meetings sponsored by the Royal Commission on Aboriginal Peoples relating to Inuit issues. The meetings were held in Panniqtuuq. My main role was to act as official note taker for a workshop on Inuit self-government. The session was of interest to Inuit leaders and drew a remarkable crowd, including Zebedee Nungak, Rosemarie Kuptana, Vince Terry, Tony Anderson, John Amagoalic, Martha Grieg, and Jaypetee Akpalialuk (then mayor of Panniqtuuq). The discussion proved highly illuminating regarding Inuit perspectives on the issue of self-government.

At the first plenary session on the first day, representatives of each of the regions explained their position on self-government. In Nunavut, the process of setting up the land claim and the new government meant that the leadership was focussing on the issue of training; having Inuit with the skills to run corporations, joint management boards, and government itself was clearly the priority. Other regions were less enthusiastic, working to establish different kinds of framework agreements and not at the stage of worrying about the nuts and bolts of setting up a government. The Inuvialuit, who are not a part of Nunavut, were looking to negotiate a regional government based on an old concept, WARM, the Western Arctic Regional Municipalities. They were on the verge of having the federal government restart negotiations with them, something that would happen later that year. The Inuit of Nunavik spoke of frustrations in implementing their land claim, which had self-government implications. The Labrador Inuit were experiencing the greatest frustration, not able to even start land claims and self-government negotiations because they were dealing with an intractable provincial government in Newfoundland. Each of the Inuit organizations was looking at a model of regional public government, rather than what they saw as 'ethnic' governments or exclusive Aboriginal governments, in order to achieve their self-government aspirations.

At the self-government workshop, Zebedee Nungak spoke early on about the question of what its goals should be.

> [T]his is a problem I had with thinking about this meeting. Do we make suggestions to the Royal Commission, and then the Royal Commission makes suggestions to the government, which it may not do anything with? Are we here to try to make history and force governments to recognize our legitimate aspirations, or do we talk a lot and nothing much happens, and even less when our ideas are floated through the Royal Commission, then floated through government. I think we should have a very free wheeling meeting, discuss everything on our minds. Self-government may be number 97 on the Royal Commission list, how can we say to them 'let's say yes, this is very important'. For instance, Labrador, when they talked yesterday, it made my heart cry. They have been dismissed for fourteen months. We're too tolerant of letting our people be treated like that. I don't want to belittle the Royal Commission.

Effectively, Nungak was arguing that the political talent assembled in the room need not be limited by the agenda—making recommendations to a body that might pass those recommendations on to another body—but, rather, should perhaps work towards establishing a self-government statement, manifesto, or declaration. This kind of statement is itself an enactment of self-government, a taking on of responsibility that reflects a determination to control the agenda itself.

By and large, although Nungak consistently returned to this theme over the day and a half of the workshop, his broadest suggestions were not followed. Discussion proceeded to the question of financing self-government, and then to the problem of barriers to self-government. On the latter issue, at the end of the first morning, Rosemarie Kuptana sounded one of her concerns, that "what's so frustrating is that there is no self-government process, but if we are going to have true self-government in Inuit lands we must think of our governments having a third order position to the other two levels of government. If it's going to have true powers or responsibility it's going to need constitutional pro-tection." The fact that self-government discussion has been so focussed on band-level self-government, on status Indians, and revising the Indian Act, which is largely the mandate of the self-government directorate in the Department of Indian and Inuit Affairs, has meant that there is no negotiating process—apart from constitutional talks—that suits the specific circumstances of Inuit, who are attempting to establish regional public governments rather than band or tribal governments.

The afternoon session, on barriers to self-government, began with a very interesting discussion that went around the table and also, therefore, around each of the regions. Near the beginning, John Amagoalic spoke of four different kinds of obstacles, focussing on the first one:

> Speaking from experience, we found that when we first started talking about land claims in the seventies our own people were an obstacle. They couldn't support something they couldn't understand. We had to spend a lot of time explaining land claims. Our problem was our own people, and the public at large. The Canadian government was reluctant to move without public support.

He added three other points, each of which he referred to in brief: "secondly, it was the existing level of government. People in Yellowknife were not enthusiastic. That was an obstacle. Not just politicians, but bureaucrats." The final two were that the "constitutional status quo only recognizes two levels of government" and, "fourthly, financing. Someone has to pay for self-government." The list identifies two kinds of obstacles, an internal one reflecting people's readiness and an external one reflecting the commitment of the dominant society.

Martha Grieg then spoke: "I can't add much more. These are the things we see, and also we deal a lot with the social issues. I want to emphasize that the people have to be ready and there has to be training." This last point was re-emphasized by the next speaker, Rosemarie Kuptana.

> We have to put things into perspective. As Inuit, we've been involved in the Canadian political process for the last twenty or thirty years and we've had to deal with many issues. Having a small population, [there are] many leaders dealing with the same issues. I see that as a main issue. We're involved in land claims, environment, self-government, constitutional reform; in order to deal with these issues there are very few educated Inuit. I see training as a major issue, particularly now that we have Nunavut.

Once again, she emphasized that "there is no process at the national level for Inuit to negotiate with the Crown self-government agreements.

There has been a process since 1986 for Indians to negotiate financing and self-government, but no process for Inuit. This is an inequity."

Others added to these themes of internal readiness and external, structural impediments to self-government. An Inuk from Baffin, saying that he had 'nothing new' to add to the discussion, spoke at length about the issue of writing.

> The major [barrier], looking at the Inuit perspective, the traditional values that haven't been written on paper by GNWT or federal government. That in my opinion is an obstacle, that's why they haven't been able to understand us. Inuit haven't been able to get their experiences or knowledge on paper. The guy on my right said there are a lot of people in the north and our representatives aren't able to visit all of us and hear our concerns. I think if all of the people were able to have knowledge or hear each of our concerns all the Inuit would be able to understand and help each other in trying to correct some of these obstacles. It is very difficult, in a sense, in the Baffin region a lot of the elders are consulted with, in dealing with big issues, we're only using consultants that have gone through universities. As Inuit, experience only comes in age, but Qallunaat attitude is that it has to be done on paper. We haven't used our elders enough to give us their opinions.

Jaypetee Akpalialuk, then mayor of Panniqtuuq (now, sadly, deceased), then spoke about the importance of tradition: "as Inuit, we have to follow the rules and laws that are given to us. In my opinion we, I feel that, we need to do the things that we never had a chance to deal with. Like, our culture is very important. Our elders and traditions, it's important that we keep them." 'Writing' traditional law and culture in order to have paper to oppose to the writing of the State: in a sense, this was also Zebedee Nungak's theme. Near the end of the discussion he suggested that "if we drafted a declaration of independence we would get noticed. Because we are such good citizens we often don't get the government's attention." Another kind of writing against the State, or a writing that would 'address' that State, that would be seen, 'noticed', that would lead to an exchange, that would become self-government.

Nungak's declaration of independence did not get drafted. Instead, a resolution was forwarded that proposed an Inuit-specific self-government process be established, and suggested how the Inuit self-government should and could be constitutionally entrenched. However, the Inuit leadership at the Panniqtuuq meetings demonstrated that incongruous combination of idealism and pragmatism, of utopian aspiration and political realism that characterizes their political project and political culture in Canada today. It is clear that self-government means very different things for Inuit than it does for other Aboriginal Canadians, yet at the level of broad visions there are also remarkable similarities. It is equally clear that meetings such as this one have the potential to themselves become exercises in self-government, staging assertions of self-determination by speaking the words and demonstrating a speech ethics that reach beyond the structural constraints imposed by the State. For a few powerful moments on several different occasions in a small Arctic College classroom in Panniqtuuq, self-government 'existed' itself.

COMMUNICATIVE COMPETENCE AND COMMUNITY COMPETENCE

Jurgen Habermas is among the contemporary social theorists who have had a great deal to say about the politics of speech. In his *Communication and the Evolution of Society*, Habermas argues that "social systems can be viewed as networks of communicative action; personality systems can be regarded under the aspect of the ability to speak and act."[11] Habermas suggests that communicative competence refers to "the ability of a speaker oriented to mutual understanding to embed a well-formed sentence in relations to reality" (98) and distinguishes between 'purposive-rational' actions and 'communicative' actions (117–118). Of the latter, Habermas states,

> communicative action is, among other things, oriented to observing intersubjectively valid norms that link reciprocal expectations. In communicative action, the validity basis of speech is presupposed. The universal validity claims (truth, rightness, truthfulness), which participants at least implicitly raise and reciprocally recognize, make possible the consensus that carries action in common. In strategic action, this background consensus is lacking.... (118)

Habermas's argument to this point provides an interesting framework through which politics in Aboriginal communities can be seen, drawing our attention to the ethics of speech in small northern communities as a central cultural politics consideration.

Unfortunately, Habermas constructs his analysis of communicative action in the context of a broad argument that seeks to preserve a deeply ethnocentric developmental or social evolutionary logic. The worst aspects of Marx's historical materialism—though borrowed in this instance from the developmental psychology of Kohlberg—are preserved in Habermas, who suggests, for example, that "apparently the magical-animistic representational world of palaeolithic societies was very particularistic and not very coherent" (104) and ranks, in his terms, Neolithic Societies, Early Civilizations, Developed Civilizations, all with conventionally structured systems of action, and The Modern Age, with post-conventionally structured domains of action (157–158). Palaeolithic societies, in this view, implicitly fall within the domain of pre-conventionally structured domains of action, though, interestingly, they are not specified in the evolutionary discussion.

Nevertheless, it is possible to suggest that concepts associated with the universal ethics of speech, that is, the final stage that Habermas proposes in his philosophical reconstruction of the stages of moral consciousness, are more relevant to the gathering and hunting mode of production than to the (post)modern era. In effect, if "rationalization," as Habermas argues, involves "overcoming . . . systematically distorted communication" (120) and if "the universal ethical principal orientation" means "at heart, these are universal principles of justice, of the reciprocity and equality of human rights, and of respect for the dignity of human beings as individual persons" (80), and if the "universal ethics of speech" implies a level where "need interpretations themselves—that is, what each individual thinks he should understand and represent as his 'true' interests—also become the object of practical discourse" (90), then this level of communicative action is probably found far more commonly in community assemblies in the NWT than in the House of Commons in Ottawa. Systematically distorted communication, speech laced through with ideological (in the vulgar Marxist sense) interest, is the order of the day in the dominant, circumscribed public sphere of the (post)modern world. A speech ethics founded on mutuality, the attempt to achieve consensus, respect for the dignity of human beings as individual persons, these are commonplace in the communities I studied.

This is one of the senses in which the communities of Liidli Koe, Fort Good Hope, and Panniqtuuq are 'ready' for self-government. In effect, to the extent that Aboriginal traditions and values still govern community politics, these communities all evidence a high degree of communicative competence and an ethics of speech that vastly surpasses that which passes as political speech in southern public forums. The officials who dominate the territorial and federal bureaucracies have no sensitivity or appreciation of this; more often than not, watching these functionaries interact with Aboriginal leaders and elders at the community level is a study in speech incompetence. Unintended disrespect, or, rather, a systemically structured disrespect, is built into the speech of these sometimes well-meaning officials. The protocols of speech that embody a speech ethics structured around mutuality itself presupposing respect: among the very few places in the world where this logic of speech can be heard to operate on an everyday basis in the public sphere are the Inuit and Dene communities in Denendeh and Nunavut.

If democracy—that is, a system whereby the members of a community themselves decide upon the course of action or direction their community will take—is the standard by which we were to assess the readiness of a community for self-government, then Panniqtuuq, Fort Good Hope, and Liidli Koe would appear to be vastly more ready for self-government than the dominant Canadian society. However, self-government as a political project in Canada's north and specifically in the three communities in question continues to flounder on systemically ethnocentric assessments of those communities. The attention to leadership that seems so prevalent in the scholarly literature is, in my view, one of the ethnocentric biases that structures too much of the discussion: citizen participation, including citizen's ability to influence the course of events between elections, would be a far better arena of attention.

FOR ERIC

Eric Menicoche provided me with my introduction to Liidli Koe, acting briefly as my research assistant and taking responsibility for boarding me. He had been a student in Native Studies at Trent University, where I got to know him and his then marriage partner, Cheryl Bonnetrouge, and their children Erica and Whitney. At Trent, he had studied community economic development, but by the time he was finished he had become more interested in dealing with the problem of drug and alcohol addiction. He returned home to Liidli Koe at about the same time I began this study. He is a courageous and determined non-drinker, often in atmospheres where there is very little social support for such a stance.

At a talk at Trent University, Ethyl Blondin-Andrew spotted Eric Menicoche in the crowd, another Dene a long way from home. She told a story about Eric: during the Dene halcyon times in the mid-seventies, when they gained international recognition in their struggle against the Mackenzie Valley Pipeline project, a group of Dene speakers toured nationally and internationally. Ethyl and Eric are in the same generation, which came of political age in that struggle against the pipeline. During one talk, an elderly woman from the crowd complimented Eric, saying that he spoke very well for such a young man and asking his age. Eric said, "I'm twenty-five thousand years old!"

He still is.

THE POLITICS OF FORM

The issue of the politics of form is crucial in the arena of Aboriginal self-government. The politics of form is raised by Aboriginal scholar Marie Smallface Marule in her important analysis of "Traditional Indian Government: Of the People, by the People, for the People," in the book *Pathways to Self-Determination*. There, she makes the following powerful argument:

> If we really want to help ourselves, we must revitalize our institutions. This does not mean that we have to return to the way we were two or three hundred years ago. Given our experience and knowledge about the failures of European institutional structures, systems, and processes, why should we repeat their mistakes? Why, for example, should we adopt an educational system that not only fails to meet the needs of its students but also alienates them in the process? Yet we are currently on a course of introducing that type of educational system into our Indian communities. I believe we are uncritically adopting European-Western institutional approaches because of our sense of inferiority. We are doing it because we do not have confidence in our ability to build something that will be workable, more appropriate to our needs, and more effective. I am convinced that Indians can find in their traditional philosophies and ideologies better and more meaningful approaches than those offered by the Canadian government. We have something to offer that even other Canadians can look to as a better alternative to their existing institutions.[12]

This is perhaps the real challenge of Aboriginal self-government, and it is nowhere stated more forcefully. In Marule's view, traditional Aboriginal political culture revolved around the notion that "authority was a collective right that could be temporarily delegated to a leader, under restrictive conditions, to carry out essential activities. But the responsibility and authority always remained with the people" (136).

Marule's argument was expanded and elaborated by Menno Boldt and J. Anthony Long in an article called "Tribal Traditions and European-Western Political Ideologies: The Dilemma of Canada's Native Indians." They argue that

> by adopting the European-western ideology of sovereignty, the current generation of Indian leaders is buttressing the imposed alien authority structures within their communities and legitimizing the associated hierarchy composed of indigenous political and bureaucratic elites. This endorsement of hierarchical authority and a ruling entity constitutes a complete break with traditional indigenous principles. It undermines fundamental and substantial distinctions between traditional Indian and European political and cultural values. The legal-political struggle for sovereignty could prove to be a Trojan horse for traditional Indian culture by playing into the hands of the Canadian government's long-standing policy of assimilation. (342)

Boldt and Long recognize that "self-government" means very different things to different people and they provide a standard by which self-government proposals and projects can be assessed. To the extent that self-government involves the adoption of Western institutional governing forms, it will work to erode the culture, values, and traditions it is being established to supposedly enact.

In Marule's, and Boldt's and Long's, view, the politics of form are of critical significance in the struggle for self-government. That means that the question of how much power will be 'devolved' or 'recognized' in Aboriginal communities as the self-government process unfolds, while not insignificant, does not solely determine what material effect the process will have. How power is deployed or distributed, how communities use whatever structural space is opened up to them in the sphere of political decision making, these are at least equally crucial questions, in the north as in the south. In each of the communities under consideration, there was strong commitment embedded in the political dynamic to community decision making, there were well-established structures of community decision making, and there was an intricate political speech ethic that remained operative. These are strong foundations for a project of Aboriginal self-government: it is crucial that the project build on these foundations rather than undermine them.

This issue can be staged by an example of children observing and learning to be successful social agents. Regardless of the substance of the decision being made—assume, for example, a decision to provide funding for Aboriginal language training at the community level—if the decision is made through the agency of a hierarchical, Western-rational, policy structure, the children will at one and the same time have their Aboriginal culture impressed upon them and undermined. While they are learning their language, they will also necessarily want to learn Western bureaucratic decision-making skills; these latter, they know, will be necessary if they are to be effective social agents. Every decision made in this manner, regardless of the substance of the decision, moves the community further away from its traditional values. The converse is equally true; every decision that enacts those traditional values, regardless of its substance, becomes an ongoing lesson to the next generation that they will have to learn a certain speech ethics if they want to be successful social actors. Aboriginal culture in this latter example becomes or remains a part of everyday life, rather than something to be trotted out on special occasions or to display for sale or in museums.

FOR BELLA

Bella T'Seleie worked as one of my research assistants in Fort Good Hope. I first met her in Yellowknife when I taught courses in Aboriginal self-government and Native Law for the fledgling Arctic College Native Studies program, which has sadly since been cancelled. She is recorded in *Denendeh* as saying the following about her background:

> I was born in Fort Good Hope in 1953. When I was two years old my mother caught TB and was taken away. I was taken care of by the people of Fort Good Hope. The people here are like that. If a child doesn't have a mother, it is everybody's responsibility to make sure the child doesn't starve. . . . The child is not taken off to some home, you know, to strangers either. I was kept by many

families until my foster parent . . . learned about my situation
. . . they were kind people and they knew I needed help, so they
adopted me. . . . I was raised in Colville Lake. In the summer we
lived in fish camps, always working together making dry fish, cutting wood, and I look back on those days as really happy. I was
happy . . . I look at Colville Lake today . . . (the people) still have
their own lives, they still have their own pride. I don't want my
people to have nothing but memories of what their life used to
be. . . . [13]

Bella's marriage partner, Frank, had been chief of Fort Good Hope and
was the son of Philip T'Seleie, who had been chief before him, who himself was son of 'old' T'Seleie, who had been chief before him, and after
whom the community school was named.

They share a log house on the bank of the Deh Cho, away from the
hustle and bustle of 'downtown' Fort Good Hope. Bella is frequently nostalgic for Colville Lake, and was one of those who confirmed my image of
that community as a particularly important place in Sahtu. Bella is a very
strong traditionalist, committed to understanding and enacting the cultural values of her people. She worked in a small house-office building next
to the community centre, in the summer of 1993, on a mapping project.
The project involved determining Dene place names in the vicinity of Fort
Good Hope. Though the various funding agencies over the years no doubt
expected more documentation of the results from her, in fact Bella worked
in a much more traditional manner, gathering the knowledge and storing
it in the rich recesses of her own powers of remembrance. Bella found,
through this project, that many of the stories and indeed much of the culture were embedded in those place names. When she talked to elders, they
would rarely just point at the map and say "this is called this"; rather, they
would tell the story of how the place came to be, why it was named, and
how it related to other places, other stories, different family networks, and
more. To do the research properly would take a lifetime, and even then
the nature of the project was such that it would never and could never be
a 'full' record, but, in spite of that, one thing was clear: Bella was the right
person to be doing it.

THE STATE IS A CERTAIN KIND OF WRITING

> Postmodernism is the name for the end of a kind of writing that begins by reading 'the name for the end of a kind of writing' as 'the name for the end of a kind of writing' and ends by reading 'the name for the end of a kind of writing' as 'the name for the end, goal, telos, terminus, finis of a kind of writing' or as the 'name for the end, goal, telos, terminus, finis of a kind of, "kinda" but not quite, class of writing,' which has among its possible readings: 'the name for non-created writing,' or 'the writing without a subject,' or 'the writing that is by no-one about no-thing.' In its end, it is 'the name for the goal of writing that is a simulacrum of itself,' its own end.
>
> —Stephen A. Tyler, *The Unspeakable: Discourse, Dialogue, and Rhetoric in the Postmodern World*

In his *State, Power, Socialism*, Nicos Poulantzas emphasized the importance to the State of writing. Noting that "there has always been a close relationship between the State and writing, given that every State embodies a certain form of the division between intellectual and manual labour," Poulantzas argued that "writing plays a quite specific role in the case of capitalism, representing, still more than the spoken word, the articulation and distribution of knowledge and power within the State. In a certain sense, *nothing exists for the capitalist State unless it is written down*—whether as a mere written mark, a note, a report, or a complete archive" (emphasis added).[14] The State cannot be addressed but in writing. Nothing happens in the sense that no events take place unless they are inscribed in the sanctioned forms, no being is recognized as existent unless it has a signature or a written status. The written, the inscribed, is a material embodiment of the State. The disjunction between how things are 'supposed to be' as they are articulated on paper, and how they are on the ground, how they play out in everyday life, is the source of endless humour in northern Canada.

The argument regarding the State as a form of writing is of particular relevance to the relationship between the State and Aboriginal people in northern Canada, where writing is a critical site of power. Poulantzas wrote that

> the anonymous writing of the capitalist State does not repeat a discourse, but plots a certain path, recording the bureaucratic sites

and mechanisms and representing the hierarchically centralized space of the State. It both locates and creates linear and reversible spacings in the consecutive and segmented chain of bureaucratization. The massive accumulation of paper in the modern State is not merely a picturesque detail but a material feature essential to its existence and functioning—the internal cement of its intellectuals-functionaries that embodies the relationship between the State and intellectual labour. (59)

The State demands to be addressed in a specific form, or series of forms, which always are concretely embodied in writing. The anonymous, trivial, form itself—the fill-in-the-blanks application form that is the ground level of the State's writing apparatus—embodies and stages this. Citizens must fit themselves into the predetermined categories of the form, abstractions that work to establish their relationship with the dominant form in its broadest sense. They thereby abstract themselves into what the State-determined categories demand. The application form is a material reflection of the whole notion of the ideology that interpellates subjects as a strategy of containment.

To the extent that community politics in northern Canada involves a mediated relationship with broader social forces, it is writing that acts as the mechanism of mediation. The modalities of writing that structure or demarcate what people can do, how they can live, in northern communities include treaties, land claims, a variety of laws—including the federal Indian Act and territorial communities legislation as well as a whole host of laws respecting hunting, fishing, trapping, and renewable resource management—policies, regulations, constitutional clauses, legal decisions, and more. One of my own 'services' to the Dene communities was to lend my writing abilities: working on a variety of funding proposals in Liidli Koe and drafting legal language for negotiations in Fort Good Hope.

From the perspective of these communities, the State is a certain kind of writing. It is anonymous writing: it has no author or signature. Even when it comes in the form of a letter, it is the office or function, not the individual, who is writing. It is the writing of comprehensive land claims. The State will respond, finally, only to writing: writing must be produced in order to get the State to act, the act involved usually itself being an act of writing. The conversations that circulate, that surround, that reflect, these documents are themselves utterly without meaning for the State unless a written commitment or embodiment is made. The writing of the State is in the most de-personal, objective, institutional, bureaucratic language possible: in its writing, rhetoric, irony, ambiguity, creativity must be tortured out of existence in favour of a semantics and a grammar that reflect instrumental rationality in its most refined (that is: banal) modality. Adorno's comment regarding this mode of writing and its political implications is worth recalling here: "the direct statement without divagations, hesitations or reflections, that gives the other the facts full in the face, already has the form and timbre of the command issued under Fascism by the dumb to the silent."[15] This form of writing then presents itself as efficient, advanced, universalist, modern, and as the standard to which all writings must conform.

If Aboriginal self-government is a politics of form, then the written form itself is a critical mechanism by which the commodity form is being incarnated. The written form inscribes possessive individualism: this too comes with, in Derrida's words, "the singularity of the signature and of the name."[16] The written form—the mark that is the vote that is the most basic and at the same time the most banal political gesture in late capitalist societies—circumscribes citizenship. While across the river from Fort Good Hope, the same trees still sway in the wind and on that ground nothing has changed, the written form has changed everything. Aboriginal title to that land has been extinguished. A signed document exists verifying this. The written form has determined that whenever the government or corporate interests want to construct their mine or oil well or hydroelectric project, they have the inscription that authorizes them to do so.

In response, another kind of writing is deployed: the syllabic writing of elders, the inscriptions on the landscape on the body, the material structure of communities incarnated in architectures and gestures, the narratives: the political declarations, the BCRs, the embodied deconstructions, the writing whose being as writing is itself encoded in its form as inscription and as text, the writing that insinuates itself within while at the same time deploying itself against other writings and other writing machineries.

FOR KAYRENE

Kayrene (Nookiguak) Kilabuk was my research assistant in Panniqtuuq. She had been a student in Native Studies at Trent University. When I arrived in Panniqtuuq in the late summer of 1993, having not been there since 1985 and not knowing if I would know anyone there, it was a great relief for me to find Kayrene at the airport, bidding a temporary goodbye to her partner Seeti Kilabuk, who was leaving on a short-term wage-work contract. Seeti is the son of Ipelee Kilabuk, one of the community's political leaders, so Kayrene had become linked to a very large and important family in Panniqtuuq. Kayrene is originally from the nearby community of Qiqiqtarjuak. She left school and settled in Panniqtuuq to raise a family with Seeti. She was trained as a legal interpreter and worked as such for the court party when they passed through town. She was working part-time as well for the hunter's and trapper's association in Panniqtuuq in 1993. In early 1994 she gave birth to a son whom she named Imo after her father; a few years later a daughter, Ina.

Because she was now a mother, she would need an amaotik in which to carry Imo around. Amaotik are the traditional pullover outer garments worn by Inuit women, with small pouches in the back, near the hood, where children can be safely and cosily carried. Kayrene's mother made her the grey nylon amaotik that she wore through the summer of 1994. It was in the Qiqiqtarjuak style and instantly identifiable as such to the people of Panniqtuuq, who admired it for its difference and its quality. Clothing, of course, is also a certain kind of writing and traces a certain kind of being. In this context, Kayrene's amaotik could be read by any Qallunaat as saying that she was, in some way, connected to the traditions of her people. To Panniqtuuq Inuit, it could be read as saying that she was, in some way, connected to the people of Qiqiqtarjuak. To Qiqiqtarjuak Inuit, it might also be possibly read as saying she was connected to a certain family, or even specifically to her mother, who made it. So, the amaotik too is a certain kind of writing, a writing that evokes being, a local embodied writing that is posed beside, within, and in some ways opposed to, the universal, abstract, totalizing writing of the State.

The amaotik has other uses than as a signifying device, of course. Qiqiqtarjuak is far less windy than Panniqtuuq, so one of the distinguishing differences that mark Qiqiqtarjuak amaotik from Panniqtuuq amaotik is that the former have shorter front and back tails, since less wind protection is required. On occasion, Kayrene—ever the pragmatist—wished that her amaotik had been made to suit the conditions she lived in, in the Panniqtuuq style.

THE STATE AND TOTALIZATION

As noted in Part One of this book, late capitalist, postmodern societies are characterized by three distinct, interrelated, totalizing dynamics. Karl Marx analyzed two of these in his *Capital*. The other has been partially analyzed in a few studies by social theorists in recent decades, the work of Nicos Poulantzas and Anthony Giddens being of particular relevance. The dynamic of capital accumulation, the piling up of abstract wealth (which, of course, does not 'pile'), is one of the three. The necessity for capital to accumulate, for abstract wealth to ever increase, remains a governing logic in the contemporary era: if capital does not increase, does not expand—and dramatically—then root structural crises that can not be resolved within the dominant systemic logic take hold. Accumulation can be facilitated by expansion, and expansion is a totalizing process. The development of the commodity form signals a second, closely related, totalizing dynamic. The commodity form refers to a relation between exchange value and use value where the quantitative, serial, abstract logic of the former dominates the qualitative, situated, embodied logic of the latter. Commodification is a continually spreading process; as more of the world becomes commodified, more capital can accumulate. The commodity form is not a form that refers only to objects: people and spaces, time and memories, are equally subject to its exigencies. And the expansion of the commodity form is not something that only takes place spatially, on the periphery of capitalist development: the interior of the human psyche is equally a battlefield for commodification. The world of generalized commodity production does not yet exist, though that world has been envisaged and characterized by a good deal of postmodern philosophy, which nevertheless underestimates the degree to which non-commodified realms of human existence persist, sometimes in self-conscious opposition to the processes of commodification. The general outline of this trajectory of thought was all established in Marx's analysis over a hundred years ago and remains as relevant to the world today as it was in his time.

One area that Marx did not closely examine was the interrelated sphere of the State as a third totalizing dynamic, essential to the operation of the other two and presupposing the same logic. In northern Canada, capital accumulation does take place, though on a relatively limited scale, largely because of cost and of the structural position of the non-renewable resource economic sector in the post-war period. Commodification takes place, particularly as it is embedded in popular culture and the money-economic sector, both of which are important in daily life in the north. But in this specific context, it is the State that acts as the crucial locus of totalization, underwriting the serialization of social life, presupposing and thereby imposing the dominant logics of instrumental rationality and possessive individualism that work together in constructing the established order.

Gidden's contribution to this analysis—which can be linked to that of Poulantzas discussed in Chapter One—comes through his focus on the importance of surveillance and deviance. Giddens has argued in *The Nation-State and Violence* that "totalitarianism . . . is a tendential property of the modern state."[17] His analysis is directed towards totalitarianism as a tendency rather than totalization as a structural feature, though much of what he says has relevance to the latter: "the possibilities of totalitarian rule depend upon the existence of societies in which the state can successfully penetrate the day-to-day activities of most of its subject population" (302). The writings of the State, and the responses it requires, can be situated in this context as mechanisms of surveillance:

> The expansion of surveillance in the modern political order, in combination with the policing of 'deviance', radically transforms the relation between state authority and the governed population, compared with traditional states. Administrative power now increasingly enters into the minutiae of daily life and the most intimate of personal actions and relationships. In an age more and more invaded by electronic modes of the storage, collation and dissemination of information, the possibilities of accumulating information relevant to the practice of government are almost endless. Control of information, within modern, pacified states and very rapid systems of communication, transportation and sophisticated techniques of sequestration, can be directly integrated with the supervision of conduct in such a way as to produce a high concentration of state power. Surveillance is the necessary condition of the administrative power of states, whatever ends this power be turned to. (309)

This is, of course, a Foucaultian analysis, with the crucial difference that for Giddens the State remains the locus of power. The example that Giddens provides is also particularly apposite. He notes that "the provision of welfare cannot be organized or funded unless there is a close and detailed monitoring of many characteristics of the lives of the population, regardless of whether they are welfare recipients or not," and suggests that this monitoring, particularly respecting those who rely on welfare, "can also be a means of regulating their activities in a co-ordinated fashion according to political doctrines promulgated by state authorities" (308). The process need not be so blatant or conspicuous: in Canada, the activities or lifestyle of welfare recipients are highly regulated by well-meaning welfare officials, who attempt to impose a State-sanctioned sense of what a 'normal' family life must be and who equally attempt to impose State-determined structures of what kind of home conditions must be maintained in order to establish social welfare eligibility.

The totalitarian tendency that Giddens writes of is, in my view, a totalizing structural feature of liberal-democratic States, certainly respecting Aboriginal peoples where they do not operate within the boundaries of the established order. It is worth remembering Hannah Arendt's insight that the foundation for the techniques of State power deployed by totalitarian regimes was invented in the project of European colonialism. The hegemonic logic of the dominant form, or all that falls within the rubric of the normal, has relevance to all citizens of liberal-democratic states. The 'forms' you cannot adequately 'fill out' mark you as a 'deviant' who must be policed. Deviancy is a necessary component of this structure, serving to consolidate an abstract-ideal 'self' in the dominant order as 'normal'. Liberal-democracy is most clearly totalitarian from the perspective of those who do not follow the dominant serial exigency—as in, Dene and Inuit in northern Canada.

The critical lesson of this for those involved in the project of Aboriginal self-government is that there will never be a 'final victory' over 'the enemy', because the enemy is not embodied in specific social agents or specific government policies or even specific constitutional structures. All these reflect an underlying logic; since that logic is totalizing, it will never stop, it will never cease to attempt to absorb and incorporate Aboriginal realities into the dominant reality. From the perspective of totalization, Aboriginal peoples, Aboriginal cultures, must equally become commodities like every other aspect of social existence, sooner or later. Any victories will only be provisional. This is a process not directed exclusively at Aboriginal peoples, though from the structural margins they experience its blunt edges. It is only when there is a foundational structural change in the established order that replaces these totalizing dynamics with something else that Aboriginal peoples will feel a respite.

FOR SUBVERSION, AN INESCAPABLE LOGIC

That which falls under the sign of resistance is as much a part of everyday life in the Aboriginal communities I worked with as that which falls under the sign of totalization. A gesture can be coded as either, depending upon the constantly shifting context. A civil servant, close to retirement, whom I interviewed in the mid-eighties in Ottawa, a verbose, blustery, no-nonsense type of the old school named Ralph Ritsie, who had run a residential school in Churchill, was proud of the fact that many of the current generation of Dene leaders had attended his school. Residential schools, 'total institutions' whose function was totalizing, generated an Aboriginal leadership who could more effectively stand against totalization and whose first demand was to end the residential school system. This points to the specific logic of resistance that takes place in Aboriginal politics in northern Canada: a logic of subversion, whereby structures or gestures or policies of the dominant order are turned against themselves, are operated so as to achieve an effect that is precisely the opposite of the one aimed for. It is as if, somehow, although all the arrows point in one direction—perhaps the very fact that there are so many arrows pointing in that direction—the reader of the sign gains a distinct, clear sense that she must turn and go the opposite way.

Subversion is one of the only forms of resistance available to those who are struggling against a dominant logic that is totalizing, that carries with it the power to define the totality, and that functions within a field of totalization. A direct confrontation will easily be smashed or smothered. Where the opponent determines the rules of the game, but does not hold all the cards, one must use every means at one's disposal; the most effective means is to play the game while subtly turning the rules against themselves. This is a difficult and risky form of resistance. It involves using the dominant logic against itself; it is risky because that logic carries hidden within it unforseen totalizing exigencies and presuppositions, including a series of attractive incentives.

Self-government itself, in its recent history, is a concept that illustrates the dynamic of totalization and subversion. It was proposed by Aboriginal peoples like the Dene, who deployed the Western language of nationhood in a determined and largely successful effort to establish their political program in the Canadian national consciousness. The concept was then 'captured' by the State and deployed to justify models that were thinly disguised versions of much older attempts at wholesale assimilation: the Sechelt Act of 1985 compared remarkably well to the 1884 Indian Advancement Act. This version of the concept was resisted by First Nations, who used the notion of inherency to establish a conceptual indeterminacy for Aboriginal self-government. There are few terms in the Canadian public space that are so widely used while being so ill-defined.

MARGINAL COMMENT ON THE SECHELT INDIAN BAND
SELF-GOVERNMENT ACT

Perhaps the accumulation of anecdotes itself comes to take on the weight of data. In any event, the following can serve as a supplement to the more extensive critique of the Sechelt Act elaborated in Cassidy's and Bish's *Indian Government: Its Meaning in Practice.*[18] A warning to gentle and sensitive readers should also preface this story: language unsuited to the sanctity of the academic text must be reported. Soon after the legislation was enacted, I met a Sechelt spokesperson at a conference. The spokesperson, a man, was eager to respond to criticism of the model and of the Sechelt, and stressed in his talk the difficulty of negotiations, the concessions they had achieved from government. Later, over coffee, he told a group of us that the Sechelt had made a flag for their band office and on the flag they had included the words, translated into Latin by their lawyer (and here's where the foul language appears): "don't fuck with the Sechelt." We laughed and thought of it as a fine comment that reflected some trace of a sense of resistance. Whether the story has a literal referent or not, after some time bothering over this anecdote, I realized its significance for me is in the fact that in the story, Latin, the cherished ancient language of the colonizers, was chosen as a means of enunciating and hiding the slogan, rather than the ancient language of the Sechelt. Here, an outwardly subversive gesture reinscribes the logic of totalization. Perhaps so too the Sechelt Act.

INDIGENISM

One interesting position that has emerged from some Aboriginal scholars in the field can be characterized as an 'indigenism' position. For Taiaiake Alfred, the indigenist position "brings together words, ideas, and symbols from different indigenous cultures to serve as tools for those involved in asserting nationhood."[19] While at pains to emphasize that indigenism "does not . . . supplant the localized cultures of individual communities," Alfred does stress that it "is an important means of confronting the state in that it provides a unifying vocabulary and basis for collective action."[20] Patricia Monture-Angus, while agreeing with much of Alfred's analysis, has criticized him for an emphasis on leadership as a solution,[21] along the same lines of some of my own comments above respecting Boldt, as well as taking him to task for an inadequate inclusion of discussion of issues and roles pertaining to Aboriginal women. Nevertheless, Alfred offers a compelling message, particularly in his understanding of the ways in which the drive to accumulate wealth vitiates traditional Aboriginal values: "without a commitment to the development of economic self-sufficiency in a framework of respect for traditional values, money can do nothing to promote decolonization and reassertion of our nationhood."[22]

This version of an indigenist position, then, recognizes the similarities that inform Aboriginal opposition to totalization, though, rather than doing so from a mode of production-based argument, grounds the analysis in similarities respecting Aboriginal values. Although the perspective is firmly rooted in Kanien'kehaka values, culture, and history—deploying, for example, the two-row wampum as a central metaphor for configuring a better way of managing relations between Aboriginal and non-Aboriginal peoples—it nevertheless offers a position that, with some modification, travels well into Nunavut and Denendeh.

ABORIGINAL POLITICS IN NORTHERN CANADA

While the struggle against totalization involves using its structures or language against itself, the struggle also depends on that which stands or can be defined or constructed as standing outside totalization. Here is where the maddening but essential (necessary and essentialist) concept of tradition takes its specific force in this field. The reconstruction of tradition—

whether 'invented' or not—within a totalizing context provides a kind of ground from which political resistance can be staged. Of course, another tradition is called forth by the servants of capital accumulation, so it is not tradition for its own sake but the substantive form of the tradition being invoked that is critical here. The Aboriginal traditions being reinvented, reconstructed, re-enacted, and revitalized in the Aboriginal cultural renaissance taking place in Canada, to the extent that they are tied to the egalitarian moment of the gatherer and hunter mode of production, substantively offer both an attractive sphere for commodification and a powerful site of resistance. It is on this terrain that Aboriginal cultural politics are being staged. Denendeh and Nunavut alike derive their specificity from the fact that, while they are now more accessible than ever before, they remain slightly to the side of the major thoroughfares of capital accumulation. Dene and Inuit continue to have direct access to the means of subsistence, and have only partially been 'proletarianized'. In *Capital* Marx continually emphasized:

> In the history of primitive accumulation, all revolutions are epochmaking that act as levers for the capitalist class in the course of its formation; but this is true above all for those moments when great masses of men are suddenly and forcibly torn from their means of subsistence, and hurled onto the labour-market as free, unprotected and rightless proletarians. The expropriation of the agricultural producer, of the peasant, from the soil is the basis of the whole process. The history of this expropriation assumes different aspects in different countries, and runs through its various phases in different orders of succession, and at different historical epochs.[23]

The extinguishment of Aboriginal title is the latest mechanism by which the State—which, it seems, has consistently played a critical role in this particular and peculiarly crucial function for capital—attempts to secure the dispossession of another sector of society in this country, Canada, in this historical epoch, postmodernism. Extinguishment is a necessary moment or phase if Inuit and Dene are to become "free . . . rightless, proletarians," sellers of labour power, human commodities.

In the distant future, culture will itself likely be the most valuable commodity. Just as signed artworks today on their own embody massive amounts of capital, in another century 'genuine' cultural artefacts and 'authentic' traditional ceremonies will have the same rarity and a collective-cultural signature-value (rather than an individual signature value). In a world of massively expanded commodity production based on even greater expansion of the commodity form into the sphere of cultural and interpersonal life, whatever traces of Aboriginality have remained will have an exponentially enormous capital value. This process has already begun, of course, but its dimensions are relatively small: we are not yet in the world of generalized commodity production that the social theorists take for granted. So, perhaps this whole politics 'merely' stages the deferral of totalization until such time as the commodity value of Aboriginal culture increases to the point where it is, literally, ir-resistible.

That future, however, is not the only one it is possible to envisage. The continued existence of societies that enact meaningful egalitarian social relations poses a specific threat to the dominant order. In spite of, or perhaps even within, their very marginality they may play a significant role in the project of structural transformation or transcendence of existing social reality. This latter possibility would then imply that this whole politics may direct itself towards shaping the future in a drastically different and opposed direction to the one outlined in the preceding paragraph.

These are the stakes in Denendeh and Nunavut today. Those without vision, the functionaries who now dominate but do not exhaust the State apparatus of the territorial governments, would like to ensure that in the north, the forms can be filled out in the same way as almost everywhere else in the world. Their job is to ensure that the paper flows. In a strange form of opposition that never confronts, in small communities scattered across the vast but well-used land, are people who have vision, and who 'see' the continuance of a way of life that has survived for years beyond memory.

A DRUM DANCE IN N'DILO

It's June 27, 1994, very late in the evening. I am with my friend Elizabeth in a canoe, gliding across the smooth, still waters of Back Bay on Tucho, at Yellowknife. We are out for our evening paddle around Latham Island. The sun is still up, but slowly, ever so slowly, setting. As we reach N'dilo, we begin to hear a steady pulse: the sound of Dene drums. We remember, then, that the Treaty 8 assembly is still convened, and one of the evening drum dances is on. We stop paddling, sit drifting and listening to the call of the drums, finally deciding not to go in and join the circle of dancers and friends, but to continue with our short trip, another circle that surrounds that of the dancers. As we pass the point of Latham Island, the drum songs still audible though faded, we catch sight of the waxing moon, near full, rising across the bay, and when we turn out of sight of the lingering sunset, the moonrise greets us. Along the other shore, we again move our paddles to the steady strong rhythm of the Dene drums, growing louder again. Finally, we reach the row of Twin Otters tied to the Old Town docks and paddle, squeezing our way, through the small tunnel under the road that connects Latham Island to Old Town, our journey at an end, though the drum songs continue long into the night, long after our passing.

EPILOGUE

still hunting stories

ONE SHOT

One time, my friend Andrew Tagak Jr. took me out with his older brother, John, caribou hunting on Baffin Island. May is one of the best times to experience Baffin Island because the worst of the cold is gone, the day is growing longer, but the terrain is still snow-covered and frozen. The dry arctic air temperatures, between minus five and minus ten degrees Celsius, have no bite and are even refreshing. The frozen ground makes travel by snowmobile still feasible. It was this trip that helped me appreciate the advantages of a treeless terrain to hunters: the Arctic is not an absence of trees so much as an open terrain. Snowmobiles are in their glory here and we charged over snow-covered hills and valleys, gaining magnificent views of broad vistas from on high, burrowing along twisting rivers down below, moving and searching, delighting in the speed in the gaze.

I had eaten enough caribou in my time that I felt no hesitation in accepting the offer to join the hunt. A large, dispersed herd had settled around Iqaluit, some even wandering through town, so we had little doubt we would find some. As we were about to leave Andrew's house, we noticed with consternation that we only had three bullets, so we decided to make a quick trip into town to get more. Andrew's father, though, Andrew Sr., stopped us in our tracks with a story about how he had been attacked by a polar bear when his snowmobile broke down and, with only one bullet, had killed it and saved his life. Three, he mildly suggested, would be more than enough for a caribou. Duly chagrined, we headed out with our three bullets.

When, after an hour or so of searching, we came across a small herd of caribou, I wondered if we were going to be able to get close enough for a good shot and if our three bullets would prove sufficient. We ran at the herd in our machines: a small group split off to our left; the larger bunch went out of sight around a hill to the right. We stopped near the base of this hill, deciding to walk around it and see if we could get close on foot. We had just stopped the snowmobile when a lone animal came trotting up, head high, skirting around the hill to rejoin the larger group. It caught scent or sight of us and stopped. There was a quiet moment. The rifle we were using was sighted slightly high, so aiming it required a bit of guess-work. The caribou seemed to offer itself to us: standing sideways, thirty-odd metres away, so still, dead still. The moment ended in a roar, the caribou crumpled. Andrew and I ran up to it; it had been hit in the heart but was still alive; Andrew quickly put it out of pain with a firm jab of his knife into its skull. He and his brother butchered it while I, useless, stood beside them, remembering with sadness the beauty of the animal. Later, I would enjoy eating and sharing its meat, sharing the story of the hunt.

FOR FUR AND WILD MEAT

The boundary mode of production is usually determined and conceived in social, political, and economic terms. It is most frequently experienced, though, in terms of values and ethics. Crossing the boundary involves hold-ing judgement in reserve or else risking the reinscription of colonial rela-tions. This is one reason why historical materialism has something to say to the issue of animal rights. While there may, in certain circumstances, be a progressive value to questioning the ethical treatment of animals by the dominant society, the same mode of questioning takes on a whole other dimension when it is exported to the treatment of animals by hunt-ing peoples. Donna Landry and Gerald Maclean, in their *Materialist Femi-nism*, subject the discourses about the fox hunt in the British countryside to critique, suggesting that in specific settings and contexts, animal rights activists do not do a service either to establishing more ethical relations between humans and animals, or in acknowledging effective microecological strategies that might involve killing animals. They open up a space from which it is possible to suggest that historical materialists, for whom ethical treatment of animals is a legitimate concern, will not easily or automatically accept the arguments of animal rights activists. Julia Emberley, in her *The Cultural Politics of Fur*, illustrates the colonial hypocrisies of a regime that for centuries encouraged Aboriginal peoples in northern Canada to harvest fur, and then more recently and with great moral self-satisfaction suggests that the whole activity should be banned. Emberley also discusses the highly politically charged value of fur as a symbolic construction in contemporary society, noting, for example, the derogatory positioning of women in many of the well-known anti-fur advertisements sponsored by animal rights activists.

The political and economic issue, at least as it regards northern Dene and Inuit hunters, is discussed at length in George Wenzel's *Animal Rights, Human Rights* and in Hugh Brody's *Living Arctic*, the former a detailed analysis of how the anti-sealing campaign affected subsistence economies in Inuit communities, the latter an eloquent defence of the rights of hunting peoples. Deployment of the concept/boundary of mode of production allows the issue to come into sharp focus. If we compare the lot of animals in ecologies controlled by gatherers and hunters, where, for the most part, they roam free, some small proportion hunted or trapped, to the lot of animals in ecologies controlled by late capitalists, where a variety of domestications, confinements, and brutalities of the worst sort are so common as to pass almost unnoticed, the hypocrisy of those who want to impose upon hunting peoples a non-violent relation to animals becomes stark. It is the duty of historical materialists to insistently question the now commonplace presumptions that fur use is somehow 'bad' and that a progressive politics demands a refusal to be complicit in the fur industry. Paradoxically, those who on a daily basis kill, skin, and butcher wild game, eating the meat and tanning the hides for still useful outer garments, have developed ways of relating to and understanding animals that put them in a far more developed ethical position on this question.

Historical materialists support the principle of Aboriginal rights, particularly the exclusive rights of Aboriginal peoples to hunt, fish, and trap—to exploit wildlife resources, in the jargon of administrators—for their own sustenance and for commercial advantage. If one wanted to *help* the political project of Nunavut, the Aboriginal project in Denendeh, the most immediately effective way to do that would be to reconstruct the market for Dene and Inuit fur products. This would result in a strengthening of the local Aboriginal economies, the economies that produce wealth that goes directly into the hands of producers.

A SHOPPING TRIP

One time, my friend Isidore Manuel took me out caribou hunting in February. I had used my mid-winter break from teaching to travel to Fort Good Hope to conduct a workshop on self-government. The short hunting trip was Isidore's way of saying masi cho. We planned to leave in the evening and overnight at a well-used warden's cabin, but could not find a part for the snowmobile, so we left early the next morning instead. By the time we reached the cabin, after a few hours along cut line trails and winter roads, cutting across frozen lakes and scooting along frozen rivers, it was close to noon. We stopped for tea and snacks, meeting there with Charlie Tobac, who had also left Fort Good Hope that morning.

Ten minutes further we encountered the hunters who had gone out the night before. Their sleds were laden with meat; within a half hour of leaving the cabin early that morning, they had come across a large herd of caribou and bagged their fill. They had only just finished butchering their kill and were on the return trip. We left them eagerly, hoping to have the same good luck. An hour or so later our eagerness had faded, replaced by regret for the fact that we had not managed to follow our original plan and been able to share in the early bird's success.

We spent hours on bush trails, snowmobile tracks, cut lines: narrow passes through the scrub spruce and pines. It was bright and not cold. The search was fruitless and my thoughts began to turn homewards rather than hopeful. As the light started to fade, Isidore and Charlie decided to try one more trail they knew of. Not far along it the noise from our machine startled an enormous grey owl out of its perch. It floated majestically through the trees as if it were gliding on the coming darkness. At the end of this trail was a lake, and there Isidore spotted caribou, though even when he gestured towards them I could not make them out. Together, he and Charlie drove them away from the centre of the lake, into the deep snow and trees near its edges; there they each shot one, dragged it out onto the

lake, and butchered it. Within an hour of spotting them, we were returning with the meat. We stopped at the cabin for fresh fried caribou heart.

The long trip back in the darkness was more enjoyable than I had anticipated. It was easier to see the contour lines in the terrain at night than in
the bright white on white of daytime. We had been successful on our hunt
and were pulling meat along behind. And, for me at least, rather than travelling towards an unknown destination, we were returning home.

There are places in the world where this mode of living continues,
thrives. There are many places in Canada where a trip to the bush store
remains a part of everyday life.

DARKNESS AT NOON

One time, I encountered the lifting of darkness at noon. For a few days
I found myself in Cambridge Bay on the south shore of Victoria Island
far above the Arctic Circle in early January. During my visit temperatures
never rose above fifty degrees below zero, Celsius. I later discovered that
this was a gift, and it resulted in the warmest winter I ever spent in Canada.
This was because when I returned to Toronto, while those of my friends
who had travelled to Cuba or Mexico or Florida waxed nostalgic about
their trips and complained about the bitter cold, I strolled around with an
open parka as if it were springtime: their trips made the remaining months
of winter even more unbearable, mine made them easy.

When I arrived in Cambridge Bay I quickly noticed that the only daylight consisted of about three hours of twilight in the middle of the day.
The rest was utter darkness. A couple of days into my research, I found
myself, swaddled in down parka, long johns, layers and layers of wool, scur-
rying quickly from building to building for my lunch break. It was midday,
and some accident led me to look, preoccupied as I was with reaching the
warmth of my destination, to the south. I saw something. A sliver of red
over a frozen sea. A coloured sky; it appeared and then was gone. Sunrise
and sunset danced together at noon for barely a minute.

Each of the remaining days of my visit, I made a point of finding some
vantage from which to watch the spectacle. Each day, the sunrise and sunset lasted a little longer, the sliver of red ever more slowly emerged and
ever more slowly settled into the distant ice. By the day of my departure,
the whole of the sun was just barely appearing over the horizon. The hours

of twilight were interrupted by something that resembled daylight and more of it was appearing every day.

What does one choose to remember: the darkness or the light? Against the mindless optimism that remains so ideologically pervasive that it is inscribed in every new object produced by capitalism, one is tempted towards the relentless, withering cynicism that has become common-place. And yet, when faced with a generalized disenchantment and a cold realization that cynicism itself has become the most powerful excuse for apathetic surrender, one determines to struggle, however fruitlessly, for ideals, however compromised. Hence, especially as we remain painfully aware of the manner in which promises are more often than not realized in their betrayal, it is as possible as it is necessary to long for something else, to continue to long in the language of the promise: a longing and a language that may not conform to the State's modality of intelligibility without betraying themselves. In the midst of that dark time the feeble stirring of a fresh sun over a frozen sea held within it a promise that the long warm bright days of summer would be returning a promise like the look in a young woman's eyes in a van Gogh painting of wretched peasant potato eaters a promise like the solemn, deliberate words that surrounded negotiations for treaties with First Nations a promise that makes cautious, delicate steps as if it were an emaciated woman in a fur coat picking her way at midnight through a back alley off Hastings Street in Vancouver a promise like that dreamed alive in birth to slowly day by day fade until crushed by the inevitable a promise like that more often than not betrayed by every new government that claims to represent the utopian hopes of the new people it helps bring into being a promise that creates that moves that inspires that is a part of establishing a future that will never but must always be its fulfilment a promise that will fade but will not in spite of the best efforts of the intellectual servants of capital disappear a promise like a pulse like an echo like a call like a sound like the sound of a drum.

ENDNOTES

INTRODUCTION

1. Stephen Greenblatt, *Marvellous Possessions; The Wonder of the New World* (Chicago: University of Chicago Press, 1991), 3–4.

2. Ibid., 4.

3. Ibid., 152.

4. Michael Asch, *Home and Native Land* (Toronto: Methuen, 1984), 94.

5. Ibid.

6. Marshall Sahlins, *Islands of History* (Chicago: University of Chicago Press, 1987).

7. Jean-Paul Sartre, *Critique of Dialectical Reason*, vol. 2, trans. Quintin Hoare (New York: Verso, 1991), 46.

8. Theodor Adorno, *Minima Moralia*, trans. E.F.N. Jephcott (New York: Verso, 1991), 103.

9. Fredric Jameson, *Late Marxism* (New York: Verso, 1990), 26–27.

10. Fredric Jameson, *Postmodernism or, The Cultural Logic of Late Capitalism* (Durham: Duke University Press, 1991), 334.

11. Fredric Jameson, *The Seeds of Time* (New York: Columbia University Press, 1994), 65.

12. Michael Taussig, *The Nervous System* (New York: Routledge, 1992), 5.

13. Jacques Derrida, *Spectres of Marx*, trans. Peggy Kamuf (New York: Routledge, 1994), 135.

14. Michael Taussig, *Shamanism, Colonialism, and the Wild Man* (Chicago: University of Chicago Press, 1987), 203.

15. Clifford Geertz, *Works and Lives* (Stanford: Stanford University Press, 1988), 144.

16. Derrida, *Spectres of Marx*, xv.

CHAPTER ONE

1. Susan Buck-Morss, *The Dialectics of Seeing: Walter Benjamin and the Arcades Project* (Cambridge: MIT Press, 1989), 273.

2. Plutarch, *Essays* (London: Penguin Books, 1992), 45.

3. Ibid., 42.

4. Jean Baudrillard, *For a Critique of the Political Economy of the Sign*, trans. Charles Levin (St. Louis: Telos, 1981), 145.

5. Joan Ryan, *Doing Things the Right Way* (Calgary: University of Calgary Press, 1995), 53.

6. Walter Benjamin, *Illuminations*, trans. Harry Zohn (New York: Schocken Books, 1978), 91.

7. Taussig, *Shamanism*, 366.

8. Ibid., 367.

9. Fredric Jameson, *The Political Unconscious* (Ithaca: Cornell University Press, 1988), 75.

10. Ibid., 89.

11. Karl Marx, *Grundrisse*, trans. Martin Nicolaus (New York: Vintage Books, 1973), 89.

12. Eric Wolfe, *Europe and the People Without History* (Berkeley: University of California Press, 1997), 75.

13. Nicos Poulantzas, *Political Power and Social Classes*, trans. and ed. Timothy O'Hagan (London: Verso, 1978), 15.

14. Jameson, *Political Unconscious*, 95.

15. Raymond Williams, *Marxism and Literature* (New York: Oxford University Press, 1977).

16. Marx, *Grundrisse*, 105–107.

17. Wolfe, *Europe and the People*, 76.

18. Jameson, *Political Unconscious*, 94.

19. Marx, *Grundrisse*, 102.

20. Wolfe, *Europe and the People*, 80.

21. Jacques Derrida, "Force of Law," in *Deconstruction and the Possibility of Justice*, ed. Drucilla Cornell, Michel Rosenfeld, and David Gray Carlson, trans. Mary Quaintance (New York: Routledge, 1992), 44.

22. Dene Nation, *Denendeh* (Yellowknife: The Dene Nation, 1984), 135.

23. Adorno, *Minima Moralia*, 62–63.

24. Jameson, *Political Unconscious*, 286.

25. Diamond Jenness, *Arctic Odyssey: The Diary of Diamond Jenness 1913–1916*, ed. Stuart Jenness (Ottawa: Canadian Museum of Civilization, 1991), 254–255.

26. Marshall Sahlins, *Stone Age Economics* (Chicago: Aldine-Atherton, 1972), 32.

27. Eleanor Burke Leacock, *Myths of Male Dominance* (New York: Monthly Review Press, 1981), 13.

28. Ibid., 133.

29. Hugh Brody, *Maps and Dreams* (Harmondsworth: Penguin Books, 1983), xi –xii.

30. Plutarch, *Essays*, 131.

31. Derrida, "Force of Law," 43.

32. Sahlins, *Stone Age Economics*, 13.

33. Marshall Sahlins, *Culture and Practical Reason* (Chicago: University of Chicago Press, 1976), 211.

34. E. Wilmsen and J. Denbow, "Paradigmatic History of San-Speaking Peoples and Current Attempts at Revision," *Curent Anthropology* 31, 5: 494.

35. Ibid., 498.

36. James Clifford, *The Predicament of Culture: Twentieth-Century Ethnography, Literature and Art* (Cambridge: Harvard University Press, 1988), 11.

37. Homi Bhabha, *The Location of Culture* (New York: Routledge, 1994), 38.

38. Ibid., 4.

39. Ibid., 207.

40. Hugh Brody, *The Other Side of Eden: Hunters, Farmers and the Shaping of the Modern World* (Vancouver: Douglas and McIntyre, 2000), 101.

41. Ibid.

42. Mark O. Dickerson, *Whose North?* (Vancouver: University of British Columbia Press, 1992), 89.

43. Ibid.

44. Ibid., 30.

45. Fredric Jameson, *Late Marxism* (New York: Verso, 1990), 41.

46. Ibid., 149.

47. Stanley Diamond, *In Search of the Primitive* (New Brunswick [USA]: Transaction Books, 1977).

48. Quoted in Jameson, *Late Marxism*, 41.

49. Mel Watkins, ed., *Dene Nation: The Colony Within* (Toronto: University of Toronto Press, 1978), 121.

50. Nicos Poulantzas, *State, Power, Socialism*, trans. Patrick Camiller (London: Verso, 1980), 81.

51. Jenness, *Arctic Odyssey*, 420.

52. Jean Briggs, *Never in Anger* (Cambridge: Harvard University Press, 1967), 96–108.

53. Jenness, *Arctic Odyssey*, 386.

54. Michael Hardt and Antonio Negri, *Empire* (Cambridge: Harvard University Press, 2001), 10.

55. Jameson, *Postmodernism*, 102.

CHAPTER TWO

1. Derrida, "Force of Law," 26.

2. Antonia Mills, *Eagle Down Is Our Law: Witsuwit'en Law, Feasts, and Land Claims* (Vancouver: University of British Columbia Press, 1994), 137.

3. Rene Fumoleau, *As Long as This Land Shall Last: A History of Treaty 8 and Treaty 11, 1870–1939* (Toronto: McClelland and Stewart, 1973), 213.

4. Minutes from Dene Assembly, July 14, 1992, p. 2.

5. Fumoleau, *As Long as This Land*, 164.

6. Jameson, *Postmodernism*, 145–180.

7. David Harvey, *The Condition of Postmodernity* (Cambridge: Blackwell, 1992), 210.

8. Ato Sekyi-Otu, *Fanon's Dialectic of Experience* (Cambridge: Harvard University Press, 1996), 72–73.

9. Nunavut Implementation Commission, "Two-Member Constituencies and Gender Equality: A 'Made in Nunavut' Solution for an Effective and Representative Legislature," December 6, 1994, p. 4.

10. Ibid., 17.

11. Jameson, *The Seeds of Time*, 61.

12. Jameson, *Political Unconscious*, 293.

13. Ibid., 285, 293–294.

14. Jameson, *Postmodernism*, 337 (but see also *Seeds of Time*, 66–67).

15. Jameson, *Political Unconscious*, 294.

16. Sartre, *Critique of Dialectical Reason*, vol. 1, trans. Alan Sheridan-Smith (London: New Left Books, 1978), 256.

17. Hugh Brody, *The People's Land* (Harmondsworth: Penguin Books, 1977), 12.

18. Adorno, *Minima Moralia*, 170.

19. Gayatri Chakravorty Spivak, *Outside in the Teaching Machine* (New York: Routledge, 1993), 177.

20. J. Irving Hallowell, "Ojibwa Ontology, Behavior, and World View," in *Primitive Views of the World*, ed. Stanley Diamond (New York: Columbia University Press, 1969), 75.

21. Ibid.

22. Winona LaDuke, *The Winona LaDuke Reader* (Penticton: Theytus Books, 2002), 79.

23. Ibid., 80.

24. Michael Taussig, *Shamanism, Colonialism and the Wild Man* (Chicago: University of Chicago Press, 1987), 447–448.

CHAPTER THREE

1. Cited in Fumoleau, *As Long as This Land,* 173.

2. Ibid., 347–349.

3. Kerry Abel, *Drum Songs: Glimpses of Dene History* (Montreal and Kingston: McGill-Queen's University Press, 1993), 240.

4. Donna Lea Hawley, *The Annotated 1990 Indian Act* (Toronto: Carswell Company, 1990), 87.

5. Ibid., 88.

6. Joan Ryan, *Doing Things the Right Way* (Calgary: University of Calgary Press, 1995), 57.

7. Dominick LaCapra, *Representing the Holocaust* (Ithaca: Cornell University Press, 1994), 202.

CHAPTER FOUR

1. W.J.T. Mitchell, "Imperial Landscape," in *Landscape and Power,* ed. W.J.T. Mitchell (Chicago: University of Chicago Press, 1994), 10.

2. Jonathan Bordo, "Jack Pine—Wilderness Sublime or the Erasure of the Aboriginal Presence from the Landscape," *Journal of Canadian Studies* 27, 4 (Winter): 121.

3. Indian and Northern Affairs Canada, *Sahtu Treaty* (Ottawa: Indian Affairs and Northern Development, 1991), 9.

4. Pierre Clastres, *Society Against the State* (New York: Zone Books, 1983), 31.

5. Taussig, *Shamanism,* 202.

6. Ibid., 203.

7. George Barnaby, "The Political System and the Dene," in *Dene Nation: The Colony Within,* ed. Mel Watkins (Toronto: University of Toronto Press, 1977), 120.

8. Indian and Northern Affairs Canada, *Sahtu Treaty,* 8.

9. Barnaby, "The Political System," 121.

10. Rosalind E. Krauss, *The Optical Unconscious* (Cambridge: MIT Press, 1993), 167.

CHAPTER FIVE

1. Jameson, *The Seeds of Time,* 23.

2. Ibid.

3. Ibid.

4. Marc Stevenson, *Inuit, Whalers and Cultural Persistence* (Toronto: Oxford University Press, 1997), 103.

5. For the decision, see my *Unjust Relations* (Toronto: Oxford University Press, 1994), 32–47; and for its background, see Peter Kulchyski and Frank Tester, *Tammarniit (Mistakes)* (Vancouver: University of British Columbia Press, 1994), 13–42.

6. Cited in Morris Zaslow, *The Northward Expansion of Canada 1914–1967* (Toronto: McClelland and Stewart, 1988), 260.

7. Brody, *The People's Land*, 74.

8. Anthony Giddens, *The Nation-State and Violence* (Berkeley: University of California Press, 1987), 252.

9. Walter Benjamin, *Illuminations*, trans. Harry Zohn (New York: Schocken Books, 1978), 255.

10. Claude Levi-Strauss, *Tristes Tropiques*, trans. John and Doreen Weightman (New York: Atheneum, 1973), 337.

11. Jacques Derrida, *Of Grammatology*, trans. Gayatri Chakravorty Spivak (Baltimore: Johns Hopkins University Press, 1976), 123.

12. Clastres, *Society Against the State*, 186.

13. Ibid., 177.

CHAPTER SIX

1. See Michael Mitchell, in Joyce Richardson, ed., *Drumbeat* (Toronto: Summerhill Press, 1989), 118.

2. Watkins, ed., *Dene Nation*, 3.

3. See Royal Commission on Aboriginal Peoples (RCAP) *Report*, Vol. Two, Part One (Ottawa: Minister of Supply and Services, 1996), 349.

4. Ibid., 340; see also 130–134.

5. Ibid., 4.6.12, 481; see also 4.6.13.

6. Menno Boldt, *Surviving as Indians* (Toronto: University of Toronto Press, 1993), 76.

7. Bill C-31, see 63–64.

8. Frank Cassidy and Robert L. Bish, *Indian Government: Its Meaning in Practice* (Lantzville, BC: Oolichan Books, 1989), 156.

9. Alan C. Cairns, *Citizens Plus; Aboriginal Peoples and the Canadian State* (Vancouver: University of British Columbia Press, 2000), 12.

10. Dominick LaCapra, *History of Criticism* (Ithaca: Cornell University Press, 1985), 140.

11. Jurgen Habermas, *Communication and the Evolution of Society*, trans. Thomas McCarthy (Boston: Beacon Press, 1979), 98.

12. Marie Smallface Marule, "Traditional Indian Government: Of the People, by the People, for the People," in *Pathways to Self-Determination*, ed. Leroy Little

Bear, Menno Boldt, and J. Anthony Long (Toronto: University of Toronto Press, 1984), 44.

13. Dene Nation, *Denendeh* (Yellowknife: The Dene Nation, 1984), 32.

14. Poulantzas, *State, Power, Socialism*, 59.

15. Adorno, *Minima Moralia*, 42.

16. Derrida, "Force of Law," 60.

17. Giddens, *Nation-State and Violence*, 295.

18. Cassidy and Bish, *Indian Government*, 135–144.

19. Taiaiake Alfred, *Peace, Power, and Righteousness; An Indigenous Manifesto* (Don Mills: Oxford University Press, 1999), 188.

20. Ibid., 88.

21. See Patricia Monture-Angus, *Thunder in My Soul; a Mohawk Woman Speaks* (Halifax: Fernwood Publishing, 1995), 15.

22. Alfred, *Peace, Power, and Righteousness*, 119.

23. Marx, *Capital*, vol. one, trans. Ben Fowkes (New York: Vintage Books, 1977), 876.

BIBLIOGRAPHY

Abel, Kerry. *Drum Songs: Glimpses of Dene History.* Montreal and Kingston: McGill-Queen's University Press, 1993.

Adorno, Theodor. *Minima Moralia.* Trans. E.F.N. Jephcott. New York: Verso, 1991.

Alfred, Taiaiake. *Peace, Power, and Righteousness; An Indigenous Manifesto.* Don Mills: Oxford University Press, 1999.

Althusser, Louis. *Lenin and Philosophy.* Trans. Ben Brewster. New York: Monthly Review Press, 1971.

Asch, Michael. *Home and Native Land.* Toronto: Methuen, 1984.

_____. *Kinship and the Drum Dance in a Northern Dene Community.* Edmonton: The Boreal Institute for Northern Studies, 1988.

Bannerji, Himani. *Thinking Through.* Toronto: The Women's Press, 1995.

Barnaby, George. "The Political System and the Dene." In *Dene Nation: The Colony Within.* Ed. Mel Watkins. Toronto: University of Toronto Press, 1977.

Baudrillard, Jean. *For a Critique of the Political Economy of the Sign.* Trans. Charles Levin. St. Louis: Telos, 1981.

Benjamin, Walter. *Illuminations.* Trans. Harry Zohn. New York: Schocken Books, 1978.

Berger, Thomas R. *Northern Frontier, Northern Homeland.* Vancouver: Douglas and McIntyre, 1988.

Bhabha, Homi. *The Location of Culture.* New York: Routledge, 1994.

Blondin, George. *When the World Was New: Stories of the Sahtû Dene.* Yellowknife: Outcrop, 1990.

_____. *Yamoria, the Lawmaker: Stories of the Dene.* Edmonton: NeWest Publishers, 1997.

Boldt, Menno. *Surviving as Indians.* Toronto: University of Toronto Press, 1993.

_____, and J. Anthony Long, eds. "Tribal Traditions and European-Western Political Ideologies." In *The Quest for Justice.* Ed. M. Boldt and J.A. Long. Toronto: University of Toronto Press, 1985.

Bordo, Jonathan. "Jack Pine—Wilderness Sublime or the Erasure of the Aboriginal Presence from the Landscape." *Journal of Canadian Studies* 27, 4.

Borrows, John. *Recovering Canada.* Toronto: University of Toronto Press, 2002.

Briggs, Jean. *Never in Anger.* Cambridge: Harvard University Press, 1967.

Brody, Hugh. *The People's Land.* Harmondsworth: Penguin Books, 1977.

_____. *Maps and Dreams.* Harmondsworth: Penguin Books, 1983.

_____. *Living Arctic.* Vancouver: Douglas and McIntyre, 1987.

_____. *The Other Side of Eden.* Vancouver: Douglas and McIntyre, 2000.

Brownlee, Robin Jarvis. *A Fatherly Eye.* Toronto: Oxford University Press, 2003.

Buck-Morss, Susan. *The Dialectics of Seeing.* Cambridge: MIT Press, 1989.

Cairns, Alan C. *Citizens Plus; Aboriginal Peoples and the Canadian State.* Vancouver: University of British Columbia Press, 2000.

Canada, Government of. *Treaty No. 11.* Ottawa: Edmond Cloutier, 1957.

_____. *Report of the Royal Commission on Aboriginal Peoples.* Ottawa: Minister of Supply and Services Canada, 1996.

Cassidy, Frank, and Robert L. Bish. *Indian Government.* Lantzville, BC: Oolichan Books, 1989.

Clastres, Pierre. *Society Against the State.* New York: Zone Books, 1983.

Clifford, James. *The Predicament of Culture: Twentieth-Century Ethnography, Literature and Art.* Cambridge: Harvard University Press, 1988.

Clifford, James, and George Marcus, eds. *Writing Culture.* Berkeley: University of California Press, 1986.

Coates, Kenneth S., and William R. Morrison. *Interpreting Canada's North: Selected Readings.* Mississauga: Copp Clark Pitman, 1989.

Cornell, Drucilla. *The Philosophy of the Limit.* New York: Routledge, 1992.

Cox, Bruce Alden, ed. *Native People, Native Lands.* Ottawa: Carleton University Press, 1988.

Cruikshank, Julie. *The Social Life of Stories; Narrative and Knowledge in the Yukon Territory.* Vancouver: University of British Columbia Press, 1998.

_____. *Life Lived Like a Story.* Vancouver: University of British Columbia Press, 1990.

Culhane, Dara. *The Pleasure of the Crown.* Burnaby: Talonbooks, 1998.

Cumming, Peter A., and Neil H. Mickenberg. *Native Rights in Canada.* Second Edition. Toronto: General Publishing, 1971.

Dacks, Gurston. *A Choice of Futures.* Toronto: Methuen, 1981.

Dene Nation. *Denendeh.* Yellowknife: The Dene Nation, 1984.

Derrida, Jacques. *Of Grammatology.* Trans. Gayatri Chakravorty Spivak. Baltimore: Johns Hopkins University Press, 1976.

_____. "Force of Law." In *Deconstruction and the Possibility of Justice.* Ed. Drucilla Cornell, Michel Rosenfeld, and David Gray Carlson. Trans. Mary Quaintance. New York: Routledge, 1992.

_____. *Spectres of Marx.* Trans. Peggy Kamuf. New York: Routledge, 1994.

Diamond, Stanley. *In Search of the Primitive; a Critique of Civilization.* New Brunswick (USA): Transaction, 1987.

Dickason, Olive. *Canada's First Nations.* Toronto: Oxford University Press, 2002.

Dickerson, Mark O. *Whose North?* Vancouver: University of British Columbia Press, 1992.

Diubaldo, Richard. *The Government of Canada and the Inuit: 1900–1967.* Ottawa: Research Branch, Corporate Policy, Indian and Northern Affairs Canada, 1985.

Emberley, Julia V. *Thresholds of Difference.* Toronto: University of Toronto Press, 1993.

Fanon, Franz. *The Wretched of the Earth.* Trans. Constance Farrington. New York: Grove Press, 1966.

Freeman, Minnie Aodla. *Life Among the Qallunaat.* Edmonton: Hurtig Publishers, 1978.

Fumoleau, Rene. *As Long as This Land Shall Last: A History of Treaty 8 and Treaty 11, 1870–1939.* Toronto: McClelland and Stewart, 1975.

Foucault, Michel. *Discipline and Punish.* Trans. Alan Sheridan. New York: Vintage Books, 1979.

Geertz, Clifford. *Works and Lives.* Stanford: Stanford University Press, 1988.

Giddens, Anthony. *A Contemporary Critique of Historical Materialism.* Berkeley: University of California Press, 1981.

_____. *The Nation-State and Violence.* Berkeley: University of California Press, 1987.

Green, Joyce. "Towards a Detente with History: Confronting Canada's Colonial Legacy." *International Journal of Canadian Studies* 12 (Fall 1995).

Greenblatt, Stephen. *Marvellous Possessions; The Wonder of the New World.* Chicago: University of Chicago Press, 1991.

Habermas, Jurgen. *Communication and the Evolution of Society.* Trans. Thomas McCarthy. Boston: Beacon Press, 1979.

Hallowell, J Irving. "Ojibwa Ontology, Behavior, and World View." In *Primitive Views of the World*, ed. Stanley Diamond. New York: Columbia University Press, 1969.

Hamilton, John David. *Arctic Revolution.* Toronto: Dundurn Press, 1994.

Hardt, Michael, and Antonio Negri. *Empire.* Cambridge: Harvard University Press, 2001.

Harvey, David. *The Condition of Postmodernity.* Cambridge: Blackwell, 1992.

Hawley, Donna Lea. *The Annotated 1990 Indian Act.* Toronto: Carswell Company, 1990.

Helm, June. *The People of Denendeh*. Montreal: McGill-Queen's University Press, 2000.

Horkheimer, Max, and Theodor Adorno. *The Dialectic of Enlightenment*. London: Allen Lane, 1944.

Indian and Northern Affairs Canada. *Agreement Between the Inuit of the Nunavut Settlement Area and Her Majesty the Queen in Right of Canada*. Ottawa: Indian Affairs and Northern Development, 1993.

_____. *Sahtu Treaty*. Ottawa: Indian Affairs and Northern Development, 1991.

Jackson, A.Y. *The Arctic 1927*. Moonbeam: Penumbra Press, 1982.

Jameson, Fredric. *The Political Unconscious*. Ithaca: Cornell University Press, 1988.

_____. *Late Marxism*. New York: Verso, 1990.

_____. *Postmodernism or, The Cultural Logic of Late Capitalism*. Durham: Duke University Press, 1991.

_____. *The Seeds of Time*. New York: Columbia University Press, 1994.

Jenness, Diamond. *The Indians of Canada*. 1930; Toronto: University of Toronto Press, 1971.

Jenness, Stuart, ed. *Arctic Odyssey: The Diary of Diamond Jenness 1913–1916*. Ottawa: Canadian Museum of Civilization, 1991.

Krauss, Rosalind E. *The Optical Unconscious*. Cambridge: MIT Press, 1993.

Kulchyski, Peter. "The Postmodern and the Paleolithic." *Canadian Journal of Political and Social Theory* 12, 3 (1989).

_____. "Primitive Subversions." *Cultural Critique* 21 (Spring 1992).

_____. "Anthropology at the Service of the State." *The Journal of Canadian Studies* (Fall 1993).

_____. "Theses on Aboriginal Rights." In *Unjust Relations*. Ed. Peter Kulchyski. Toronto: Oxford University Press, 1994.

_____, and Frank Tester. *Tammarniit (Mistakes)*. Vancouver: University of British Columbia Press, 1994.

LaDuke, Winona. *The Winona LaDuke Reader*. Pentiction: Theytus Books, 2002.

Landry, Donna, and Gerald MacLean. *Materialist Feminisms*. Cambridge: Blackwell, 1993.

LaRocque, Emma. *Defeathering the Indian*. Agincourt: The Book Society of Canada, 1975.

Leacock, Eleanor Burke. *Myths of Male Dominance*. New York: Monthly Review Press, 1981.

_____, and Richard Lee, eds. *Politics and History in Band Societies*. Cambridge: Cambridge University Press, 1982.

Leopardi, Giacomo. *Pensieri.* New York: Oxford University Press. 1984.

Levi-Strauss, Claude. *Tristes Tropique.* Trans. John Weightman and Doreen Weightman. New York: Atheneum, 1973.

Lukacs, George. *History and Class Consciousness.* Trans. Rodney Livingstone. Cambridge: The MIT Press, 1981.

Macklem, Patrick. *Indigenous Difference and the Constitution of Canada.* Toronto: University of Toronto Press, 2001.

Macpherson, C.B. *The Real World of Democracy.* Toronto: CBC Enterprises, 1965.

Marule, Marie Smallface. "Traditional Indian Government." In *Pathways to Self-Determination.* Ed. Leroy Little Bear, Menno Boldt, and J. Anthony Long. Toronto: University of Toronto Press, 1984.

Marx, Karl. *Grundrisse.* Trans. Martin Nicolaus. New York: Vintage Books, 1973.

_____. *Capital.* Volume One. Trans. Ben Fowkes. New York: Vintage Books, 1977.

Memmi, Albert. *The Colonizer and the Colonized.* Trans. Howard Greenfeld. Boston: Beacon Press, 1972.

Milloy, John. *A National Crime.* Winnipeg: University of Manitoba Press, 1999.

Mills, Antonia. *Eagle Down Is Our Law; Witsuwit'en Law, Feasts, and Land Claims.* Vancouver: University of British Columbia Press, 1994.

Mitchell, W.J.T. "Imperial Landscape." In *Landscape and Power.* Ed. W.J.T. Mitchell. Chicago: University of Chicago Press, 1994.

Monture-Angus, Patricia. *Thunder in My Soul; A Mohawk Woman Speaks.* Halifax: Fernwood Publishing. 1995.

Morris, Alexander. *The Treaties of Canada.* Saskatoon: Fifth House Publishers, 1991.

Morrison, R. Bruce, and C. Roderick Wilson, eds. *Native Peoples: The Canadian Experience.* Toronto: McClelland and Stewart, 1986.

Nadasday, Paul. *Hunters and Bureaucrats: Power, Knowledge, and Aboriginal-State Relations in the Southwest Yukon.* Vancouver: University of British Columbia Press, 2003.

Oakes, Jill, and Rick Riewe. *Culture, Economy, & Ecology: Case Studies in the Circumpolar Region.* Millbrook: The Cider Press, 1994.

Petitot, Emile. *The Book of Dene.* Yellowknife: Department of Education, 1976.

Plutarch. *Essays.* London: Penguin Books, 1992.

Poulantzas, Nicos. *Political Power and Social Classes.* Trans. and ed. Timothy O'Hagan. London: Verso, 1978.

_____. *State, Power, Socialism.* Trans. Patrick Camiller. London: Verso, 1980.

Rasmussen, Knud. *Across Arctic America.* Fairbanks: University of Alaska Press, 1999.

Raunet, Daniel. *Without Surrender. Without Consent.* Vancouver: Douglas and McIntyre, 1984.

Ray, Arthur. *Indians in the Fur Trade.* Toronto: University of Toronto Press, 1974.

Ridington, Robin. *Little Bit Know Something.* Vancouver: Douglas and McIntyre, 1990.

Rollason, Heather. "Studying Under the Influence: The Impact of Samuel Hearne's Journal on the Scholarly Literature About Chipweyan Women." Master's thesis, Trent University, 1995.

Rushforth, Scott, and James S. Chisholm. *Cultural Persistence.* Tucson: University of Arizona Press, 1991.

Ryan, Joan. *Doing Things the Right Way.* Calgary: University of Calgary Press, 1995.

Sahlins, Marshall. *Stone Age Economics.* Chicago: Aldine-Atherton, 1972.

_____. *Culture and Practical Reason.* Chicago: University of Chicago Press, 1976.

_____. *Islands of History.* Chicago: University of Chicago Press, 1985.

Said, Edward. *Orientalism.* New York: Vintage Books, 1979.

Sartre, Jean-Paul. *Critique of Dialectical Reason.* Volume 1. Trans. Alan Sheridan-Smith. London: New Left Books, 1978.

_____. *Critique of Dialectical Reason.* Volume 2. Trans. Quintin Hoare. New York: Verso, 1991.

Scott, James. *Weapons of the Weak.* New Haven: Yale University Press, 1985.

Sekyi-Otu, Ato. *Fanon's Dialectic of Experience.* Cambridge: Harvard University Press, 1996.

Shewell, Hugh. *Enough to Keep Them Alive.* Toronto: University of Toronto Press, 2004.

Slattery, Brian. "Understanding Aboriginal Rights." *The Canadian Bar Review,* 66 (1987).

Smith, David M. *Moose-Deer Island House People.* Mercury Series. Ottawa: National Museum of Man, 1982.

Spivak, Gayatri Chakravorty. *Outside in the Teaching Machine.* New York: Routledge, 1993.

_____. *A Critique of Postcolonial Reason.* Cambridge: Harvard University Press, 1999.

Stevenson, Marc. *Inuit, Whalers and Cultural Persistence*. Toronto: Oxford University Press, 1997.

Taussig, Michael. *The Devil and Commodity Fetishism in South America*. Chapel Hill: University of North Carolina Press, 1986.

_____. *Shamanism, Colonialism, and the Wild Man*. Chicago: University of Chicago Press, 1987.

_____. *The Nervous System*. New York: Routledge, 1992.

_____. *Mimesis and Alterity*. New York: Routledge, 1994.

Tennant, Paul. *Aboriginal Peoples and Politics*. Vancouver: University of British Columbia Press, 1990.

Tobias, John. "Protection, Civilization, Assimilation." In *Sweet Promises*. Ed. J.R. Miller. Toronto: University of Toronto Press, 1991.

Tyler, Stephen A. *The Unspeakable: Discourse, Dialogue, and Rhetoric in the Postmodern World*. Madison: University of Wisconsin Press, 1987.

Watkins, Mel, ed. *Dene Nation: The Colony Within*. Toronto: University of Toronto Press, 1978.

Weaver, Sally. *Making Canadian Indian Policy*. Toronto: University of Toronto Press, 1981.

Wenzel, George. *Animal Rights, Human Rights*. Toronto: University of Toronto Press, 1991.

Whittington, Michael S., ed. *The North*. Toronto: University of Toronto Press, 1985.

Wilmsen, E. and J. Denbow. "Paradigmatic History of San-Speaking Peoples and Current Attempts at Revision." *Current Anthropology* 31, 5.

Wolfe, Eric R. *Europe and the People Without History*. Berkeley: University of California Press, 1982.

Zaslow, Morris. *The Northward Expansion of Canada 1914–1967*. Toronto: McClelland and Stewart, 1988.

INDEX

A

Abel, Kerry 131

Aboriginal rights 3, 12, 100, 146, 196, 233, 244, 249, 277

Aboriginal title 12, 80, 82, 89, 90, 91, 98, 99, 146

Adelson, Naomi 114

Adorno, Theodor 24, 26, 29, 43, 59, 60, 111, 263

Agreement in Principle 86, 87, 88, 138, 139, 145, 146, 159

Akpalialuk, Jaypetee 197, 250, 253

Akpalialuk, Leah 207

Akwesasne 232

Alaska Native Land Claim 92

Alberta 57, 185

Albuquerque 114

Alcoff, Linda 35

Alfred, Taiaiake 249, 270

Amagoalik, John 93, 102, 250, 252

Anderson, Tony 250

Angmarlik 83, 212

Angmarlik Centre 199–203, 206

Angmarlik, Pauloosie 36, 143, 212, 213, 214–222

Animal rights 276–77

Animal Rights, Human Rights 277

Anishnabe 101, 113, 196

Antoine 125

Antoine, Gerry 139–141, 145

Antoine, Jim 87, 136, 137, 138–141

Antoine, Jonas 87, 122

Arctic Bay 207

Arctic Circle 152, 187, 189, 279

Arendt, Hannah 227, 267

Arnaqaq, Meeka 208, 223

As Long as This Land Shall Last 81, 124

Asch, Michael 10–11

Assembly of First Nations 102

Assiniboine 101

Attagoyuk 191

Auyuittuq 189, 190, 192, 194, 198, 202

B

Baffin Island 9, 14, 187, 189, 274

Bahktin, M. 106

Balicki, Asen 21

Band council 102, 131, 132, 133–46, 155, 157, 162, 234

Barnaby, Charlie 164, 182

Barnaby, George 62, 63, 66, 102, 156, 170, 172–76, 178, 180, 184

Barnaby, Joanne 102

Baudelaire, Charles 227

Beaufort Sea 10, 86, 184

Beaulieu, Archie 110, 112

Being Alive Well 114

Benjamin, Walter 20, 32, 44, 207

Berger, Thomas 79, 89, 173, 237, 248

Bhabha, Homi 53, 246

Bish, Robert 241–43, 269

Blacklead Island 201

Bloch, Ernst 106

Blondin, George 33, 36, 97–98, 167

Blondin, Gina 33–35, 55

Blondin, John 33

Blondin–Andrew, Ethyl 33, 102, 159, 257

Boas, Franz 21, 204

Boldt, Menno 238–40, 241, 244, 249, 258, 270

Bonnetrouge, Cheryl 256

Bordo, Jonathan 151

Borrows, John 245

Breynat, Bishop 124, 131

Briggs, Jean 69

British North America Act (1867) 56, 80

Brody, Hugh 21, 35, 41, 42, 49–50, 54–55, 78, 109, 277

Brown, Bern Will 166, 168

Brown, Beverly 212

Bruce, Wyndham Valentine 85

Buck–Morss, Susan 32

C

Cairns, Alan 235, 243–49

Calvino, Italo 18

Calder, Frank 80

Cambridge Bay 165, 279

Canada Arctic Resources Committee 185

Capital 79, 89, 265, 271

Carrothers Commission 58

Cassidy, Frank 241–43, 269

Catholique, Annie 84, 85

Central Eskimo, The 204

Charlottetown Accord 93, 103, 175

Charter of Rights and Freedoms 233

Chipewyan 10, 12, 95, 105

Citizens Plus 243–50

Civilisation Act 131

Cizek, Petr 184

Clastres, Pierre 164, 215–16

Cleary, George 160, 169

Cli, Bonnie 135

Cli, Rita 135, 140

Clifford, James 53

Clyde River 223

Colonialism 19, 61, 64, 70, 71, 73, 83, 123, 148, 151, 267

Colonial nominalism 151

Colville Lake 5–7, 8, 157, 158, 159, 168–69, 185, 260

Committee for Original People's Entitlement 61, 86

Communication and the Evolution of Society 254

Communist Manifesto, The 40

Conroy, Henry A. 124–26

Conspiracy of Catiline, The 29

Cooper, Scott 212

Corbiere 234

Cournoyea, Nellie 93, 102

Cree 10, 86, 101, 196

Cree-Naskapi Act 232

Critique of Dialectical Reason 23, 27, 107

Critique of Postcolonial Reason, A 21

Cruikshank, Julie 70

Cultural Politics of Fur, The 277

Culture 12–13, 16, 19, 20, 23, 32, 34, 37, 43, 53, 70, 71, 74, 78, 103–04, 112, 129, 154–55, 193, 195, 233, 245, 246, 247, 250, 258, 259, 271

Culture and Practical Reason 51

Cumberland Sound 187, 193, 200, 202, 225

D

Dante 143

Davis Inlet 111

Decolonization 88, 148, 168, 247

Deh Cho (Mackenzie River) 10, 13, 14, 34, 74, 81, 84, 87, 95, 120–22 123, 124, 127, 138, 139, 149, 152, 153, 154, 158, 159, 161. 164, 166, 171, 183–84, 260

Dehcho region 10, 12, 13, 126, 185

Dehcho Tribal Council 95, 96, 137, 140, 146

Deline 33, 55, 97, 159

Denbow, James 52

Dene (Dehcho) Assembly 84, 86, 87, 94, 95, 139, 146, 147

Dene Cultural Institute 97, 102

Dene (Deh Cho) Declaration 86, 95, 96, 146, 147, 148, 248

Dene law 141–44

Dene Nation 61, 82, 84, 86, 94, 96, 97, 102, 160, 174

Dene Nation 62, 172

Denendeh 10, 11, 12, 13, 25, 54, 77, 82, 84, 101, 120, 229, 233, 235, 237, 256, 259, 270, 271, 272, 278

Derrida, Jacques 25, 27, 42, 50, 78, 215, 220–22, 263

Detah 72

Dialectics of Seeing, The 32

Diamond, Stanley 59

Dickerson, Mark 55, 57–58

Doctor, Gabe 230

Dogrib 10, 12, 84, 95, 96, 100, 105, 110, 143, 230, 233

Doing Things the Right Way 143

Dunne–za 49

Dupont, Deborah 145

Durkheim, Emile 106

E

Eagle Down Is Our Law 78

Emberley, Julia 224–26

Empire 71

Enfranchisement Act (1869) 131

Engels, Frederic 40

E–Numbers 83

Epic of Asdiwal 189

Erasmus, Bill 85, 95, 96, 102

Erasmus, Georges 95, 102, 235

Etuangat, Aksayuk 212

Extinguishment 81, 86, 87, 89, 91, 95, 96, 98–100, 130, 138, 146–47, 271

F

Fajber, Elizabeth 31, 168–69, 272

Fanon, Franz 88

Fanon's Dialectic of Experience 148

Flaherty, Robert 69

Fort Good Hope 5, 14, 15, 19, 22, 79, 96, 127, 151–85, 255, 256, 259, 260, 262, 263, 278

Fort Norman 159, 160

Fort Providence 34, 74

Fort Resolution 84

Fort Simpson 14, 19, 22, 31, 65, 74, 84, 87, 119–49, 155, 158, 178, 185

Foucault, Michel 56

Frobisher Bay 92

Frobisher, Martin 92

Fumoleau, Rene 81, 84, 124–25

G

Galeano, Eduardo 166

Geertz, Clifford 27

Gender 13, 69–71, 83, 93, 133–35

Giddens, Anthony 56, 206, 265, 266–67

Good Hope (Ontario) 111

Governance Act 234, 235, 240, 242

Grassy Narrows 111, 112, 122
Green, Joyce 229
Greenblatt, Stephen 7
Grieg, Martha 250, 252
Grundrisse 40
Gully, Suzanne 158
Gwi'chin 10, 11, 12, 94–96, 98, 105, 160

H
Habermas, Jurgen 254–55
Hallowell, J. Irving 113
Hardt, Michael 71
Harvey, David 88
Haudenosaunee 196, 232
Hay River 81, 84–85, 97
Hearne, Samuel 70
Helm, June 10
Henderson, Sakej 249
Hodgson, Stuart 55, 58
Home and Native Land 10
Housing 153
Hudson Bay 9
Hudson's Bay Company 123, 191, 192
Hunting 23, 41, 43–51, 54–55, 89, 103, 106, 190, 193, 201, 235, 237, 262, 264, 275–79

I
Indian Act 14, 80, 131–32, 134, 135, 157, 196, 231, 233, 238
Indian Advancement Act 242, 269
Indian Agent 81, 130–31
Indian Brotherhood of NWT 125
Indian Government 241, 269
Indians of Canada, The 21
Inuit law 212–22

Inuit Tapirisat of Canada 61, 86, 93, 102
Inuit, Whalers and Cultural Persistence, 193
Inukjuak 93
Inuktitut 9, 12, 14, 102, 105, 196
Inuvialuit 10, 11, 12, 86, 87, 95
Ipperwash 69
Iqaluit 58, 92, 94, 194
Iroquoian nations 131
Irwin, Ron 100
Ishulutak, Elizabeth 102
Islands of History 51

J
Jackson, A.Y. 201
James Bay and Northern Quebec Agreement 98, 232
James Bay Cree Cultural Education Centre 235
Jameson, Fredric 13, 24–25, 27, 37–38, 40, 44, 59, 72, 88, 106–07, 188, 189
Jean Marie River 125
Jenness, Diamond 21, 44–46, 69, 70

K
Kakfwi, Everette 162, 169, 170, 176, 179, 180, 181, 182, 183
Kakfwi, Rita 154, 166, 168
Kakfwi, Stephen 87, 95, 96, 159, 160, 180
Kakisa 133, 140
K'ashogot'ine 15, 79
Kanesatake 68
Karpik, Jonasie 102
Kekerton Island 192, 201, 204–05
Kilabuk, Aittaina 224, 225

Kilabuk, Ipelee 187, 209, 224, 226, 264

Kilabuk, Kayrene 28, 200, 215, 216, 220, 223, 224, 226, 263–64

Kilabuk, Michael 208

Kilabuk, Seeti 264

Kitikmeot 9

Kivilliq 9

Krauss, Rosalind 109, 177

Kunuk, Zacharias 112

Kuptana, Rosemarie 93, 102, 250, 251, 252

Kusugak, Jose 94

L

LaCapra, Dominick 149, 245

LaDuke, Winona 113–14

Lafferty, Jean 135

Lafferty, Marie 138

Lakota Sioux 77

Lamonthe, Ethyl 135

Lamonthe, Rene 84–85

Land claims 12, 13, 22, 61–62, 80, 82, 85, 87, 89, 90–92, 98, 103, 126, 131, 232, 234, 262

Landry, Donna 276

Landscape 18–19, 20, 120–22, 151, 154, 171–72, 190, 194, 201, 202, 229

LaRocque, Emma 249

Leacock, Eleanor 48–49, 50

Lee, Richard 52

Leopardi, Giacomo 119

Lethbridge 238

Levi-Strauss, Claude 215

Liard River 14

Life Lived Like a Story 70

Liidli Koe 15, 119–49, 155, 158, 182, 183, 255, 256, 262

Living Arctic 277

Lockhart, Felix 84

Long, J. Anthony 258

Lost His Canoe 110

Lukacs, George 25

M

Mackenzie, Alexander 123, 159

Mackenzie highway 127

Mackenzie Valley Pipeline 4, 79, 152, 184, 257

Maclean, Gerald 276

Manitoba 28, 34, 101

Manuel, Isidore 158, 169–70, 172, 176, 180, 181, 182, 183–84, 278

Manuel, Millie 183

Maps and Dreams 49

Marule, Marie Smallface 257–58

Marvellous Possessions 7

Marx, Karl 23, 25, 38, 40–41, 79, 89, 106, 255, 265, 271

Marxism 22, 23, 24, 37, 38, 79, 88, 113

Masazumi, Barney 153, 157, 175

McMichael Gallery 201

Menicoche, Eric 28, 256–57

Menicoche, Lorayne 135, 145

Métis 9, 10, 11, 14, 20, 21, 57, 64, 65, 74, 87, 95, 96, 101, 102, 122, 127, 129, 130, 136, 152, 155, 159, 160, 163, 231

Métis Nation 61

Milloy, John 34

Mills, Antonia 78

Minima Moralia 24, 29

Mimesis and Alterity 108

Mitchell, W.J.T. 151

Mode of production 37–42, 47, 49, 50, 51, 54, 71, 103–04, 270, 276, 277

Monture–Angus, Patricia 270

Morrow, William 81, 82, 97, 125

Moss, John 190

Municipal Council 155, 160

Munn, Henry 114

N

Naechag'ah 120, 123, 128, 149

Nahendeh 120, 121, 136

Nakashuk, Mosesee 207, 208

Names 20, 21, 37, 79, 83, 120, 123, 260

Nanook of the North 69

National Crime, A 34

National Indian Brotherhood 96

Nation-State and Violence, The 260

Native Studies 15, 21, 28, 83, 256, 263

Native Women's Association 61, 136, 102

N'Dilo 72, 272

Ned, Annie 70

Negri, Antonio 71

Nelson Commission 82

New Yorker, The 137

Nisga'a 80, 100, 233

Nisga'a Agreement 100

Norman Wells 57, 81, 152, 159, 178, 183, 185

North to Alaska 7

Northern Frontier, Northern Homeland 89, 237

North West Company 123

Northwest Territories 8, 9, 10, 11, 17, 28, 33, 34, 56, 57–58, 64, 81, 82, 83, 86, 90, 91, 95, 101, 102, 103, 104, 105, 110, 185

Norwegian, Bertha 133–35

Norwegian, Herb 102, 138, 139, 140–41, 145, 147–48

Norwegian, Joseph 125

Norwegian, Leo 119, 121, 141–44, 168, 182

Norwegian, Louis 125–26

Norwegian, Mary-Louise 31–32, 135

Nunavut 8, 9, 10, 11, 12, 13, 17, 21, 25, 54, 56, 58, 64, 69, 74, 77, 82, 83, 90–92, 96, 101, 103, 104, 105, 191, 193, 197, 229, 233, 235, 249, 250, 256, 270, 271, 272, 278

Nunavut Agreement in Principle 90–91, 95, 96

Nunavut Final Agreement 91, 98

Nunavut Implementation Commission 92, 94

Nunavut Tungavik Incorporated 92, 94

Nungak, Zebedee 250, 251, 253

O

Oakes, Jill 91

Of Grammatology 220

Okalik, Paul 102

Okpik, Rosie 195–96, 200, 224

Optical Unconscious, The 109–10

Origins of Totalitarianism, The 227

Other Side of Eden, The 35, 54, 78

Ottawa 9, 55, 57, 58, 87, 91, 168, 223, 255, 268

P

Pangnirtung Fiord 187, 190, 198, 199, 202

Panniqtuuq (Pangnirtung) 14, 15, 19, 22, 28, 83, 127, 187–226, 250, 253, 255, 256, 263, 264

Parker, John 62

Parti Quebecois 248

Pathways to Self–Determination 257

Patterson, Dennis 33, 58
Pauktutit 61
Penner Report 232
People of Denendeh, The 10
Peoples Land, The 109
Peterborough 195
Petitot, Emile 153
Pierrot, Jim 171
Pimaatisiwin, 112–15, 226
Plutarch 35–36, 50
Poison Stronger Than Love, A 112
Political Unconscious, The 44
Pope John Paul II 128–29
Postmodernism 88, 92, 247, 261, 265, 271
Poulantzas, Nicos 39, 66–69, 89, 261, 265
Public Archives of Canada 84–85
Purgatorio, 143

Q
Qiqiqtarjuak 189, 223, 264
Quebec 86, 248

R
Reserves 82
Resistance 68, 147–48, 155, 236, 268, 271
Resolute Bay 93
Riewe, Rick 91
Ritsie, Ralph 268
Roads 72–75, 127, 129, 152, 154
Rollaston, Heather 70
Rousseau, Jean–Jacques 106
Royal Canadian Mounted Police 57, 142, 210, 211

Royal Commission on Aboriginal Peoples 234–37, 243, 246, 248, 249, 250
Royal Geographical Society of Great Britain Island 82
Royal Proclamation of 1763 89
Ryan, Joan 36, 143

S
Sahlins, Marshall 23, 46–48, 49, 50–51
Sahtu (Great Bear Lake) 10, 33, 84, 94, 95, 96, 159
Sahtu Region 12, 14, 159–61, 184, 260
Sahtu Treaty 98, 99, 160, 161, 162, 169–71, 172, 175
Said, Edward 246
Sallust 29
Samooh, Chief (Moses David) 79
Sartre, Jean–Paul 21, 23–24, 27, 106, 107
Saskatchewan 57, 245
Sechelt Act 232, 269
Seeds of Time, The 106, 188
Sekyi-Otu, Ato 88, 148
Self-determination 232, 236
Self-government 12, 13, 16, 18, 22 81, 86, 87, 92, 119, 132, 136, 137–38, 143–44, 146–48, 155, 160, 172, 174–75, 176, 177, 197, 230–73, 278
Shamanism, Colonialism and the Wild Man 119, 166
Shamattawa 111
Shandley, Kathryn 77
Shkilnyk, Anastasia, 112
Sibbeston, Nick 62, 65–66, 136
Sidney, Angela 70
Simon, Mary 93, 103
Simpson, George 123

Slavey 10, 14, 94–95, 105, 120, 140, 141, 152, 157

Smith, Kitty 70

Solway, Jacqueline 52

Sophocles 50

Sioux 101

Sowdloapik, Sakiasie 210–11, 212, 213

Spectres of Marx 28, 222

Spivak, Gayatri Chakravorty 21, 113

State, Power, Socialism 66–68, 261

Stevenson, Marc 193

Stone Age Economics 46

Stories 8, 14, 18, 19, 23, 32–33, 37, 42, 121–22, 141, 142–43

Subversion 23, 25–26, 27, 268–69

Supreme Court of Canada 80, 82

Surviving as Indians 238

T

Tacitus 46

Tagak, Andrew 275

Tagak Jr, Andrew 275–76

Tammarniit 70

Taussig, Michael 25, 26, 32, 36, 108, 109, 114, 119, 166, 190

Tautuajuk, Hannah 223

Terry, Vince 250

Tester, Frank 70

Thanadelthur 33, 70

Tli'chon 233

Tlicho Treaty 100, 233–34

Tobac, Charlie, 164, 278

Tobac, Henry 171

Tookoome, Robert 28

Toronto 34, 201

Totalitarianism 67, 206, 267

Totality 24, 25, 38

Totalization 17, 21, 23, 24, 25, 27, 28, 59, 66–68, 90, 101, 236, 265–68, 269, 270

Totalize 17, 24, 25, 67, 69, 71, 99, 107, 154–55, 230, 236, 243, 245

Treaty 5, 6, 80, 82, 84, 85, 88, 99, 101, 124–26, 128, 130, 131, 132, 137–38, 140–41, 145, 146–47, 155, 233, 237, 280

Treaty Eight 81, 82, 125, 146, 272

Treaty Eleven 57, 81, 124–25, 130, 137, 146

Trent University 28, 58, 91, 97, 113, 226, 256, 257, 263

Tristes Tropiques 215

T'Seleie 260

T'Seleie, Bella 28, 158, 183, 259–60

T'Seleie, Frank 15, 77, 79, 102, 114, 155, 164–65, 182, 183, 185, 232, 260

T'Seleie, John 183

T'Seleie, Philip 260

T'Seleie School 153

Tucho (Great Slave Lake) 10, 272

Tulita 159, 185

Tungavik Federation of Nunavut 86, 90

Turpel, Mary Ellen 249

Tusi Ko (Dry Loon) 158–59

Tyler, Stephen 261

U

Unspeakable Discourse, The 261

Uqqurmiut Artists Co–operative 192

V

Van Camp, Richard 28

Vancouver 74, 280

Victoria Island 82, 165, 279
Virginia Falls 121

W
Wahshee, James 28, 62
Wakeham, William 204, 205
Washington 168
Watkins, Mel 62
Weber, Max 67
Wenzel, George 277
Western Arctic Claim 12
When the World Was New 97
White Paper, The 231, 242, 249
Whose North? 57
Williams, Raymond 40
Wilmsen, Edwin 52

Witsuwit'en 78–79
Wittman, Tara 194
Wolfe, Eric 39–41
Women 32, 33, 36, 48–49, 52, 69, 70,
   93, 94, 110, 131, 133–35, 140,
   162, 223, 231, 234–35, 264, 270
Wright, Paul 36

Y
Yakelia, Norman 160
Yamoria: The Lawmaker 97
Yellowknife 9, 28, 35, 55, 58, 72–75,
   103, 109, 145, 146, 168, 181,
   183, 223, 229, 252, 259, 272
Yukon Territory 8, 56, 233
Yupik 9, 10

Gun Grudge

Gun Grudge

Walt Coburn

Thorndike Press • Chivers Press
Waterville, Maine USA   Bath, England

This Large Print edition is published by Thorndike Press, USA and by Chivers Press, England.

Published in 2003 in the U.S. by arrangement with Golden West Literary Agency.

Published in 2003 in the U.K. by arrangement with Golden West Literary Agency.

U.S. Hardcover   0-7862-5154-9 (Western Series)
U.K. Hardcover   0-7540-8964-9 (Chivers Large Print)
U.K. Softcover   0-7540-8965-7 (Camden Large Print)

The text of this Large Print edition is unabridged.
Other aspects of the book may vary from the original edition.

Set in 16 pt. Plantin by Al Chase.

Printed in the United States on permanent paper.

British Library Cataloguing-in-Publication Data available

Library of Congress Cataloging-in-Publication Data

Coburn, Walt, 1889–1971.
  Gun Grudge / Walt Coburn.
    p. cm.
  ISBN 0-7862-5154-9 (lg. print : hc : alk. paper)
  1. Large type books.   I. Title.
PS3505.O153G86 2003
  813′.52—dc21   2002044745

Gun Grudge

1: Alone

Big Jim Merchant was dying — dying of that malady so common among cattle rustlers such as big Jim, a malady known along the Mexican border as lead poisoning. There were four leaden slugs buried in big Jim Merchant's tough body but not a whimper left his tightly-drawn lips. Nor did his grey eyes, bloodshot and pain-seared, show a flicker of fear as he lay on the bunk in the log cabin, taking snapshots at the men out yonder who had finally run him to his hole.

He looked at his son who crouched there by the door, a Winchester in his hands. He was wondering what would become of Howard, when death had claimed his only friend.

"Howdy!" he called. "Howdy, fetch me another dipper full of water, son. I'm almighty thirsty."

Howard Merchant, better known as "Howdy," brought the water. He was a slim, long-muscled young fellow of perhaps seventeen. He had the same grey eyes as had Jim Merchant, the same straight, clean-cut features, the same quick smile that had won the cattle rustler friends, even among some of his enemies.

"You sufferin' much, Dad?"

"Not so much. Keep outa line with that window, son. Better sit down on the floor. I got somethin' to tell you, Howdy, before I cash in my chips."

"You mean, Dad, that you're a-dyin'?"

"An hour or two, three at the outside, and I'll be pullin' out for the big range. You'll be left alone. No tears now, old pardner. Like I always told you, when things look the worst, grin or whistle or cut a pigeon wing. Shucks. Howdy, it ain't so bad, this business of dyin'. Not when you've played your string out on this range. It's like a man that's bin in the saddle two-three days and nights without sleep so that he's plumb weary. Then he beds down and drops off to sleep. Just like that is the way I'll be agoin', son.

"But it's you that I'm thinkin' about. You'll be left alone. Mebbe so it would 'a' bin better, if I'd let the law take you away from me like they aimed to, and put you in that reform school. But it looked too much like the penitentiary to me. So I taken you away from 'em and let you ride with me. Mebbe so I done wrong, but it seemed to me like the right thing to do."

"I've had a swell time, Dad. Gosh, we've

8

had fun. I'll never go to no reform school."

"In the hole under the floor, son, is enough money to last you a long time. Git it and shove it down in your boots. How long till dark?"

"An hour, I reckon."

"That's lucky. Use the tunnel we dug from under the floor to the barn. Take along some jerky and them cold biscuits. You better ride the Ginger geldin'. He's grain-fed and fast and he'll carry you plumb into Mexico without drawin' a long breath. When you leave the barn, lay along that horse's neck. Give him his head. There ain't a man among that bunch of snakes out yonder that'll be able to hit you, unless it's a plumb accident. Head for the Reyes ranch in Chihuahua. Old Rafael Reyes will take care of you. Foller his advice and go straight from here on. You've seen what lays at the end of a rustler's trail. It's a losin' game, son, no matter how you look at it. Come dark, you're quittin' this game for keeps. Promise me that, Howdy."

"It ain't hard to promise that," he answered, looking old and wise far beyond his years. "It's bin fun, but I'd a heap rather go a straighter trail — But I ain't leavin' you here alone, Dad."

Jim Merchant smiled. He had been expecting that. He laid a blood-smeared hand on the young fellow's shoulder.

"No, son, you have to go. Stayin' here till I cash in will only pile the odds against you. You can't do me any good by stayin'. I might hang and rattle until daylight. You'll need every hour of darkness between here and the Mexican border. Come dark, you pull out. I'll hold off the skunks till the time comes for me to go yonderly."

Howdy's square jaw tightened. "You wouldn't quit me, as long as I was livin'. I ain't quittin' you." And big Jim Merchant knew that there was nothing that he could put forth in the way of argument to make his son change his mind.

Now the men out yonder were peppering the cabin again, though no man among them dared risk his life by charging the cabin. Jim Merchant was a dead shot. His son, Howdy, was almost as deadly with a gun as his father, though Jim had made him promise to shoot only at their legs or arms, for he did not want him ever to become a killer.

"Dig up that money from under the floor, Howdy."

The young fellow obeyed. His heart was like a lump of lead under his ribs. Already he felt alone in a world that was unfriendly.

What good was money when Jim Merchant was dead? Howdy fought back the tears that stung his eyes like acid. There was an aching lump in his throat as he took the money from the tobacco can and stuffed it down in his boots. Jim Merchant watched him, a soft smile on his grim mouth.

In an hour darkness would come. When Howdy was not watching, Jim Merchant loosened the tourniquet and bandage that bound a deep wound in his leg. He felt the warm wetness of the flowing blood, as it flowed afresh, soaking the blankets and sougans under the canvas tarp. An hour and Jim Merchant would be dead. And Howdy would be free to leave the cabin.

Dusk closed in on the little cabin there in the pines. Outside, the men called to one another in cautious tones. When darkness came, they would close in on the cabin. Howdy, sensing their plan, set his jaws and his eyes hardened to the colour of cold steel.

They were not law officers, those men out yonder. They were cattle thieves, the same as Jim Merchant. Their errand here, an errand of red death, was not one of justice or law but one of vengeance. Jim Merchant had killed the brother of the leader, a renegade known as "Black Mike" Guzman, a half-breed Mexican, in a quarrel over the

11

matter of three aces in a stud-poker game. Now Black Mike was here to collect the lives of Jim Merchant, and his son, Howdy, by way of payment with interest.

Half an hour later Jim Merchant was getting weaker. He felt horribly thirsty and had Howdy put the pail of water and the dipper alongside the bunk. His whole body, racked with the pain of his wounds, was burning with fever. But he would not let his son see how badly he was suffering. Was it getting dark, he wondered, or was the shadow of death creeping across his vision? He felt dizzy and weak. He fumbled with the cartridges that he shoved into the magazine of his Winchester. Now he called out:

"Is it gittin' dark, Howdy?"

"Pretty dark, Dad. Can't hardly see my front sight."

"Come over here a minute, son." Jim Merchant's voice sounded weak and far away to his own ears. Howdy felt something tighten about his heart — something cold and heavy and hard. He knew that his father was dying now; that it was only a matter of minutes.

The young fellow sat on the edge of the bunk, his two hands holding Jim's right hand that felt hot and dry.

"I'm leavin' you now, Howdy. Be a good,

honest man, son. Play a square game, always. So long. So — long — Howdy."

Jim Merchant sighed like a man utterly tired. His eyes closed, there in the dusk. He had gone.

Tears, scalding hot, trickled down the smoke-grimed cheeks of his son. He rubbed them away and made a terrible effort to grin, as Jim Merchant would want him to grin. Then he folded his father's arms across his chest and pulled the tarp up high so that it covered the dead man's face. He lifted the planks that led to the tunnel that he and Jim had made for just such emergencies. Now he was in the black passageway that led to the barn.

The barn was dark. The four horses there were eating hay. Howdy made no sound but moved there in the darkness until the horses caught the scent of him. Then, saddle in hand, he slipped into the stall alongside the rangy sorrel horse called Ginger. Saddling and bridling the big gelding was a matter of seconds. The young fellow slid his carbine into the saddle scabbard. Then he led the big gelding out of the stall. The shod hoofs made no sound on the dirt floor. The darkness inside was thick, filled with the odours of stables. Howdy mounted and eased the big horse alongside the door. There was a heavy wooden latch to be lifted by a rawhide thong.

Now, from out yonder, came the sudden burst of shots, men yelling, guns roaring! They were charging the cabin. Howdy lifted the thong, kicked open the door. Now he gave the big sorrel horse free rein and there was the pounding of flying hoofs.

Not a shot followed his flight. So intent on getting into the cabin were those outlaws that they did not even notice the young fellow's escape.

Low along the sorrel's neck; the wind fanning his hot face; his blood pounding through his veins; now he looked back across his shoulder. Yellow flames pierced the black sky. They had fired the cabin. They would race back to their shelter and wait for the trapped pair to run out, only to be shot down. But they would be disappointed. The flames would cremate the body of big Jim Merchant. And by the time they discovered that the rustler's son had escaped, Howdy would have all the head start he needed to beat them to the Mexican border.

The heavy .45 six-gun in its holster beat against Howdy's slim flank and he tied it down with a buckskin string he found in his pocket. The big belt that had been his father's was so large that he had wrapped it twice around his slim waist. For Jim Merchant was a giant of a man. The gun gave Howdy a certain manly feeling. He pulled his Stetson hat across his eyes at an angle. His eyes were smarting from powder smoke and unshed tears. His throat ached a lot and he felt a little sick at his stomach. But he forced a grin.

It seemed to Howdy that he'd never again feel hungry or that he would ever laugh out loud any more. With Jim Merchant gone, he was plumb alone — alone, riding through a moonless night, drifting south towards Mexico where he would find shelter at the Reyes rancho.

Howdy recalled the Reyes rancho — its rambling white-washed adobe buildings, its patio filled with fruit trees and flowers and birds that sang from dawn until dusk; dark-skinned vaqueros in their Mexican trappings and silver-crusted saddles; Don Rafael, tall, straight, white of hair and beard, a dignified old man with black eyes that shone with the brightness of youth from under heavy brows. And there were women there, grown women and giggling, shy-mannered little girls who peeked from behind the corners of the buildings at the tawny-haired, grey-eyed gringo child who

15

hotly resented their presence.

Howdy's face felt hot, even now, at the memory of those little girls who peeked at him with a bold shyness. Howdy had never spoken to a girl in his life and, save for the women at the Reyes rancho, the only women he had ever come in contact with were the women who sometimes were to be found in the border cantinas and saloons — women with painted lips and shrill voices who drank like men and smelled of heavy perfume that choked his nostrils.

The thought of again seeing the women and girls at the Reyes rancho made him squirm uneasily in his saddle. He reckoned that, before he made the long, long ride down into Chihuahua, he would look around some. Perhaps he could get a job with some cow outfit, wrangling horses. That was more to Howdy's liking. The thought of holding down a job with some big outfit sent a pleasant thrill through him. He savvied horses and cattle. He could ride fairly well and was handy with a rope. For all his slim build he was tough-muscled and stronger by far than he appeared to the eye.

2: Ribs

There was hardly a square mile of the Arizona and New Mexico country that Howdy Merchant had not ridden across with his father, even as he knew Sonora and Chihuahua, down in Mexico. And in such matters as teaching his son to remember landmarks, brands, and the faces of men, big Jim Merchant had been a hard taskmaster. And so it was that the seventeen-year-old Howdy knew this part of the Southwest as most boys his age might know their own back yards. And he could read brands with the best cowman on the border — brands, earmarks, dewlaps and wattles. He could work a herd with the best of cowhands, even when the critters' hair was long and they cut cattle by the marks.

Over to the eastward lay the boundary that marked the beginning of the Circle Dot range. But Howdy had no intention of swinging over there. The boss of the Circle Dot had little love for any man bearing the name of Merchant, because Jim Merchant had been in the habit of helping himself, when the need demanded, to fresh horses

17

from the Circle Dot remuda. As a result that outfit had posted a reward of five hundred dollars for the capture, dead or alive, of Jim Merchant. And while there had been no mention made of Jim's son, still Howard had been wise enough to know that the Circle Dot outfit would be more than glad to lay hands on the horse thief's son.

No, better keep plumb clear of that Circle Dot country. Better lean over westward aways; in towards the ragged peaks of those mountains that marked the Muleshoe Bar range. The Muleshoe Bar outfit was not so hidebound. Big Jim Merchant had sold that layout more than one bunch of stolen cattle. A tough outfit was the Muleshoe Bar. Their cowboys were a close-mouthed, hard-riding crew. Some of the best ropers and riders in the country drew top wages there. For the cattle that ranged in the canyons and cedar breaks of the Mescal Mountains were wild and snaky. It took good cowboys and fast horses to catch those renegades.

There were a hundred and one strange tales told of the Muleshoe Bar outfit and the men who worked there. Some of those tales were none too savoury. Yet any man who had held a job for a year with that outfit was considered a sure enough cowhand in any man's country. And at the rodeos the

Muleshoe Bar cowboys usually rode home with the first money in the roping, riding and bulldogging events. They were, first and last, wild cowboys. When a man rode a string of Muleshoe Bar horses, he was sure enough mounted. And if he couldn't tie down his share of wild steers, he was fired.

Howdy recalled the night that he and his father had stayed at the home ranch at the foot of the Mescal Mountains. They had dropped a hundred head of Mexican cattle in a lower pasture. Jim seemed to know most of the cowboys gathered in the bunkhouse. He had shaken hands with a tall, hawk-featured man with black eyes and the straight black hair of an Indian.

"Howdy," his father had told him, "shake hands with the fastest cowhand in the Southwest, Black Jack Hardin. This is my young un, Black Jack."

And Howdy had shaken hands very gravely with this dark-skinned, hawk-nosed, thin-lipped man who was the boss of the Muleshoe Bar.

Later, bit by bit, he learned more about "Black Jack" Hardin who was a Texan and the son of a Texan. Most of those tales concerned deeds of daring with rope and gun. For besides being a fast cowboy in the rough country, Black Jack was a killer. He had taken an active part in several big range wars — Texas, New Mexico, Arizona, Wyoming. Howdy was given to understand that it was up in Wyoming, where the sheepmen and cattlemen had spilled blood across Johnson County, that Jim Merchant had known Black Jack Hardin. For, like Hardin, Jim Merchant had been a gun toter in more than one range feud.

Howdy remembered his promise to his dying father that he would go straight. Yet he was tempted to ride over to the Muleshoe Bar Ranch and ask Black Jack Hardin for a job. Wrangling horses was honest enough. Even if, perhaps, some of the horses in that big remuda had been stolen, still it was not any crime to wrangle 'em. A man didn't need to be a thief in order to hold down a job with the outfit. And it was a safe bet that as long as he worked for Black Jack Hardin, he'd be secure from the long arm of the law that wanted to collar the son of Jim Merchant. He'd be safe, also, from the bounty hunters at the Circle Dot. Jingling horses, even for the Muleshoe Bar, was no crime. And he'd be learnin' things that a cowboy needed to know.

Determined now to chance his luck, Howdy, using the stars to guide him, headed for the Mescal Mountains.

Daylight found him at the home ranch at the foot of the ragged peaks where the wild cattle roamed. The big corral was filled with milling horses. The cowboys were roping out their mounts for the morning's circle. Lucky for Howdy that the outfit was not out on the roundup, but was camped here at the home ranch, working the lower country where the more gentle stuff ranged.

The young fellow rode boldly up to the corral. Several cowboys glanced at him curiously, but asked him no questions. Now Black Jack Hardin, leading a rangy brown gelding, came out of the corral. He stared hard at the slight young figure on the big sorrel. Then he walked over to where Howdy still sat his horse.

"Ain't you Jim Merchant's kid?"

"Yes, sir. I'm Howdy Merchant."

"Jim sent you to see me?"

"No, sir. I just come of my own accord. I'm huntin' work and I wondered if you needed a horse jingler."

"Where's Jim?"

"Dead. Mike Guzman and his snakes ketched up with us. Dad got killed. I got away in the dark."

"And now you're alone, is that it, button?"

"That's the size of it, yes, sir."

21

"You're purty young to be ridin' the grub line."

"I got money," said Howdy, flushing a little. "I ain't bummin' anything. But what I got I'd as soon salt down. I ain't scared of work."

Black Jack Hardin looked at him without smiling. He seemed to be studying Howdy, and reading his thoughts.

"Turn your horse in with the remuda, button. Then go on over to the cookhouse and tell that grub spoiler to take the wrinkles outa your innards. Then you better bed down a while. And if I was you, I'd wash that shirt. You look like you'd bin butcherin' a beef. When we git back this evenin', we'll see about that job."

Black Jack walked away to saddle his horse. Thus dismissed, Howdy did as the Muleshoe Bar boss had told him. The cook, a heavy-paunched, bald-headed man with freckled arms, proved to be good-natured and he took a vast delight in feeding the young fellow who suddenly made the astounding discovery that he was exceedingly hungry.

Howdy liked this fat cook who brought forth pie and doughnuts and some strawberry jam. And while he ate, the cook, whose title was "Ribs," kept up a running fire of talk.

"It ain't often I gits a chance to augur any-body around this ranch," he explained. "Black Jack pays top wages but he shore makes them waddies earn their coin. They don't git a chance to swap lies acrost the table. It's eat and run, daybreak till dark. When a man hires out to this slave-drivin' outfit, he don't need no bed, just a lantern. I git no chance to even know the boys. They wolf down their grub; then hit a lope. And nighttime they're too weary to set around argurin'. It's plumb lonesome fer the cook. I'm quittin' here afore long." Ribs sighed heavily as he began carrying out the dishes.

Howdy grinned a little. The fame of Ribs, the Muleshoe Bar cook, was widespread. Since he had first cooked for the outfit, some fifteen years ago, he had been making that same promise that he would quit. He would cuss the outfit from all angles, yet would fight any man who spoke a word against that same outfit. Once every three months Ribs would get drunk, beautifully, gloriously drunk. Then he would go back to work. And he was rated as the best roundup cook in the country.

Howdy helped Ribs with the dishes, car-ried in wood, fetched water from the well, and swept out the dining-room — this, in spite of the fact that Ribs protested. Then the cook showed him a rolled bed in the room off the kitchen.

"Bed down, sonny. The gent that owned that hot roll got killed a week or so ago in Nogales. He tried to beat a Mex saloon man outa his gal. He come out second best. Now bed down and git some shuteye. And gimme that shirt. I'll rustle a new one for you."

Howdy slept soundly, though his sleep was crowded with wild dreams. It was past noon when he awoke suddenly. From the kitchen beyond there came the sound of voices.

"Nope," he heard Ribs saying in a voice that was strangely harsh and gruff, "nobody of that description has bin here, I tell you. I ain't seen no baldfaced young feller. And I ain't feedin' nobody till Black Jack and the boys come in. If you and your men is hungry, you better ride on to somewheres where they're runnin' a short-order joint. My orders is to feed nobody except at meal-times."

"We ain't et since last night," growled a voice. "We're old friends of Black Jack's. I'm Mike Guzman from down in Sonora."

"You might be the King of Russia but you still couldn't git grub till it comes time for the boys to eat."

"We struck young Merchant's sign and it

24

led this way. He come here, Fatty."

"My name ain't Fatty," came the voice of Ribs. "I don't know nothin' about no fellow named Merchant. And if you don't git outa my kitchen, this sawed-off scatter-gun I'm a-holdin' will go off mighty sudden and I'll put in the rest of the afternoon scrubbin' what's left of you off my clean floor. Hit the trail, Mr. Mike Guzman. Because if Black Jack was to git back early, which he sometimes does, and if I was to tell him that you was tryin' to horn your way into my clean kitchen, he'd make you and your gang hard to ketch. Git!"

There followed the clumping of boot heels and the jingle of spurs; then the thud of hoofs as Mike Guzman and his gang rode away. Ribs opened the door to find Howdy crouched behind some cases of canned goods, his father's six-gun in his hand. Ribs chuckled until his fat paunch shook.

"I bet you'd use that cannon, too. Well, they done pulled out, button. Guzman is scared of Black Jack. He wouldn't've dared set foot on the place if he'd thought Black Jack was within twenty miles of here. But he follered your sign here and he knows I lied to him. He ain't goin' to give up so easy. Them half-breeds is like that. You should've seen his eyes booger out when I pulled that shotgun outa the empty flour bin where I keep 'er. He like to knocked down a hip gettin' out the door in a hurry.

"How about a little grub, son? You look kinda ga'nt. It'll take me a week to put any taller on them ribs of yourn. And here's a flannel shirt that I taken outa Shorty Jones's war sack. It shrunk up on him till he can't git into it and he was sayin' only yesterday that he aimed to take it to town and shove it down that storeman's throat. It'll just about fit you."

"But what'll Shorty Jones say?"

"Nothin'. He'd be givin' it to you hisse'f if he was here. Crawl into it, Howdy."

Rested and well fed, Howdy felt a lot better. He knew his way around a kitchen and was peeling potatoes when Black Jack Hardin rode up alone. Howdy, on a bench outside the kitchen door, grinned a little. The Muleshoe Bar boss nodded to him and went into the kitchen. Then Howdy heard them talking in lowered tones. Presently Black Jack came outside, a cup of black coffee in one hand, a brown-paper cigarette in the other.

A grim man, this ranch boss, not given to smiling often. But a faint smile twitched at one corner of his thin-lipped mouth as he

26

looked at Howdy peeling potatoes.

"Ribs tells me you bin makin' a hand around his kitchen. How'd you like to he'p him steady?"

"I'd a heap rather be ridin'," admitted Howdy, hiding his disappointment behind a wistful sort of grin, "but if that's the job that's open for me, I'll take it."

"Then you're hired. There's worse jobs than helpin' the cook. Ribs used to be as good a cowboy as ever spurred a pony down a mountain, till he got crippled up so's he couldn't ride. You kin learn a lot from Ribs, just by listenin' careful. Ribs tells me Guzman was here."

"Ribs run him off."

Black Jack grinned. "He ain't the first un Ribs has run off, son. Ribs is bad medicine when he's got a gun in his hand. Yet, you kin learn aplenty from that ole pot rassler. He's bin a wart hawg in his day."

Black Jack sipped his hot coffee. Howdy kept on peeling potatoes.

"Just what do you intend to make outa yourse'f, Howdy?"

Howdy Merchant looked at the older man. "I promised my dad when he was a-dyin' that I'd go straight. Outside of doin' that, I ain't had hardly time to think 'er out."

He talked like a man. Cheated of his boy-hood, he had always been with grown men, men who rode the dim, twisted trails that the outlaw follows. His was a wisdom far beyond his years.

"Goin' straight, are you, Howdy? Well, that's the ticket. But whatever made you come here? This is a purty tough outfit for a button your age. You know the rep we got."

Howdy nodded. "He'pin' the cook can't be no crime. And knowin' how I feel, I don't reckon you'd be askin' me to do anything wrong. I've heard Dad say he'd a heap rather trust you than he would a lot of them cow outfits that claim they're so almighty honest. I'd be proud to stay here, sir."

"You're stayin', son. And don't call me 'sir' no more. I ain't no banker ner politician. You're welcome to stay on. Later on, when we pull out on the roundup, mebbe so I'll be able to stake you to a string of horses. Right now I'm full-handed."

Now several of the Muleshoe Bar cowboys rode up to the corral, jerked the saddles from sweat-marked horses, and came over to the cook shack. There was the sound of horse bells as the day wrangler brought in the remuda. The cowboys, jerking off their leather chaps, washed at the bunkhouse.

Inside the cookhouse, Ribs was busy.

28

Black Jack joined his men and they squatted around on their spurred boot heels, talking. Howdy took his peeled potatoes into the kitchen. Ribs winked broadly and jerked a thumb towards the group outside.

"It's gonna be a tough evenin' fer Mike Guzman and his gang, son."

"How do you mean, Ribs?"

"Somehow Black Jack got word that Guzman and his outfit was campin' not far from here. He's takin' a few of the boys along to smoke Mike off the Muleshoe Bar range. Black Jack thought a heap of big Jim Merchant, sonny."

Howdy made no reply. He did his work around the cookhouse and waited on the table where Black Jack and his picked cowboys ate an early supper in silence.

The young fellow was at the carbine in the saddle scabbard, when the boss and his men led fresh horses from the corral. Black Jack looked at Howdy, scowling a little.

"Travellin', button, or just goin' somewhere?"

"If you're goin' after Mike Guzman, I'd be proud to go along. It was his bullets that killed my dad. I'm hopin' to line my sights on his briskit."

Howdy's voice shook a little. Still terribly fresh in his heart was the pain and sorrow of losing his father. His grey eyes were hard now — Jim Merchant's eyes.

Black Jack laid a hand on his shoulder. His voice was almost gentle as he spoke.

"My game, this time, son. My quarrel with Mike Guzman goes back a long ways. You better stay home this trip. You're kinda young to be gunnin' for anybody. Killin' men is bad. After the first man you kill, it comes almighty easy to jerk a trigger. Jim wouldn't want you to turn out ornery. So you just jerk that hull of yourn off that geldin' and leave all the fireworks to us boys."

Howdy obeyed, but he was disappointed. Ribs joshed him a lot and when the rest of the cowboys came in Howard almost forgot that he had wanted to go with Black Jack. These wild cowboys, a reckless, hoorahing crowd, plagued the cook and one another. They talked of the steers they had roped that day and of the wild races they had had. Howdy, learned in the ways of cowboys, did not intrude himself into their company. And after a time, when they learned that this young fellow, with the grey eyes and yellow hair, was not "mouthy" or bold, they included him in their talk. So Howdy became one of them.

Black Jack and his men got back at daybreak. No man of them mentioned anything about the night's ride. But Black Jack, reading in Howard's eyes the question he so wanted to ask but did not because he would be violating a cow-camp rule for younger fellows who trail with men, smiled crookedly and shook his head.

"Mike got away. They'd pulled stakes when we got there. Mike's hard to ketch. I reckon that's why he's lived as long as he has."

"I bin thinkin' 'er over careful," said Howdy. "I don't aim to be a killer, but if ever I cut Mike Guzman's sign, I'll do my best to kill 'im."

3: The Call

So it was that Howdy Merchant came to the Muleshoe Bar. And there he remained for four years, cook's helper, horse wrangler, then cowboy. And at the end of the four years, men said of Howdy that he was the fastest cowboy on the Muleshoe Bar payroll. He drew top wages and rode a string of the best horses that wore the Muleshoe Bar iron. Nor was his ability confined to the roping of wild cattle. Howdy had cow savvy. He was, as Black Jack told the owners who paid half-yearly visits to the ranch, a natural born cow-hand. And when Black Jack was away, it was Howdy who ramrodded the outfit.

Four hard riding years had made the slim young figure into a man, wide-shouldered and narrow-flanked, with rawhide muscles and the agility of a panther. He was a good bronc rider. He could catch more wild cattle than any two men in the outfit because he not only was fast and rode top horses, but he outguessed the big renegade steers that had to be hunted as a hunter stalks deer or mountain sheep.

At the rodeos along the border, Howdy

Merchant hung up some records that no man could beat. Be it calf roping, steer roping, bulldogging or bronc riding, the tawny-haired young cowboy was always in the money. Better than six feet tall in his socks, he was a hard man to handle in a fight, though he had very few fights of his own choosing. But cowboys in town are cowboys in town and most of the rough-and-tumble battles that Howdy had been involved in were of another man's making. He was not one to stand back and see a friend get the worst of it.

Not once during the four years he spent with the Muleshoe Bar had he met with Mike Guzman. But occasionally the news drifted into camp that the half-breed was plying his lawless trade on both sides of the border. He had picked himself a crew of renegades who would stop at no crime. Guzman was rapidly gaining a sinister repu-tation. He was a power along the border. He stole from Mexican and gringo alike. He laughed at the laws of both the United States and Mexico. And, as is often the case with such outlaw leaders, he gained a host of sympathizers among the Mexicans and certain Americans.

With cunning foresight, Mike Guzman gave a certain per cent of his lawless earnings to those who might, now and then, be of use to him. He became known as a friend to the poor, robbing the rich and giving to the poor. Such was the aim of the clever-brained Mike Guzman. When the law followed hot on his trail, he could always find refuge among the people whom he had befriended. He became a legendary figure along the border. The superstitions had it that he bore a charmed life. Babies and horses, dogs and pet goats were named after him. Many a candle burned for him in the little adobe churches or before the little images in the homes of the peons.

A big, handsome, swashbuckling, swaggering caballero, this Senor Mike Guzman. As fortune favoured him and he became wealthy, he decked himself out in the finest clothes that money could buy. Favouring the Mexican mode of dressing, he was a resplendent figure as he rode down the dusty streets of the border towns — jacket and wide-bottomed trousers of the softest suede leather; silk shirt; a sombrero crusted with gold and silver stitching woven into intricate design; glove-fitting boots; huge rowelled spurs covered with silver; a beautifully carved belt and holster and a silver-handled gun. His saddle was the finest that could be made of leather and silver. He rode the finest horses money could buy.

In the cantinas from Algadones to Juarez, Mike Guzman was well known. He spent freely. The dance-hall girls fought for his smiles. Gamblers, saloon men, entertainers all greeted Don Mike, as they called him, with an unfeigned enthusiasm. And why not? Did he not throw money away with both hands? Was he not the greatest spender along the border? Aye, aye!

And all was towards an ultimate end, this two-handed spending. For often enough, Mike Guzman needed protection of these men and ladies of the border resorts. More than once they had hidden him away while the law officers searched vainly for his hiding-place. It was useless for the law to hunt for Don Mike Guzman in any of those border towns. For why should these people give such a magnificent spender over into the hands of law officers who never paid for a drink?

So had Mike Guzman increased his power during the four years that Howdy Merchant spent learning the cow business at the Muleshoe Bar. Mike Guzman, renegade, half-breed, had become Don Mike, chief of the rustlers and smugglers along the border; even as Howdy Merchant, the slim, ragged young fellow, had become Howdy

Merchant, the best all-around cowboy in the Southwest.

Then, from down in Chihuahua had trickled a bit of news that made a change in the life of Howdy. The news came by a roundabout course, vague, disturbing, uncertain in detail. It concerned the welfare of the Reyes family who had been the great friends of big Jim Merchant in former years. It was Black Jack who told Howdy. Black Jack had been on a trip to El Paso.

"Did Jim ever mention the Reyes family to you, Howdy?"

"Yes. He wanted me to go down there when he died, but I never got that far. I'd clean forgot about the Reyes ranch. Why?"

"Old Rafael Reyes was Jim's best friend, back about the time you was born. I never knowed the whole story but Jim told me that there was nothin' he wouldn't do for old Rafael Reyes. Well, in El Paso, I got to talkin' with a man from down in that country. He tells me that old Rafael Reyes is bein' robbed blind. One of his sons was killed a while back. They're runnin' off his horses and stealin' his cattle."

"Who is doin' the stealin' and killin', Black Jack?"

"The feller claimed that Mike Guzman was the big boss."

Howdy's eyes hardened. "I reckon it's about time that half-breed snake was tromped into the dirt, Black Jack. I'm goin' after him. The work is about caught up with for a few weeks. If it's all right with you, I'll take a little pasear down into Chihuahua."

Black Jack nodded. He knew what Howdy's reaction would be when he heard that Mike Guzman was persecuting the Reyes family. But he felt that Howdy should know.

During the four years that Jim Merchant's son had spent with the Muleshoe Bar, Black Jack had never asked of him anything that was not honest. He had taken Jim's place as guardian of this boy who had come there. And while Black Jack had sometimes dealt in wet cattle brought up from Mexico by nameless riders, he had never once let Howdy handle those stolen cattle.

"Howdy, you're buckin' a tough game down there," he said gravely. "You'll be just a gringo there in Chihuahua and Mike Guzman has a heap of friends down there. You'll have no backing from the United States. You'll git little help from the Mexican rurales because Guzman has friends among 'em. Fact is, a brother of his is a rurale captain down there. You kin see what you're up against. One lone gringo against that pack."

37

Howdy nodded, smiling grimly. "I know about what kind of a game I'm buckin', but just the same, I got to go down there."

"Yeah. You know that country, I reckon. If it was me, I'd cross the border at about Hachita, New Mexico. Foller along the east slope of the Sierra Madres, along the Casas Grandes River to the town of Casas Grandes. Let your whiskers grow. Ask at the Cantina Juarez where the Trainor ranch is. There's a Texan tending bar there. He goes by the name of Jones. Tell him who you are and that I sent you there. And before you go to the Reyes rancho below Casas Grandes, have a pow-wow with Jeff Trainor. He'll tell you all the news and stake you to a fresh horse or cartridges or whatever you need. Jeff knowed Jim Merchant before you ever thought of bein' born. And he'll do all he kin to he'p you."

Howdy had heard of Jeff Trainor and the men who worked for him — a hard lot. Exiled from their own country, they lived in Mexico, sheltered by the rocky cliffs and deep canyons of the Sierra Madres — outlaws, renegades, men such as Jim Merchant had been. Howdy had given his promise to his father that he would go straight. Now it seemed that fate was throwing him into the midst of the toughest outlaws in the country.

"Just because you herd with Jeff Trainor and his boys," said Black Jack, as if reading the younger man's thoughts, "is no reason why you'll have to turn out bad. Jeff won't coax you into no deviltry. I wouldn't be sendin' you there if there was any other way out for you. Alone against Mike Guzman, you wouldn't last a week. But with Jeff and his boys, you'll have plenty protection. Jeff shore hates Mike Guzman. And he'll be expectin' you, Howdy."

"Expectin' me?"

"The feller that told me about the Reyes trouble was one of Jeff Trainor's men. And knowin' how you'd take the news I fetched back, I sent word by him that you'd be showin' up there one of these days. Only that the owners is about due down here and will want to have a long medicine talk and look around for a couple of weeks, I'd go along with you and let Shorty rod the spread. I'd shore like to take that pasear." And he grinned twistedly, his eyes glittering.

4: Cantina Juarez

Yellow lights gleamed in the black-purple night. The high peaks of the Sierra Madres stood out boldly, proudly, against the moonlit sky — a night meant for lovers and for men who know and understand the silence of the desert and mountain peaks.

Howdy, his face covered with a bristle of sand-coloured whiskers, clad in flannel shirt and denim jumper, Levi overalls and leather chaps, pulled rein at the outskirts of the little Mexican town that sprawled at the foot of the high mountains. He rode his big sorrel and a stout mule carried his bed and meagre camp outfit. He was dust-powdered, gaunt, shabby.

Faintly the muffled noises of the town came to him. He caught the sound of music, the jumble of voices. Evidently a *baile* or fiesta was in progress; some Mexican holiday, perhaps; some saint's day to be celebrated with music and dancing and the drinking of too much mescal. How those hardworking, sombre, cowled padres must quiver with fear and shame! — mass and candles and chanted hymns at the morning mass, knees bent in prayer; at night the music of guitar and fiddle and the dancing of red-slippered feet; scarlet flowers; dark eyes inviting love under a silver moon; the odour of cheap perfume and Mexican cigarettes; the odour of mescal and pulque and tequila; laughter, the shuffle of feet; the tinkle of spurs; outside in the darkness, men's voices; perhaps a hotly flung curse; the glitter of steel blades in the moonlight; blood, as red as the lips of the senorita they fought for, spilling into the yellow dust.

Past the adobe house where the *baile* was in full swing, rode Howdy Merchant, on down the street. The light from the saloons and cantinas splashed the dust. From those places there sounded the voices of men, all speaking the Mexican tongue. Now and then a tipsy vaquero staggered on unsteady legs from one place to the next. There was the call of a keno banker. Horses stood patiently at the hitch-racks. A motley assortment of mongrel dogs, flea-covered, were forever scratching. Burros strayed aimlessly about. A Chinese, white-aproned, placid, stood in the doorway of a tiny restaurant, pulling slowly at a long-stemmed pipe with a tiny metal bowl.

There was music in the Cantina Juarez; a violin in the hands of some musician with a soul for music, playing some song of Mexico, that throbbed like a living pulse — "Morir Sonando" — "To Die Dreaming." The music of that violin seemed to cleanse the place of other, more ribald sounds; to fit in somehow with the stars and the mountains. Howdy sat his saddle, listening. Now the music was silenced. Howdy stepped off his horse and into the Cantina Juarez.

A dozen men, perhaps, were standing at the bar. The musician, his violin tucked under his arm, was having a drink with the vaqueros. They were all Mexicans. Now their eyes fixed dark, suspicious glances on the shabby gringo who boldly entered the place, chaps swishing, spurs jingling. A Mexican was tending bar, a fat Mexican with sleek black hair and small black eyes.

Howdy slid a ten-dollar bill across the bar. In the Mexican language, and with that suave manner of politeness common even among the illiterate of Mexico, he asked them all to join him in a drink. They accepted gravely, though it was plain that they put little trust in this unshaven gringo. One of the group, a heavy-shouldered, pockmarked Mexican, who was heavily armed and wore two cartridge belts, was eyeing Howdy with an almost hostile glance.

"Salud, senors," Howdy lifted his glass.

42

"Buena salud!" they drank with him, all save the pockmarked man with the two cartridge belts who deliberately poured his drink out on to the floor. There was an uneasy silence. Howdy turned to the fat bartender.

"There is," he asked, speaking the Mexican tongue with a fluency rare even among the border cowboys, "perhaps an Americano named Jones who works here?"

"Jones, the *Tejano,* senor?" The fat bartender smiled faintly and shrugged. "The Senor Jones is no longer here."

"Do you know where he went?" asked Howdy, a feeling of uneasiness creeping over him. The other Mexicans were listening to his every word. There was a leering grin on the face of the pockmarked fellow.

"That," smiled the bartender, pocketing the ten-dollar bill that Howdy had laid on the bar, "is not for me to say. His destination depends very much upon the manner in which he lived and the number of sins written against him. The Senor Jones was killed only last night. It is very bad luck for any *Tejano* to call Don Mike Guzman a lying greaser."

This brought a laugh from the other Mexicans. The pockmarked Mexican laughed a little too loud. The other vaqueros seemed to watch him and the bartender for their cue to laugh or be silent.

Howdy Merchant had lived on both sides of the border long enough to know that he was in a tight spot. The oily-haired barkeep was becoming suavely insulting. The pockmarked man was openly an enemy. The others were little better than dumb cattle. If it came to a fight, which now seemed most probable, he must deal with the bartender and the pockmarked man.

"This *Tejano*," continued the bartender, and his smile was like a thick-lipped snarl now, "was perhaps your friend, no?"

"Not exactly, no." Howdy had unobtrusively shifted his position so that his back was to the wall.

"But, then, why did you ask for him?"

"That," said Howdy, "is perhaps more my business than it is the business of others. I gave you a ten-dollar bill for the drinks that amount to less than half of that. I am now waiting for my change, if you please."

"There is no change, gringo."

"No?"

"No."

"Is this the hospitality that Casas Grandes extends to strangers? Is it the habit, then, for the Cantina Juarez to rob those who come here?"

The pockmarked man shoved past his companions. He stood on stocky legs, his hands on his two guns, leering up at the tall gringo.

"The Cantina Juarez does not like the smell of a gringo. You have had your drink. Now go, before something might happen to you. Is that plain enough for your gringo ears?"

"Plenty plain, hombre."

The heavy-set Mexican had made the bad mistake of coming a little too close. Howdy's fist had suddenly shot out. There was a dull, sickening crack as that hard fist, driven by all the weight Howdy knew how to put into a straight left, collided with the pockmarked jaw.

The man's eyes rolled back in their sockets. His knees gave way under him and he went down as if hit with a sledgehammer. That jaw would need setting.

There was a six-gun in Howdy's hand now. He was grinning unpleasantly and his eyes were tiny slits of steel-coloured light. The vaqueros, bunched together, knives glittering in the lamplight, eyed the gringo with a mingling of hatred and fear.

Now the heavy-paunched bartender

reached under the bar. But even as his thick hand came up, holding a .45 automatic, Howdy's gun spewed fire. With a howl of pain, the bartender stared with wild eyes at a hand that was now a bloody smear, two of the fingers shot away. The automatic lay on the floor, its butt smashed by the cowboy's bullet.

Howdy had noticed a heavy trapdoor behind the bar. This, he knew, led to the cellar where the liquor was kept. It was fastened by a heavy padlock.

"Open that trapdoor, hombre," he growled at the moaning bartender. "If it is not open in ten seconds, you die." He now faced the sullen-eyed vaqueros.

"So you would murder a lone gringo, no? Even as the *Tejano* Jones was murdered, perhaps! Coyotes! Yellow-backed dogs! Followers of Mike Guzman who is no more than a coyote trying to play the wolf. Pouf! One small gringo can lick an army of such cowards."

The bartender had the trapdoor open. Howdy's grin twisted upward at one corner. "Put my ten dollars back on the bar. Pronto, you fat son of a hog. That is right. Now when these very tough hombres pass around the end of the bar, give each of them a push. A strong push, so that they will go down

46

into the cellar. They do not need the stairway, those very tough hombres who are the Mike Guzman fighting men. Now, coyotes, move fast. Single file. Around the end of the bar. Oily one, give each a good push. Hard, or I'll shoot your ears from the side of your fat face. March, coyotes!"

One by one they passed around the end of the bar. One by one they were pushed into the black space. It was a drop of perhaps fifteen feet — groans and curses as they piled up in confusion down there. Now only the bartender remained.

"Throw down the sleeping one who was so brave. Drop him down the hole, then jump down after him. Move fast, you thick-skulled clown."

The unconscious man was dumped into the cellar. The fat bartender, his face now discoloured by a greenish pallor, stood staring down into the black cellar.

"I am of a heavy build, senor. Such a jump might mean injury to my legs."

"Then land on your thick head!" cried Howdy, and kicked the man violently from behind. A gasping cry and the fat one landed on top of the others below. Now the cowpuncher slammed shut the trapdoor and snapped the padlock shut.

Leaving the Cantina Juarez, Howdy again

was in the saddle, riding at a running walk down the street. He was loath to leave the little town without getting some sort of information regarding the trail that would take him to the Jeff Trainor place. To start out blindly was worse than folly. Surely, he told himself, there must be some Americans here in the town who were friends of Jeff Trainor's. And besides, it was better to stay in town for a few hours. When someone heard the commotion in the cellar of the cantina and liberated the men down there, friends of the pockmarked man and the greasy bartender would be taking the trail in pursuit of the bold gringo. They would naturally surmise that he had left town in a hurry.

Howdy grinned widely. He touched the big sorrel with the spurs. The mule quickened its pace. Now they were racing down the street that was splashed with light from the windows and open doors. For good measure Howdy shot a couple of times at the stars. Now men and a few women came piling out of the houses. They saw a gringo and a big sorrel, followed by a pack mule, tearing down the street and headed for the open country.

A few minutes later, Howdy had gained the open country. Plenty of Mexicans had seen him apparently in headlong flight. That was good. Doubling back, he entered the edge of town from another direction. But he left his horse and pack mule in a brush thicket and entered town on foot, keeping to the dark streets, if the crooked roadways could be so dignified by such a label, and after half an hour of maneuvering he was crouched in the black shadows alongside the adobe building that was the Cantina Juarez.

In front of the cantina was gathered a score of men, all Mexicans. Three or four were wearing the soiled and wrinkled uniform of the rurales, the mounted police of Mexico. All of them were jabbering at once with many gestures. Gun-barrels gleamed in the lamplight of the cantina. The bartender, his injured hand swathed in white bandages and held high, was loudly bewailing the loss of his fingers and was cursing all gringos and that one in particular.

Now a man on a handsome black horse rode up. They greeted him with a babel of shouts. There was no mistaking that resplendent figure — Don Mike Guzman. He held up his hand for silence.

"Some one among you with a sober tongue will tell me what all this excitement is about."

The bartender nominated himself spokesman. With many wild gestures and moaning, he told of the coming of a wild gringo who had all but murdered half a dozen of them. The gringo had then left town in a great hurry, headed south — a friend of the Jones *Tejano*.

A dozen excited Mexicans added to the yarn. They told how the gringo had shot at them, nearly killing half a dozen people. Howdy, listening to the wild, exaggerated tales, grinned to himself in the darkness.

Mike Guzman barked staccato orders. Men piled into their saddles. The rurales joined the vaqueros. Brandishing guns and machetes, they left town at a gallop, Mike Guzman riding in the lead, leaving a swirling cloud of dust in their wake and followed by wild cheers from the men and women who stood on the street. Of all the populace the moon-faced Chinaman in his doorway was the only one who seemed unperturbed. He pulled thoughtfully at his long-stemmed pipe, his face a round mask.

5: Senorita

"Senor!" Howdy whirled, his gun cocked. "Do not shoot, senor. I am your friend," came the whispered reply in the Mexican language.

"Who are you, then? Speak quickly or there'll be a bullet in your hide. Who are you?"

"I am the one who was playing the violin when you entered the cantina. Before the trouble starts, I slipped out the back way. Because once, when such a fight starts, a very excellent violin gets broken for me and nobody ever pays for a new one. And good violins are rare."

"You say you are my friend. Why?"

"Because, senor, you are the enemy of that devil in human form, that Mike Guzman. Pah! I spit to cleanse my tongue of the sound of his foul name. Some day I shall kill that bragging beast. But I am of small stature and he is strong and built for fighting." The voice of the small Mexican shook with emotion.

"Why do you hate him, then?"

"It is something I cannot tell you now,

senor, because whenever I let myself think too much about it, I go loco. Loco! I drown my grief with mescal until I am unconscious."

"How did you know I was here?" Howdy changed the subject as a thin note of hysteria crept into the little musician's whispering voice.

"I was hiding here when you came. I was hoping that the accursed Mike Guzman would pass this way. Then I would bury this knife between his shoulders."

Howdy caught the gleam of a thin-bladed stiletto, also the glitter of the little man's darting black eyes.

"Mike Guzman and his men have gone," said the cowpuncher.

"*Si, senor.* And it is as if the *Senor Dios* has this night sent you here. You are big, senor, and strong and with a heart of great courage. You hate this Mike Guzman. Ah, senor, I dread to put to you that request for fear it will be refused. But, if only you would do this favour, you shall be many times rewarded here on earth and in heaven. If you have a sister, a sweetheart, a wife, a mother, you will understand why I go on my knees to beg of you this favour. I will gladly pay you money, all the money I have, which is a few thousand pesos. I will give my life to you to keep or do with as you will. I will —"

"But what is it that you would ask of me, my friend?" asked Howdy, a little amused at the man's fervour, yet moved by the passion of his pleading.

"It is not for me that I ask, but for the deliverance from Mike Guzman's foul hands of the most beautiful, the most gentle, the most saintly of Mexico's senoritas. The vile beast has her held prisoner at a house not far from here. With her is an old hag who is foul of tongue and slovenly. Guarding the place are two of Guzman's most vicious men."

"And the lady is what to you?" asked Howdy shrewdly.

"She is my cousin. But she is also more than that, for when the revolution robbed me, as a child, of my home and my parents, it was her father who gave me shelter and was as my own father to me. So is this senorita as dear to me as if she were my own sister. Ah, senor, if you could but understand how terrible it is for her, as pure and as free from evil as a nun, to be held by that beast of a man whose very glances leave her soiled."

The little musician was speaking from the depths of his heart. Howdy's lips were pulled to a thin line. He shifted his gun so that it was ready for instant use.

"After we get her out of the house, what then?"

"Senor, you'll do this thing?"

"Why not? Sure, I'll give it a try." Howdy's eyes were dancing now. He unconsciously spoke his own tongue.

"The *Senor Dios* will reward you, senor. And my uncle, Don Rafael, will most surely reward you. Rafael Reyes is, in spite of the thieving Guzman renegades, a wealthy man."

"Do you say that Rafael Reyes is your uncle?"

"*Si, senor!* You know him?"

"I was at his rancho when I was a child. I came there with my father. We were there a week."

"You had yellow hair and rode a blue roan horse?"

"You were there then?"

"*Seguro!* Certainly! And we had never before seen anyone with yellow hair. Ah, senor, no less than Our Lady of Sorrows has sent you here this night."

"When we get the senorita free," repeated the practical Howdy, "what then?"

"I will have horses waiting. Two horses, for I shall go with you and do my share of the fighting in case we should meet enemies."

"My horse and pack mule are near here in

a brush patch. I'll slip the pack off the mule. It's a good bed but I'll get another. We'll need to make fast time."

"Your horse is fresh, senor?"

"Fresh enough to carry me across Mexico," said Howdy, grinning. "Let's go."

Howdy waited for ten minutes while his newly found friend got the two horses and met him at the brush patch.

"You stay here with the horses," Howdy told him. "I'll take care of the two guards."

The little Mexican, whose name proved to be Ricardo Reyes, begged Howdy to let him share the risk of rescuing his beloved cousin, but the cowpuncher shook his head.

"You just point out the house, Ricardo. I work better alone."

From a safe distance, Ricardo pointed out the adobe casa where the daughter of Rafael Reyes was held prisoner. The cowpuncher nodded grimly. They saw the two sentries who walked in opposite directions around the house, halt and light cigarettes, then move on. They were stalwart men, these guards, and wore serapes and huge straw sombreros. Around the crown of the sombreros was wrapped a white band, the badge of loyalty to Mike Guzman, so Ricardo explained.

"When I get inside," said Howdy, "I'll take care of the old hag. I'll be with you in a few minutes if luck is on my side. Have the horses ready. *Adios* for a little while."

"May the *Senor Dios* give you luck, senor."

Cautiously, without making a sound, Howdy wormed his way through the black shadows, keeping close to the wall of an adobe corral where some horses and mules, undoubtedly the property of Mike Guzman, were eating hay. From the adobe wall across to the shadowed wall of the casa was a distance of perhaps twenty-five feet.

Timing carefully the passing of the two guards, Howdy learned that they met at the front and at the rear of the white-walled casa. The wall across from the corral was at the side of the house. It was also in the shadow. Alongside the wall of the house was an old pepper tree. Now the guards were meeting in front of the house. Howdy leaped from the shadow of the corral. A moment later he was up in the big tree, hidden in the feathery foliage. Now the guard passed under him, walking lazily. Howdy, breathing a little fast from the swift climb up the tree, let the guard pass on. Now the two guards met at the rear of the casa which was shadowed, passed, went on.

They met once more in the moonlight at the front of the building. Howdy's crouched figure went taut. Here came the guard. Now he was directly underneath the tree. Howdy, gripping his six-shooter, leaped. The Mexican went down as the cowboy's weight struck his shoulders. Once, twice, Howdy's gun-barrel thudded against the man's skull. The man lay as if dead. Howdy now put on the unconscious guard's serape and the big sombrero with the white muslin band. Taking the guard's carbine, he stalked on. Now he rounded the corner of the house, wrapped in the serape, the wide brim of the sombrero throwing his face in the shadow.

The second guard approached slowly. Howdy kept on at a lazy pace. Now the two were passing. Whirling suddenly, Howdy swung the short-barrelled carbine like a club. The man went down with a smothered grunt — another cracked skull.

Now to gain entrance to the house! Still wearing the serape and sombrero, he cautiously tried the rear door — locked. Someone was moving about in the kitchen — the old woman who was the senorita's companion and jailer, no doubt. Howdy rapped boldly at the door with the barrel of the carbine.

"*Quien es?*" snapped a sharp, whining, shrewish voice. He heard the shuffle of her heavy sandals.

"A note from Don Mike. There has been trouble at the Cantina Juarez," replied Howdy, speaking Mexican and muffling his voice. "A gringo who was perhaps loco or drunk has — Woman, would you keep a man here shouting through barred doors like a lunatic? Take you this message that he has written and —"

The bolt slid back. The door opened a little ways. Howdy gave the door a quick jerk that pulled the slatternly old hag almost into his arms. Now he threw the serape over her head, smothering her profane cries. Jerking her none too gently inside the house, he tied her arms and legs and gagged her with a strip of the dirty serape. The old hag fought with surprising strength but the cowboy had her tied securely in a few seconds. From the woman's girdle he took a bunch of keys. With the kitchen lamp to light his way, he went into the hallway.

"Senorita Reyes!" he called, not too loudly. "It is a friend of Ricardo's, come to take you home. Which room are you in?"

A moment of silence, then a girl's strained voice. "Here! At the end of the hall."

Now Howdy found the huge key that

58

fitted the lock. The heavy door swung open. And there in the lamplight, tall, white of cheek, wide-eyed, stood a girl dressed in black. Black! Her hair was as black as the dress she wore. Her lips were pomegranate red, her eyes soft brown. Never, in all his life had Howdy Merchant seen so beautiful a woman. Her beauty stunned him for a moment. She was staring at him uncertainly.

"Who are you, senor?" she asked in a voice that was almost a sob.

Howdy felt his face grow red. "I'm a friend of your father's, and your cousin sent me here. Hurry, because we have to go as fast as we can."

For a long moment her dark eyes searched his. Then, as if satisfied with what she read there in his grey eyes, she picked a black mantilla from the bed and came towards him. "I am ready, senor."

Now they were out of the house. Howdy hurried her past the two men who lay unconscious there alongside the house. He felt her shudder as he guided her past, holding her arm in his left hand, his gun gripped in his right.

At sight of them, Ricardo gave a glad cry. Sobbing brokenly, the senorita was in his arms.

"We'd better git goin'," said Howdy, almost gruffly. "No time to waste."

"Quite so," said Ricardo. "Ah, Shirley, thank the Blessed Virgin for this friend of ours tonight. Only for him you would be there in that ugly casa."

Confusedly Howdy interrupted. "Let's git goin'."

They were in the saddle now, two men and a girl. The mule followed without being led.

"They'll be watching the trails that lead south," said Howdy. "They think I headed that direction. We'll have to head either for the border or take to the mountains."

"The hardest part of the business," agreed Ricardo, "lies before us. The Reyes rancho lies to the south. They will never let us get as far as the border. The mountains must be our only chance to elude them."

"Where is the Trainor ranch?" asked Howdy.

"South and west of here. They'll watch that trail, senor, because Jeff Trainor is a *Tejano* and hates all Mexicans. He would not give my cousin and me shelter from Mike Guzman because he hates us, even as he hates Mike Guzman. The mountains, then; that is our one chance."

"Then we'll take to the mountains," said

Howdy, grinning. "It'll be hard on the lady, though, livin' like coyotes up there."

"Any hardship, senor," replied the senorita, forcing a brave little smile, "is better than being Mike Guzman's prisoner. For a week, now, he has kept me there. Threatening me, taunting me, telling me that when he had bled my father for the big ransom money, he would not keep his part of the bargain, but would keep me until he grew tired of me. Then he would slit my throat, or give me to his men. Gladly, senor, will I endure the hardships of the mountains. I cannot find the words to tell you my gratitude tonight. You came as if sent by God in answer to my prayers."

Howdy's ears were burning. He was afraid of women, especially beautiful women. More to change the subject then anything else, he put his next question.

"Your cousin called you 'Shirley,' senorita. That is an odd name for a lady of Castilian blood."

"Yes. I was named for a beautiful Americano lady who died at our rancho many years ago. She was the wife of a Texan, a *Tejano*, who was my father's great friend."

"The name of this *Tejano?*" asked Howdy, the cords of his throat tightening.

"Merchant. James Merchant."

"Yes." A husky note crept into the cowboy's voice. "I am the son of that James Merchant. My mother's given name was Shirley. To me it is the most beautiful name in the world."

6: That Mule

Dawn crept across the sky and they halted at a little spring that gurgled from the granite boulders. There was feed for the horses. The little park was surrounded by junipers. It was an ideal camping spot that Ricardo had guided them to.

"We're out of luck for something to eat," said Howdy, "but there should be game here. I'll take my Winchester and see what I can find."

"The sound of a rifle shot might carry to the ears of enemies," said Ricardo. "There are Yaquis here that are worse than Guzman's wolves. Besides, I think we have enough food. I prepared for that."

From the large saddle pockets of his saddle and the senorita's, Ricardo brought forth jerky and pinole, which is a corn meal, penoche cakes that are brown sugar, and salt. Even a small skillet came from the spacious pocket.

In the light of the sunrise, Howdy had a good look at his companions. Shirley Reyes, happy now, the fright gone from her eyes, was more beautiful than he had thought.

She smiled and laughed a little and made fun of Ricardo for bringing along his precious violin.

Ricardo, his slight frame weighted down by crossed cartridge belts and a heavy automatic on each hip, joined in her mirth. He was a handsome young caballero, for all he was slight of build, though his features were finely chiselled, sensitive, almost too perfect. He had the eyes of a dreamer, an artist. And yet there was courage there, also, the courage of a man who, though his very soul revolts at the sight of spilled blood, will fight to the death for his honour or the honour of those he loves.

Howdy felt awkward and uncouth in the eyes of this beautiful senorita. He was all too conscious of his unshaved jaw, his tousled hair, his jumper and overalls that were faded and soiled. He tried to find an excuse to get out of sight for a little while.

Shirley, perhaps, sensed his embarrassment, because she came over to where he squatted by the little camp-fire and sat opposite him.

"And so," she spoke in English, with the trace of an accent that was vastly charming, "you are that yellow-haired boy who came, so long ago, to our rancho. We were afraid of you because never before had we seen a boy with fair skin and grey eyes and yellow hair. I think we were very rude, were we not, peeking from behind trees and around the buildings at you. And you scowled very fiercely and would not even look at us. Though, when we got over our fright, Lupe and Margarita and Bonita and Rosita, we made eyes at this gringo boy who would have none of us."

"I was plumb scared," admitted Howdy, grinning. "I'd never seen any little girls before."

Shirley nodded. "As I grew older, I thought of that. But at the time I thought you were just very haughty and fierce and swaggering. You did swagger, I swear you did. And you had a gun on your saddle. Lupe, my older sister, had a fight with me about who would marry you. I pulled her hair.

"And before you left, I stole a very beautiful red silk neck scarf that you had left in your room. I still have it. And that is not all, Senor Gringo. I used to pray on my knees every night before the little image of Our Mother, asking her to send you back to me." She laughed gaily, then the laugh became a soft smile.

"Those prayers," she said, looking at him across the fire, "were answered, but not quite in the way the little girl who prayed so hard expected them to be answered. Just the same, you have now changed so much. You are still afraid, are you not?"

"I reckon I am," grinned Howdy.

Shirley laughed; Ricardo joining in her mirth. "Ricardo, this bold gringo who breaks heads of evil men and is very much of a big, strong warrior, is afraid of one little harmless girl. He calls me 'ma'am' like I was a skinny teacher of the schools with perhaps big-rimmed glasses and a wart on my nose. Have we not known him many years? Has he not saved me from worse than death? Yet he would treat me like I am ugly and wrinkled with perhaps a crooked nose and crossed eyes.

"Ricardo, you must give Howard lessons. And I can well assure you, Howard, that, though he may not be so big around the chest and so high up from his boot heels, still, that Ricardo *sabes* the ways to make the hearts of the senoritas flutter like the wings of a bird. When the moon is so round and like silver, then this caballero puts on his best Sunday clothes and rides away with that violin under his arm. And under some fair senorita's barred window, he plays. You shall hear him play tonight, Howard, when the moon comes up."

"And Shirley will sing for you, Howard," put in Ricardo. "He has already heard me play, cousin. There in the Cantina Juarez where I amused those drunken swine, pretending to be but a wandering musician. Even that Mike Guzman threw me a peso, not knowing who I was."

"And you took it?" Shirley's eyes grew angry for a moment.

"Would you have had me throw it back in his face and so reveal the fact that I was his enemy? I am keeping it. I hope to cram it down his throat some day."

"Be sure that he is well tied, Ricardo, and that he does not bite off a finger," she teased him, her eyes filled with laughter now.

"Sometimes, Howard, this very beautiful cousin of mine can be provoking. She is too old to spank any more. The best a man can do is to ignore it. But if she promises to behave, then I will tell her how a single Americano defeated almost a dozen men in that cantina."

"I will be good, Ricardo. I promise not to bait you further. Tell me the story. Oho! Look you, Ricardo, at the ears of our good friend Howard! They are red. Quick, Ricardo! The story." And she clapped her hands gaily.

Ricardo gave a vivid recital of the

cowpuncher's fight in the cantina. Howdy's self-consciousness gradually left him.

"And all this time, cousin, where were you?"

"Outside, peeking through the window," came the shameless reply. "I saw the storm coming. I had no desire to be included in the slaughter of those Mexicans. My violin was my only weapon. Lucky for me I left, no? For I would have been pushed into the cellar with the others."

Now they ate breakfast which Howdy prepared, all save the tortillas which Shirley made, patting them out with her own fair hands. When breakfast was done, Ricardo took the serapes from his saddle and Shirley's and made her lie down.

"Rest while you may, cousin. Who knows when we may be forced to ride on once more."

There was no use hiding the fact that danger surrounded them; it was better that she should know. The senorita was brave. If she feared death, she hid that fear well. When she was asleep, the two men walked to a high point some distance away. Howdy had taken the powerful binoculars from the leather case on his saddle. With the glasses, they could plainly see the town below and the desert beyond. They took turns scanning the lower country.

Groups of horsemen rode the trails, combing the country for the escaped gringo and for Shirley Reyes. It was doubtful if Mike Guzman connected the two events. The girl's escape, no doubt, was blamed on some Mexican, who was loyal to the Reyes family. Rafael Reyes had many staunch friends. Even now, Ricardo mentioned the fact.

"A friend has taken word to my uncle Rafael," he said, "that we have rescued Shirley and will protect her with our lives. I took that liberty, Howard."

"That was right." Howdy now swept the rough slopes of the mountains behind them, but could see no trace of any human being.

"The Yaquis," he told Ricardo, "are not easy to see, but I reckon they'll be locatin' us before long. We'll move camp after sundown. I know a place, if we can find the trail after dark. It's dangerous goin' and the trail is rough and steep, but, if there's a moon, we'll tackle it. Let's see, the moon showed about eleven o'clock last night. It'll be later tonight. But with a moon, we can cover the distance in four hours. It's risky, but not half as risky as bein' caught here by the Yaquis."

"You have been here in the mountains

before, then, Howard?"

"Some years ago. But I remember the trails. I was with my father then, and he made a good teacher. Supposin' you go back and ketch up on your shut-eye, Ricardo. I'll stand guard till noon, then you can go on watch. I'll wake you at noontime."

While Ricardo and the girl slept, Howdy tried to figure out some definite plan by which they could reach the protection of the Reyes ranch, some sixty miles distant — a sixty miles patrolled by Mike Guzman's renegades and by squads of hard-riding rurales under Mike's brother. To be sure, when the governor or the president or someone higher in authority than Captain Ramon Guzman should learn that the rurale captain was aiding and abetting his brother Mike in his lawless trade, then most assuredly Captain Ramon Guzman would stand with his back to the adobe wall and be shot. But until that fatal day, Captain Guzman would work with his brother Mike, sharing the rich profits from many sources. And until that dawn when the firing squad snuffed out the life of that captain of rurales, Mike Guzman's enemies were his enemies.

Back in the mountains were the Yaquis. Crafty, cruel, brave in the face of death, those Yaquis obeyed no law save the laws made by Yaqui chiefs. Warlike, at home in the rocky fastness of the mountains, they waged endless war against all men save their own people. Deep in their hearts was a deep, bitter, relentless hatred for the Mexicans. For centuries they had fought the Mexican. Driven back into the mountains by armies that outnumbered their dwindling warriors, they were making a last fierce stand against the hated Mexican. Few were the Yaquis ever taken alive. And may the *Senor Dios* have mercy on the luckless Mexican who fell into their hands. For the Yaqui had many modes of exquisite torture that made the blood of the Mexican people run cold at the very mention of tales told of Yaqui torture.

No Mexican in his right mind ever strayed into the deep canyons behind the Casas Grandes. Those who did never returned. Occasionally, some badly frightened vaquero would bring word into town that the Yaquis had raided this ranch or that, had driven off cattle and goats, had stolen horses, had killed the men and children, and stolen the women who were worth having. But the rural captain never followed the raiders into the mountains. He had seen troops of Mexico's seasoned cavalry put to

71

headlong flight by those same Yaquis. He had seen bodies of soldiers after they had been put to torture, then turned loose to die in the desert. Right there in Casas Grandes was an example that might make the bravest man in all Mexico shudder.

This old man, a hopeless cripple now, had been a gallant figure, brave, bold, handsome, an officer who had finished with high honours at Mexico's West Point. He had led his men in an attack upon a Yaqui stronghold. Of the troop, he was the only one to survive — better if he had been killed.

Vaqueros had found him, half alive, insane, wandering on the desert, barefooted, naked, his body a mass of festering wounds; his eyes gouged out and the sockets filled with sand; his tongue cut out. Though he lived, life was torment, because, in that eternal darkness that was his life, he lived over and over those horrible days of torture at the hands of the Yaquis. From his tongueless mouth came horrible sounds. He crawled about on his hands and knees through the dust, like an animal. And while his age, as measured by years, was not more than thirty, his matted hair was as snow.

Children ran screaming at the sight of him. Women shuddered and turned away, crossing themselves. Even the strongest of

72

men went sick at their stomachs when that horrible wreck of a human being crawled down the street, mouthing his terrible cries of agony. One of his boyhood friends watched over him whenever he escaped from the house where he was kept. This old friend would get a bottle of mescal and pour it down the tongueless throat. The liquor would stupefy the poor wretch so that he could be taken back to his house.

And inside those walls, he was cared for by the sad-eyed woman who had been his beautiful bride. She looked after this scarred, demented creature who had been the most dashing cavalry officer in Chihuahua. With nunlike devotion, she tended his wants. Her beauty fading, her eyes seared by suffering, washed by tears, her hair almost as white as that of the man, she gave her life to this pitiful, horrible wreck.

Howdy had seen the man years ago. He had heard the grisly tale. He had never forgotten. And now, when he thought of Shirley, a shudder crept along his spine. He told himself that, before she should fall into the hands of the Yaquis, he would kill her with a merciful bullet. He almost regretted their flight from the little town. What could he and the little Ricardo do against a war party of Yaquis?

Those Yaquis were said to be well armed. These rough mountains were their playground. Perhaps, even now, cruel black eyes were watching the woman and two men who had the temerity to venture here. Building a fire that morning had been a foolish act. For little escaped the ever vigilant eyes of the Yaqui scouts.

Uneasy now, Howdy scoured every rock, every point, every open space on the mountainside. Now he tensed, his jaws tightening. For high up on the slope, he saw three men riding mules, travelling single file along a narrow trail. Yaquis!

Howdy made his way back to camp. It was nearly noon, and Ricardo was gathering wood for the fire. Shirley still slept. Howdy motioned Ricardo to join him.

"We'll have to pull out now. Just sighted three Yaqui scouts. By the way they acted, they haven't spotted us yet. And we'd better take to cover before they do. We'll work back towards town, following around the foot of the mountains, down the river. Then, after we rest our horses below Casas Grandes, we'll make a race for the Reyes rancho, under the moon, about two nights from now. Better wake Shirley and tell her we have to ramble along. I'll fetch the horses."

"You've had no sleep, Howard."

"Sleep? Man, if I had ten feather-beds piled up here, I couldn't shut an eye. Not with those Yaqui devils riding the ridges! I'll ketch up when we reach your uncle's ranch."

"If ever we do reach there."

"Sure we'll git there. Shucks, I've bin in tights that make this look like a kid's game of hide and seek. Grin, Ricardo, ole-timer."

Howdy saddled the horses. He wolfed some food, joking and laughing as if it were a real picnic. But when they were in the saddle, he handed Shirley a little pistol.

"Better keep this, Shirley."

"Thank you, Howard." She smiled at him. She asked no questions. He volunteered nothing. Both understood why he had given her the little double-barrelled pistol.

The trail narrowed. Howdy rode in the lead, Shirley behind him. Ricardo brought up the rear.

Now, upon the mountainside, high above them, there sounded the faint crack of a rifle; after a few moments, another shot, nearer them; and from the broken canyons and ridges below them, a third shot.

Howdy pulled up, his mouth a grim line. "No use hidin' it from you, Shirley. Those shots relayed the news that they'd located

75

us. Whoever is below will be watchin' for us. We'll have to shotgun the hill when they open up on us. I savvy these Yaquis poco plenty. They'll be waitin' upon the sides of that canyon we have to pass through. Once they think they've got us bottled up, they'll open up with all they have. That's what they plan. And there in that canyon is where they aim to mop up on us. The others are trailin' us from behind, so we can't turn back, which will give 'em the idea that they have us in a tight trap, which they have. And it is up to us to find a hole in that same trap."

Howdy grinned a little, his grey eyes narrowing. "Got to locate a weak spot in their trap," he mused aloud, rolling and lighting a cigarette. "Then ride down the mountain like we had a bunch of wild cats tied on to the tails of our horses. I'd give a purty if it was only dark. Then we could risk a run down the canyon and — Dog-goned if I ain't gittin' slow-witted as a sheep-herder. That's our ticket to home. We'll outfox these Injuns. Let's go. We're pickin' us a nice place among the boulders where we kin make a good stand and keep the trail open below. I know the place, too. We'll give 'em a lickin' they'll talk about for a few weeks."

Howdy, setting a brisk pace, led the way. Quitting the main trail, he took a twisting course that finally brought them out on a point that was a sort of natural fortress. Surrounded by giant granite boulders, there was a grassy opening some twenty feet in diameter. The grass was thick and tall. There was but one way of gaining the spot, and that was the steep trail that climbed a twisting course, so steep that in places a rider had to dismount and lead his horse up over boulders. From where they were, they could stand off a hundred men.

"Keep outa sight," Howdy cautioned Shirley and Ricardo. "The Yaquis behind us might, in their hurry, run past the sign that tells 'em we quit the main trail. They'll keep on goin', thinkin' we're ahead of them. And by the time they trail back here, it'll be gettin' along to'rds dark. They might even run past the sign a second time, though that would be askin' just too much of Lady Luck. From here, we kin see the war-party that's follerin' us."

Howdy, his glasses glued to his eyes, watched the trail down which they had come. Now he swore softly under his breath. Coming down the trail, riding single file, were half a dozen Yaquis, heavily armed, all riding stout mules. They looked formidable enough. They wore cotton shirts, overalls, and big straw sombreros.

77

Filled cartridge belts were across their chests. They carried side arms, machetes, rifles; as well equipped as the Federal army.

Now they were passing along the foot of the slope. They had passed the rocky spot where Howdy had led his companions off the trail. He heaved a big sigh of relief, but all too soon.

The mule belonging to Howdy, long ears at attention, nostrils twitching, had caught the scent of the mules below. Before anyone could smother the noise, he split the mountain silence with loud, discordant braying. From below came replies from his kind. The Yaquis pulled up. They were looking up at the rocky point that hid the three.

Howdy's anger and chagrin ended in a crooked grin. Tragic as it was, that chorus of braying bordered on the ridiculous.

"That's our signal," said Howdy grimly, cocking his carbine. "Let 'em have it, Ricardo. Take your time. Shoot to kill." Now his Winchester cracked. A Yaqui pitched from his saddle. Now the cowpuncher was shooting rapidly. Ricardo was following Howdy's advice and taking careful aim.

Below was confusion. Mules were stampeding. Riders trying to get into shelter. Now they scattered into the brush and rocks. But along the trail tore three riderless mules.

7: The Yaqui Chief

Before sundown more Yaquis had come to increase the odds against the three trapped enemies of the warlike Indians, until perhaps they numbered twenty or more, down there in the brush and rocks. Bullets threw bits of granite into Howdy's face. A few among those Yaquis could shoot. Whenever one of them was careless or reckless enough to show himself, the cowboy's gun would crack.

Howdy kept up a line of bantering talk. Hiding his fears behind a grin, he raised the hopes in the girl's heart. She knew the gravity of their situation, yet she showed no fear. She was ready, if it came to the worst, to use the stubby little derringer. But until that final moment of despair, she would keep her nerve and smile. She even offered to handle a rifle, but Howdy shook his head.

"Every cartridge we have is shore valuable. You might miss a few. Anyhow, shootin' Yaquis ain't what you might call a lady's job. You just sit in the shade and watch the fireworks. Come dark, we'll bid these fightin' Injuns a fond good-bye and pull out for a safer climate. We might even have breakfast at Casas Grandes. Ricardo, will you kinda hold their attention for a few minutes? I want to look around a little. If there's any other way down from this place except the way we come up, then we'll be in luck."

Howdy, crawling on hands and knees, sometimes wriggling like a snake on his stomach, wormed his way through the brush and boulders. He had left his carbine behind and his only weapon was his six-gun. Keeping hidden, he descended the steep slope until he was close enough to the enemy to hear them talking back and forth. Crouched in a brush thicket, he listened. They were speaking the Mexican language.

"On foot — as soon as it is dark. By the only trail that leads up there."

Now another voice, deeper, more harsh of tone. It was the voice of a man accustomed to giving orders.

"The woman must not be killed. Just the gringo and the Mexican dog."

Now Howdy caught a glimpse of the Yaqui chief, a giant of a man, with a face that was terribly scarred. Both ears had been cut off, giving him an animal look; a shock of black hair sprinkled with white; teeth like ivory; a pair of fierce black eyes that glittered from under scarred brows.

The lips were thin, cruel, pulled down at the corners. Man or woman could expect no mercy from this earless Yaqui who, no doubt, had suffered at the hands of the Mexicans.

Even as far north as the Muleshoe Bar Ranch, the cruelty, craftiness, and bravery of the earless Yaqui had been recounted. He was called "Nono" — Nono, which means the ninth. Probably, he was the ninth of his family to rule with iron hand this tribe of Yaquis. Warrior, victor of countless battles with rebel and Federal troops, nemesis of the rurales, enemy to all men save his own people, hater of Mexicans, despiser of the gringo — that was Nono.

"Dark — on foot — by the main trail," Howdy mused. "Capture the woman — kill the gringo and the Mexican dog."

Now he gave a start. The huge Nono stood in an opening behind some giant boulders. Now another man stepped into the clearing, a man with fair skin and blue eyes. The two spoke rapidly in Mexican.

A white man trailing with these savage Yaquis? It seemed an impossibility. Yet there was the man; blue eyes, fair-skinned, freckled somewhat by the sun, a reddish tint to his light-brown hair. Like Nono, he was dressed in cotton shirt and dungarees.

Filled belts crossed his chest. Two Luger pistols hung from holsters, a Mauser rifle in the crook of his arm. A wide-bladed machete was shoved into the sash he wore. Across one shoulder hung a folded serape, its once brilliant colours faded. He seemed to be a lieutenant under the terrible Nono.

"The canyon is still guarded?" asked the chief.

"*Si, Si!* Nobody can come up or go down. Four picked men guard the trail."

"*Bueno!* Go back to the canyon and wait there. Kill any who pass up or down the trail. That is all, Blanco."

The blue-eyed man departed as suddenly as he had come. Now Nono stood there, his fierce black eyes staring up at the rocks that sheltered Shirley and Ricardo. So close was the Yaqui chief now, that the cowpuncher dared not move a muscle for fear of attracting the giant Yaqui's attention, in which event Howdy determined to kill this scarred chieftain and as many more as he could before they captured him or killed him. But he would like to live long enough to kill that white man who had dropped to such a low level that he lived with the Yaquis.

Then he was given a second shock. Three more fair-skinned men with blue eyes filed

82

past the giant Nono, no doubt following the lieutenant Nono had called Blanco. They talked to one another in the Mexican language. White men, yes! Yet there was something queer about them. They did not act like white men. Were they, perhaps, men who had been captured as babies by the Yaquis and raised among them?

White men, yet their ways and movements were those of an Indian; their manner of walking, their carriage, their gestures. Yet they were white men. It was puzzling. Now Howdy recalled a vague tale that he had heard of a party of Russian colonists there on the Gulf of California in Sonora, north of Guaymas — Russian refugees. They had been driven from their native land, had landed there on the gulf coast, and begun to farm that fertile land. Then some ravaging disease had wiped them out, save a few who had quit the colony and found refuge among the Mexicans. Some of them had intermarried, that was certain. Some of their children had been raised by Mexican families. Then, perhaps, the Yaquis had raided the village, had stolen some women or children. For the Yaquis sometimes rode as far as the Gulf.

Howdy decided that those blue-eyed, fair-haired men he had seen must be from that old Russian colony. What else? He wished the Yaqui chief would move on.

Instead, Nono had moved closer to the brush patch that hid the cowboy. Nono seemed to be thinking; for his forehead was criss-crossed by wrinkles, and his dark hands twisted and clenched as he stood staring up at the spot where Shirley and Ricardo were hidden behind the rocks. Now the big Yaqui squatted on his heels. He was wearing crude sandals made of bullhide and buckskin. His bare feet were as black as those of a Negro. The man removed his sombrero, and Howdy saw that the heavy hair covered a well-shaped head. The thick, hard muscles of the Yaqui's shoulders bulged and rippled under the faded blue cotton shirt. From where he crouched, Howdy could almost reach out and touch the man's back.

Now a crazy notion tempted Howdy, a plan so bold, so daring, so foolhardy, that it made him grin humourlessly.

"Don't act the fool, cowboy," he told himself. "Don't play the bone-head."

Yet, even as he told himself that only a man gone loco would think twice about such a harebrained scheme, he was gathering himself for a quick leap.

Muscles taut, his weight bunched, every

nerve, every muscle co-ordinating, he gathered himself, staring hard at that broad-shouldered back, the earless head with its thatch of iron-grey hair that was as coarse as the mane of a horse — the man squatting on his heels, there in the shelter of the rocks, alone.

From up above, came the crack of Ricardo's rifle; from the shelter of the brush and boulders below, the answering roar of Yaqui Mausers; and there before him, Nono, the earless giant, his back to the crouching cowboy. Howdy could kill the man where he squatted and be gone before any of the Yaquis below discovered the dead body of their chief.

Howdy's thumb was on the hammer of his gun. Murder? It would be justified murder — the life of this earless torturer of women and men and children against the life of Shirley Reyes.

But it was not murder that Howdy planned. Only cowards and fools do murder.

A loco idea, so Howdy told himself, yet it was such loco ideas, boldly executed, that turned defeat into victory.

"Here," he grinned mirthlessly, "goes nothin'."

With a leap, he was on the big Yaqui's

85

back. His gunbarrel rapped against that black-thatched skull with a dull thud. A second rap, and the big frame went limp between Howdy's legs that were wrapped around the big Yaqui's ribs.

A minute's quick work, and the big Yaqui's hands were fastened behind his back. There was a gag in Nono's mouth that bit cruelly into his cheeks, cutting the slitted mouth till the blood trickled. Stripped of his guns, machete, and an ugly-looking hunting knife, the big Yaqui lay on the ground, senseless. Howdy had pulled the heavy bulk of bone and meat into the shelter of the brush. Now he squatted on his heels, waiting for the Yaqui leader to waken. Howdy had the big Yaqui's knife in his left hand. His grey eyes were hard, merciless. Now Nono moved a little. The eyelids twitched. Now a pair of black eyes stared into the grey eyes of the gringo cowboy. Howdy grinned. The black eyes were opaque, unfathomable. What white man could ever read what lay behind the eyes of a Yaqui? The giant lay without moving a muscle. Now Howdy spoke, his voice but a faint whisper. He used the Mexican language.

"In a few minutes I turn you free. I give back to you the life that I could have taken with a bullet or a knife. You hate a Mexican named Mike Guzman. That Mexican is also my enemy. The Mexican with me and the senorita who is his cousin have been badly used by Mike Guzman. We escaped from Casas Grandes and came here because there was no other place to go.

"You are Nono, a Yaqui. You are chief among the Yaquis. Between you and me there is no quarrel. You are a big man. You are big of body and big of brain. It was the father of this Mike Guzman who put those scars on your face. It was the father of that same Mike Guzman who sent your ears to the City of Mexico, no? I have come to Mexico to kill that same Mike Guzman. If you are the chief of your people, you are, therefore, a man of wisdom.

"You and I have this common enemy. For the injury I have done you, I am sorry. But it was the only way that I could use to talk to you. Now that I have talked, and you have listened, I will now see how much I have won."

Grinning, Howdy cut the gag and the strip of rawhide that bound the hands of the giant Yaqui. He gave back to the Indian his weapons. Then he stood back, rolling a cigarette, which he lighted. The Yaqui chief stared hard at this bold gringo. His swarthy

87

face was like a mask, the black eyes smouldering. Now Howdy offered the Yaqui tobacco and brown papers.

For a long moment, the big Yaqui stared at this gringo. Then his lipless mouth widened in a smile. He accepted the tobacco and papers.

Howdy had done the impossible. Together, the two men smoked in silence.

"I will tell my men," said Nono, "that you and the senorita and that little Mexican are free to go. You travel to the Reyes rancho?"

"How did you know that?"

"Because, senor, I know the name of the senorita. You are a bold man, senor. You are also a brave man. And you are the only gringo who ever believed that a Yaqui might have what is called honour. It is because of that, that you and your friends will go safely. But the night will be dark. You are hungry, and your horses need rest. I am but a poor man, a Yaqui, hated and hunted by Mexico. But tonight, senor, I will show you and the senorita and the Mexican hombre that Nono, the chief of the Yaquis, can be a man. You will all stay at my camp. You will be safe. And when you leave for the Reyes ranch, my men will go with you."

"That," said Howdy, moved by the Yaqui's fervour, "is too much to ask of you."

"When I say that I will touch the hand of a gringo," said the giant Yaqui, "it means that I give to him my friendship and the protection of my mountains. You might have killed me. But you did not. You gave me back that life which was in your hands. I shake hands with a brave man."

8: Danger Trail

To Shirley Reyes and Ricardo, it seemed no less than a miracle, because the Yaqui Nono, about whom countless tales of cruelty were told, had never been known to make a friendly gesture towards Mexican or gringo.

"You are sure, Howard," questioned Shirley, when the cowpuncher brought the word that they would camp that night with Nono's Yaquis, "that this is not some Yaqui trick?"

"The Yaqui may be cruel and ornery, Shirley, but he's not a liar. I'll risk it, since he's given us his word that we'll be safe. And that is more than I'd trust Mike Guzman."

It was getting dark when they went down the trail. In a clearing by a crystal spring, they found Nono standing alone beside a blazing fire. He greeted Shirley and her cousin with grave dignity. He had tied a silk scarf around his head so that his lack of ears would not be noticed. Scarred though he was, the Yaqui's face had dignity and character. Here was no common man. They sensed the magnetism there in those black eyes, the power absolute that was his

90

among his people.

Beyond the brush and rocks, a second fire burned. There was the savoury odour of broiling meat and coffee.

Nono made no apology for the simple fare that he gave them. A king does not apologize; that was his attitude. Shirley never left Howdy's side. If the Yaqui noticed the senorita's lack of trust, he hid the knowledge. In fact, he all but ignored her and her cousin. When he spoke, it was always to Howdy. Plainly, he tolerated the girl and Ricardo because they were friends of the cowboy.

After supper, the men smoked. Now that blue-eyed, fair-haired lieutenant appeared. Nono gave the man a few brief orders, and he retired as suddenly as he had come.

"A gringo?" asked Howdy.

The faintest trace of a smile widened the mouth of the Yaqui. "An Indio. His people live to the far south."

"I have heard my father speak of a tribe of blue-eyed Indians," Shirley told the cowpuncher. "Their history would be an interesting study."

Ricardo brought out his violin. As he played, Nono became silent, sitting squat-legged beside the fire. A hush fell over the Yaquis at the other fire.

Shirley edged closer to Howdy and her hand crept into his. She smiled up at him as a child might smile. The cowboy held her hand, a strange warmth creeping through his veins, her shoulder touching his, her hand clinging to his hand, the perfume of her black hair filling his nostrils. Above them, the moon was round and white. The music of the violin throbbed out its songs of love and sorrow and happiness. Never had Howdy listened to such playing. Ricardo was touched by genius. The Yaqui chief seemed lost in the spell of the music such as he had never heard. Now his eyes looked through the firelight at Shirley and Howdy.

"Your woman?" he asked.

Howdy's hand held hers tightly. "Yes," he said boldly, "my woman." He spoke the lie that Shirley's safety might be doubly assured. No harm could now befall her.

Her hand squeezed his with a quick, understanding pressure. She smiled up at him, just a tiny trace of deviltry in the brown depths of her eyes. She was thanking him, and she was laughing at him, just a little. But Howdy felt like a man given a glimpse of paradise.

"You have compromised yourself, Howard," she said in English, whispering into his ear. "Be careful that I do not hold you to that bold statement."

Now he did that which afterwards he marvelled at. He put his arm across her shoulder and so held her. He felt her shiver a little and grow tense as if she were going to draw away. Then she relaxed. Her mass of dark hair was against his broad shoulder.

"Was that quite fair, Howard?"

"I reckon not, Shirley. Shall I let you go?"

"No. I — need your strength, my friend, and the protection of your arm. Perhaps I shall go to sleep like this."

Now Nono watched them, an amused look in his eyes. Ricardo smiled as he played for them. Nono finally rose and stalked away without a word. The three were left alone there beside the fire. Howdy felt that uneasy sensation of being watched from the darkness. His back against a giant boulder, he sat there, Shirley in the shelter of his left arm. Ricardo, upon the pretence of borrowing a cigarette, now sat beside the cowboy. He played softly on his violin, improvising, his dark eyes dreaming. After almost an hour, Nono returned. He had probably been inspecting the guards. In his arms he carried tanned deer and goat hides and several new, gaily coloured serapes. These he put on the ground beside Howdy.

"You will sleep here, senor. The fire will

be kept blazing. No harm will come to you so long as none of you leave this camp. But my guards have orders to kill anyone who comes or goes along the trails. You are, in a way, prisoners, but so long as you do like I say, no harm will come to any of you. At daylight, we start out for the Reyes rancho!"

"But will it be safe to cross from the mountains through that desert and mesa country except after dark?" asked Howdy. "Mike Guzman and the rurales are hunting for us there."

"There may be fighting," came the indifferent reply. "I would be glad of the chance to meet those raiders under Mike Guzman. My Yaquis and the white Indios fear no man."

From this, Howdy now began to understand that Nono planned a bold march by daylight through the very heart of the enemy country; that he anticipated a fight with Mike Guzman's renegades and the rurales under Mike Guzman's brother.

"These skins and serapes are clean," said the Yaqui chief, looking at Shirley. "You do not need to be afraid of getting bugs."

She laughed a little. "Thank you, I am not afraid. Not even of the little bugs."

"No. You are a brave woman. But not so brave as the Yaqui women. You have not

94

ever known what they know about being hunted and killed like coyotes."

He left them alone once more. Howdy and Ricardo spread the skins and serapes. Howdy helped Shirley get her tight-fitting boots off. Then, Shirley between them, they lay down, fully clothed except for their boots, to sleep fitfully beside the fire that silent-footed Yaquis kept ablaze. At daybreak, they were wide awake and ready to eat breakfast, consisting of broiled beef and coffee and tortillas of coarse meal. Half an hour later, they were in the saddle. And they needed no one to tell them that the trail ahead would be a danger trail.

9: The Hermit Doctor

With his own hand, Mike Guzman had killed the two guards who had, through their stupidity, let the Senorita Reyes escape. The old hag who had been in the *casa,* had been found the next day with her ugly throat slit from ear to ear. So did Mike Guzman exact payment for careless mistakes on the part of those who served him. Also another Mexican lay dead not far from a water hole between Casas Grandes and the Reyes rancho. The dead man had been that friend of Ricardo's who had volunteered to take to Don Rafael Reyes the news of his daughter's escape.

Better, perhaps, if that messenger had been allowed to get through, because the news of Shirley's imprisonment had spread like a prairie fire before a strong wind. Men who had taken no sides against the swaggering Mike Guzman now rode to the Reyes rancho to offer their services to the white-haired old man who grieved over his daughter's absence from home as if she were already dead.

"Because," he told them at the rancho, "Shirley will most assuredly take her own life before the foul hands of Mike Guzman can soil her. *Si, senors,* my daughter is dead. It cannot be otherwise. And now I go to find her murderer and kill him. With my own hands, I shall kill him."

So, at the head of half a hundred vaqueros and neighboring ranchers who had suffered heavy losses at the hands of this hard-riding cattle thief, old Don Rafael, as he was often called, rode to avenge his daughter.

Thus it was that, on that morning when Howdy, Shirley and Ricardo rode with the Yaquis, the same sunrise found Don Rafael at the head of his armed riders.

Mike Guzman, his eyes red and slitted from lack of sleep and too much mescal, rode like a man gone mad. Those who were luckless enough to fetch him bad news, were abused. Without sleep, hardly tasting the food cooked for him, he rode from one scouting party to another. Changing horses often, leaving his last horse sweat-caked and cruelly spur-marked, drinking mescal as if it were water, he hunted for Shirley. He cursed his luck.

Now he began to connect the gringo stranger, who had come to the Cantina Juarez, with the escape of the girl, because somehow he had learned that the gringo's name was Howard Merchant and that he had come from the Muleshoe Bar outfit in Arizona. He also learned the real identity of that little violinist who had hung around Casas Grandes. Shrewdly putting together these things, Mike Guzman found the correct solution to his puzzle. This hated gringo, son of big Jim Merchant, had again crossed Mike Guzman. Mike vowed grisly vengeance if ever he could capture the luckless Howdy.

But Don Rafael and Nono were not the only leaders who were anxious to meet Mike Guzman and his renegades. Up in the mountains, Jeff Trainor got word that Jones, the Texan, had been murdered by Mike Guzman. Jones, contact man and friend of Jeff Trainor, would be avenged.

But Jeff Trainor was in no position to attack Mike Guzman openly, with only a handful of cowpunchers there at the Trainor ranch. Brave, hard-fighting cowpunchers, to be sure, but they were sadly lacking in numbers. Under Mike Guzman's command, there was a small army, augmented by the rurales. Jeff Trainor must, therefore, mark time until he could take the powerful Mike Guzman unawares. Now, on top of the news that Jones had been killed by the treacherous Mike, came word that a gringo cowboy had been in trouble at the Cantina Juarez, and had treated some of Mike's men a trifle roughly. Then the gringo cowboy had stolen the daughter of Rafael Reyes from the *casa* where Mike had held her prisoner. The gringo and the senorita had escaped. They had vanished. Mike Guzman was offering fabulous rewards for the return of the girl and for the severed head of the bold gringo.

"I'm bettin'," said Jeff Trainor, "that this cowpuncher is none other than the Howdy Merchant feller that Black Jack 'lowed would be comin' down here. Well, he's shore made a fast start and he must be a wart hawg. Wish we knowed where to locate him. If he ain't gone to'rds the Reyes rancho, then he must 'a' took to the hills. And if he's taken to the hills, then the Yaquis will pick him up, and it'll be good night, cowboy."

Then a bit of news that sounded like some drunken cowboy's dream, came to Jeff Trainor. A cowpuncher brought word that at an hour past sunrise this morning, he had been up on a pinnacle with a pair of field-glasses. And he had seen the earless Nono and his Yaquis riding down out of the mountains. Riding with the Yaquis, apparently at ease and content, rode a gringo cowboy, and a girl who answered the description of the Reyes girl. The cow-puncher had his guns. He and the girl were not, so far as he could tell, prisoners.

"What kinda taranchlar juice you bin hittin'?" asked Jeff Trainor, grinning.

"It's the truth, Jeff. And with the cowboy and the gal was a little Mexican feller I've seen at Casas Grandes. That little gent that played the fiddle for us the last time we was in town. It was shore the same Mexican, Jeff. I'd swear to it. Him and the gal and the cowpuncher was ridin' along just like they belonged with them Yaquis."

"There's a ketch in it somewhere," said Jeff Trainor. "It don't sound right. Them Yaquis don't like gringos, and they hate Mexicans. It don't make sense, feller."

But when the cowboy took Jeff Trainor to a high point, and Jeff Trainor saw with his own field-glasses, then he had to admit that the cowpuncher was right.

"But there's a ketch in it somewheres," persisted Trainor, who did not believe in miracles. "Looks to me like the gal and this Howdy boy and the Mex fiddler is due for trouble. Black Jack asks me to do what we kin for this feller. So we better saddle up and take a li'l ole pasear down yonder. Kinda cold trail them Yaquis. I smell trouble, boys, and trouble aplenty."

So, taking care to stay far enough behind, Jeff Trainor and his cowboys trailed the Yaquis across the river and on to the mesa beyond, then across miles of mesquite and cactus; dusty, sun-blistered miles that were hard on men and horses.

The Yaquis were pushing hard along the trail. Nono's advance scouts, spread far ahead and flanking the main column, kept careful watch. Once or twice, they reported small scouting parties, but there was no trouble until almost noon when they came suddenly upon a little party of vaqueros and rurales. The fight was brief, fierce, and without quarter asked or given. Now the Yaquis pushed on, a little tipsy with the glory of that victory. Not a man of the enemy had escaped alive. Nono had, with his own machete and Luger, put a quick end to the wounded. But he had, before killing them, learned from their dying lips the approximate position of Mike Guzman's main body of fighting men, also where Mike's brother and his rurales were.

When that little skirmish had started, Nono had quickly sent to the rear a dozen of his best warriors. These, so the leader of them explained to Howdy, were to be under the white man's command. Their orders from their chief had been to protect, with their last breath, the lives of the three who were the guests of Nono.

Shirley, frightened a little by the shooting, stayed close by Howdy. Around them in a circle, the Yaquis sat their horses, their guns in their hands, ready to die for the three persons they no doubt hated in their primitive hearts. But such was their loyalty to their chief, that they obeyed him without comment whatsoever.

Once, when the fighting came near them Howdy left Shirley in Ricardo's care and joined the Yaqui bodyguard. This brought gleams of savage satisfaction from their black eyes. This gringo was no coward. He did not hide behind their shelter, but took his place, as a brave man should, among them. And when he dropped a charging Mexican from the saddle with a bullet through each of the rider's shoulders, they nodded their approval of the gringo's marksmanship.

The Yaquis took what was worth taking from the enemy dead. Nono sent back a Yaqui with a message for Howdy to join him at the head of the column. This the cowpuncher did, though he was loath to leave the girl behind with only the rather inefficient Ricardo to protect her.

But it was not the chief's aim to keep

Howdy up there at the head of the column.

"Ahead of us about twenty miles is Mike Guzman and most of his men. To the west of them ride the rurales. They ride towards the Reyes rancho. Word has come from there that old Rafael Reyes is on his way to meet that hombre Guzman. With old Reyes are fifty men. It will be a hard fight. Now we are not riding so hard. Let them do their fighting. Then we shall finish off that hombre Guzman and those others who wear the rurale uniform and obey the brother of Mike Guzman. Tell the senorita that she is safe. Why did you lie, senor, when I asked if she was your woman?"

"Because, my friend, I thought she would be safer."

Nono nodded. "But some day, if you both live, she will be your woman, no?"

Howdy grinned. "If she'd marry a cowboy, yes."

"I do not think you need to worry about that," replied the Yaqui chief, speaking English with hardly a trace of accent.

"You speak English?"

"Yes. I learn it from a gringo who was once my friend, a man who came to live here in the mountains because your gringo law wanted him. He had books, and I had him teach me to read and write and talk. He mined much gold, that man. He was here twenty years. Then he died, and I had lost that friend. He was a good man, even though he was not a fighter. He never used a gun except to kill for meat. He was no coward, that man. I saw him look at death, and smile. He was not afraid to die. I was sorry when he died, because he was a wise teacher and a good friend. He was a doctor and his medicines cured many Yaquis I brought to him. He is the only gringo except you that ever had my hand in friendship." Then he dismissed Howdy with a gesture.

"Go back, my friend, to your woman."

Howdy rode back and joined Ricardo and Shirley. The girl made no effort to hide her joy at seeing him again.

"Do not leave me again, Howard. When you are not here, the eyes of those savages look so evil and wicked that I am frightened."

Howdy laughed. But Ricardo was inclined to agree with his cousin.

"They are afraid of you, Howard. They only hold me in contempt. No sooner had you gone, than they seemed to change. Their eyes were more bold and they whispered among themselves. I do not trust them."

"I won't leave you unless I'm forced to,"

said Howdy, staring searchingly at the Yaquis and two of the blue-eyed Indios who made up their personal bodyguard. "I'd trust the Yaquis, though, further than I'd trust the blue-eyed gents. I never had anything to do with a blue-eyed, tow-headed Injun. It ain't right for an Injun to be light-complected, that a-way. Dog-gone it, an Injun had oughta look like an Injun."

Shirley laughed softly. Howdy talked a lot of nonsense for some time. He did not want her to know that her father was leading a cavalcade of armed men to meet Mike Guzman. But Shirley was not so easily deceived.

"What is it, Howard, that you are trying so hard to hide from me?"

Trapped in a web of his own weaving, the cowpuncher grew red and confused. Then bluntly, for he was unused to subtlety, he told her that Don Rafael was carrying the fight to Mike Guzman. Instead of being frightened, this daughter of the don smiled proudly.

"For all his years, my father is a far better soldier than that border dog he goes to fight. I pray to the Senor Dios for my father's safety and for his great victory."

Fingering the mother-of-pearl rosary with its little gold cross, Shirley's lips moved in prayer as she rode. Howdy and Ricardo rode behind her.

"Did you ever hear of a white man who lived with the Yaquis?" asked the cowboy. "A doctor?"

"Many times. And many different tales." Ricardo smiled queerly at Howdy. "Have you not heard the true story, or at least the story that Don Rafael tells and the story your father knew?"

Howdy shook his head. "Never heard of him till Nono mentioned him."

"That is strange, because, in a way, the story concerns you."

"How do you mean, Ricardo?"

"When that doctor came to Mexico, he met Don Rafael Reyes. He told a strange and tragic story to Rafael, my uncle. And together with some money and certain documents, he gave into the keeping of my uncle, a child. Rafael raised this child as his own. She married James Merchant, your father. It was for her that Shirley Reyes was named."

"This doctor's daughter was my mother?"

"Yes. Doctor Macklin, for that was his real name, then hid himself in the mountains with his books and the burden of his bitter memories. Few men save the Yaquis ever saw his face. They said that he found much gold, and that he lived a hermit's life. And there he died, somewhere in the mountains, without a man of his own race to grip his hand."

"Why did he hide away like that, Ricardo? What had he done?"

"That," said Ricardo, "is something that only my uncle Rafael can tell you."

"I wonder if that's why my father wanted me to go to the Reyes rancho?"

"Perhaps. It is most likely, Howard."

"Do you reckon that Nono suspects that the hermit was my grandfather?"

"*Quien sabe?* Who knows? There is a mystery behind it all that no man save Rafael Reyes can unravel. I have heard him, many times, express the wish that some day the son of James Merchant would return to the rancho. Don Rafael feared, perhaps, that he might die before you came. And the secret of Doctor Macklin would be buried with him."

Howdy nodded. "I'll be back in a little while. There is something I want to ask of the Yaqui chief. I won't be gone long."

10: The Ruby Stiletto

Since childhood, Howdy had wondered, as any boy might wonder, about the mother of whom big Jim Merchant had so many times spoken. She had died when Howdy was small. His memory of her was vague. But he knew that his father had worshipped her, that her death had been tragic, and that there was some dark mystery behind it all, a mystery that had to do with Jim Merchant's turning outlaw. It had always greatly puzzled Howdy, and, while the years spent at the Muleshoe Bar Ranch had blurred his curiosity and crowded out much of his boyhood dreams, he had never ceased to think about that mystery that his father had kept from him. He had always wondered why Jim Merchant spoke of Rafael Reyes as his nearest friend and the friend whom Howdy should seek. Now he wanted to find Rafael Reyes and learn the secret that he had steadfastly kept all these long years.

He caught up with Nono, who scowled at him in an almost unfriendly manner. "Your place," said the chief bluntly, "is behind with the woman and the little Mexican.

Why do you ride up here, then?"

"To tell you," said Howdy quietly, "that I am the grandson of Doctor Macklin."

The Yaqui's face did not change expression. The black eyes, fierce, penetrating, stared hard at the white man.

"That is why you came into the mountains, then?" The Yaqui's voice was harsh.

"No. I just now learned from Ricardo Reyes that Doctor Macklin was my grandfather. Until you spoke of him, I had never heard of him."

"How does that little Mexican know so much?"

"From his uncle, Rafael Reyes, who raised Doctor Macklin's daughter. She became the wife of my father, and my mother."

"Prove what you say," said Nono fiercely.

"Don Rafael Reyes holds the only proof."

"Many men would like to be the grandson of Doctor Macklin," said Nono. "Many men would risk death and torture to be proven the grandson of Doctor Macklin. You are not the first man who has said that he bore that relationship to the hermit who was my friend. Others have made that claim. Do you know what became of them? They died. I killed them with my own hands. Just as I must kill you if you do not prove what you say. Now go back to your woman and the little Mexican. Speak no word to any man about what you said to me. If you do not prove, through Rafael Reyes, what you claim, then you will die."

"That's fair enough. But if we're goin' to see Rafael Reyes alive, we better git there in time to he'p him clean up on this Guzman tribe."

"We double our speed from here on." Nono gave sharp commands. The column of Yaquis hit a long trot. They leaned forward as they rode, eyes glittering, faces set, eager for battle against the enemy they hated.

Now Howdy rejoined Shirley and Ricardo. He grinned a little.

"I got Nono to shake a laig. We'll git there in time to be lendin' Don Rafael a helpin' hand."

Briefly, Howdy told Ricardo and Shirley of his conversation with the Yaqui chief. They listened carefully. Shirley's face looked oddly pale, and her eyes were wide with fear. But Howdy did not notice, so engrossed was he in this new mystery.

"So," he said lightly, "if Don Rafael can't produce the proof that I'm Doctor

Macklin's grandson, it looks like I'll have to do battle with our Nono amigo."

"Howard," said Shirley huskily, "why did you not talk to me before you spoke so freely to that terrible Yaqui? *Madre de Dios,* you have surely signed your own death warrant."

"How come, Shirley?"

"Because, Howard, those documents that you need are gone. They have been stolen. There is only the spoken word of my father to vouch for what you say."

"And the word of a Mexican," added Ricardo bitterly, "is of no value to the earless Nono, the chief of the Yaquis."

"When were the papers stolen, Shirley? And also tell me who stole 'em."

"When? *Quien sabe,* Howard. The papers were in a steel box that was buried somewhere under the floor of our little chapel at the rancho. My father had had no occasion to look for them. They had been buried there many years. A few weeks ago, for some reason which he did not reveal, father removed the tile beneath which the steel box had been hidden for many years. The box was gone. In its place was a Spanish stiletto that was covered with old bloodstains. He showed me the dagger. Under the ugly stains, the steel was covered with finely

111

etched inscriptions. The handle was of pearl and gold, beautifully set with rubies."

"What did it mean, Shirley, that knife?" asked Howdy.

"That I do not know. But I am sure that father knew, because he was terribly upset. It is my opinion that he knew the owner of that dagger with its old bloodstains. You know, of course, the manner of your mother's death, Howard?"

Howdy shook his head. "Dad never told me."

"She was stabbed to death one night in the patio there at our rancho. Her murderer was never found, so far as I know. It is my belief, Howard, that this dagger that was found where the steel box had been buried, was the same dagger that killed your mother. While it may sound like the silly idea of an imaginative girl, I cannot help feeling that the same dagger had to do with some terrible tragedy in the life of Doctor Macklin. I feel that my father knows that, because after he had shown it to me, his face was the colour of dead ashes.

" 'May the son of James Merchant, the grandson of Doctor Macklin,' he said in a voice that made me shudder, 'be brave and strong and able to meet that which fate holds in wait for him. May the Senor Dios lend him the strength of hand and the stoutness of heart to do that which Rafael Reyes is now too old to do.' "

11: The Indio

Mystery inside a mystery! Howdy was a little bewildered by the knowledge of these things. Here he was, on the eve of discovering that secret behind his life, so deep that his father had never told him. But, with the revelation of that secret, it would appear that something sinister, dangerous and of powerful nature would confront him. Would it be his task to take up the short end of some terrible feud? What did that jewelled dagger with its bloodstains mean? If that was the knife that had killed his mother, then it was obviously up to the son to kill the owner of that knife or be killed in the attempt.

A few weeks ago, Howdy Merchant had been a carefree cowboy, roping wild steers, riding broncs, swapping yarns across campfires. He found himself wishing now that Black Jack was here to sort of advise him. He felt young and too inexperienced to cope with something that he did not at all understand. Mystery and knives and hidden documents were altogether beyond his ken. Yet he felt himself drawn into its dark intrigue as if by some unseen hand.

He was riding behind Shirley and Ricardo, deep in thought. Now, for some reason, guided by some strange instinct that becomes a sort of sixth sense to men who live in the mountains and on the desert, he turned his head quickly.

Behind him rode one of the blue-eyed Indians. Howdy's quick turn surprised the man who was glaring at the cowboy's back, a half-drawn Luger pistol in his hand.

In a flash, Howdy's gun covered the surprised Indio.

The blue-eyed man dropped his gun. Fear blanched his face. "Don't shoot!"

"So," said Howdy grimly, "you speak my language. And you've bin stickin' close enough behind to mebbe so ketch what we've bin talkin' about. I ketch you when you're just about to sink a nice hunk of lead between my shoulders. Now, mister, you'll talk, or I'll shoot you square between them off-coloured eyes. If you're an Injun, I'm a Chinaman."

"Don't shoot!" The man broke into the Mexican tongue now. He explained rapidly that he knew but half a dozen words of English. That he was an Indio. That he had been examining the gun to see if it was fouled by the dust. He had meant no harm. If the Senor Americano doubted his honesty, then the Senor Americano could shoot him now. But he would be killing a man who had done no harm.

Now another blue-eyed Indio came up, followed by the black-eyed, cruel-lipped Yaquis. Their hands were on their guns. Their eyes stared at the gringo cowboy. And Howdy knew that he was looking into the eyes of death itself.

They had halted. Shirley's face was white as chalk. Ricardo's slim hand held a gun. If this was the end, then they would die together. A tense, dangerous movement. Howdy's grey eyes were hard, steady, a little contemptuous. His thumb pulled back the hammer of his .45.

"The first man to die, mister," he told the blue-eyed fellow, "will be you. Tell those others to go back where they belong. You're the lieutenant, and they'll do what you say. I'm speakin' plain American gringo talk, mister, and you're understandin' every word I say. Call off your dawgs, feller, and behave, or I'll put a bullet into your spine where it hurts. It'll take you hours to die and every second will seem like ten years, because when a man's shot in that certain spot, he suffers torture. My daddy taught me never to forget a man's face. I'm recollectin' your face, understand, even if you ain't wearin' a beard. You might pass for an Indio with the Yaquis, but I read your brand different. Do I win?"

The man touched his lips with a dry tongue. His eyes showed fear. He nodded and gave the others a quick, hoarse order in the Mexican tongue. They dropped back sullenly.

"From here on," said Howdy, "you ride in front of me. I reckon you know what'd happen to you if I told Nono that you wasn't an Indio? That you used to ride with Mike Guzman's gang, and that you're a border skunk that was so low-down that you couldn't trail with your own kind? You might fool these blue-eyed Injuns, and you might fool the Yaquis, but you ain't foolin' me, because I got good reason to remember you. You was with Mike Guzman the night my dad was killed and the night I got away from you. I'd kill you now only that I'm goin' to need you after a while. But if you want to keep on livin', stay in front of me and act peaceful. One little careless mistake on your part, and you'll die slow and hard — hear me?"

The man nodded. "I'll behave, Merchant."

"Do them others back there savvy gringo talk?"

"No."

"Then you kin tell me some things I want to know."

"About what?" asked the man.

"First, what are you doin' here with these Yaquis?"

"Gettin' what I can. I seen a chance to work in and I did. I quit Guzman."

"That's a lie. The truth, you snake, or you'll git what I promised you."

"Mike sent me."

"A dirty spy, huh?"

The man nodded. "But I'm an Indio, the same as the others. Only I was brought to the border when I was a baby, by some Mexicans. I was raised at Juarez and El Paso. Then I went back to my own people and lived there some. Mike sent me here to find out things."

"What things, you double-dealin' snake?"

"About a gold mine. But I ain't found out nothing. Nono don't let nobody know where he gets gold from."

Now Howdy felt that the man was telling something of the truth. He was running down another clue that had to do with Doctor Macklin's gold.

"What made Mike think the Yaquis had gold?"

"Who, in this end of Mexico, does not know it, senor? It is no secret that the great

Nono comes in to town with lumps of gold the size of a man's fist. Mike wants to find that mine. So he sent me here to join the Yaquis. And, believe me, it is no easy life. No sleep, no good grub, no mescal or women. Always on the move. I'm sick of it. I hope I can run away and get back to Juarez where I can get a job in town. I can tend bar and gamble and have fun there."

"And knock drunken cowboys on the head," added Howdy. "You're just a snake, feller. A stool pigeon, a squealer, a pale-eyed dog with a yellow back. Ride on ahead or I'll shoot you in the back. The sight of you turns a man's stomach."

When the man had ridden on, Ricardo smiled thinly. "Too bad, Howard, you did not kill that blue-eyed one. He will make you bad trouble."

Howdy nodded. "He was too cowardly to kill, my friend."

"And cowards are always more dangerous than brave men."

12: The Brush

They crossed the Santa Maria River and pushed on, keeping to a steady trot. This was the western boundary line of the big Reyes grant. At the river, when they watered their horses, Nono joined them. Howdy noticed that the treacherous Indio had disappeared, and the cowboy reckoned that the man had run away, driven by the fear that this hottempered gringo would tell the Yaqui chief that there was a Guzman spy in camp.

Ignoring Shirley and Ricardo, Nono addressed Howdy. "Has your woman any friends at Galena, a few miles below here on the river?"

"None that I would trust," Shirley replied.

"There will be fighting inside an hour," said the Yaqui harshly. "A woman will be in the way."

Shirley's eyes blazed. "We are not here of our own will, Yaqui."

Howdy's hand was on his gun. But the Yaqui chief merely smiled thinly. It was a smile that might mean almost anything. Then he mounted his horse and resumed his place at the head of the moving column.

"I am sorry, Howard, that I spoke so," said Shirley, "but I am not accustomed to being so rudely addressed by Yaquis."

Howdy nodded. "I *sabe*, Shirley, but talkin' back to him don't he'p us much. Gosh knows, I hate to see you here. But we'll make the best of it. When the fight starts, Ricardo and I will be with you. As long as we're alive, nobody will ever hurt you."

Now Nono sent back word for Howdy to join him at the head of the column.

"Tell your chief," said the cowpuncher grimly, "that my place is here with my woman, and I'm staying here."

"Those who disobey the orders of Nono, die," said the Yaqui.

"Tell Nono that I stay where I am."

The earless chief did not send back any reply to Howdy's bold defiance of his orders. They rode along as they had been riding, guarded by the Yaquis and one blue-eyed Indio who seemed uneasy. They had missed that other blue-eyed one who had made his escape. A surly mannered Yaqui had taken charge in the Indio's absence, and he eyed Howdy with venomous eyes.

Now, from the distance, came the unmistakable sounds of rifle fire. Advance scouts had already brought back the news that Mike Guzman and Don Rafael were engaged in a hard battle on the banks of the Rio Carmen. Another scout brought word that the other Guzman and his rurales were moving in on the Reyes forces from below, maneuvering to make a flank attack.

Now the Yaquis were more restless than ever. These fearless warriors of the Sierra Madres were itching to stain their hands with Mexican blood. They were working themselves up to that fighting pitch. They were as wicked-looking a crew as ever a man could imagine, and they loved fighting.

Now the column moved along faster. Even their chief could not fully control them as they pressed forward.

The fighting was nearer now. Mike Guzman's men on this side of the Rio Carmen, Rafael Reyes and his vaqueros on the opposite side. But the captain of the rurales was late. Coming in by a roundabout course, his arrival was delayed. In a black rage, Mike cursed the lateness of the rurales. Those vaqueros under Rafael Reyes were fighting like men who meant to win or die. A number of Mike's men, wearied and disgusted by the past few days of searching for a woman and a gringo about whom they cared nothing, their nerves rubbed raw by their leader's ill temper, were putting up a listless fight. Mike Guzman, half-drunk, perhaps a little insane, cursed them. Two or three times he had ordered them to cross the river and attack, but they had refused to move from their shelter. To cross that river meant that they would lay themselves open to the deadly gunfire of the enemy. Mike Guzman raved like a man gone mad. He had killed two of his officers who had dared question his judgment.

Now came that which chilled the blood of his men, the dreaded Yaqui war cry. Completely demoralized, they were caught between two enemies, just as the rurales began their flank attack on the Reyes army.

Pandemonium broke loose. The din of the battle was terrific now, though, save for the attacking Yaquis who made no attempt to conceal their movements, the men were fighting from shelter. The rurales, on foot now, were fighting from behind trees and rocks. Under the relentless charge of the Yaquis, many Guzman followers were taking to the river or fleeing madly up or down the river — only to be caught by the Yaquis who raced pell-mell after them.

Now a lone man raced for safety,

mounted on a splendid, fleet-footed horse. The silver trappings of his saddle glistened in the bright sunlight. Mike Guzman was running away!

With wild yells of dismay as they took to their heels, the Guzman renegades were in headlong flight, spurring for safety. Made desperate by fear, they shot their way through the Yaqui line. Their horses, fresher than those of the Yaquis, were now widening the distance between them and the blood-thirsty Yaquis.

At the start of the attack, Howdy and Ricardo had placed themselves alongside the girl. Their guns covered their Yaqui bodyguard.

"Go!" Howdy barked at them. "Pronto! Leave us alone!"

They exchanged glances, nods. These warlike Yaquis had no desire to linger behind with the three captives. With a wild yell, they spurred ahead to join the battle.

"Come on," said Howdy. "Follow me."

They turned back now, hunting a place where Shirley would be safe from the flying bullets that droned and snarled above them. Now they found a dense clump of brush and, hiding their horses as best they could, they crawled into the shelter. Shirley, white, badly frightened, leaned against Howdy's shoulder. He felt the wild beating of her heart.

"We're safe here," he said, grinning, though he knew that they could not remain hidden long before someone would find them.

They could hear the screams of men dying, the blood-curdling yelling of the Yaquis, the rattle of rifles. Now a man on horseback came tearing past. Howdy's gun raised. He took careful aim, then, with a muttered curse, he lowered his carbine.

"That," he said bitterly, "was Mike Guzman."

"Why did you not shoot, then?" cried Ricardo.

"Because, my friend, I don't kill from ambush. I don't shoot men in the back."

"But that one! That yellow dog! That vile beast! *Madre de Dios,* and you let him pass because you do not shoot from the brush!"

The Mexican's words were like a whiplash. Howdy's nerves pulled taut; he turned on Ricardo like a fighting dog.

"Who are you, anyhow, to tell me when to shoot? My kind of men aren't murderers. Get that and get it, now!" For a moment, the two men faced one another. Howdy's fist was clenched. Then Shirley moved between them.

"Have we not enough trouble without this — this silly quarrelling?"

Howdy turned away, still seething with anger. Ricardo glared at the cowboy's back for a moment, then the anger died from his eyes.

"I am a fool, Howard. Forgive my words. You have been brave. Only for you, we —"

"Then let's forget it," said Howdy, without turning his head, "and keep quiet. Here comes a smear of 'em."

Crouched, tense, they waited there in the brush. Men on horseback were tearing past. Now, behind them, the yelling Yaquis.

"Looks like Guzman's wolves are mostly coyotes," muttered Howdy.

The fighting on this side of the river was about over. Across on the other side, the rurales were likewise faring badly. The Reyes men were driving them back.

From the shelter of the brush, Howdy saw Nono ride past, shouting orders to follow and kill the Guzman riders. Now the firing dwindled to a few scattered shots, the groans of wounded men, shouted orders from across the river.

"Ricardo," said Howdy, "I think it's safe enough now for you to slip around and get word to your uncle that we're here. I'll stay with Shirley."

Ricardo nodded. The next moment he was gone. Shirley and Howdy were left alone.

"You must not think too badly of poor Ricardo," said the girl. "He is not like you, accustomed to fighting. He is more expert with the violin than the gun. Please, Howard, do not remember what he said."

"We was both kinda excited, Shirley. Ricardo's a game little rooster. He just ain't cut out for this kind of a racket."

"Ricardo would not have hesitated to shoot Mike Guzman in the back. He does not understand your code. I am glad, Howard, that you have such a code. That you are such a brave man."

Her hand had gripped his. Her dark eyes were soft, alight with some emotion that made the cowpuncher suddenly reckless. His arms went around her. His lips met hers. Nor did Shirley resist that embrace. Rather, she returned the fervour of that kiss.

"The Yaqui," said Howdy huskily, "called you my woman. Was he right, Shirley? Will you marry me?"

Shirley covered her face with her hands. "Howard, Howard," she whispered brokenly, "what have I done? May the *Senor Dios* forgive my sin."

"What sin, Shirley?" he asked, almost roughly.

"The sin of loving you. Because I do love you, my Howard. No, no, do not kiss me again. It is wrong, my Howard."

"Why is it wrong?"

"Because I am betrothed to another. One of my own people. We are soon to be married."

"You love him, Shirley?"

"Love him? No. But we are Castilians. For many years it has been arranged between our families that I should marry Camillo Vasquez. I cannot disobey the wishes of my parents. It is arranged by them. It was very wrong for me to let myself love you."

"But you do love me, Shirley?"

"It would be a lie to say that I do not love you. But now you must help me put that love from my heart."

"I'll be hanged if I will." Howdy's arm reached out for her again. But a shout from near-by made him draw back from his purpose.

With a glad cry, Shirley had leaped from the brush. Now she was in the strong arms of a tall, white-maned, white-bearded man. Tears wet the cheeks of Rafael Reyes as he embraced his daughter.

Now another man had ridden up, a younger man, straight-backed, handsome, arrogant of eye and bearing. This swaggering young caballero swung from his saddle. Now he was embracing Shirley. He kissed her almost fiercely, then let her struggle from his embrace.

"Are you not glad to see me?" he asked, a little petulantly.

"Of course I am, Camillo. I am — upset and quite exhausted and not myself."

Howdy bit back some muttered curse and crawled from the brush. Don Rafael greeted him warmly, embracing him.

"Ricardo told me, Howard, about how bravely you have acted. I can never be free of my eternal debt to you, my son."

Now Rafael Reyes introduced Howdy to the young caballero, whose dark eyes studied the gringo cowboy with a none too cordial glance.

"I am likewise in your debt, senor," he said, measuring his words, "for rescuing my fiancee."

"Keep the change," said Howdy. "You missed a good show by not being there when it happened."

A dark flush mounted the cheeks of Camillo Vasquez. "I would have saved you your trouble had I known that my fiancee was in danger. I was working with the rodeo, gathering cattle that we took away from Mike Guzman." His voice was cold, formal, unfriendly. Howdy itched to take a good hard swing at that red mouth that twisted in a faint sneer.

Now Ricardo came up, his cased violin under his arm, his white teeth flashing, dark eyes alight. "I tell you, uncle," he cried impetuously, "Howard is the bravest man I have ever known. He did not even fear the Yaquis."

"Ricardo makes a lot out of a little thing," grinned the cowpuncher, enjoying Camillo's unguarded scowl. "It wasn't much at all, Don Rafael."

"But it was, though, father," cried Shirley. "We are all of us deeply in his debt."

Howdy felt his ears getting hot. He was glad when a score or more of Don Rafael's men rode up.

Now, from the other direction there rode a solitary figure. It was the earless Nono, riding alone. In silence, they all watched his approach. The Mexicans, some with drawn guns, others ready to draw. But the Yaqui chief came on, contemptuous of their hostile attitude.

Now Nono pulled rein. Howdy spoke to Rafael Reyes.

"Don Rafael, the chief of the Yaquis rides

here alone and under a truce. Tell your men that."

Don Rafael did so. Now the fearless chief faced Howdy. His black eyes glittered with reddish lights. There was blood on his hands and his clothes and the ugly-looking machete.

"In a week's time, Senor Gringo," he said coldly, "I will ask for that proof to the claim you made. I have already told you the penalty you must pay if you have lied. But if you can, as you claim, show proof of your claim, then you will be the richest man in Chihuahua. Adios."

Nono whirled his horse and rode away at a lope, without a single backward glance.

"Of what claim did he speak, my son, if I may be so bold as to ask?"

"I told him that I was the grandson of Doctor Macklin."

Rafael Reyes gave a sharp exclamation. His dark, seamed face took on an ashen pallor. He seemed about to speak, then thought better of it.

"Tonight, my son," he said hoarsely, "you and I shall talk. You and I — alone." He turned his horse and nodded for Howdy to ride with him. As the cowpuncher mounted his horse, he glanced at Shirley and Camillo Vasquez. Shirley was pale, her

131

eyes filled with pain. But Camillo was smiling and the expression on his face was one of triumph that the cowboy did not like.

Scowling, angry, but filled with a dogged determination to fight this thing through, the cowboy joined Don Rafael. The thought of Shirley riding alone with the red-mouthed, arrogant, handsome Camillo put him in a bad humour. Never in his life had he so ached to hit a man.

"And I will, before I'm done," he told himself. "I'll pound that grin off his mouth. I'll close his purty eyes. And I'll make that map uh his over into what'll look like yesterday's battleground."

"It is good to have you with us, Howard," Don Rafael was saying. "I hope you will always remain."

Plainly, Don Rafael did not care to open the subject of Howdy's ancestry until that night. The old Mexican had regained his self-composure and, as they rode, they talked of cattle and horses and the thieving of Mike Guzman.

"I hoped to find his body among the dead, Howard, but the black-hearted rascal got away. They are too well mounted for the Yaquis. We'll hear more from him, I'm afraid."

"He had a close escape this time, sir. Mebbe so he won't be so lucky the next trip. I came down here to he'p you all I could. So far I haven't had much chance to do anything. With Mike Guzman and his brother dead, the others will not have the grit to keep on. And the rubbin' out of two men don't sound like too hard a job."

Rafael Reyes smiled tolerantly. "More difficult than you imagine, my son. He is powerful and has protection."

To Howdy, the older man's tone was that of a man beaten. He was too old to carry on an active campaign. Capturing Mike Guzman was a job that required youth.

"I am, as you perceive, Howard, no longer young." Don Rafael seemed to read the cowboy's thoughts.

"Camillo Vasquez is young enough." The words slipped out of Howdy's mouth before he thought.

Don Rafael shot him a shrewd, sidelong glance.

"You do not like Camillo."

"No more than he likes me, sir."

"That is too bad, my son. I had hoped you two would become real friends. He is like one of the family, betrothed, as you perhaps know, to my daughter. And I always think of you as my own son. I am sorry you cannot like him."

"I'm sorry on your account, sir. But I pick my own friends, and he don't just happen to be among 'em. I'd be a liar if I said I'd try to like him."

Don Rafael nodded slowly. "It is best, always, to be truthful."

"I don't like to hurt your feelings, sir. And if I see that my bein' at the ranch makes things unpleasant, I'll pull out, of course. I figgered on stayin' just long enough to wipe out this Mike Guzman. When he's planted, I'll ride on back to the outfit where I belong."

"You belong with us, Howard. When you speak of leaving, you make an old man very sad and lonely. We will talk of something more pleasant, no?"

"Yes, sir." Howdy rolled and lighted a cigarette. He felt that he had hurt this fine old man more than he had ever intended. He had spoken like a young, thick-skulled idiot. Now he told Don Rafael as much, forcing a grin to hide the dull ache in his cowboy's heart.

Don Rafael's understanding smile forgave him. "I know your father, Howard. You are very much his son."

13: The Story

That night, Howdy Merchant heard, from the white-bearded lips of Rafael Reyes, the story of Doctor Macklin and his daughter who had become the mother of Howard Merchant.

"I first came upon Doctor Macklin and the six-year-old child when he was outfitting in El Paso, preparing to go into Mexico. My wife was with me, and the child had taken an instant fancy to her there in the store where the doctor and I were both purchasing camp supplies. The doctor, a handsome, grey-haired man of perhaps forty, seemed strangely perturbed about the child making friends with my wife. He spoke to the little girl with what, to us, seemed an unjustified harshness. Then I caught a strange look in his fine brownish eyes. It was a look of fear. Terrible, panic-stricken fear. And he hurried away with the child without completing his purchases.

"It was very odd, and, on our way to the rancho, my wife and I spoke of it several times. At that time we did not know his identity, of course. But his strange behaviour was not easily forgotten, and the man's eyes haunted me. But as this was the last part of our honeymoon, we were not too greatly absorbed in the man and child. Back at the rancho, with the fiestas and the entertaining of our many friends who came to welcome us, we were quite busy. And so it was that we had almost completely forgotten the incident in the store at El Paso when the man and child came back into our lives.

"Some vaqueros brought in the man and child. The man was more dead than alive, but the child was quite healthy. He had starved himself of water that she might not suffer. Lost, their mules strayed, they would have died had not my vaqueros found them.

"For many days the man lay ill, half-delirious. And I knew that it was not only exhaustion, hunger, and thirst that kept him ill. For in his delirium, he tossed and moaned and cried out aloud about blood on his hands. We feared for his sanity. Obviously, he was haunted by some terrible secret. And I felt that something of the secret was in the heavy oiled-silk package that I had taken from his money-belt and put away.

"The child, who said her name was Shirley Macklin, seemed to worship my wife. They became inseparable. We grew to love her as our own.

"One night, in a rational hour, the sick man told me something of his story, fearing that he might die with the secret untold. He knew us to be his friends and was moved beyond words by Shirley's deep affection for my wife.

"He said that his name was Doctor Macklin. He had a splendid practice as a surgeon in New York City. He had fallen in love with a famous actress, Shirley Sanderson, and that love had been returned. They married, and she retired from the stage. A year later, their girl baby was born and they were supremely happy. His practice increased. He became famous as a surgeon. But as his practice increased, he was taken away from home more and more. His wife, longing for the social activities of her former life, perhaps piqued by the lack of attention given her by this man who would come home at all hours of the night, too utterly exhausted to talk, became discontented.

"He was too busy, too ambitious, too weary of body and brain to notice her discontent — until one night he returned home to find her gone. She had taken the baby, then three years old. There was a letter there on his pillow from her. She was going away somewhere. She would apply for a divorce. Then she planned to resume her career as an actress.

"The blow was a terrific one to the surgeon. Too late he realized that he had neglected her, that he had sacrificed love for ambition — an old story, to be sure. It smashed Doctor Macklin. It shattered his nerves, wrecked him completely. He gave up his practice. Closing up his home, he set out to find the woman he loved and his child. For almost three years, he hunted her in vain. He did not know that she had obtained a divorce in some foreign country and had remarried.

"His health broken, his lungs ravaged by tuberculosis, he was forced to seek the dry climate of the Southwest. His lungs were healing. He was convalescing. And it was when he was sitting in the sunlight at an Arizona sanitorium, that he saw his former wife and his child. The woman was but a white shadow of the beautiful Shirley Sanderson. She was dying.

"So they were united once more, but only for a few days, for she died there in his arms, forgiving, forgiven. And Doctor Macklin was left with the care of the little child Shirley.

"It was from the child he learned the causes contributing to the death of his former wife. The doctor and nurses, under the fierce questioning of Doctor Macklin, now told him the truth. Her second husband, a blackguard from somewhere in South America, scion of a powerful and wealthy family, had tired of her. He had beaten her, starved her, insulted her in every conceivable manner. On a trumped-up charge of infidelity, he had divorced her and literally kicked her out of home, practically penniless, with a small child to support. Some kind friends had discovered her and the child starving in a tenement house. These friends, members of the theatrical profession, had given her money and sent her to Arizona.

"Now began another long trail for Doctor Macklin. Leaving the child in good care at Tucson, he purchased a revolver and set out to find this blackguard. He found him in New York. And there, in the man's palatial home, he sent six bullets into the heart of that human cur. Then he fled New York, found his child, and came into Mexico.

"But the family of the South American were, as I said, powerful and wealthy. They hired many detectives. Even at my rancho, Doctor Macklin was no longer safe. It was then that he gave the child into our keeping and buried himself in the Sierra Madres. I never saw him after. Now and then, news of the hermit of the Sierra Madres reached us but, as he sent us no word, we never connected the hermit with our Doctor Macklin, not until, years later, a Yaqui brought a sealed letter of unusual bulk and a leather sack filled with pure gold nuggets. The letter bore my name. It was a lengthy epistle that thanked us, at great length, for what we had done for him and for his daughter. He seemed content to live out his life among the Yaquis, shutting himself from the world, even from the child he loved. Perhaps he was not quite right in his mind. Certainly, he'd had enough tragedy to crack his brain.

"The gold was used to educate the child Shirley. She loved Mexico, and could ride with the best vaquero. Books bored her. Her love was all for horses and cattle and the life of the open range. Nor did it surprise us when she announced her desire to marry Jim Merchant, a neighbour of ours over on the Rio Carmen. Because we were very fond of this young cowman, and because he was of her own people, we approved the marriage, though she was hardly more than a child, and he was not yet twenty. But then, here in Mexico, we marry young. Ah, what a grand fiesta that was, here at the rancho! Even friends from as far away as Arizona and Texas came. And there, Howard, was where we made the very grave mistake, because it was announced widely in the papers that Shirley Macklin Reyes, adopted daughter of Rafael Reyes, was married to James Merchant, cattleman. And this bit of news finally reached the notice of some of the members of that family of the South American.

"We had forgotten that those relatives of the dead South American might still seek revenge, and we were all away on the big fall rodeo, when the tragedy happened. Shirley was staying at our rancho with her baby boy. Save for a few servants, no men were at the rancho. Shirley had put her son to bed and had gone into the patio to watch the moonlight. And it was there they found her, the following morning, stabbed to death.

"Jim Merchant was like a man stricken with some terrible malady that left him without tongue or without the power to move, when he heard of his wife's death. Stunned, bewildered, he was like that at the funeral and for many days afterwards. No man ever heard him laugh again. One morning, almost a month after his wife's death, Jim Merchant had gone. No need to tell us where or why he had left. Gone with him was the jewelled dagger that had been found buried in Shirley Merchant's back.

"Almost a year passed, and we heard no word of Jim Merchant. Then the El Paso papers were filled with the news of the killing of two wealthy South Americans who had a ranch in California. They had been shot down by a cowboy who was breaking polo ponies for them. He had given them a chance to use their guns, but had killed them. A third and younger brother he had let live. To this third brother, he handed a jewelled dagger stained with old blood. Then he had mounted the best horse they owned and had ridden away. There was a picture of this cowboy on the front page, taken at some rodeo. It was a good likeness of Jim Merchant.

"Another year passed. Then, one morning, when I went to the corrals, there was Jim Merchant. He looked ten years older. His hair had become very grey, and his eyes had lost their laughter. He was now, as we knew, an outlaw with a price on his head. He had found a good hiding-place and had come to get his son. You were still a small boy, Howard. He carried you away in his arms. You were too young then to re-member it now.

"Later, you rode here with him. When we begged him to leave you with us, he said that must be for you to decide. You chose to go with your father. And that, my son, is the story."

"All but the theft of the box and that dagger put in its place," said Howdy, after a long silence.

"Yes. That is something I cannot understand. I buried the steel box under the floor of the chapel years ago, many years ago, perhaps twelve or fifteen years ago, Howard. Besides the documents proving that you are the legal grandson of Doctor Macklin, there was a fair-sized fortune in gold and securities that had been your mother's, and which Jim Merchant wanted you to have when you became of age. The thief who stole that strongbox got away with perhaps a hundred thousand dollars or more."

"And it was just lately that you found out the box was gone?"

"Yes. I was in Casas Grandes about two weeks or so ago. A Texan who tended bar at the Cantina Juarez told me that you were probably on your way to pay me a visit. One of Jeff Trainor's men had told him. The cowboy had met a friend of yours in El Paso, so this Texan Jones said. Beyond that, I could learn nothing more.

"When I returned home, I decided to dig up the buried strongbox. Loosening the old tiles, I lifted them from their places. Instead of the box, which was of considerable size, there was but a gaping hole. And in that hole was the dagger that had taken the life of your mother."

14: Camillo — A Busy Bee

That was the strange tale told by Don Rafael Reyes to Howdy Merchant as the two men sat together in the private study of the old don. For a long time, the two were silent, Howdy smoking thoughtfully, Don Rafael sipping his wine and puffing at his cigar.

"What was the name of this South American family?" asked Howdy.

"The name is Duarte."

"The name of the youngest son, the one my father left the dagger with?"

"Alphonso Duarte. If you read the papers you find his name often enough. He is worth millions. And he is known as a heavy spender, a drunkard, an excellent rider, and his last escapade was in France when he wounded some Italian in a duel with swords. He has a racing stable, polo ponies, beautiful estates in California and Canada and in South America. He has one of the finest yachts afloat, a villa in the Riviera, a home in Bermuda. It is hardly possible or probable that such a young man would take the trouble to steal that box, if that is what you mean."

"But he had the dagger, sir."

"Yes. Yes, that is true. Alphonso Duarte had the dagger. But it taxes the imagination, my son, to think that such a young spendthrift and lover of luxury would bear the discomforts of such a task as coming here to steal that box and its contents. Besides, it has been said that he hated his older brothers and was not at all grieved at their passing. Perhaps that is why Jim Merchant spared him."

"Well, I give 'er up," said Howdy, shrugging. "But it puts me in a tight fix with the Yaqui chief. He's bad medicine, and he means just about what he says." He grinned and got to his feet.

"I reckon there's nothin' more to be said about it tonight, anyhow. And I know that you're tired and need some rest."

Howdy left Don Rafael in his study and walked out into the moonlit patio.

It was a beautiful night, with a sky that was thick with stars. The ancient tile fountain tinkled like the chiming of tiny silver bells. There was the odour of orange blossoms. The old tiled walk wandered among the tropical fruit trees and shrubs and flowers. And Howdy thought of that beautiful girl who had been his mother, lying there on the old tiled walk, her blood

146

staining the pathway. He felt sad and alone and strange here. The large patio was so beautiful, yet so unlike anything in his own life that had been exiled from beauty and softness. He thought of Shirley Reyes and the love she had confessed for him. He had hoped with a sort of aching hopelessness, that Shirley would be somewhere here in the patio. He gave a quick start as he heard someone moving towards him from the shadow of the bushes. Then, the next instant, his heart sank. It was Ricardo, not Shirley, who walked towards him.

"Shh!" whispered Ricardo. "I have been waiting for you, Howard. There is something I must tell you. Let us go to the corrals where the walls have no ears."

There was no mistaking the tenseness of little Ricardo's voice. Howdy followed him, out through the heavy old gate and towards the corrals.

Once he had made certain there were no eavesdroppers, Ricardo smiled a little confusedly. "You'll think I'm a fool, Howard. But I felt that I could not sleep until I had talked to you." His voice trembled a little with emotion. He gripped Howdy's hand in a fierce, strong pressure.

"Can you, first, forgive me for that so foolish remark I made that angered you?"

"Great gosh, Ricardo, that's forgotten, plumb. Both of us got excited."

"I cannot forget. I asked you to shoot a man in the back. But you do not shoot men in the back. That is because you are brave and strong of heart. And that is more than can be said of a certain fine-feathered game-cock that struts about sneering insults and making fun of one because that one does not fancy killings and bloodshed, getting drunk and picking quarrels with a knife blade. *Por Dios,* Howard, I promise you that before I see that strutting rooster marry my cousin, I will learn to shoot the *pistola,* and will, myself, challenge him to fight the duel. Since we were little boys, he has never failed the chance to humiliate me. Ah, and I am not blind, my good friend! I am not blind to what I read in her eyes and yours, there at the Yaqui camp when death hovered in the shadows and I played for you two those songs. I may not know one end of a gun from the other, Howard, but I know love when I see it. Ah, my friend, do not look so confused. I wish you luck and happiness, and I will do all that it is possible for such a misfit as I to do, to make your happiness come true."

Out of breath, Ricardo paused. His eyes, large and dark, were alight with strange, glowing fires. Howdy fought back an almost overwhelming desire to laugh, so wrought up had the little violinist become. Now Howdy saw the dark eyes narrow. Ricardo's voice dropped to an almost inaudible whisper.

"That strutting one, whom we shall not soil our tongues by naming, Howard, is not the mere braggart and swaggering caballero that he appears. There is in him a streak of villainy. And it is I, Ricardo Reyes, who shall prove it. I shall prove it to Don Rafael and to my cousin who must loathe his cursed touch. I tell you this, Howard, that you may take fresh hope. I will prove to my uncle and to any who will listen, that our gamecock is but a filthy buzzard."

"What has he done, Ricardo?"

Ricardo smiled knowingly. "That is something I must not mention until the proper time. Then I shall shout it to the four winds and cram the words down the throat of the blackguard. I will tell you this much, but you must not let it be known further. He is a secret friend to Mike Guzman. And he has been sharing the profits gained by Guzman from cattle stolen from Rafael Reyes. When the time is ripe, I shall throw proof of that in his pretty face!"

For all his slightness and his gentleness,

Ricardo Reyes now was all fighter. His eyes blazed, his voice shook with anger. Then he relaxed. He smiled as if ashamed of his outburst.

"For you, Howard, I would gladly risk my life. Because to me there is nothing so dear as my beloved cousin Shirley. I would give my life, my honour, my soul, to see her happy. I know, as well as does my dear cousin know in her heart, that you are the only man she loves or that she ever will love. And now, my friend, we must separate and go to our beds before someone finds us and suspects. That gamecock has his spies. Say no word of this to anyone, not even Shirley. I promise you, Howard, that unless I am killed by some murderer, I shall make you two happy."

Howdy, moved by the fervour and loyalty of the little musician, gripped his hand. "If it comes to fighting, Ricardo, that's my job. And if there's risk, you'll have to share it with me. Promise me that."

"I promise, Howard. Take hope. Keep a silent tongue. Await your time. *Buenas noches, amigo.*"

15: Some Little Night

But the moonlit night was to hold for Howdy Merchant still another surprise. When Ricardo had gone, leaving the cowpuncher there in the deep shadow of the old adobe corrals, Howdy watched his erstwhile companion blend into the shadows of the night.

Sleep now seemed impossible. Thoughts milled in his brain, like cattle milling after a stampede. He tried to make sense of it, but everything seemed jumbled and confused — Doctor Macklin, the murder of his daughter, Jim Merchant's scarred, broken life. Howdy understood now why his father had been the sort of man that he was. He told himself that he would carry on where Jim had left off. He was needed here — the Guzmans, Nono the Yaqui, and now the swaggering Camillo Vasquez, traitor to Rafael Reyes, if one could believe Ricardo, and certainly Ricardo was no liar. This sneering, black-eyed devil marry Shirley? Not while Howdy could prevent such a thing.

Howdy did not know how long he had been squatting there in the deep shadow, minutes or hours. He was abruptly jerked from his deep musings by the low-pitched, clear-noted call of a night bird. Now it sounded again. And Howdy, his nerves already strung to tautness, told himself that no bird had voiced that call. He waited. Now he thought he saw the shadow of a man there near the long adobe stable. Now that shadow moved again. It crossed a moonlit space. There was something familiar about that figure with its straw sombrero and its serape. Now the man's face lifted for an instant. Howdy gave a slight start of surprise.

The man was the blue-eyed Indio lieutenant who had run away from the Yaqui band. Had the Indio come here to kill him by way of revenge? If so, why had he given that signal? Had he brought along others to help him?

Howdy swore softly when he remembered that his guns were inside the house. Weaponless, he crouched low, determined to fight as long as there was life in his body. Let the blue-eyed Indio come close enough, and he'd make him over into something harmless.

Now another figure passed the moonlit strip — no mistaking that one, Camillo Vasquez. The two met there in the shadow.

"What in the name of the devil and his imps brings you here, fool? The risk is great. Don Rafael would not let you off with a mere flogging if he caught you here again. He has already warned you, Blanco, that if ever you set foot on the place again, he would have you shot. And what in Satan's name would he think of me if he caught me talking to you in the middle of the night? What news brings you here?"

"Some night I will slit the neck of that Rafael Reyes," muttered the Indio. "He had me flogged like a dog. I am no dog. Before ever a Spaniard set foot in Mexico, my ancestors were here. My people are as old as the pyramids here in Mexico, as old as the holes in the cliffs. No Spaniard can lay the lash across my bare back until the blood runs in a puddle at my feet. I shall kill him some night."

"Lower your voice, fool! Would you wake the whole household?"

Both spoke in Spanish. Howdy listened with both ears. What more was he to learn?

"I swear I will cut that Spaniard's heart from his ribs!"

"In due time, Indio. Not tonight. Again, what brings you here?"

"There is a gringo here. If ever you hope to get the gold you want, that gringo must

153

die. And that is not all. You will never get to marry that Senorita Reyes unless the gringo dies."

"What fool's talk is this?" asked Camillo, with a snarl.

"I care not for that word 'fool,' senor. It is not well digested. Nor do I lie when I say that with my own eyes I saw him hold her close to him at the camp of the Yaquis. With my own ears I heard the gringo claim her as his woman. With the same pair of ears I heard her admit that claim. I speak the truth, senor."

Howdy saw the Indio step backward a pace. There was a long, thin-bladed knife in his hand, its point in the Spaniard's ribs. Camillo's hand dropped away from his own knife. The Indio laughed unpleasantly, softly.

"I repeat, senor, I speak but the truth. The gringo must die, no?"

"He'll die, never fear. Now vamoose. Get back to the Yaquis."

"I cannot return to the Yaquis. The gringo recognized me as one of Guzman's riders. He has no doubt told Nono. I have no wish to be cut up alive and my pieces thrown to the buzzards. I ride from here to join Mike Guzman once more."

"You located the gold?"

"No. Only Nono knows where the gold is buried. That earless one knows well how to guard a secret. And now, patron, I need money. Not one peso in my pockets. I have risked my life and nearly lost it at the hands of that gringo. I need money."

"Money to get you drunk, eh?"

"Money to spend as I please, senor. Perhaps, as you say, I will get drunk. But mescal never loosens my tongue. I will never tell all that I know about the brave senor, Camillo Vasquez."

"Blackmail," said Camillo through his teeth. "Here's your money. Go!"

"*Adios, senor.*" There was a shade of mockery in the Indio's lowered voice. He went as silently as he had come. Now Camillo went back to the house. Once more, Howdy was alone.

"Take 'er all around and crossways," said the cowpuncher, grinning, as he slipped through the shadows to his own room, "it's bin some little night."

He undressed in the dark and climbed into bed, only to lie awake until dawn, despite the fact that he was utterly tired and needed sleep. Morning found him weary of brain, and his eyes ached. A *mozo* brought an earthenware jar of warm water, and, when he had shaved, he stood in a sort of box-like compartment while the same *mozo* doused him with cold water. A brisk rub-down, and he felt refreshed and ready to face what the new day might hold for him. It was not yet breakfast-time, and he walked out into the patio that was filled with the fragrance of flowers and the songs of birds. There was the constant whir of humming birds. The first rays of sunrise touched the blue-tinted walls.

"Good morning, Howard!"

Howdy gave a quick start. He had not seen Shirley, all but hidden in the foliage where she sat on a bench. He dropped down beside her, and, for a moment, their hands met in a clasp that was like a caress.

"I went to bed early, Howard. I knew that father would keep you talking until late. And I had no wish to sit and listen to — to a certain person." She made a funny little grimace that brought a grin to Howdy's face. Then he frowned.

"Was he ugly to you — about me, Shirley?"

"Camillo can be very sarcastic at times, and he is the most jealous man imaginable. Sometimes I loathe him, but I should not be talking so about the man I am to marry. That is wicked."

"You'll never marry him," said Howdy.

"But I must. It is the wish of my father, Howard."

"Well, we won't cross that crick till we git to it, Shirley." Howdy looked down at her, his eyes drinking in her beauty with a thirsty look that made the girl blush a little, though her eyes admitted that she did not at all mind the worship of the cowboy.

"Shirley," he said in a low tone, "if I can prove that Doctor Macklin was my grandfather, that Yaqui will hand over a lot of gold. At least, that's the way I figure it out. And then I'll no longer be just a stray cowboy without anything to offer you. I'm going to prove to that Yaqui, somehow, that the doctor was my grandfather. And that's not all I aim to do. But I'll have to work fast. That's why I'll have to be hitting the trail after breakfast."

"You mean you are leaving here?"

"It's a case of have to. I've got a heap of work to do."

"Where do you go when you leave?"

"That's hard to say. But I can't win a thing by sitting around here in the shade whittling a stick."

"I am afraid for you, Howard. What can one man do against so many enemies? They will kill you!"

"I hope not, honey. But I'm afraid for

157

you. Don't, for any reason, leave this ranch. And don't trust Camillo Vasquez. He's bin told that we love each other."

"I was going to tell him that, myself, Howard. I could not live a lie, and I intended telling him that, while I will marry him, I do not and cannot ever love him. But who told him? Ricardo?"

"No. The blue-eyed Indio. They met last night. But tell nobody. I told you because I wanted you to be on your guard. Watch Camillo. He makes snake tracks wherever he travels. Don't let him know that you suspect anything. Just keep your eyes and ears open. And — here he comes now."

Camillo Vasquez came along the tiled path. He halted when he saw them on the bench and bowed mockingly, his black eyes narrowed, an ugly smile on his handsome face.

"I beg your pardon for so rudely interrupting such a delightful little scene." His voice was harsh, insulting.

"Don't let us keep you, senor," said Howdy quietly.

"We are both guests under the roof of Don Rafael," said Camillo stiffly. "I hope, senor, that I shall have the pleasure of meeting you elsewhere at a more convenient time."

"Any place, and any time. Just now I have something to say to Shirley that concerns only us two," said Howdy. "As you said, you sort of horned in. Don't trip over your spurs on the way out."

"You are insulting, Senor Gringo!"

"Just outspoken, Senor Greaser!"

"Please!" said Shirley, her voice losing its softness. "You are both forgetting yourselves."

"Your pardon, senorita," said Camillo, and stalked off, his spurs chiming with an angry noise. Howdy chuckled.

"I'm sorry I let him git my temper riled, Shirley. But the sight of that snake does somethin' to me inside. Good thing I'm goin' away. If I stayed here more than a few hours, I'd have to take that nasty-mouthed caballero out behind the barn and give him a good old-fashioned gringo whippin'. Gosh, you're shiverin'."

"I am afraid, Howard. Afraid for you. Camillo Vasquez is a very dangerous man. He is a man who never forgets an insult. You would not be the first man he has killed in a duel. He will choose knives instead of guns. He has killed several men in such duels, but he has never been even scratched. And they were also men who were skilled with a knife."

"I hate a knife," admitted Howdy, who had the average American's loathing for that sort of weapon. "Dagos and greasers fight with knives."

"You forget, Howard, that I am also a — greaser."

She would have risen, but Howdy held both her hands. "You are no greaser. Neither is Don Rafael. Greaser is a mongrel coyote, a coward, a treacherous yellow dog that bites when you think he's friendly. I called Camillo Vasquez a greaser because he called me gringo. Shirley, I'd sooner have my tongue jerked out by the roots than to say one word against you or your people. You know that."

"Ah, Howard, this business of gringo and greaser, it is bad. It is the hatred that goes back to the wicked old days of Santa Ana and the Alamo. Your father was a Texan, a *Tejano*. In your heart there is, perhaps, that hatred for Mexico. I fear, Howard, that for you and me, there can never be happiness. Only sorrow and an ever lurking bitterness, hidden away like an ugly image. Howard, what if we should be married and something should unveil that ugly image, that feeling of gringo and greaser? That would, indeed, be a tragedy. I should die of grief. Between us there is that invisible barrier of race. I am

160

afraid for us, my Howard." Tears stood unshed in her dark eyes.

What Howdy might have said or done was interrupted by the appearance of Ricardo who, when he saw them, tried to slip away unseen. Howdy, however, called to him, and the young Mexican came with an eagerness that was a little pathetic.

After a little talk, Ricardo told Howdy that Don Rafael wished to see him for a few minutes in his study.

Howard found the old Spaniard in a state of excitement. He seemed very much disturbed.

"What is it, sir?" asked Howdy quickly. "What has happened?"

"The dagger. The jewelled dagger, Howard. I had it here in a secret drawer of this old cabinet. It has vanished. It is most strange, my son, because only I know the hidden spring that releases the secret panel. The dagger has vanished. It is a sign! A sign of death!"

16: Howdy Rides Again

Once again, Howdy Merchant rode alone. Behind him lay the Reyes rancho. Ahead of him the ragged peaks of the Sierra Madres pushed their forbidding peaks against a turquoise sky.

In his heart was a strange mingling of sadness and joy, of hopelessness and determination. With him rode the memory of Shirley's farewell as the two stood alone in the patio. The warmth of her lips on his, the pitiful embrace of her arms about his neck, her tears wetting his cheeks — so they had parted.

Alone, pitted against powerful enemies, the odds piled against him, how could he hope to win? Yet, he fought off that sinking sensation of defeat. At least he knew those enemies. Knew them for what they were, and he was, therefore, fore-armed. Now, as he let his horse, one of Don Rafael's best geldings, follow the twisting trail that was fringed by cactus, mesquite, and cat-claw brush, he maintained a careful vigilance. His hand was on his gun, or near it. So, when a man on a big bay gelding suddenly confronted him, Howdy's gun covered the rider. The man on the bay horse was a short, unshaven man with twinkling blue eyes.

"H'are you, Howdy Merchant," called the rider, lifting his hands. "I bin layin' along the trail for you some time."

"Who are you?" asked Howdy.

"Right now my name is Jeff Trainor. I've used other names."

With a grin of relief, Howdy shoved his gun back in its holster. "I'm gittin' kinda boogery down here in this country of yourn." He shook hands with the renegade, who was laughing silently.

"Don't blame you, young feller. You bin kinda outa the skillet and into the fire since you landed. I was hopin' they wouldn't run a knife into your back before I got a chance to see you. The boys is camped on the Rio Carmen at Jim Merchant's old place. We bin playin' tag with the Yaquis on one side, Mike Guzman up the river, and the rurales below us. Had more fun than a three-ring circus. We run Mike and what the Yaquis left of his coyotes plumb into town. Run 'em right into their holes. Then we dodged the Yaquis and slipped down the river to give the rurales some fun. It ain't often us boys git a chance to celebrate, but we shore howled like wolves this time. Picked up some good hosses, filled our hide with Guzman's beef, got lit up on the best that we could grab at the Cantina Juarez, and we're just wonderin' what we kin do next to make this part of the neighbourhood safe fer the gringo. Any stray idees you might have rattlin' around in your skull, turn 'em loose. Because we're r'arin' to go. Jest a-r'arin', Howdy!"

He was a genial rascal, this Jeff Trainor. Howdy had no trouble liking the little outlaw who, for all his joking and laughing and caper-cutting, was reputed to be deadly enough when he chose. It took a brave man and a born leader of men to pilot the renegades that called him their chief.

All the way to camp, Jeff kept up a line of talk that had Howdy grinning. He seemed to know every move that Howdy had made since he had ridden into Casas Grandes. He got a lot of fun out of teasing Howdy about Shirley Reyes.

"I bin down here fer a long time, but I still got to find the gal that'd look at me twice, excep' them senoritas that work in the cantinas. And here you blow down here like a dad-burned tumbleweed and grab off the purtiest young lady in Mexico, bar none. And when I says purty, I shore means purty, and when I says lady, that shore goes as it lays. They tell me, though, that she's all signed up to git married to this Camillo Vasquez greaser. Howdy, if you beat that coyote's time, I'll make you a weddin' present of five hundred head of steers, even if we have to steal 'em from ole man Reyes hisse'f. That Vasquez is jest as pleasant to take as a dose of strychnine, hear me? He plays both ends agin' the middle, and if ole man Reyes 'ud git hisse'f measured up fer a pair of magnifyin' specs, he'd read the snake brand on that gent. A man that'd steal off his friends, off folks as trust him, needs the kind of medicine the Yaquis hand out. Fact is, Howdy, I had 'er in mind to rope and hawg tie this Vasquez thing and hand 'im over to Nono fer Christmas, whenever they celebrate a Yaqui Christmas. But now that you're here, I'll turn the deal over to you. Dog-gone, boy, you're the livin' spittin' image of big Jim. Only now and then I kin see your mother's smile."

"You knew my mother, Jeff?"

"Boy, I shore did. I've et more than one meal there at Jim's place on the Rio Carmen. And she treated this outlawed cow-servant like he was actually a human bein'. I'm white-headed and I've bin in a lot of places between Mexico City and Calgary, Canada, but I never was treated as good as your mammy treated me. I used to set you on my knee when you was a yearlin'. You cut your fust tooth on the barrel of my six-gun. Didn't Jim ever tell you about the times I used to drop in there at the ranch?"

"No, Jeff, I never heard him talk, to speak of, about the ranch on the Rio Carmen."

"No!" Jeff's mouth tightened, and the laughter left his eyes. "No, I don't reckon he did, Howdy. When she died, it come mighty near killin' Jim. And it was almighty tough on us that knowed her. She was a good woman. She treated us boys like we was real men instead of what we actually was. I reckon there wa'n't a man of us that wouldn't'a' bin ready to take the long trail Jim Merchant took when he pulled out from here. And you're her son. Which means, boy, that we're your friends." Jeff blew his nose with much gusto and pulled a bottle from his chaps pocket. There was an odd mistiness in the eyes of the little outlaw, but he was grinning.

"Drink, Howdy?"

"Just a nip, Jeff. I ain't ever punished the stuff much. Half a dozen drinks in my life would cover the list. Here's luck."

Jeff took the bottle. "Here's luck aplenty, Howdy Merchant."

Now they rode through the trees to the

166

camp on the river bank. A man, who was shoeing a horse, quit his work and wiped the sweat from his forehead.

"Black Jack!" yelled Howdy. "Black Jack, you darned old son of a gun!"

"Knowed you'd git into a tight," drawled Black Jack, hiding his emotions behind a one-sided grin, "so I follered you down. And from what they tell me, I made the right move."

17: The Chief Comes

Vasquez was twisting his slim black moustache between thumb and forefinger. "Always," he said, "it has been considered very evil luck to make an enemy of me. If you are in the mood for praying, Shirley, then you better offer up a few prayers for the soul of your gringo lover. Under the roof of your father I could not kill him. But tonight, perhaps, I shall find him and teach him how a caballero resents such insults. As for you, it will be very wise in case he runs too fast for me to catch him, and sneaks back here like the coyote, if you see nothing of him. Because a man's honour is a sacred thing and you are soiling it by this silly affair with a common gringo cowboy."

"Honour?" Shirley's dark eyes blazed with anger. "Since when have you become a man of honour?"

"Eh? What is that?" Camillo's eyes narrowed. "What are you trying to say? As usual, I suppose, you have been listening to the loose-tongued lies of your little bandy-legged cousin? Only that he is your cousin has kept me from twisting his head from his skinny little neck. Pah! What can a caballero do against such a puny little enemy whose weapons are a fiddle and a wagging tongue? He had better use more care in his silly choice of gossip or I may forget that he is your cousin and turn him across my knee for a sound spanking."

"So? Ricardo is no swaggering braggard nor is he in the habit of picking quarrels with men and killing them. He is no match physically for you, I am most sorry to say. Otherwise, he would have long since held you to a strict accounting. Why do you try to hide your mistakes and your brutality behind the honourable name of your father? Since you give advice so freely, let me repay you in your own sort of coinage. Choose your companions with better wisdom, for one thing. It is hardly becoming of a Vasquez to associate with certain men who are known rascals."

"More of your crazy cousin's lies!" exclaimed Vasquez.

"So? Then, why do you seem so upset if they are lies? Oddly enough, it was not Ricardo who told me that last night you met a man there by the corrals. The man was that blue-eyed Indio who was with the Yaquis. I recall the Indio now as being the same one whom my father caught once in some sort of treachery and had him flogged and sent away from the rancho. Does a real caballero meet such men under the shelter of the night? You should have used more caution, Camillo. What would my father say if he knew of that last night's meeting?"

"You had some queer sort of nightmare," said Camillo, desperately trying to laugh off the bad situation. "It comes of listening to the silly tales of Ricardo and the love words of the gringo."

"If it was a dream, Camillo, then that dream also disturbed the sleep of another. Odd, no, that two separate persons should have the same exact dream? Next time you must meet a renegade Indio, you had better choose a more isolated hiding-place."

"So," cried Camillo, white-lipped now, "you and the gringo were sharing together the moonlight? Well, let me warn you, take care how you stain the honour of a Vasquez. You are to be my wife. Death comes to any man who seeks to interfere. I ride to avenge personally my honour and the honour of your father." Camillo, booted, spurred, armed, swung off for the stable. But something of his usual swagger was lacking.

Shirley saw him mount his horse and ride away alone. Fear gripped her heart with a cold, clammy hand. She knew that

Camillo's words were no idle boast. He would kill Howdy if he could. The weapons would be knives. A lonely spot, no witnesses, and Camillo Vasquez would be the one who rode away from the spot. It had happened before. It might easily happen again if Howdy were so foolish as to accept Camillo's challenge. And certainly that grey-eyed cowpuncher was not the man to evade a dangerous issue.

She must send Ricardo to warn Howdy. But a frantic search found no trace of that little fellow. Ricardo was nowhere to be seen. His horse and saddle were gone.

"You seem agitated, my daughter," said old Don Rafael.

"It is nothing, father. I was looking for Ricardo. He should not ride away alone, telling nobody where he has gone. Supposing the Guzman men find him?"

Rafael frowned. He tugged thoughtfully at his drooping white moustache. "It is, perhaps, my fault, daughter. I foolishly told him that someone had, during the night, stolen the jewelled dagger. The news of the theft upset Ricardo greatly. He hinted that he knew the thief. He went so far as to say that he would recover the dagger and perhaps the steel box and the documents proving that Howard Merchant is the

171

grandson of the late Doctor Macklin. The money and securities, so Ricardo said, would be gone. He was almost irrational. Never have I seen him so strange. He answered disjointedly, evasively when I put questions to him. Where did Camillo ride? I wanted him to go with me to where the vaqueros are gathering steers. Last night I spoke to him about it, and he acted like he was hardly listening to me. Has some strange malady of madness struck this rancho that everyone is so upset? I cannot understand it."

Don Rafael was not easily upset. Like most of his race, he was a man who liked to enjoy the more quiet things of life — sunlight and the shade of a big tree; music and good wine and laughter; fine horses to ride at the rodeos when the cattle were gathered for branding or shipping. Dissension or anything that marred the smoothness of existence was disquieting to the old don. He liked to see Shirley happy and laughing. He liked to hear the music of Ricardo's violin. He enjoyed the swaggering of Camillo who was so splendid a figure on a horse or on the ground, and he had welcomed Howard Merchant as his own son.

Now Shirley was upset, Ricardo had ridden off somewhere. Howard Merchant had gone on some mysterious errand. It was all very disturbing. Why had Camillo ridden away? Why was his daughter acting in such an agitated manner?

"Something troubles you, my daughter."

"It must be," said Shirley, offering a silent little prayer to atone for the kindly lie, "that being kidnapped and rescued and all has frayed my nerves, father."

"Of course, of course. And now, since Camillo has gone, and Howard rode away so suddenly, I will have to be content to sit around and twirl my moustaches."

Shirley forced a laugh as she led her father to a shady seat in the patio. She found him a fresh cigar, a bottle of wine and a book from which she read aloud to him. And all the time she was thinking of Howdy and Ricardo and Camillo.

Don Rafael dozed a little. Shirley kept on reading, scarce knowing what it was that she read. Suddenly she looked up to see Nono the Yaqui standing there in the patio — tall, straight of back, an imposing, stern-eyed figure.

Speechless with surprise, Shirley quit reading, the leather-bound book slipping from her hands to the tiled walk. Don Rafael blinked, startled into wakefulness. Now the Yaqui chief advanced. He held out something in his lean brown hand. At sight of the object, Shirley and her father gasped.

It was the jewelled dagger, and the blood that stained the sinister weapon was fresh blood.

"Where — where did you find this dagger?" asked Don Rafael tensely.

"I took it from the back of a man, senor."

"What man, Yaqui?"

"From the dead body of a blue-eyed Indio who was a spy for the Senor Mike Guzman. He was a deserter from my camp. He was here last night, because I followed him here. At daylight I came upon him, lying in the trail, this dagger in his back."

18: Heavy Odds

At the camp of Jeff Trainor the gringo cow-boys squatted about on their boot heels, smoking, talking, sipping black coffee from tin cups. They were waiting for darkness. Jeff Trainor, Black Jack and Howdy conversed in low tones. The hour was past sunset and within a short while darkness would creep along the Rio Carmen to shield their movements.

News had come to their camp that Mike Guzman and his brother had joined forces at Casas Grandes. Their main camp was at the edge of the little town. Mike Guzman's scattered forces, while somewhat shot to pieces and demoralized, had been again gathered and now Mike, the wily one, was plying them with enough mescal and pulque and marijuana to steady their broken courage and make them over into fighting men. The rurales, likewise bolstered by the false courage that comes in bottles and husk cigarettes, were now eager to do battle once more. But it was their intention to use more caution this time.

"We will wait until Camillo gets here,"

Mike Guzman told his brother.

"This must be the end of things," growled the bad-tempered Captain Guzman. "Already there is an army officer coming from the city of Chihuahua to relieve me. With him ride men of his own choosing who hate me. My game here is coming to a close. Let us steal what cattle we can, and the best horses in the Reyes remuda. No more of this dangerous business of kidnapping old Rafael's daughter. That was what spoiled things for us. That foolish business made for us too many enemies. An idiot's plan, that kidnapping."

"At the time," replied Mike, sneering at his brother, "you were willing enough. Had it not been for the coming of that cursed gringo, Merchant, all would have gone well. Rafael Reyes would have sent the ransom money with Camillo. Camillo would have made a pretty play at rescuing her. We would then have been rich enough to leave this country and still forever afterwards bleed our handsome Camillo when we needed a few hundred pesos. He would never have dared refuse us."

"Me, I like not this bragging Camillo," complained Captain Guzman. "He is treacherous. If he would double-cross Rafael Reyes, who has been to him like a father, then he would not hesitate to slit our throats. He is not overfond of me, I know that. Nor does the swaggering gamecock care for you, because he has always been jealous of anyone who looked twice at that daughter of Rafael Reyes. How do we know but what this last defeat we suffered from the Reyes vaqueros and from the Yaquis was not the sly doings of Camillo Vasquez? What proof have we that he did not mean our ruin?"

"He does not dare go against us," Mike's voice was an angry snarl. "We know too much about him."

"And it is that very knowledge," argued Captain Guzman, "that would cause him to hate us and want us out of the way. He fears our power over him. And speaking of the devil, look yonder!"

Camillo rode up to the camp, tossed his reins to one of the men, and greeted the two Guzmans with a thin smile of welcome. Camillo's eyes were hard and bitter. He was a little drunk and in an ugly temper.

"Your wolves turned into coyotes when they heard a Yaqui yell," he began, sneering. "Their courage slipped out of their hides at the first Yaqui charge."

Mike Guzman laughed unpleasantly. "How were we to know that the Yaquis were coming? We were cutting the Reyes men to pieces when the Yaquis attacked from the rear. How did it happen that these spies we had with the Yaquis did not get word to us of the attack? You have bragged much of that Indio called Blanco. Why did he not do his work?"

Camillo shrugged. "He will make no more such mistakes."

"No?" Mike Guzman lifted an eyebrow. "No?" he repeated.

"No. Blanco died last night. He paid the price that all men pay who make the mistake of threatening Camillo Vasquez. I left a knife in his white carcass."

"Another of your little duels?" asked Mike Guzman, with a sneer.

"The man sought to blackmail me. But we waste time that is very valuable. Below here, on the Rio Carmen, the gringos are camped. They are only a few against our many. It is my plan to attack them tonight."

"And since when," asked Captain Guzman, "have you become the leader here?"

"I am footing the bills, *senor capitan.*"

"Perhaps. And you are running none of the chances with death that we take. Since you are so eager to attack the gringos, there is a place for you at the head of the column.

Let us see the kind of soldier that Camillo Vasquez says himself to be."

"Are you trying to insult me?" cried Camillo.

Captain Guzman shrugged his trim shoulders. "I was merely giving you the opportunity to fight with us. If that is an insult, then take it as such."

"Have a care with your words," said Camillo. "I have killed more men in duels than you ever shot in battle."

"And you would challenge me to fight, then?" Captain Guzman's laugh was like a slap across the face. "I have heard much about these duels of yours, Camillo. They have an unpleasant odour."

"What do you mean?" Camillo's face was livid with anger.

"Por Dios," exclaimed Mike Guzman, "put an end to this quarrelling. Is this the time to be trading insults?"

Captain Guzman and Camillo stood facing each other, both angry. Mike Guzman stepped between them. His growl became a smile and he held a bottle of tequila in his hand.

"Wash away your words with this. We cannot afford to have these hombres see us quarrelling. It is bad for discipline, as you both know. Drink and forget it."

The quarrel thus averted, all three men drank. But the seed of trouble was planted, a seed that might easily bear fruit at some future date.

"How many gringos are camped on the Rio Carmen?" asked Mike.

"No more than twenty, counting Merchant and one they call Black Jack, who is new to the Trainor gang."

"Black Jack, eh?" Mike's eyes narrowed. "I would give much to find that certain *Tejano* at the end of my gun. No more than twenty? We have a hundred men, all ripe for the smell of gringo blood. Tonight at the hour of midnight we will come at them from all sides. And this time there will be no rear attack from the Yaquis, because I have news that they are back in their hills. Besides that earless Nono has no love for the gringos. Tonight at midnight they get a big surprise there at their camp on the Rio Carmen."

They did not notice a little figure hidden under the shadow of a huge straw sombrero, a faded serape pulled across his face. Now, that small figure melted into the darkness. On foot he made his way to the edge of camp, staggering drunkenly as he walked. But once beyond the edge of camp, his gait became swift and sure of foot. He mounted a horse that was hidden in the brush and rode away alone. It was some hours later when this lone rider was challenged by one of Jeff Trainor's outposts.

"*Quien es?*" barked the guard.

"Ricardo Reyes, a friend of Howard Merchant's. I bring important news from the Guzman camp."

"But Howdy Merchant ain't here now."

"Not here?" Ricardo's voice was a husky sob. "Then let me speak to the Senor Trainor."

"He ain't here, either. There's only a few of us boys here and we'll be gone in half an hour."

"The Guzmans plan an attack here at midnight. I rode here to warn my friend, Howard."

"You're some late, pardner. Howdy was speakin' about you and I know you're all right. So I kin tell you where they went. They're plannin' to ride into Casas Grandes and make some hard luck fer the Guzman spread. With 'em is Major Nunez of the Mexican army with a few rurales. He's got orders from the governor to arrest the Guzman brothers. I reckon it'll mean the firin' squad fer them two jaspers."

"How many men, all told, under the Senor Trainor and Major Nunez?"

"Twenty-five — thirty."

"But there are more than a hundred under the Guzman banner."

The cowpuncher lit a cigarette, his unshaven face spreading in a wide grin.

"Twenty of the boys are Texans, mister. Some of 'em has bin Rangers along the border. I don't reckon the odds bother 'em much."

"*Tejanos,*" said Ricardo, nodding his head. "They are fighters, *si.*"

"Texans," nodded the cowpuncher. "They'll feel plumb bad if they ain't fightin' big odds."

19: To Casas Grandes

The thud of shod hoofs, the creak of saddle leather and the faint jingle of spurs; here and there a cigarette glowing like a firefly in the darkness; a murmur of subdued voices — so they rode, those Texans, to meet the Guzman forces at Casas Grandes; boldly, carelessly, with a contemptuous grin for the odds that they would meet.

Riding in the lead with Jeff Trainor, Black Jack and Howdy Merchant was Major Francisco Nunez, as able and honest an officer as ever was given a commission by *El Presidente* himself. Here was a man who personified the law of Mexico; a man who had the interest of his country at heart, a man who had, in various ways, gained the respect and friendship of the Americans who now rode with him; a gentleman and an officer; a leader of picked men; a fighter who knew and understood border conditions and had many times shared meals and blankets with the Texas Rangers and the hardworking men of the United States border patrol. Here was a man who hoped to see the fulfillment of a

183

dream — a dream of friendly relations between Mexico and the United States;
Mexico, ripped and torn by the leaden bullets and steel blades of revolutions; the
United States, striving for a friendly relationship with its neighbouring country
south of the Rio Grande.

Such men as Major Nunez, such men as
Howdy Merchant hoped for an understanding without that bitter and fatal feeling
which so often existed — no gringo-against-
greaser feeling, but an understanding between two peoples who were equally good
and bad.

Too much had been said and done to increase that enmity along the border. Too
many men, spurred by greed and lust and
selfish gain, had traded on those two names,
"gringo," "greaser," names thrown as a
bomb or as a knife might be thrown, shat-
tering the friendship of the true Mexican
and the true citizen of the United States.
Outlaws, rebels, gun runners, smugglers,
men who dealt in stolen cattle and horses,
those were the gentlemen of high-handed
lawlessness who kept alive a malignant
flame along the border.

"Cigarette, major?" asked Jeff Trainor.

"Thees tobacco you smoke, Senor Jeff,"
said Major Nunez, "ees too weak *por* me.

Ees a long time since we meet, you and I. Ees a great pleasure *por* me, my old frien'."

"And for you and me, both, Francisco. Hope we kin do what we set out to do when I come down here."

Major Nunez nodded. Better than any man in Mexico did Francisco Nunez know Jeff Trainor. He knew Jeff, not as an outlaw, but as an old friend. He knew many things that most men in Chihuahua never guessed. For instance, he knew that Jeff Trainor was not the outlaw that men claimed him to be. Moreover, he knew why Jeff Trainor chose to be known as an outlaw rather than a man of honour.

Even Black Jack had never guessed that Jeff Trainor was an armed and able missionary of peace here in the broncho State of Chihuahua; that Jeff Trainer, supposed outlaw, was something quite the opposite; that Jeff Trainor, in the interests of cattle owners on both sides of the border, was here in Mexico for an honest purpose; that, for several years there in the Sierra Madres, this grizzled little fighter who had once been a Ranger, was working out one of the most difficult problems that was ever given a man to solve.

Black Jack and Howdy were just beginning to understand Jeff Trainor and what he

185

had risked so much to accomplish; namely, the wiping out of rustlers who were becoming an ever-increasing menace to both countries.

Tonight, pinned to the grey flannel shirt of Jeff Trainor, was a gold badge with blue lettering. For Jeff Trainor was an officer of the law, border law; a law that must use the utmost precaution to work out its problems; a law that could be enforced only by men of great courage and honesty. Last night, and for many nights and days, Jeff Trainor had been looked upon as an outlaw with a following of desperate men. Tonight he became Jeff Trainor, an officer of the law, leader of a band of deputies whose true worth had been proved in a hundred and one tight places.

Black Jack grinned at Howdy Merchant. "I reckon it'd tickle big Jim Merchant to know that his kid was ridin' with the law."

Howdy nodded. His heart, his conscience was clear tonight. He was following the wishes of his father. He was following an honest trail. Even if that trail ended in death, he had travelled it like a man. And what more could any man ask of Fate?

Tonight the stars seemed bright to Howdy. Instead of being alone in a hopeless fight, he had the support of men who were bound by a secret oath to enforce the law. He had the aid of real men; men who talked little but were never slow to act. He had given Jeff Trainor and Major Nunez what information he had concerning the Guzmans and the double-dealing Camillo Vasquez. Oddly enough, they seemed little surprised at the duplicity of Camillo. Questioned, Jeff chuckled softly to himself.

"Howdy, that Vasquez gent has showed his hole card a long time ago. I bin stealin' cattle from Rafael Reyes for a long time and splittin' the proceeds with Camillo. Then he figgered that Mike Guzman had more drag than me. He throws in with Mike. Which was just what we bin a-waitin' for. The dough I got from the Reyes cattle is in the bank under a special account, to be turned over to Don Rafael at the right time. Camillo's cut is Rafael's losin'. But in order to git this Camillo sport in the right place, we had to let Don Rafael take a losin'. Now we got Camillo where we want him. We got the Guzmans with him. And when we're done with 'em, they'll learn that they ain't big enough or tough enough to lick two nations. The graft was good. It kep' gittin' better. Now, just when they figger that they're booked to win the big stakes, we cut in and corral the whole works."

"Just where," asked Howdy, "do the Yaquis figger?"

It was Major Nunez who replied to that question. "The Yaquis and thees earless Nono, they count as they have always counted here in Mexico, senor. Always they have been enemies. They weel die enemies. *Por* why? Because they cannot be otherwise. It ees een their blood. So long as there ees one Yaqui left, one true Yaqui, that one weel fight the Mexicans onteel he ees die. Because that ees the way of the real Yaqui."

"Then we'll be fightin' the Yaquis, major?"

"*Quien sabe?* Why knows, my frien'? I 'ave 'ope to meet thees Nono once more. Ees ten years now seence I meet heem. I am taken prisoner by that same Nono, who has no ears because a Mexican who was the father of the two Guzman hombres ees cut off the ears from thees same Nono and send the ears away so that the governor ees geeve heem the commission een the rurales. Thees business of losing the ear makes out of thees Nono Yaqui one bad enemy *por* Mexico. So, senor, when I am so onlocky to be capture, thees Nono promise to send the both of my ear to *El Presidente*. That night I 'ave the beeg chance to escape. I take heem, only to be once more capture and thees time the Yaqui Nono ees take the knife and cut me een many places. Not to keel me, onderstan', but to make me so that, when I am send back to Chihuahua Ceety I shall never forget the taste of the Yaqui knife. Aye, when I find thees Nono, I weel take the knife and cut heem and send heem back to the Yaquis weeth the note stuck to hees skin weeth cactus needles. I beg the senor now *por* the match to light thees leetle cigarette."

20: Trainor's Message

It was a wild-eyed and exhausted Mexican who brought Jeff Trainor's message to the Guzmans and Camillo Vasquez at their camp. This message was brief and to the point. It was written in pencil on the back of a letter written for the governor of Chihuahua to Jeff Trainor, his trusted friend. The letter bore the official stamp of the coat of arms of Mexico. It bore the governor's signature. And on the back of this official letter Jeff Trainor had pencilled his message to the Guzmans and Camillo Vasquez.

"Senors," so the letter read, "we are coming to take you dead or alive in the name of the government of Mexico. Expect us tonight."

The letter to Jeff from the governor explained Jeff's status as an officer.

"A trick!" cried Camillo. "A gringo trick!"

"He has not enough men to hurt us," said Mike Guzman, sneering as usual. "Let them come along with their threats. We will wait here for them and give them a hide full of bullets."

Only Captain Guzman of the rurales was silent and morose. Here lately he had felt uneasy. Rumours, as vague as the rustling of leaves, had reached him. Certain officials whom he had met had been an edge too polite of manner, and their eyes were veiled. Now Captain Guzman, studying both sides of Jeff Trainor's letter, read his fate written in blood. He rose, carefully brushed his uniform, and strode away to where his men were sitting around their camp-fires. Camillo's eyes followed the rural officer.

"Your brother is, perhaps, frightened."

"He has been within arm's reach of death many times," Mike Guzman replied, in defence of his brother's honour, "and never yet has he flinched. When the gringos attack, it will not be Captain Guzman who runs away. Could I be that certain regarding the courage of a certain swaggering braggart, then I would be happy."

"Enough of your infernal insults," replied Camillo, through gritted teeth. "You dare not meet me alone, with only our knives to defend us."

"No? We shall see about that after the gringos are cared for in the proper manner. And because I know how you have killed those men you fought, I shall be fore-armed against your cowardly tricks. Now, Camillo, you are here in my camp. You will take orders from me and from my brother."

"And what if I do not choose to take orders from you two, what will happen?"

Mike Guzman gave some signal. A dozen heavily armed men stood at Camillo's back. Mike Guzman smiled.

"You will obey my orders, senor," he told Camillo softly, his right hand slipping the safety on his Luger pistol, "or I shall now take the extreme pleasure of shooting you through the head. Make a quick choice, my friend."

Camillo ran his tongue across dry lips. The insolent swagger was gone. He was looking into the cold eyes of death and he knew that Mike Guzman would not hesitate to shoot if he felt inclined.

"You — win — Mike."

" *'Sta bueno.* Then go under escort into town. Tell them at the Cantina Juarez that we will all be in town and to get music and women and much mescal for a big *baile.* Now move pronto. A big *baile.* The biggest that Casas Grandes has ever seen. Vamoose!"

"A *baile!*" gasped Camillo. "At such a time as this, when the gringos are coming to attack? Have you lost your brains?"

"Obey the orders I give. Speak when I

give you leave to talk. Now get out of my sight before I spill your brains down your face." Mike turned to an elder.

"Give orders to mount. Tell Captain Guzman to report to me at once. Pronto, hombre, or I'll shoot the ears off your thick head."

Black Mike was shouting orders, laughing, cursing, swinging the flat blade of his machete against the legs of those who were sleeping off their pulque; kicking them into life, cursing them into their places, singing a ribald marching song that his men took up in drunken chorus.

To Captain Guzman Mike outlined his plans. The captain of the rurales shrugged and nodded dubiously. But Mike Guzman was fired with his wild plan.

They would ride into town. There, some of the rurales and renegades would dance and drink and make merry. But a lot of others would be stationed at certain spots along the street, where they could cut down the gringos.

Now Mike had the messenger who had delivered Jeff's letter brought before him. He gave the man back the letter. Then he gave orders that the luckless man be taken along the back trail to a spot where the gringos would be certain to find him. At that spot the messenger was to be staked out by his hands and feet. He was to tell the gringos, when they found him, that a little party of Yaquis had so mistreated him and left him to die. He was to let the gringos think that the message had not been delivered. He would likewise inform the gringos that tonight Mike Guzman was celebrating his birthday by giving a great *baile* in town. Mike slipped some gold coins into the messenger's pocket and gave him a bottle of tequila. Also he gave the man a few words of warning.

"Fail me, hombre, and I will have you pulled apart by wild mules."

With the camp left in such a state that the enemy would think the Mexicans were merely in town to celebrate, Mike took every man of them and rode boldly into Casas Grandes. Once in town, he placed certain picked men in command of squads that would lie hidden in the shadows of the dark side streets. Others who were already too drunk to fight well, he sent into the cantina to celebrate.

Now the revelry was in full swing. The orchestra played with hardly a pause. The dance was fast and merry. Men called loudly for more drinks. Overhead the big kerosene lamps shed a yellowish, smudgy glow across the smoke-laden room.

"Where's that Camillo?" Mike asked the men who had come to town with the caballero. They shrugged. Camillo, they said, had been dancing and drinking and laughing with the others. Was he not out there on the dance floor?

Camillo was not on the dance floor. Nor was he to be found after a swift search. Camillo Vasquez had taken some opportune moment to slip away from the cantina. He had mounted his horse and ridden away. He had no appetite for this fight that was to come. Besides, now that Mike Guzman had become openly hostile towards him, the gay caballero decided that he was safer almost anywhere than here within range of Mike Guzman's Luger.

Mike and his brother took part in the festivities for a while, then vanished to take their positions along the darkened streets where their warriors lay in wait for the gringos who would ride into that carefully laid ambush.

21: Suspicious Gringos

True to Mike Guzman's ingenious planning, Jeff Trainor and his men found the messenger who had been staked out. The man's wrists and bare ankles were cruelly cut by the rough rawhide thongs. In his pocket was the letter that he told Jeff he had been unable to deliver. He begged them not to kill him. These Yaquis had waylaid him, caught him unawares, and treated him cruelly. The saints above would bear witness it had not been his fault that he had not delivered the message to Mike Guzman who was even now in Casas Grandes with all his men celebrating a birthday. He had learned that much from the Yaquis.

"Mike's celebrating his birthday, is he?" said Jeff Trainor. "Putting on a big *baile*, is he? Well, cowboys, that makes it all the easier for us. They'll be drunk as fools by the time we hit town."

Jeff turned loose the Mexican with orders to go where he pleased so long as he did not go to town. When the Mexican had gone, Howdy shook his head, making a wry face.

"You're the boss, Jeff, and it ain't the

place of a young bonehead like me to be buttin' in, but I'd bet a hat that *paisano* high-tails it for town and reports that we're on our way there."

"Sure he will, Howdy," grinned Jeff. "He'll never slack a lope till he gits there. But I wanted him to think that we'd take Mike by surprise. I wanted him to figger we believed he'd not go near town. That way, as soon as we git near town, and a man goes in alone to look over the layout, he can tell whether this *baile* is on the level or is it just another slick trick that Mike is pullin'. He likes to set traps, that gent does. And this smells like one to me. Major, have you a man that kin put on some old clothes and slip into Casas Grandes?"

"*Si, senor.* I have one man who ees smarter than the fox. If there ees the trap set, then thees man weel soon find that trap."

"There was somethin' about that Mexican's story that didn't sound real to me," said Black Jack.

Jeff nodded. "Nor me, Black Jack. And when I frisked him for the note I found some gold money that wasn't on him when I sent him with that note. That Yaqui attack don't look right, either. They'd've tortured him more than that. No, I figgered he was lyin'. Mike's layin' a trap. And so it's up to us to ride into that trap. But we'll ride a-shootin'."

It was when they were waiting for the spy to return from his dangerous mission that Ricardo caught up with them. The little Mexican was excited and mysterious. He told Howdy about seeing Nono bending over the body of a dead man. The dead man was the blue-eyed Indio. Nono had plucked a dagger from the dead Indio's back while Ricardo, hidden within a stone's throw, watched. It was the dagger that had been stolen from Don Rafael's secret panel.

"It was that sneaking Camillo who stole it, Howard. It was that same Camillo who killed the Indio. But what was that earless Yaqui doing there? He was alone. He took the dagger and looked at it. Then he talked to the sunrise in some lingo that I did not understand. Mostly, these Yaquis here speak the Mexican language. When he had done with his strange talk to the sun, he got on his horse and rode away with that cursed dagger. He rode towards the Reyes rancho. I fear he meant harm, because he is a bad hater, that Yaqui."

"Why didn't you stop him?"

Ricardo's hands went out in an empty gesture. "Forgive me for being a dunce,

Howard. In my haste to find out a secret I have long suspected, I forgot to bring any weapons of any kind. I was unarmed. So I rode to find you. Howard, I fear for the life of my uncle and for the safety of my cousin. The earless Yaqui is a devil in human form.

"I followed you. I thought you had gone to the Guzman camp, one against them all. But I learned that you were not there, that you were with the Americanos on the Rio Carmen. The Guzmans and Camillo were there. They were planning an attack. I rode to warn you. Our trails passed in the night. So I returned to find you here. But one thing I learned. The steel box and what it holds are not, as I supposed, in the possession of Camillo. Once Camillo had the box, but not now. It has fallen into evil hands. The thing carries a curse, Howard, a curse that is stained with the blood of men."

"Who has the box now?"

Ricardo shivered as if struck by a chill. "I am the only man alive who knows where it is now hidden, because I buried it at dark tonight. I dug it up, Howard, from the spot where the earless Nono buried it before he took the knife from the dead Indio's back. Nono had the box. It is locked. There is but one key to that box and Camillo Vasquez has that key. That I know."

"More riddles," frowned Howdy. "How did Nono get the box?"

"*Quien sabe?* It is my belief that he found it where Camillo buried it. Camillo, I am sure, took the box from under the chapel floor. He and I and Shirley were small children when it was buried there by my uncle. We were playing some child's game there in the shadows behind the pews and confessional box when Don Rafael buried the box. Hidden, not daring to move, we watched. Camillo, the oldest and boldest, shoved Shirley and me into the dark confessional box. He crept closer after whispering a warning in my ear that he would cut out my tongue and burn out my eyes with hot coals if I peeked or told of what we saw. He said that Uncle Rafael was burying Spanish gold and jewels and much rich loot that had belonged to the old pirates. He was ever strong with imagination.

"Shirley was too young to comprehend or remember. Throughout the years that followed, I never forgot that evening there in the chapel that was almost dark — the deep breathing of my uncle as he laboured; my hand over Shirley's mouth to keep her from crying aloud or giggling; Camillo, ever the bold one, spying on my uncle.

"But as years passed, I dismissed the memory as only some labour my uncle had been doing there behind the heavy pews. I thought no more of it for years until recently when Don Rafael told us that a steel box had been dug up from the chapel floor and that dagger left in its stead. Then I suspected Camillo. I know he found the key that was with the box, a large steel key that fitted the ancient Spanish lock. I have seen it in his room when he was changing clothes and putting things from one pocket to another. Always he carried that key. And when he and I were together at the university he was spending far more money than he got from home. Camillo stole the money from the box, but I think he left the documents. Perhaps he intended replacing the box but never got the proper opportunity.

"I think he buried the box about three miles from the ranch in an old mine shaft. It is my belief that the Yaqui saw him and stole the box, because he was coming from that shaft with the box when he came upon a dead Yaqui almost at the same time that I found the dead Indio. I had hidden when he appeared along the trail. In front of him was the box, tied to his saddle, an awkward, clumsy burden for a man to carry far. Perhaps that was why he buried it again and rode on towards the Reyes rancho with the dagger."

"But if the dagger had been left there under the chapel floor, instead of the box," questioned Howdy, "and Camillo was the thief, how did he git hold of the dagger that, the last we know, was given to the youngest of the South American brothers, Alphonso Duarte, the day my father killed Alphonso's two brothers in California?"

Ricardo shook his head, bewildered. "*Quien sabe, quien sabe?* But now, Howard, what must we do? Don Rafael and my cousin Shirley are in danger. I feel it. I know it. Can we not do something?"

Jeff Trainor, Black Jack and Major Nunez had been listening. Now Jeff laid a hand on Howdy's shoulder.

"Ricardo is right. You better slip on back to the ranch and see what the Yaqui is up to. I'll lend you what men you'll need."

"I'll go alone, Jeff. If Nono fetched his Yaquis, then you haven't enough men to spare to do good. But if he's alone, I reckon I kin handle him without too much trouble. I hate to miss the show at Casas Grandes but this means —"

"Ride to it, cowhand," said Jeff, grinning. "Give the lady our best regards. Now hit the trail, you wart hawg, and good luck to you.

Me'n' Black Jack and the major will mop up the sidewalks with the Guzmans and their Camillo *compadre*. See you later."

22: Dig Deep, Hombre

Rumour, like the faint whispering of a coming storm, crept through the dark streets and alleyways of Casas Grandes. It was a rumour that struck terror into the hearts of the poor people of the little adobe town. The gringos were coming! There was to be a battle, a big battle, here in their yards, on their very doorsteps! The streets would be filled with horses and men, horses that ran amok, men who killed one another. Ah, *Madre de Dios!*

Little Casas Grandes had seen, during the past years that had been torn by a dozen revolutions, several such fights. They had seen their homes destroyed, their children trampled under the shod hoofs of stampeding horses, their husbands and brothers and lovers shot down.

It was the women who bore the burden of these battles — black-clad women, praying with trembling lips, their eyes pleading to the little *santos* in their niches; some already widowed, black-shawled, suffering in dumb-like silence as they gathered their few belongings and hushed the children with whispered words. Here and there some woman sobbed aloud. But the older ones, those who had seen blood on their doorsteps, went about the business of evacuation without complaint.

True, orders had been given that no man, woman or child was to leave town. But these followers of the Guzmans were mostly men of Casas Grandes, men who owned wives and mothers, sisters and sweethearts there. They pretended not to see the huddled little groups that crept into the night from darkened doorways, headed for the safety of the foothills. Now the stifled whimper of a child; mute farewells in the black shadows; dried tears; bare feet shuffling silently in the dust; burdened with heavy loads wrapped in blankets; their little homes left to the will of the men who fought to kill — so those women of Casas Grandes slipped into the night.

This same rumour had filtered into the Cantina Juarez. A dancing girl sought to slip out a side door. One of Mike Guzman's men shoved her back roughly.

"Dance!" he growled at her, his eyes sullen and without mercy. "Go back and dance!"

"The gringos are coming!" she screamed in a shrill voice. "I will not be trapped here!"

She sprang at him like an animal but he knocked her senseless with the barrel of his gun. She lay there on the grimy floor, a crumpled, pitiful heap of cheap red silk. A drunken man laughed harshly. Another scowled at the man who had struck the blow. The other dancing girls no longer laughed. Their red lips were bloodless under the smudged colouring. Their eyes, the saddest eyes in the world, were dark with a fear. They huddled together like animals. The gringos are coming, the gringos.

One of the rurales stepped to the platform where a badly frightened orchestra had quit their playing. "Play, hombres, or we shoot you where you sit. Play, fools!"

Discordant music came from their string instruments. The fat one who played the bull fiddle had turned a greenish colour. Sweat beaded their foreheads. But they played for their very lives under the guns of the Guzman renegades. The terrified dancing girls were dragged roughly on to the dance floor. The men who danced had a crazy, desperate look in their eyes. They were in all stages of intoxication. Many were doped with that marijuana smoke that makes fighting men of cowards. In an hour some of them would be lying here dead. But now they would dance.

The orchestra was generously supplied with mescal. At the gruff command of the rurale sergeant in charge, they struck up the wild, barbaric, swinging tune of Mike Guzman's marching song. The men who danced caught up the tune and sang the ribald verses. There was the heavy odour of cheap musk perfume, smoke, spilled liquor, sweat; women's faces, white and drawn and tired, daubed red across the cheekbones, eyes filled with a sullen hopelessness; men's faces, unwashed, unshaven, somehow all alike; paid to die, those men who served under the two Guzmans. The atmosphere was thick and close almost to the point of suffocation. It was only the guards at the doors who were able to breathe pure air.

Now the night outside was filled with the sound of gun-fire, shouts, pounding hoofs. The guards at the door clubbed back the desperate women. Now those guards went down like shot beef; now men in their places, men who let the women pass but held back the Guzman warriors. These newcomers were gringos, grim-lipped, cold-eyed gringos who barked sharp commands in the Mexican tongue.

"Surrender!" they roughly commanded. "Get out of here, you women. Pronto. The back door. Here, take this dead un along with you as you go."

Here and there a Guzman follower showed fight. The guns of the gringos cracked. The suddenness of this surprise attack cowed the renegades. Three or four swift-moving gringos were quickly disarming the Guzman men. Guns were thrown behind the bar in a pile. The men stood facing the wall, arms held high. Disarmed, they were like so many sheep. Their stupid brains, dulled by drink, had not reacted quickly enough to the sudden turn of things. Now, their weapons gone, it was too late to fight. They could only wait for death, dumb-lipped, blank-eyed, to be shot down by these gringos, these *Tejanos*.

"Good work, boys," called Black Jack. "Just ride close-herd on 'em. I'll go and see how the game goes outside."

The street was filled with men who ran and dodged. Crimson spurts of gun-fire split the shadows apart. Some on horseback fled headlong. Others cried out in surrender to the gringos.

Outside, as well as in the cantina, the plans of Mike Guzman had gone wrong. The gringos had not, as he had planned, come riding down the street in a crowd. They had come from all sides and on foot.

Before the Guzmans were aware of their presence, the hated gringos had piled in on them from the darkness. Mike and his brother were among the very first to feel the force of the gringo attack. Guns had been shoved in their faces by men who seemed to spring out of the ground behind them. Both of them had fought for a brief moment. But they had gone down, stunned by the blows that had been thrust across the head. Ropes bound them hand and foot. The two Guzmans were prisoners.

The leaderless renegades lost all stomach for the fight. The guns of the gringos were spewing fire from all sides.

Less than fifteen minutes of fighting and Casas Grandes belonged to the invaders. Oddly enough there were not more than three or four men killed, because the gringos had fired over the heads of the rene- gades — that, by order of Jeff Trainor and Major Nunez.

Now the Cantina Juarez was packed with unarmed and docile prisoners. To these men Major Nunez made a speech. It was quite a long speech and, as this soldier of the wars talked, fear left the eyes of the men who listened. This officer of rurales was not going to have them shot down against the adobe wall. He was giving them back their lives, offering them peace and prosperity if they would go to work on their farms. There would be no more fighting here. No man save his own rurales would be allowed to own any kind of a gun. The penalty of owning a gun or even ammunition was death.

Their faces brightened. This soldier who talked so grandly was sent by the governor. His word was absolute law. A law they must obey under the penalty of death. Under his rule their women and children would be safe. Their homes would be safe. Was this not better than a few pesos a month, only to be shot down in the end?

Major Nunez finished his talk. There was a hush. Then the cantina was filled with the husky cheering of these men who had been so near death.

Dawn was coming. Still the prisoners were under guard but they smoked and talked and were as happy as children.

Now, at the far end of the street, Mike Guzman and his brother were led from an adobe house. A squad of rurales marched with them to the high adobe wall behind the little chapel.

The ropes that bound their arms were untied. They finished their cigarettes. Now the two brothers embraced.

Captain Guzman saluted Major Nunez. "We are ready."

"Is there any last word?" asked the major.

"Tell them," said Mike Guzman, twisting his moustache and smiling insolently, "to shoot well. Do not mark my face. There will be more than one tender senorita who will wish to put a last kiss on my dying lips."

The brown-robed, sandalled padre who had shared their last hours now signed them with the cross and shuffled away, his sad eyes deep with suffering. He had seen others placed there at that wall, within a stone's throw of his little patio garden. They knew how to die, these soldiers of Mexico.

There came the rattle of breech bolts, the staccato commands, the brief burst of gunfire. Then as the echo of the shots died, the bell in the little chapel tolled slowly.

A wrinkled, bent-shouldered man, caretaker of the Casas Grandes old cemetery, spat on callous hands and picked up his spade. In the pocket of his cotton jeans were gold pieces. That Senor Mike Guzman paid well for his last bed.

"Dig deeply, hombre. Make the grave wide enough for two." The old man smiled grimly.

23: Again the Yaqui

Young Merchant rode as hard as he dared push his horse. Beside him rode little Ricardo and dawn found them within sight of the Reyes rancho. At sunrise they pulled up at the corral and swung from the backs of their weary horses. All seemed quiet and peaceful enough. Perhaps a little too quiet, thought Howdy, as he dismounted.

Nor was he far from wrong. In his study, old Don Rafael lay on the floor. There was an ugly-looking bruise above one ear and he was bound hand and foot. The study had been ransacked. The place was littered with papers. On the desk was a half-emptied bottle of tequila. Camillo Vasquez had thus repaid the fine old don for the countless favours bestowed upon him. He had robbed Don Rafael after knocking him senseless.

He had been in the midst of this cowardly affair when Shirley, aroused from a fitful sleep by her father's muffled outcry, had interrupted him. The silk handkerchief had slipped from his face. At sight of the girl that face had distorted horribly. The man's eyes were red, congested with hate and greed.

Before she could move, before she could cry out, Camillo had dragged her inside, had gagged her and bound her tightly.

"The old man has gold and I need it," he said thickly. "You'll save his life if you tell me where he keeps it. I'm in a rush. Your gringo lover is dead and your tongue-wagging cousin is dead," he lied. "I'll loosen the gag and you can tell me where the old devil keeps his money."

"You beast!" hissed Shirley. "You vile, ungrateful dog! After all he has —" Her words were silenced by a vicious slap that brought blood to her lips. Her eyes blazed with anger.

"Where's his money?" Camillo stepped to the unconscious Don Rafael. His long-bladed knife was at the bare throat of the old man. Murder glittered in his madman's eyes.

"It is in leather sacks," she told him, fearful for her father's life. "In the panel behind the book-shelf. Push the wooden peg from which hangs the portrait of your own father. His eyes are watching you."

Camillo laughed shortly and tightened her gag again. Now he pushed on the wooden peg. A panel swung open. There, in a small compartment were leather sacks tied with buckskin strings, a dozen, all told.

Camillo dumped the sacks into his serape which he fashioned into a carrier. Then he cut the rope that tied Shirley's ankles.

"Unless you want to see the throat of your father slit from ear to ear, you'll come with me."

He gripped her arm tightly. The pain stung her but she did not care. Nothing mattered now. He had told her that Howard and Ricardo were dead. She went with him without fighting, because she knew that the man was drunk and mad and that he would not hesitate to do murder. Perhaps, so she swiftly reasoned, she could persuade him later to return with her and the money. Or she might somehow escape. To cross this crazed man now would be worse than folly.

He had her horse saddled in a few minutes. Now he freed her hands and lifted her roughly into the saddle. Then he lashed the serape with its gold to his saddle and boldly lit a cigarette. For a brief moment in the darkness his face, twisted, leering, triumphant, was revealed. Then the match was snuffed out.

Shirley, watching him with a sort of hypnotic stare, gave a little start. For there, beyond Camillo, until that moment hidden by the darkness, was the crouched figure of a man, a man who lifted his hand in a gesture behind Camillo's back. That gesture meant for her to keep silent. Shirley had, in that brief moment, recognized the crouched figure. It was the earless Yaqui, Nono.

Now Camillo mounted his horse. He ordered her curtly to ride ahead of him. His cigarette glowed in the darkness.

Now, as she rode, Shirley recalled the strange visit of the earless Yaqui that morning. He had shown Don Rafael the dagger. Then he had told Don Rafael that he wanted some words alone with him. So Shirley had left them there in the patio.

After almost an hour she had been summoned to the patio by her father. The earless Yaqui had gone. Don Rafael looked tired and older by ten years and he was visibly upset.

"I find, my daughter," he told her, "that I have done you a great injustice. I have promised your hand in marriage to a thief and a man who has violated every trust I have placed in him. You are now released from that contract of marriage. If Camillo Vasquez ever again sets foot on this ranch, I shall have him flogged. I shall, with my own hands, administer the flogging. But that his father was my friend, I should kill the dog with my own hands. Try to forget the scoundrel."

"That, my father," she had said quietly, "is not so easily done. I shall remember him, yes, but not as a lover. I have never loved him. Of late I have grown to fear and loathe him. Respect for your wishes has kept me from breaking the betrothal."

While Don Rafael had not revealed the source of his information, Shirley knew that it was through the earless Yaqui that her father had learned the truth.

She had asked about the dagger. Don Rafael had told her, almost curtly, that the earless Yaqui had kept the grisly weapon.

Now, as she rode ahead of the treacherous Camillo, she knew that somewhere behind them the Yaqui was following. Though she wondered how he could keep track of them in the darkness without his horse's hoofs betraying his presence.

Mile after mile they travelled. It was an hour until dawn. Camillo called a halt so that he might divide the burden of the money between the two horses. The gold was heavy.

Camillo shifted the gold to his own satisfaction. He took a bottle from the saddle pocket and dug at the cork with his knife.

Now he gave a choking cry. There sounded the brief threshing of two men locked in desperate grips. Then all was quiet. The deep voice of Nono, the earless Yaqui, broke that stillness.

"Ride back to your rancho, senorita. Wait there for the coming of the Senor Howard Merchant. Tell him to ride alone to this spot. I will be waiting here for him."

He had come closer now. Camillo lay motionless on the ground. Shirley noticed that the tall Yaqui was naked save for a breechclout. In his hand was a knife. Nono had followed them on foot.

It was sunrise when she reached the ranch. She found Howdy, Ricardo and her father saddling fresh horses. To them she gave the brief recital of her capture and rescue and the earless Yaqui's message to Howdy.

Don Rafael showed little surprise at the message. "The Yaqui is right, my son," he told Howdy. "Go alone. Trust the Yaqui because he is your friend. He is repaying his debt to your dead grandfather. Whatever else he may be, that Yaqui is a man who keeps his word. Go, son. May the *Senor Dios* send you back safely to us." He embraced Howdy, his dark eyes misty with unshed tears.

Now Howdy faced Shirley, who stood beside her father. He held out his two hands and she came to him.

"Sir," he said to Don Rafael, "when I come back, I would like to ask your permission to marry your daughter. We love each other."

A smile broke the solemnity of Don Rafael's leathery face. "I have given that permission before you asked it, my son. Now go with God."

24: A Secret Dies

A merciless, blistering, unshaded sun; two men, naked save for loin clothes, each with a knife in his hand — so Camillo Vasquez, renegade scion of a proud name, faced the earless Nono.

"It is my understanding," said the Yaqui, "that you have killed many men in such a duel. I give you the chance to kill one more. But before we fight, let me tell you that I know how those men were killed. Perhaps you will also kill me as you killed those others. *Quien sabe?*"

Camillo Vasquez shivered a little, though the sun was blistering his bare skin. The black eyes of the Yaqui mocked him. He read death in those eyes. Yet, had he not met some of the most skilful knife men in Mexico? Had he not left them lying there on the ground dying? Hadn't his trick worked many times before? This Yaqui could not be so fast. He was old. The scars of many years marked that bronzed, lean, muscled body. Yet he had felt the grip of those sinewed arms and knew that the Yaqui's muscles were like steel fibres. Dare he risk it? Dare he chance that trick that he had practiced so many times? That trick of throwing his knife with the speed of a bullet, so that its blade went hilt-deep into the heart of the luckless man who faced him? The Yaqui was anticipating that throw. He knew the trick that had won Camillo those duels. Nono, the jewelled dagger in his lean brown hand, stood ready.

"Come, senor, we waste time. Fight, thou!"

Camillo's wrist twisted in that practised, sliding whirl. The knife shot like a silver streak. But Nono stood there, unharmed. That lithe, bronze body had slid sidewise as Camillo's knife sped at him. He stood there for a moment, his earless head erect, the deeply lined face masklike. Camillo, unarmed now, naked, stripped of his fine clothes, robbed of his swagger, his courage drained, fell on his knees, begging brokenly for his life, while Nono stood there like some pagan statue, contempt in his black eyes.

"Tell me, coward, how came you by this knife that you changed for the treasure box that was buried in Don Rafael's chapel? Speak, coward! Speak or off go your ears."

"It was given to me by Alphonso Duarte. He and I met at school in New York."

"Look upon it, then, for the last time." Nono held the dagger in the palm of his hand, so that the sun made the blade and its blood-bathed jewels glitter.

"You'd kill me, Yaqui? You'd kill an unarmed man?"

"No. You are too cowardly to kill. You would not even fight with the courage of a peon. You, the son of a Vasquez, a coward. I, Nono, the Yaqui, despised by your people, spit on you!"

Camillo, whipped to fury by the Yaqui's insults, was on his feet. If this must be his time to die, then he would die as a Vasquez should die. He slapped Nono across the earless head. The Yaqui stepped back. He picked up Camillo's knife that had buried itself in the sand. He returned it to the Spaniard with a thin smile.

"Now, Senor Vasquez, we fight!"

"We fight, Yaqui!"

There, under that merciless brassy sun, they fought; knives ripping and slashing, bodies twisting, turning, dodging; advancing, retreating, attacking, countering, until their naked torsos ran red with blood and they swayed with dizziness.

Camillo was the first to fall but, even as Nono bent over him, Camillo, hate in his red-shot eyes, gasped his last breath, carrying with it a curse.

Nono dressed his own wounds with strips of cloth torn from the fine linen of the dead caballero.

So Howdy Merchant found them, the dead man and the dying man. The Yaqui indicated the dead body of the last of the Vasquez line.

"He died fighting, senor. At the last, he proved himself a brave man. At the Reyes rancho is a paper showing where the steel chest is hidden. It contains gold, much gold for you and the senorita. The papers you seek are with the gold. I have waited long for your coming, so that I could give to you that which belongs to no other man. It is the fulfilment of my promise to the man who was my friend and your grandsire. One key to the chest is in the pocket of that dead one. Here, my son, is the other key. There were two keys, though no man knew the existence of the one given me by your grandsire. Please take them both.

"And now you will return to the Reyes rancho. When the sun goes down, I die. Do not return to this spot. My Yaquis will come for me at sundown after I am dead."

Howdy looked at the wounded Yaqui who suffered his pain without a grimace. "Can't I do something to help you?"

"No. Get the key from the pocket of the dead one. Then go. What hours are left me, I want to spend alone. Go, white man."

Nono refused Howdy's hand in parting. The Yaqui's black eyes burned strangely. "Go! What I have done pays a debt. For you and all gringos I have nothing but hate. I but paid a debt, can you not understand? Let me die as I must die. Alone. When the sun sets. Go!"

And so Howdy left the dying Yaqui who stood facing the lowering sun, a naked, bronze statue, stained with blood.

What debt Nono owed to Doctor Macklin, no man would ever know but he had paid the debt with all that a man can pay.

At the Reyes rancho Howdy told his tale to Don Rafael who nodded grimly. If Don Rafael shared any part of Nono's secret, he never mentioned a word of it.

The jewelled dagger was buried with the body of Camillo Vasquez. And when Don Rafael died, some years later, he asked that the history of that fatal weapon never be mentioned within the walls of the old hacienda. This promise Shirley and Howard kept. Even when news came that Alphonso Duarte, last of the Duartes, had been killed in an automobile wreck, neither Howdy nor his wife made mention of it to one another.

The strongbox with its two keys is buried under the chapel floor. Its gold made Howdy Merchant wealthy beyond his dreams.

Every year, at Christmas time, Ricardo Reyes, world-famous violinist, pays a visit to the old Reyes rancho where he spends most of his time with Howdy's eldest son, Ricardo Merchant, who promises to be a musician as well as a splendid young vaquero. Black Jack, the foreman, claims he's going to make a world's best roper out of the boy.

"Providin'," adds Black Jack, with the privilege accorded him there, "he don't up and git married and spend the rest of his life makin' love to his wife, like one young gent I once spent a lot of time learnin' how to ketch a wild steer."